"Romance, suspense, danger, action-packed excitement, hot hot men, and on top of all that, a couple that sizzles all throughout the book . . . Sexy as hell." —The Reading Cafe

"I cannot wait to see where Ms. Feehan takes us next."
—Fresh Fiction

"Packed with adventure . . . Not only is this a thriller, the sensual scenes rival the steaming bayou. A perfect 10."
—Romance Reviews Today

"Daring . . . Fresh . . . Who knows what the next book will bring?" —HeroesandHeartbreakers.com

"Explosive! The sexual chemistry is literally a scorcher."
—Fallen Angel Reviews

"The fastest-paced, most action-packed, gut-wrenching, adrenaline-driven ride I've ever experienced."
—Romance Junkies

"Wow! . . . Made me hungry for more." —The Best Reviews

"Sultry and suspenseful . . . swift-moving and sexually charged . . . In short, it is an electrifying read."
—*Publishers Weekly*

"Intense, sensual and mesmerizing." —*Library Journal*

"[An] erotically charged romance." —*Booklist*

"Brilliant. The sexual energy . . . is electrifying. If you enjoy paranormal romances, this is a must-read."
—Romance at Heart Magazine

Titles by Christine Feehan

POWER
GAME

CHRISTINE
FEEHAN

JOVE
New York

A JOVE BOOK
Published by Berkley
An imprint of Penguin Random House LLC
375 Hudson Street, New York, New York 10014

ISBN: 9780399585463

Berkley hardcover edition / January 2017
Jove mass-market edition / June 2017

Printed in the United States of America
1   3   5   7   9   10   8   6   4   2

Cover illustration by Craig White
Cover design by Judith Lagerman
Cover background photographs: Sunrise on the Bayou © Greg Guirard / Stockbyte;
Dutch Marines © VanderWolf Images / Shutterstock.com; Storm Clouds © Dudarev
Mikhail / Shutterstock.com; Chameleon Skin © designmethod / Shutterstock.com
Book design by Kelly Lipovich

For Neil and Lisa Benson of Pearl River Eco Tours, two people I consider very good friends. Thank you for everything, and we're missing you like crazy!

FOR MY READERS

Be sure to go to christinefeehan.com/members/ to sign up for my PRIVATE book announcement list and download the FREE ebook of *Dark Desserts*. Join my community and get firsthand news, enter the book discussions, ask your questions and chat with me. Please feel free to email me at Christine @christinefeehan.com. I would love to hear from you.

ACKNOWLEDGMENTS

With any book there are many people to thank. This one took a *lot* of help! Neil Benson of Pearl River Eco Tours: Thank you for the many hours out on the boat, both day and night. All the crazy adventures that allowed me the necessary research for this book. The time spent getting distances and names correctly! I appreciate your help so much. Thanks to Lieutenant Commander 04 Patrick Schuette for your help with medical issues in the field. To Myiah Castillejos for her help with ranks needed for the PJs. I have Specialist Jason Hutton especially to thank for all his help with this book. I couldn't have come up with such a great mission— thanks for making it real and reading the fight scenes over and over until I got the details right. Any mistakes made are strictly my own. Thanks to Domini for her research and help with editing.

THE GHOSTWALKER
SYMBOL DETAILS

SIGNIFIES
shadow

SIGNIFIES
protection against evil forces

SIGNIFIES
the Greek letter psi, which is used by
parapsychology researchers to signify
ESP or other psychic abilities

SIGNIFIES
qualities of a knight—loyalty,
generosity, courage and honor

SIGNIFIES
shadow knights who protect against
evil forces using psychic powers,
courage and honor

nox noctis est nostri

THE GHOSTWALKER CREED

We are the GhostWalkers, we live in the shadows
The sea, the earth, and the air are our domain
No fallen comrade will be left behind
We are loyalty and honor bound
We are invisible to our enemies
and we destroy them where we find them
We believe in justice and we protect our country
and those unable to protect themselves
What goes unseen, unheard, and unknown
are GhostWalkers
There is honor in the shadows and it is us
We move in complete silence whether
in jungle or desert
We walk among our enemy unseen and unheard
Striking without sound and scatter to the winds
before they have knowledge of our existence
We gather information and wait with endless patience
for that perfect moment to deliver swift justice
We are both merciful and merciless
We are relentless and implacable in our resolve
We are the GhostWalkers and the night is ours

1

Bellisia Adams stared at herself in the mirror. Beside her was JinJing, a sweet woman, unaware that the man she worked for was an infamous criminal or that the woman beside her was no more Chinese than the man on the moon. Bellisia's hair was long and straight, a waterfall of silk reaching to her waist. She was short, delicate-looking, with small feet and hands. She spoke flawlessly in the dialect JinJing spoke, laughing and gossiping companionably in the restroom during their short break.

She kept her heart rate absolutely steady, the beat never rising in spite of the fact that she knew just by the heightened security and the tenseness of the guards that what she'd been looking for this past week was finally here. It was a good thing too. Time was running out fast. Like most of the technicians in the laboratory, she didn't wear a watch, but she was very aware of the days and hours ticking by.

JinJing waved to her and hurried out as the chime sounded, the call back to work. Anyone caught walking the halls was instantly let go. Or at least they disappeared.

Rumor had it that wherever they were taken was not pleasant. The Cheng Company paid well. Bernard Lee Cheng had many businesses and employed a good number of people, but he was a very exacting boss.

Bellisia couldn't wait any longer. She couldn't be caught in the restroom either. Very carefully she removed the long wig and lifelike skin of her mask and rolled them into her white lab coat. She slipped off the laboratory uniform, revealing the skintight one-piece bodysuit she wore under it—one that reflected the background around her. Her shoes were crepe-soled and easy to move fast in. She removed them and shoved them in one of the pockets. Her pale blond hair was braided in a tight weave. She was as ready as she'd ever be. She slipped out, back into the narrow hallway the moment she knew it was empty. Acute hearing ensured she knew exactly where most of the technicians were on the floor. She knew the precise location of every camera and just how to avoid them.

Once in the hall, she climbed up the wall to the ceiling, blending in with the dingy, off-white color that looked like it had seen better days. As she moved from the hallway of the laboratory to the offices the wall color changed to a muted blue, fresh and crisp. She changed color until she was perfectly blending in and slowed her pace. Movement drew the eye, and there were far more people in the offices. Most of them were in small, open cubicles, but as she continued through to the next large bank of offices, the walls changed to a muted green in the one large office that mattered to her.

She could see the woman seated, facing away from her, looking at the man behind the desk. Bernard Lee Cheng. She was very tempted to kill him, take the opportunity of being so close and just get the job done. It would rid the world of a very evil man, but it wasn't her mission, no matter how much she wished it were. The woman, Senator Violet Smythe-Freeman—now just Smythe—was her mission, specifically to see if the senator was selling out her country and fellow GhostWalkers, the teams of soldiers few even knew existed.

There was no way into the office, but that didn't matter. She moved slowly across the ceiling, hiding in plain sight. Even if one of the men or women on the floor happened to look up they would have a difficult time spotting her as long as she was careful to move like a sloth, inching her way to her destination. She positioned herself outside the office over the door. Muting the sounds around her, she concentrated on the voices coming from inside the office.

Cheng faced her. Even if she couldn't hear his every word because he'd soundproofed his office, she could read lips. He wanted the GhostWalker program. Files. Everything—including soldiers to take apart. Her stomach clenched. Violet's voice was pitched low. She had the ability to persuade people to do what she wanted with her voice, but Cheng seemed immune.

She wanted money for her campaign. Maurice Stuart had named her his running mate for the presidential election. If elected, she planned to have Stuart assassinated so that she would become president. Cheng would have an ally in the White House. It was a simple enough business deal. The origins of dark money never had to be exposed. No one would know.

Violet was beautiful and intelligent. She was poisonous. A sociopath. She was also enhanced, one of the original girls Dr. Whitney had found in orphanages and experimented on so that he could enhance his soldiers without harming them. She used her looks and her voice to get the things she wanted. More than anything, she wanted power.

Cheng nodded his head and leaned forward, his eyes sharp, his face a mask. He repeated the price. Files. Ghost-Walkers.

Bellisia remained still as Violet sold out her country and fellow soldiers. She told him where to find a team and how to get to them. She also told him there were copies of the files he wanted in several places, but most were too difficult to get to. The one place he had the best chance was in Louisiana, at the Stennis Center.

Cheng responded adamantly, insisting she get the files for him. She was just as adamant that she couldn't. He asked her why she was so against the GhostWalker program.

Bellisia tried to get closer, as if that would help her hear better. She wanted to know as well. Violet was one of them. One of the original orphans Peter Whitney had used for his own purposes—a "sister," not by blood but certainly in every other way. She'd undergone the same experiments with enhancing psychic abilities. With genetics, changing DNA. There was no doubt that Whitney was a genius, but he was also certifiably insane.

Violet's murmured response horrified Bellisia. The woman was a GhostWalker snob. Superior soldiers were fine. DNA of animals was fine. Enhancement met with her approval, but not when it came to the latest experiments coming to light—the use of vipers and spiders. That was going too far and cheapened the rest of them. She wanted anyone with that kind of DNA wiped out.

There was a moment of silence as if Cheng was turning her sudden burst of venomous hatred over and over in his mind, just as Bellisia was. Bellisia could have warned Violet that she was skating close to danger. Violet was a GhostWalker. Few had that information, but with that one outburst, she'd made a shrewd, extremely intelligent man wonder about her. He had a GhostWalker right there in his laboratory.

Violet, seemingly unaware of the danger, or because of it, swiftly moved on, laying out her demands once again. The two went back to haggling. In the end, Violet began to rise, and Cheng lifted a hand to stop her. She sank down gracefully, and the deal was made. Bellisia listened to another twenty minutes of conversation while the two hashed out what each would do for the other.

Bellisia calculated the odds of escaping if she killed the

senator as the traitor emerged from Cheng's office. They weren't good. Even so, she still entertained the idea. The level of the woman's treachery was beyond imagination. She despised Violet.

A stir in the office drew her attention. Guards marched in and directed those in the smaller offices out. She glanced into the hallway and saw that the entire floor was being cleared. Her heart accelerated before she could stop it. She took a slow breath and steadied her pulse just as the siren went off, calling everyone, from the labs to the offices, into the large dorm areas.

Lockdown. She couldn't get to the restroom to retrieve her uniform, lab coat and wig before the soldiers searched, nor did she have enough time remaining before the virus injected into her began to kill her. She also couldn't remain in one of Cheng's endless lockdowns. He was paranoid enough that he had kept workers on the premises for over a week more than once. She'd be dead without the antidote by that time. Cheng would be even tighter with his security once the clothes and wig were discovered.

She began the slow process necessary to make her way across the ceiling to the hall. She couldn't go down to the main floor. Soldiers were pouring in and every floor would be flooded by now. She had to go up to the only sanctuary she might be able to get to. There were tanks of water housed on the roof that fed the sprinkler systems. That was her only way to stay safe from the searches Cheng would conduct once her clothes were found. That meant she had to take the elevator.

Cursing mentally in every language she was fluent in— and that was quite a few—she hovered just above the elevator doors. The soldiers would go into the elevator and that meant she had to be very close to them. The men were already on alert and gathering in front of the elevator. The slightest mistake would cost her. Although she could blend into her environment, it took a few seconds for her skin and hair to change. Her clothing would mirror her surroundings, so she would have the look of the elevator over her body but her head and hands and feet would be exposed for that couple of seconds.

Heart pounding, she slowly edged over to the very top of the elevator. Should she try to start blending into that color now, or wait until she was inside with a dozen guards and guns? She had choices, but the wrong one would end her life. Changing colors to mirror her background was more like the octopus than the chameleon, but it still took a few precious moments. She began changing, concentrating on her hands and feet first until she appeared part of the doors.

A ping signaled that she only had seconds to get inside and up the wall to the ceiling of the elevator. She waited until soldiers stepped into the elevator and slipped inside with them, clinging to the wall over their heads. The door nearly closed on her foot before she could pull it in. The men crowded in, and there was little space. She felt as if she couldn't breathe. The car didn't have high ceilings, so they were mashed together and the taller ones nearly brushed against her body. Twice, the hair of the man closest to her— and it was just her bad luck that he was tall—actually did brush against her face, tickling her skin.

She rode floor to floor as men got off to sweep each, making certain that all personnel did as the siren demanded and went immediately to the dormitory where they would be searched.

The last of the soldiers went to the roof. She knew this would be her biggest danger point. She had to exit the elevator right behind the last soldier. It was imperative that all of them were looking outward and not back toward the closing doors. She was a mimic, a chameleon, and no one would be able to see her, but once again it would take precious seconds to complete the change in a new environment.

She crawled down to the floor and eased out behind the last man, her gaze sweeping the roof to find the water tanks.

There were six banks of them, each feeding the sprinklers on several floors. She stayed very still, right up against the wall until her skin and hair adjusted fully to the new background. Only then did she begin her slow crawl across the roof, making for the nearest tank while the soldiers spread out and swept the large space.

Up so high the wind was a menace, blowing hard and continuously at the men. They stumbled as it hit them in gusts. She stayed low to the ground, almost on her belly. She stopped once when one of the soldiers cursed in a mixture of Mandarin and Shanghainese. He cursed the weather, not Cheng. No one would dare curse Cheng, afraid it would get back to him.

Cheng considered himself a businessman. He'd inherited his empire and his intellect from his Chinese father and his good looks and charm from his American movie star mother. Both parents had opened doors for him, in China as well as the United States. He had expanded those doors to nearly every country in the world. He'd doubled his father's empire, making him one of the wealthiest men on the planet, but he'd done so by providing to terrorists, rebels and governments classified information, weapons and anything else they needed. He sold secrets to the highest bidder, and no one ever touched him.

Bellisia didn't understand what it was that drove people to do the terrible things they did. Greed. Power. She knew she didn't live the way others did, but she didn't see that the outside world was any better than her world. Maybe worse. Hers was one of discipline and service. It wasn't always comfortable and she couldn't trust very many people, but then outside her world, the majority didn't seem to have it much better.

The cursing soldier stopped just before he tripped over her. She actually felt the brush of the leather of his boot. Bellisia eased her body away from him. Holding her breath. Keeping her movements infinitely slow. She inched her way across the roof, the movements so controlled her muscles cramped in protest. It hurt to move that slowly. All the while her heart pounded and she had to work to keep her breathing steady and calm.

She was right under their noses. All they had to do was look down and see her, if they could penetrate her disguise. She watched them carefully, looking out of the corners of her eyes, listening for them as well, but all the while measuring the distance to the water tanks. It seemed to take forever until she reached the base of the nearest one. For*ever*.

She reached a hand up and slid her fingers forward using the setae on the tips of her fingers to stick. Setae—single microscopic hairs split into hundreds of tiny bristles—were so tiny they were impossible to see, so tiny Dr. Whitney hadn't realized she actually had them, in spite of his enhancements. Pushing the setae onto the surface and dragging them forward allowed her to stick to the surface easily. Each seta could hold enormous amounts of weight, so having them on the pads of her fingers and toes allowed her to climb or hang upside down on a ceiling easily. The larger the creature, the smaller the setae, and no seta had ever been recorded that was small enough to hold a human being— until Dr. Whitney had managed unwittingly to create one.

Her plan was to climb into the water tank and wait until things settled down and then climb down the side of the building and get far away from Cheng. She was very aware of time ticking away, and the virus beginning to take hold in her body. Already her temperature was rising. The cold water in the tank would help. She cursed Whitney and his schemes for keeping the women in line.

The girls had been taken from orphanages. No one knew or cared about them. That allowed Whitney to conduct his experiments on the female children without fearing repercussions. He named them after flowers or seasons, and trained them as soldiers, assassins and spies. To keep them returning to him, he would inject a substance he called

Zenith, a lethal drug that needed an antidote, or a virus that spread and eventually killed. Sometimes he used their friendships with one another, so they'd learned to be extremely careful not to show feelings for one another.

She started up the tank, allowing her body to change once again to blend in with the dirty background. The wind tore at her, trying to rip her from the tank. She was cold, although she could feel her internal temperature rising from the virus, her body beginning to go numb in the vicious wind. Still, she forced herself to go slow, all the while watching the guards moving around the roof, thoroughly inspecting every single place that someone could hide. That told her they would be looking in the water tanks as well.

A siren went off abruptly, a loud jarring blare that set nerves on edge. It wasn't the same sound as the first siren indicating to the workers to go immediately to the dorms. This was one of jangling outrage. A scream of fury. They had found her wig, mask and lab clothes. They would be combing the building for her. Every duct, every vent. Anywhere a human being could possibly hide.

She had researched Cheng meticulously before she'd ever entered his world. It was narrow, rigid, autocratic, with constant inspections and living under the surveillance of cameras and guards. Cheng didn't trust anyone, not his closest allies. Not his workers. Not even his guards. He had watchers observing the watchers.

Bellisia was used to such an environment. She'd grown up in one and was familiar with it. She also knew all the ways to get around surveillance and cameras. She was a perfect mimic, blending into her environment, picking up nuances of her surroundings, the language, the idioms, the culture. Whitney thought that was her gift. He had no idea of her other abilities, the ones far more important to the missions he sent her off on. All the girls learned to hide abilities from him. It was so much safer.

The guards reacted to the blaring siren with a rush of

bodies and the sound of boots hitting the rooftop as they renewed their frenzied searching. She kept climbing, using that same slow, inch-by-inch movement. It took discipline to continue slowly instead of moving quickly as every self-preservation cell in her body urged her to do.

She relied heavily on her ability to change color and skin texture to blend into her surroundings, but that didn't guarantee that a sharp-eyed soldier wouldn't spot her. The pigment cells in her skin allowed her to change color in seconds. She'd hated that at first, until she realized it gave her an advantage. Whitney needed her to be a spy. He sent her out on missions when so many of the other women had been locked up again.

She gained the top of the tank just as one of the soldiers put his boot on the ladder. Slipping into the water soundlessly, she swam to the very bottom of the tank and anchored herself to the wall, making herself as flat as possible. Once again she changed color so that she blended with tank and water.

She *loved* water. She could live in the cool liquid. The water felt soothing against her burning skin. In the open air, she felt as if her skin dried out and she was cracking into a million pieces. She often looked down at her hands and arms to make certain it wasn't true, but in spite of the smoothness of her skin, she still felt that way. The one environment she found extremely hostile to her was the desert. Whitney had sent her there several times to record its effects on her, and she hadn't done well. A flaw, he called it.

The soldier was at the top of the tank now, peering down into the water. She knew each tank had soldiers looking into it. If they sent someone down into the water, she might really be in trouble, but it appeared as if the soldier was just going to sit at the edge to ensure no one had gone in and was underwater. Once it was dark, the soldiers should have completed their search and she should be able to slip up to the surface and get air.

Right now she was basking in the fact that the water was helping to control the temperature rising in her from the virus. Whitney had injected her every time she left the compound where she was held, to ensure she would return. She'd always managed to complete her mission in the time frame given to her, so she had no idea how fast-acting the virus was. The water definitely made her feel better, but she didn't feel good at all. Her muscles ached. Cramped. Never a good thing when trying to be still at the bottom of a water tank with soldiers on the lookout above her.

Night fell rapidly. She knew the guards were still there on the roof and that worried her. She had to be able to climb down the side of the building, and she couldn't even get out of the tank as long as the guard was above her. She also needed air. She'd risked blowing a few bubbles but that wasn't going to sustain her much longer. She needed to get to the surface and leave before weakness began to hit. She had been certain the soldier would leave the tank after the first hour, but he seemed determined to hold his position. She was nearly at her max for staying submerged.

Bellisia refused to panic. That way lay disaster. She had to get air and then find a way to slip past the guard so she could climb down the building, get to the van waiting for her and get the antidote. She detached from the wall and began to drift up toward the surface, careful not to disturb the water. Again, she used patience in spite of the urgent demands her lungs were making on her.

After what seemed an eternity, she reached the surface. Tilting her head so only her lips broke the surface, she drew in air. Relief coursed through her. Air had never tasted so good. She hung there, still and part of the water so that even though the guard was looking right at her, he saw nothing but water shimmering.

A flurry of activity drew the guard's attention and she attached herself to the side of the tank and began to climb up toward the very top. She was only half out of the water when the shouted orders penetrated. They wanted hooks dragged through the containers to make certain no one was hiding in them with air tanks. So many soldiers tromped up onto the roof that she felt the vibrations right through the container. Spotlights went on, illuminating the entire roof and all six containers. Worse, soldiers surrounded each one, and more climbed up to the top to stand on the platforms.

Bellisia sank slowly back into the water, clinging to the wall as she did so, her heart pounding unnaturally. She'd never experienced her heart beating so hard. It felt as if it would come right out of her chest, and she wasn't really that fearful—yet. Her temperature was climbing at an alarming rate. She was hot and even the cool water couldn't alleviate the terrible heat rising inside of her. Her skin hurt. Every muscle in her body ached, not just ached, but felt twisted into tight knots. She began to shiver, so much so she couldn't control it. That wasn't conducive to hiding in a spotlight surrounded by the enemy.

She stayed up near the very top of the tank, just beneath the water line, attached to the wall, and made herself as small and as flat as possible. There was always the possibility that she could die on a mission. That was part of the . . . adrenaline rush. It was always about pitting her skills against an enemy. If she wasn't good enough, if she made a mistake, that was on her. But this . . . Peter Whitney had deliberately injected her with a killer virus in order to ensure she always returned to him. He was willing to risk her dying a painful death to prove his point.

He *owned* them. All of them. Each and every girl he took out of an orphanage and experimented on. Some died. That didn't matter to him. *None* of them mattered to him. Only the science. Only the soldiers he developed piggybacking on the research he'd conducted on the girls. Children with no childhood. No loving parents. She hadn't understood what that meant until she'd been out in the world and realized the majority of people didn't live as she did.

All of the girls had discussed trying to break free before Whitney added them to his disgusting program to give him more babies to experiment on. The thought of leaving the only life they'd ever known was terrifying. But this—leaving her to die in a foreign country because she was late through no fault of her own. She had the information Whitney needed but because he insisted on injecting her with a killer virus before she went on her mission, she might never get that information to him. He liked playing God. He was willing to lose one of them in order to scare the others into compliance.

Something hit the water hard, startling her. She nearly jerked off the wall, blinking in protest against the bright lights shining into the tank. Her sanctuary was no longer that. The environment had gone from cool, dark water—a place of safety—to one of overwhelmingly intense brilliant light illuminating the water nearly to the bottom of the tank. A giant hook dragged viciously along the floor, and she shuddered in reaction.

A second hook entered the water with an ominous splash as the first was pulled back up. The next few minutes were a nightmare as the tank was thoroughly searched with hooks along the bottom. Had a diver with scuba gear been hiding there, he would have been torn to pieces.

She let her breath out as they pulled the hooks back up to the top. They would leave soon and she could make the climb out of the tank and across the roof. Already she could tell she was weaker, but she knew she could still climb down the side of the building and get to the van where Whitney's supersoldiers waited to administer the antidote to the poisonous virus, reducing it to a mere illness instead of something lethal.

The hook plunged back into the water, startling her. She nearly detached from the wall as the iron dragged up the side of the tank while a second hook entered the water. This was . . . *bad*. She had nowhere to go. If she moved fast to avoid the hook, she would be spotted. If she didn't, the hook could tear her apart. Either way, she was dead.

The sound, magnified underwater, was horrendous on her ears. She wanted to cover them against the terrible scraping and grinding as the point of the hook dug into the side of the tank. She watched it come closer and closer as it crawled up from the bottom. The other hook came up almost beside it, covering more territory as they ripped long gouges in the wall.

She tried to time letting go of the wall so neither hook would brush against her body and signal to the men on the other end that there was something other than wall. She pushed off gently and slid between the two chains, trying to swim slowly so that movement wouldn't catch eyes. She stroked her arms with powerful pulls to take her down, still hugging the wall as best she could below the hooks. If she could just attach herself on the path already taken, she'd have a good chance of riding this latest threat out.

The advantage of going deeper was that the light didn't penetrate all the way to the bottom. She just had to avoid the hooks as they plunged into the water and sank. Once she was deep enough, the soldiers above her wouldn't be able to see even if she did make a jerky movement to prevent the hook from impaling her.

She made it about halfway down when the hooks began their upward scraping along the wall. Once again she stayed very still, the sound grating on her nerves, her heart pounding as the huge hooks got closer and closer. This time she did a slow somersault to avoid getting scraped up by either hook. The dive took her lower into the tank. She didn't see how they could possibly think anyone could stay underwater that long, and by now certainly they would have discovered a scuba tank.

The soldiers were thorough, plunging the hooks deep and dragging them up the walls without missing so much as a few inches of space. Bellisia realized they had to have perfected this method of searching the tanks by doing it often. That made sense. The tanks were large and Cheng was paranoid. No doubt the many floors and laboratories were being searched just as thoroughly.

There, in the water, listening to the sound of the chains scraping up the walls, she contemplated the difference between Cheng and Whitney. Both had far too much money. Whitney seemed to need to take his research further and further out of the realm of humanity and deeper into the realm of insanity. No government would ever sanction what he was doing, yet he was getting away with it. At least his motive, although twisted, was to produce better soldiers for his country.

Cheng wasn't affiliated with his government as far as she could tell. He worked closely with them, but he wasn't a patriot. He was out for himself. He seemed to want more money and power than he already had. She'd researched him carefully, and few on the planet had more than he did. Still, it wasn't enough for him. Yet he had no family. No one to share his life with. He didn't work for the sake of knowledge. He existed only to make money.

Bellisia was aware of her heart laboring harder and the pressure on her lungs becoming more severe. That was unusual. She'd taken a large gulp of air and she should have had quite a bit of time left before she had to rise, but it felt as if she'd been underwater a little too long, even for her. Of course Whitney would find something that would negatively impact her ability in the water. He didn't want her to use that means as an escape route.

She had no choice but to begin her ascent. She tried to stay to the side of the tank they'd already dredged. It was terrifying to be in the water as the large, heavy hooks slammed close to her again and again. It was inevitable, given the many strikes the soldiers made at the water, and it happened as she was just pushing off the wall to allow her body to rise slowly, naturally. A hook hit the bottom of the tank and was jerked upward and to the left, right across her back and arm. She folded herself in half to minimize the damage, but it hit hard enough to jar her, even with the way the water slowed the big hook down.

She felt the burn as the point ripped her skin open. It was a shallow wound, but it stung like hell and instantly there was blood in the water. She had to concentrate to close those cells to keep from leaking enough blood that the soldiers would notice. Under her skin she had a network of finely controlled muscles that aided her in changing the look and feel of her body's surface skin. Now, she used them to squeeze the cells closed and prevent blood from pouring into the water, at least until the spotlights were turned off.

It seemed to take forever as she continued to rise, her lungs burning and her muscles cramping. All the while the horrible splash and scraping of the hooks continued. Twice she had extremely close calls, and once more the tip barely skimmed along her body, hitting her thigh, ripping her open. It was much harder to control the bleeding this time as she was weaker and needed to break the surface before her muscles went into full cramps.

She was relieved when the hooks were pulled from the water and the soldiers began to climb down the ladders back to the roof. Instantly she kicked the remaining four feet to the surface and took in great gulps of air. She clung to the side for several long minutes, resting her head against the wall while she tried to breathe away the inferno inside her. She couldn't keep doing this for Whitney. She wouldn't survive. He made them all feel as if they were nothing. She knew she wasn't alone in wanting to escape because they all talked about it, late at night when one or two could disrupt the cameras and recording equipment and they were alone in the dorms.

She had tried planning an escape with her best friend, Zara, but before they could attempt to carry out their plans, Zara was sent on an undercover mission and Bellisia was sent to ascertain whether or not Violet was betraying Whitney. Whitney had set Violet up as senator, taking over when her husband had been killed. Whitney didn't trust Violet, but Bellisia suspected that he had paired them together. If that were the case, then that physical attraction evidently didn't stop Violet from conspiring against the man who had experimented on her.

Bellisia began her slow climb out of the water tank. She would have to dry off before she could make the trek across the roof to the side of the building. If she didn't, one of the soldiers might discover the wet trail leading to the edge. The platform around the tank was warm from the high-powered lights, and she lay down, allowing her body to change to the color of the dingy planks.

She didn't dare sleep, not when soldiers still guarded the roof, but they seemed content with pacing the length of it in patterns, checking every place that could possibly hide a body over and over. She realized the soldiers were as afraid of Cheng as she and the other women in her unit were afraid of Whitney. Life was cheap to both men, at least other people's lives.

She began her slow crawl down the side of the tank once she felt she wouldn't leave behind a trail. Her body was hot now, so hot she felt as if her skin would crack open. Her muscles cramped, and she couldn't stop shaking. That didn't bode well for crossing the roof, but at least it was very dark now that the spotlights had been turned off. If she shook when a guard was close, hopefully the darkness would conceal her.

It took her just under forty minutes in the dark to climb down the side of the building. The virus he'd given her was vicious, her fever high, her insides searing from the inside out. For someone like her, someone needing more water than most people, it was sheer agony. It was as if he'd developed the strain specifically for her—and he probably had. That only strengthened her resolve to escape.

She rested for a moment to get her bearings and plan out her next step. She needed the antidote immediately, and that meant putting herself back in Whitney's hands. She had no other choice. Bellisia made her way across the lawn to the street where the van was waiting for her. It was parked one block down to be inconspicuous, one block away, which put it right next to the river.

She was staggering by the time she reached the vehicle, and Gerald, one of the supersoldiers sent to watch over her, leapt out to catch her up and jump back into the van. He placed her on a gurney and immediately spoke into his cell to tell Whitney she was back. She closed her eyes and turned her face away, as if losing consciousness.

"I need the information she has," Peter Whitney said. "Get it from her before you administer the antidote. Take her to the plane immediately. Your destination will be Italy."

Her heart nearly jumped out of her chest. She knew several of the women had been taken there to ensure they became pregnant. The GhostWalkers had destroyed his breeding program in the United States. No way was she going to Italy.

"Whitney needs a report," Gerald said.

She kept her breathing shallow. Labored. Eyes closed, body limp.

"Bellisia, honey, come on, give me the report. You need the antidote. He won't let me give it to you until you give him what he wants."

She stayed very still. Gerald and his partner Adam were her handlers on nearly every mission. The three had developed a friendship of sorts, if one could be friends with their guards. She knew how to control her breathing and heartbeat, and she did both to make him think she was crashing.

"We're losing her, Doc," Gerald said while Adam caught at her arm, shoving up the material of her bodysuit.

"Be certain. She could be faking," Whitney warned.

"No, she's out of it. She got back way past the time she was supposed to. We might be too late to save her. They locked the building down and she was still inside." Gerald's voice held urgency.

"Did you see Violet or any of her people going in or coming out?" Whitney demanded.

"I never saw Senator Smythe. I have no idea if she was there or not," Gerald said. Bellisia wasn't altogether certain he spoke the truth. He may very well have seen the senator, but Gerald and Adam didn't always like the way Whitney treated the women.

"Be sure Bellisia is really out."

Gerald prodded her. Hard. She made no response.

"She's burning up. And she's bleeding on her back and thigh."

"Inject her. She'll need water."

"Adam, give her the antidote fast. We'll need water for her."

She felt the needle and then the sting of the antidote as it went in. She stayed silent, uncertain how fast it was supposed to work. She hated needles; the sensation of them entering her skin often made her nauseous. The double row of muscles caused the needle to spread a terrible fire through every cell.

"Doc says get her water."

Adam held up a bottle. "She's not responsive enough to drink." That showed her how upset on her behalf Adam was—he knew she would need to be submerged in water. He wasn't thinking clearly.

"Not drink. Pour it over her."

The cool water went over her arm and then her chest. She nearly lost her ability to keep her heart and lungs under control, the relief was so tremendous.

"That's not enough. Get the bucket and fill it up at the river."

Adam threw open the double doors to the van and hopped out. Her acute hearing picked up Whitney hissing in disapproval. He didn't like that they'd parked by a river. That was her signal to move.

She leapt from the gurney, onto the ground right beside a startled Adam.

"Grab her," Gerald yelled.

She raced across the street with Adam rushing after her. The tips of his fingers brushed her back just as she dove right off the edge into the river. Water closed over her head, the cool wetness welcoming her.

2

Grace Fontenot rocked gently back and forth in the creaking rocking chair, holding her pipe and surveying the view. She'd lived sixty-seven years on the Fontenot land and eighty-two years in the swamplands and loved every minute of it. Her bones told her she was getting up in age, but she still had plenty of work to do. She had boys to raise. It didn't matter that they were grown men; they'd never had a home or love, and she was determined they'd have both before it was her time.

Her husband had built their house with his own two hands and with the help of his father, right there in this exact spot so she could always look out on the river. Her grandsons had modernized the structure, making it more comfortable. Insects droned continually, a beautiful music to wake to every morning. Water lapped at the pier and the wind played through the cypress trees, adding to the symphony that had been hers all those years ago when she'd first chosen her man. And she'd chosen well. She had no regrets.

She'd lost her husband, son and daughter-in-law in an

accident, but she had four grandsons to look after, so she'd kept going. Her grandsons had brought more men to her— men with death in their eyes, torment. Men who had seen and experienced things they never should have had to see or experience. Those men served their country in ways most couldn't fathom. She didn't ask what they did, because her knowing didn't help them. They weren't the kind of men to share much.

She gave them a home. Someone to come back to. Someone to remind them of what they fought for. They were tight, her boys. She had nine more of them now to worry about. She also had acquired two daughters when two of her grandsons had married, and now she had three great-granddaughters. Later, Trap, one of the other men in her grandson's squadron, had married and his wife, Cayenne, became a daughter to her.

Nonny puffed on her pipe. She didn't ask a lot of questions because she knew better. She knew her boys were involved in some government program that changed them. Like anything government, she was fairly certain it wasn't good. Her great-granddaughters were products of a failed experiment, a mix of human DNA with viper DNA. The three girls had been scheduled for termination, just as their mother, Pepper, and Cayenne had, but her boys had gotten them all out safely and brought them home.

She bit down on her pipe, holding back the Cajun curses she wanted to spit out at the lunacy of such experiments. Of the secrecy of them. Secrecy meant monsters could get away with things that should never have been done to human beings, all in the name of producing the perfect soldier.

"Nonny? Pepper said you were looking for me."

The quiet voice interrupted her thoughts. She never heard him coming. No one ever did. Ezekiel Fortunes was a challenge. She might be old, but she figured that gave her an advantage. He was a man of few words. He had strange, amber-colored eyes. Sometimes they were cool, like a potent shade of whiskey. Other times they were gold, like an antique from the Renaissance, an age of swords and deception. Sometimes they were liquid and molten, like the blaze of lava pouring down a mountain.

His eyes were too old and far too devoid of feeling—unless he looked at his two brothers, then those eyes blazed with life. With love. He was capable, he just wasn't aware of it. He was street smart. Jungle smart. Desert smart. The man was definitely a challenge. She had to walk softly with Ezekiel.

"Nonny, everything all right?" His voice was low, soft, almost gentle, but there were no soft, gentle edges to this man.

She rocked some more and nodded her head while she took another puff of her pipe, studying him. Ezekiel was stunning. A man's man. He looked rough and dangerous. There was no hiding either fact because the evidence clung to him like a second skin. He didn't just look those things, he *was* both, and no one was silly enough to challenge him.

Ezekiel had black hair, longish, because he never bothered to cut it. He was in the military and she thought it a good thing that he was in the special unit of GhostWalkers and wasn't required to have a military haircut, because she was fairly certain Ezekiel wouldn't follow the rules. He made the rules. His shoulders were broad and his arms bulged with muscle. He had a thick, muscular chest that narrowed through his rib cage into his hips. He was quiet on his feet, so silent that most times she never knew when he was close.

Nonny nodded. "Yes, Ezekiel, I need another favor if you don' mind."

His eyes rested on her face, and she calmly took another puff from her pipe, keeping the shiver to herself. Those eyes were penetrating. Eyes that could see right through to a man's soul. Or a woman's. She shivered again, deep inside, and his eyes darkened, as if he saw that. Still, she had to be brave. Someone had to save Ezekiel. He was too willing to sacrifice himself for those he loved.

He'd lived on the streets, responsible for his two younger brothers and later, two other boys. He used his fists to fight for food for them. He'd fought grown men to keep the predators off them, all the while insisting all of them go to school. How he kept it from the schools that they were street children she had no idea. The three boys—Mordichai, Malichai and Ezekiel—were tight and they rarely talked about their past other than to occasionally crack jokes. Ezekiel never was the one to make the joke, and she rarely saw him smile. If he did smile, it never, not once, reached his eyes.

She had to go careful. Very careful. This was a game, their own version of chess. Ezekiel was extremely smart, but more, he was street smart. She took the pipe from her mouth and regarded him with her failing eyesight. "I know you've been to town a time or two already since the other boys left, but I forgot a few fixin's when I made the list for you. Guess my age is finally catchin' up with me." Throwing her age at him was always a plus. He couldn't argue with that.

His gaze jumped to hers and stayed there. Made it impossible to look away. She was very glad she was past eighty and knew how to keep a poker face. He didn't believe a word she said—most likely because it wasn't the truth. She just knew it was imperative Ezekiel Fortunes go to New Orleans, into the French Quarter. Why? She didn't know, only that he *had* to go. He wouldn't have liked it one bit if she'd tried to tell him she had the second sight and her visions were all about him.

He didn't respond. He wasn't going to make it easy on her. She didn't mind. She quite enjoyed her little game with him. "I made a list of ingredients. You'll have to get them at the specialty store in the French Quarter. It's right off of Jackson Square. You know the one I'm talkin' about. All the spices . . ." He was nodding, but his gaze never left her and that look was difficult to face, but she did it. For his sake.

"Been there three times in the last week, Nonny."

She liked that he spoke low. Velvet soft. His voice was like that, but it carried a menace that sent chills creeping down her spine, and she wasn't afraid of very much.

"I know. I just forgot."

He shook his head. "You don't forget things."

That much was true, but she was old. "I'm not gettin' any younger."

"Still too young to forget."

See? She loved their game. He countered her every move. He was gentle about it, deceiving his opponents into thinking they had him, but she knew better. She knew he wasn't buying into her story at all. She loved that about him, so much so that she took her pipe out of her mouth and smiled at him. "Nice of you to say that, Ezekiel. Sad truth is, I do forget a few things now and then."

He was going to let her get away with it. His face didn't change. Neither did his eyes, but his energy did. She knew he was letting it go because he cared about her. He might never admit that to her, but she didn't need the admission from him. It was enough that she knew. Now, she had to come clean. Confess. She'd made a mistake that could have cost them all and he had to know.

"I took the boat out yesterday and tried to get into the area near Stennis, but a gunboat turned me back. Soldiers lookin' grim and threatenin' an old lady."

She watched him carefully. He was protective of those he called family, and she believed she had found her way into that inner circle. His face didn't change expression, but his eyes did. They went from amber to Renaissance gold. Not a good sign with Ezekiel. She didn't want to be one of those boys threatening her.

"Nonny"—he spoke more gently than ever—"you know better than to go there. If you need something, I'll get it for you. That area is restricted."

She lifted her chin at him. "These waters have been my

home for over eighty years. No one ever told me where I could go or when."

He nodded. "I appreciate that, Nonny, I don't like being told what to do either, but the canals and waterways around Stennis are closed for a reason. Why did you try to go there? What was so important?" Patient. Soft. That was her Ezekiel at his most lethal.

"I needed a plant called black nightshade. It only grows there, and I lost the ones I transplanted. They died when the floods came. I have to plant on higher ground. I need that particular plant for my pharmacy. It can be poisonous and I have to be very cautious with it." She was careful not to sound stubborn. She'd learned Ezekiel didn't do well with "no" or stubborn. Even the three little girls, Wyatt's girls, had learned that and they were just babies. Ezekiel wasn't nearly as easygoing as he liked to appear. She'd learned coming up against him was like coming up against a rock. He was immovable.

"You should have told me. I'll get it for you," he offered.

So sweet. That was her Ezekiel. He would too. He'd go into the swamp and dig up even the foulest-smelling plant and bring it to her if she asked him.

"Someone already left it on our doorstep." She watched him closer than ever, because if there was a time for him to get angry with her, now was that time—and she'd deserve it.

He stiffened. His eyes slashed at her. All that merciless gold. "Repeat that."

"I found the plant on my doorstep this morning. It was in a box. I asked Pepper and the girls and they hadn't done it. Neither had Cayenne. They were the only ones I told about the plant except the boys in that gunboat."

"Did you ask Malichai?"

She nodded. "I asked all the boys. No one knew I wanted the plant, and they certainly didn' go out and get it for me. It was packed in soil very carefully. I thought maybe you . . ."

He shook his head. "I didn't. If someone else penetrated

our security, we have to know who it is. The girls are at risk.
Cayenne and Pepper and even you, Nonny. Wyatt, Gator,
hell, all of us, would do just about anything to get you back
if someone took you."

She puffed on her pipe, not wanting him to get riled. Just
how to say it? "I doubt that anyone bringin' a plant means
to harm us." It was an excuse. As a rule, she didn't make
excuses for mistakes, but she felt strongly about the waterway. It was a highway for Cajuns. For the people living in
the swamp. Her people. They could use the land for whatever
they wanted, but it was a crime to take away the canals and
bayous.

His expression didn't change, but his eyes did. There was
a glow to the gold now, as if any moment the color would
turn to that one that meant the volcano might erupt. "It's a
matter of security. I realize you've always led your life a
certain way and it must be difficult to have all these changes,
but we're building a fortress for a reason."

She wasn't a child, and she wasn't addled either. She bit
down on the stem of her pipe to keep from retorting back.
For just one moment the glow in those eyes mellowed. Just
a moment. Was it a glint of humor after all? She couldn't be
certain, but she was fairly sure he'd just moved another piece
on their invisible board. He'd scored, taken one of her
pawns. It was time to capitulate. She nodded. "I'll be more
careful."

Ezekiel studied Nonny carefully. The old lady was playing him. He just couldn't figure out her game. He sighed. He
wasn't the type of man to allow himself to get played, yet
he knew he was going back into town just to please her. She
wasn't making any sense, when she was usually as practical
as they came.

Nonny was the type of woman a man could always count
on. Steady. She didn't freak out no matter what happened
around her. A knife and a shotgun were always close. They
just didn't make women like her anymore. He'd never known

there were women like her in the world, so if she wanted to play him for some reason, he was willing to be played.

"I'm well aware Dr. Whitney is tryin' to kidnap Wyatt and Pepper's daughters," Nonny said with a little sniff.

He'd upset her. He resisted the urge to press his fingers to the inside corners of his eyes. Hard. He didn't know how to talk to women. He'd never had time to learn, and now it was too late. He didn't have charm. He wasn't interesting. He was a soldier. He was damned good at being a soldier. He was a medic and he was damned good at that as well. But women . . .

"I know you're aware, Nonny. Of any of us, you would be the one to be aware. It's just that anyone slipping through our security has to be a GhostWalker or one of Whitney's supersoldiers. Just the fact that they knew which plant you needed bothers me. They had to be watching you."

She pulled the pipe from between her lips with a little unladylike Cajun curse. "I didn' think about that. I didn' tell the soldiers *which* plant I needed. Someone had to have seen me pull up the dead one from the field by Trap and Cayenne's house."

Ezekiel didn't think anyone else would refer to the huge factory-sized building in the swamp as a "house." Trap had converted it to use as a home, so he supposed it could be loosely labeled that. Still, Nonny included Trap and Cayenne in her family circle.

"I had four plants growin' and all of them were dead. Black nightshade is rare in these parts. I don' see it much growin' in the wild around here anymore."

"But the plant was on the doorstep this morning?"

She nodded slowly. "I'm sorry, Ezekiel. I should have told you right away. I figured whoever brought it to me wasn' a threat."

He couldn't blame her. She was sweet and kind. She couldn't conceive of the evil a man like Dr. Peter Whitney was capable of. Still, she was smart. Very, very smart, and it would never do to underestimate her. She looked innocent enough, but she was very good at this game.

"I'll take a look around, try to backtrack whoever it was." He knew that was useless. He always scouted around the house and property. There hadn't been any tracks. Just in case, he would ask Cayenne to move into the house until the others came back. The other members of his team had been pulled into an extraction mission, leaving only Ezekiel, Mordichai, Gino and Draden to guard the women and children.

She nodded. "It will be good to have Cayenne here. Trap doesn't like her on her own when he's gone. Says she goes down to the basement and stays alone. He worries."

"Cayenne isn't a woman you have to worry too much about, Nonny." Clearly Nonny was more worried about Cayenne than Trap. If Trap was afraid for his woman, she'd be put somewhere safe and made to stay there. Trap didn't mess around when it came to Cayenne and her safety.

"I know she can take care of herself," Nonny agreed, "but she's spent too much of her life alone. It will be good for her to come here. I like havin' her around."

There it was. The simple truth. What made Grace Fontenot so special. She'd taken Cayenne into her world without hesitation and now that she was there, Nonny wanted her close. Ezekiel wanted Cayenne close for a completely different reason. Mordichai, Gino and Draden would protect the women and children, and Pepper would help if needed, but violence made her physically ill. Not so Cayenne. She was as lethal as they came, and Ezekiel wanted her nearby to help protect Nonny, Pepper and the triplets if needed.

"Give me your list, and after I get things settled here, I'll go into the Quarter and get these urgently needed spices."

She pinned him with a stern eye. "Are you bein' sarcastic, Ezekiel Fortunes?"

"Yes, ma'am, but I'm willing to pretend I believe you desperately need these spices or we won't be having any dinners for the rest of the week."

She gestured toward him with her sweet-smelling pipe. "Much obliged, Ezekiel." She put the pipe back in her mouth and commenced rocking.

Ezekiel shook his head, watching her for just a few moments longer. She looked relaxed and very pleased with herself. She was up to something, but he still couldn't figure it out yet. He enjoyed their little sparring sessions, although she should have told him about her plant immediately. He was responsible for security at the Fontenot home while the rest of his team was in the field, but more, nothing could happen to Nonny. She was the heart of their world. She had no business approaching the no-trespassing zone at Stennis, not when he could easily get in and get whatever she needed.

He went straight to the kitchen door where the box with the plant had been found after texting Cayenne that he needed her and to pack a bag. She didn't ask him why; she simply texted back the time she'd be there and that was in under an hour. Cayenne was a no-nonsense soldier and one they all knew they could count on. It was telling that Nonny hadn't asked her to go into town for the imaginary, can't-live-without spices.

Puzzles bothered him. He didn't like what he didn't understand and even as he backtracked around the house, and farther out into the yard, his mind kept worrying at why Nonny repeatedly sent him into town. She was a direct woman. Ordinarily, she just came out and said what was on her mind, but this time . . .

There it was. A brush against a branch had left the small leaves on the bush bruised. Not crushed. Bruised. Whoever had gone through that very narrow trail had been relatively small. Definitely light on their feet. He crouched down and studied the ground. The narrow path leading through the brush passed quite close to the dog kennel. He followed that track, paying close attention to the leaves spilling out into the space. Most were pristine, but there were a few that had that same bruising. He could see a small blemish near the top of the kennel where existing dirt had been smeared by a light touch. Someone had gone up the side of the fence onto the roof of the kennel and into the yard.

The dogs were loose at night, running free in the yard, but closed up in the kennels during the day. The dogs hadn't sounded off at all, nor had they attacked, and they had to have been in the yard at the time the plant was delivered. Unease snaked down his spine. Few people in the world could get through the security at the Fontenot compound. Those few were enhanced soldiers. Dr. Peter Whitney's experiments.

Abruptly he spun around and stalked back toward the house. He didn't expect to find much, but there was always the possibility of a screwup. He might get lucky—except he didn't. The cameras had recorded glimpses of the dogs rushing the area near the kennels but then halting abruptly, tails wagging before turning away. He studied the feed over and over, trying to catch a single glimpse of the intruder and failing. He saw the box with the plant appear in the footage twice—rather just the corner of the box, but who carried it was another matter.

He studied that little corner of the box, trying to determine by where it was positioned just how high in the air it was. That might give him an idea of the height of the person carrying it. He went back and forth between the two frames, scrutinizing carefully. He was still working on it when his brother Mordichai came in.

"Nonny just told me."

"Someone definitely penetrated the security last night." Ezekiel pointed to the screen where he'd frozen the frame. "They came through the water. I backtracked them to the edge of the pier."

"We have a camera trained on the water."

"No boat, Mordichai, and there wasn't a ripple in the water for as far back as forty-five minutes. I'm going to have you go back even further, just in case, but you aren't going to find anything."

There was a brief silence as they both pondered the significance of that. "Shit. We're in trouble, aren't we?" Mordichai said. "I should have known that bastard wouldn't leave us alone no matter what he said."

"What if it isn't Whitney trying to reacquire Pepper and the triplets? What if it's the same person who tried to kill Cayenne? Because we know that wasn't Whitney."

"Violet. That fucking bitch. She's one of us. A Ghost-Walker."

"She's not one of us. Not now, not ever. Whitney enhanced her, but she couldn't possibly have passed a psych eval. Whitney brought the women from the orphanages, and he didn't feel the need to test them before he enhanced them. He just used them for his experiments so he wouldn't make mistakes on his soldiers. If he'd tested her, he would have seen she was a sociopath and out for herself," Ezekiel said. He tapped the screen with the picture frozen. "I have to get going, but Cayenne should be here any minute. Stay sharp. Keep the girls close. You'd better warn Pepper. She might not like violence, but she'll kill if she has to in order to protect her daughters and Nonny, so use her as a last resort."

"Are you that worried?"

Ezekiel frowned, thinking it over. It was possible Whitney had orchestrated the other team members to be out on missions in order to reduce the size of the guards around the women and children, but he doubted it. He almost believed Whitney would leave them alone. The man wanted to see what Wyatt and Pepper could do with their three daughters, all capable of injecting venom when biting.

"I just think we should be extra vigilant. We've got someone, obviously enhanced, watching us and penetrating security. Nonny said they had to be watching her when she goes to harvest the plants because they knew which plant had died that she needed. She went to Stennis to try to dig up another one."

Mordichai's eyebrows shot up. "They turned her back?"

"Said they weren't nice about it. I'll have a talk with the guards and warn them they don't want a lesson in manners."

Mordichai grinned at him. "That'll go over big."

Ezekiel shrugged. "It won't hurt them to learn to be polite, especially to an eighty-plus-year-old woman who has lived her entire life here." There was an edge to his voice he couldn't prevent. No one was going to fuck with Nonny and get away with it. He'd pull rank if he had to, but he'd rather beat the shit out of them. His brothers always retained the lesson when it had been delivered that way. "She's got me on another bullshit run to the store for her. Not just a grocery store, where I could stay closer to home, she wants me to pick up items only found at a specialty store in the Quarter."

"What's her game?"

"I haven't figured that out yet, but it's important to her or I wouldn't go."

"Wyatt says she's got the second sight."

Mordichai smirked a little, and Ezekiel resisted the sudden urge to punch him. "If she does, she should just tell me what the hell she's seeing instead of making me go into town when I'm needed here."

Ezekiel glanced once more up at the screen and then froze, staring. "Upper right corner, Mordichai, right by the nearest cypress trees. Right *inside* them. You see anything?"

Mordichai stepped closer and peered at the small flat screen. "Maybe. A ripple for sure. Run it slow."

Ezekiel did, frame by frame. Something made the water ripple outward. For one moment something came up out of the water, but it was impossible to tell exactly what he was seeing because it was the exact color of the water, even rippled like water. Then it reached up to grasp the root of a gum tree sticking out of the ground just up from the shore. He saw a hand. A human hand. It was small, not a man's.

He let out his breath. "You see what I'm seeing? That's a woman, Mordichai."

"What the hell is she?"

"I saw her hand *before* she touched the root. The moment she touched it, her hand disappeared." He took the recording back to the moment the hand was in midair and froze the screen. "Definitely a human hand, a woman's or child's. I think a woman."

"Another one of Whitney's fuckups he sent here for termination?"

Ezekiel shook his head and reached out to the screen, running his finger along the knuckles of the hand as if by touching it he could figure out just who it was. Enemy or ally? "I wouldn't refer to them as fuckups, not in Wyatt or Trap's hearing. If this is someone scheduled for termination, Pepper and Cayenne didn't know about her or they would have told us."

Mordichai shrugged. "That doesn't mean anything. The ones scheduled for termination were kept apart because they were deemed too dangerous. Cayenne was never let out of her cell unless they were testing her. Even then they transported her drugged. The girls admitted there could have been others they didn't know about."

Ezekiel turned away from the screen and stared out the window into the swamp. He liked the peace of it. The way the world disappeared and there was only the sound of nature. The insects. The alligators. The wind in the trees. Birds. He never wanted to see another city as long as he lived. He could make his base here. He would. But first, they were going to have to ferret out every secret and destroy every enemy sent their way.

He was born for battle. He knew that. He didn't like it, but he knew he was too good at it to be anything else than what he was. His friend Wyatt had found a woman and settled down with Pepper and their triplets—meaning as settled as any GhostWalker could ever be. Trap had followed. That had been a complete shock. Trap wasn't the kind of man to ever settle. Cayenne, his woman, wasn't the type of woman most men could ever live with. One bite and it could be the end, but Trap got off on that.

Ezekiel accepted that no such woman existed for him, one who could understand his need to protect his family and his fellow soldiers. That need drove him and always would. Wyatt had a woman content to stay home and raise her children. She would protect them if she was forced to, but it wasn't in her nature. Trap had a woman just the opposite. She would fight by his side, and throw herself into every dangerous situation without hesitation. He knew neither woman would suit him. He needed a Nonny, and it didn't seem like there were any women like her left in the world.

"You all right, Zeke?"

Mordichai rarely called him Zeke these days. It was a leftover-from-childhood thing, but one that twisted at his heart. He shot his brother a careless smile. He didn't feel like smiling. He felt dead inside sometimes. All around him the swamp teemed with life. Wyatt's little girls made him long for something he couldn't have. He didn't want his brother seeing into him. Seeing that he'd hit some kind of wall and wasn't certain where he was going or what he was doing anymore. "Just a little tired."

Those three little girls. So beautiful. Running around as if they didn't have a care in the world. He liked to listen to them play together. Their little voices laughing while they made up imaginary games. His hand was always near a weapon, and he liked knowing he could protect them from any harm. He couldn't imagine men wanting to destroy those three babies.

They crawled in his lap when he was reading, demanding stories from him. He gave them stories when no one was around. Hell, he'd told his brothers stories when they huddled together in the dark of an alleyway. He knew stories, and he had an imagination. He just didn't like showing it to anyone. It made him feel vulnerable, and he had never liked that feeling.

The three little girls were very intelligent. Too intelligent for their own good. Fortunately, so were Pepper, Wyatt and Nonny. They had to be to stay one step ahead of the girls. He took the triplets out with him on the river whenever he was familiarizing himself with the waterways. He told the others he wanted them to learn as well, but it was really to tell them stories and have fun with them. Sometimes they snuck into town and he bought them snowballs. As far as he knew, they didn't ever tell Wyatt, because he was fairly certain he'd never hear the end of it.

Aside from his two younger brothers, he'd never been around children. Ginger, Thym and Cannelle made him realize he wanted a family of his own. He just wasn't the type of man to have one.

"Were you out on the roof again last night?" Mordichai persisted. "You don't need to be. We post a guard every night on a rotation, and most nights Draden goes running. I don't think he actually sleeps. Ever."

"I like to take a look around," Ezekiel admitted. "Without the rest of the team to guard the girls, I just want to be extra vigilant." That sounded lame and gave away more than he wanted to. Mordichai knew him too well to allow him to get away with too much.

"You're getting restless again." His brother made it a statement.

Ezekiel shrugged. It was never good when he got restless. All around him bad things happened. He usually went off by himself. It was much safer that way. Still, there were the three little girls, the women and Nonny to hold him there at least until his team came back.

"Last time . . ."

"Yeah. I know." He didn't want his brother to say it aloud. He knew what happened. How many men he'd hurt. How close he'd come to really losing it. "I'll take off if I need to. It's better out here. Not so many demons." That much was the truth. It was far better living on the edge of the swamp, right along the river where the wind called to him and he felt as if he could breathe.

"Whitney's enhancements made it worse."

There was no denying the truth of that. What had been born and bred in the streets and alleyways of the city had grown into a monster inside of him. When he'd been chosen for psychic and physical enhancement, he hadn't realized the extent of what would be done to him, or the complications it would create.

"I handle it," he said softly, needing to reassure his brother as he'd always done. Mordichai studied his face, so Ezekiel kept his features carefully blank. He was handling it, but the need in him was growing and it was ugly.

"You almost killed them," Mordichai reminded softly.

"They started it." Why he felt compelled to defend himself he didn't know. He never defended his actions. What the hell was wrong with him? He needed to get away for a while, at least be alone until the need building in him passed. "I've got to pick up the spices for Nonny or we won't be eating. At least that's what she claims."

He didn't wait for his brother to reply. He found Nonny on the porch in her rocking chair. "The girls?"

"Pepper put them down for a nap. She's watchin' them. You know they're little escape artists." Nonny sounded proud, a smile in her voice.

"Keep the shotgun close. Something's not right. Early this morning I received orders to go to work at Stennis. That's fairly standard, and usually I would consider it a good thing, working so close to home, but with most of the team gone, now I'm worried. We're getting shorthanded around here."

Nonny took the pipe from her mouth. He noted the spicy tobacco wasn't lit. She was just chewing on the stem, an indication that she was worried. The knots in his guts tightened. Nonny wasn't a woman prone to worry.

"I always have the shotgun handy, and I'll tell Pepper to keep the girls close." Her eyes bore straight into his. "You stay safe, Ezekiel. Mind your surroundin's and stay cautious, even when you aren't with us."

"I will." He held out his hand for the note for the spices.

She hesitated. Not long. No more than a split second, but he saw it and felt it in his gut again. She put the scented notepaper in his hand, and he shoved it into his pocket without looking at it. It was a crap list, but he'd get it for her.

"It's important you stay alert even when you aren't watchin' over us," she reiterated. "We need you. You're important to us."

That monster in him rose fast and ferocious. He could feel it deep inside waiting to consume him. His fingers closed one by one until he had made two tight fists, the need so strong he held himself still so he wouldn't give himself away. So she couldn't see.

He was always needed. He was always so important. As a shield. A protector. He was born into that role, and there was no getting around what he was. Even Nonny saw it. What they never saw was the why of it. Why he was so fucking good at being a shield. He hoped to hell the ones he loved never did.

3

Ezekiel walked straight down the narrow, uneven side-walk, head up, eyes moving restlessly, quartering the entire area out of sheer habit. Jackson Square was alive with tourists and street vendors. Dozens of street artists displayed their paintings and crafts as well as played music and mimed. He didn't like painted faces of men or women who could be anyone. He was a target. He would always be a target. He accepted that fact, even walking down a street filled with laughing people.

He didn't belong there and he never would. More, he didn't want to. Nonny, however, wanted these damned spices, so he would crawl through hell for her if that's what it took.

He was a hunter first and always. That was bred in him. Enhanced in him. He could follow a trail better than almost anyone. Some said he had the eyes of an eagle and a sense of smell equal to a polar bear's. It was close to the truth. Once he was set on a trail, few escaped him. Here, in the Quarter with the jazz players and the mimes and the street

artists fighting for a small piece of the pie, it was more difficult to separate scents and spot the enemy.

Aromas from various small cafés and restaurants assailed
him. Perfumes and the sweat of the street performers. The
sweet smell of weed competed for space with tobacco. The
river was close, and he could smell that and the ships that ran
up and down it with their loads of cargo. The fish. The cars
and horses. His mind processed it all, separating and cata-
loguing automatically.

The wind shifted minutely just as he was about to enter
the store where Nonny bought all of her Cajun spices—at
least the ones she didn't make herself. The scent stopped him
in his tracks and he whirled around, for the first time in his
life losing focus on his primary mission. He *had* to track that
scent. Turning away from the spice shop, he followed the
wind up toward the street opposite the Café Du Monde.

Out in the open, away from the shelter of the buildings,
the wind was capricious, blowing in small eddies, stopping
and starting from a different direction. One moment it
seemed to be coming off the river and the next it was down
from the Café Du Monde. He didn't stop moving, filled with
a purpose he didn't understand and therefore was leery of,
but he knew he had to catch the scent again.

A small restaurant right on the corner was tucked into
the space between two shops. Tables were on an outside
balcony on the second story as well as a few on the street
and more inside. A waitress laughed softly as she served
two women what appeared to be strawberry lemonade and
some fluffy pastry. The waitress was small and slight. Her
hair was pulled back away from her face, hidden under a
rolled handkerchief. Her accent was very Cajun, as if she'd
been born on the bayou and stayed there growing up. Soft.
Sexy. A slow drawl that crawled inside a man and wrapped
itself tight until he couldn't ever forget that sound.

More, for him, it was the elusive scent he couldn't quite
name. She smelled—delicious. Sexy. Everything her voice

promised. He didn't know how to saunter. To be casual. He didn't date. He didn't show interest in women. What was the use when he was a soldier? He was gone on a moment's notice, and his woman would never know where he was. Still, knowing that, his feet refused to move and he simply stood there, inhaling her, taking the scent of her deep.

It wasn't as if she was strikingly beautiful. She was . . . nondescript. Hard to describe other than she was small. He couldn't take his eyes off of her. The more he took her in, the more he saw of her. Why hadn't he noticed her bone structure? It was amazing and her skin flawless. Like silk or satin. More, her skin appeared dew fresh, as if the morning mist had enveloped her and left her skin looking like the petals of Nonny's exotic flowers.

The rolled handkerchief covered most of her hair, but the sun struck her at an angle and he could see the shine, gloriously blond, so pale it appeared to be like the finest vintage of a fine white wine. He instantly had the need to touch her skin, to bury his fingers in that thick mass of hair peeking out beneath the triangle of cloth. When he found he'd taken a step toward her, he forced himself to halt, his hands curling into two tight fists against his thigh.

He didn't have a reaction to women. When one caught his eye, she was always tall, with dark hair and decidedly curvy. He passed over them quickly, because in his world, men like him didn't have a woman of their own. But this one . . .

Her eyes were large, a beautiful, startling blue. Framed with blond, almost blue-tinged very thick lashes. The color made her eyes even more exotic. He was certain she wore blue mascara, but there were no clumps or any other indication that her lashes weren't naturally that color.

His body stirred. Not just stirred—every cell in him reacted to her. It was damned embarrassing. He wasn't a teenager. He'd had control of his body since he was a young kid. Now, he doubted if it would be safe to take a step.

He found he wanted her to look at him. Not just look, but

really see—and that was dangerous for both of them. He knew he shouldn't. He knew better. He was not only a hunter, he was a soldier and a damned good one. Things like this— things so unusual—were suspect, but he couldn't walk away, no matter how many times he told himself to do so.

She glanced up at him and stilled, like a doe caught in the predatory stare of a lethal cat. As if for just a moment she recognized the hunter in him and the prey in her. Those exotic long lashes fluttered and then she flashed a small smile.

"Would you prefer a table outside or inside?"

For a moment all he could do was stare at her. He felt like a fucking imbecile. A table? Why the hell was she going on about a table? A bed maybe, but a table? He didn't need either. A wall would do.

"Outside will do." He was never that comfortable in- doors. He'd lived on the streets for years, and then traveled to the world's hotspots, most of the time where there were no accommodations. He was used to that life, and being inside often made him feel trapped. He remembered man- ners. He'd beaten etiquette into his brothers and yet his man- ners were damned rusty. "Thank you."

Her small smile in response made his cock jerk and pulse with demand. Shit. He was totally out of control, and not once in his life had that ever happened. Suspicion slithered down his spine. He kept his features blank and nodded to- ward the only table that afforded him any kind of cover while still allowing him to see anything coming at him.

Did she hesitate just for a split second before she turned and walked toward the table, indicating that he follow her? Was he so suspicious, even of a random waitress working the dinner rush? That was insane. No one could have known he would be in town at this precise hour and then randomly walk over to grab a bite to eat. He took a deep breath and inhaled her scent. A mixture of vanilla and orange. *Good Lord*, she smelled good.

"Thanks," he murmured politely and took the menu from

her. He had a wild urge to run his finger along the back of
her hand and touch her skin just to see if it was as soft as it
looked. If he stooped so low, he'd be descending into the
world of creepy stalker and that was just plain unacceptable.
But he liked looking at her. And inhaling her. He knew he'd
like touching her.

He watched her walk away. It was strange that when he'd
first seen her he thought she was nondescript. She was viv-
idly alive, a shimmering, beautiful woman he couldn't take
his gaze from. For the first time in his life, he decided he
was going to sit back and be normal. Just enjoy the moment.
It would probably never come again, but right now, he was
simply a man appreciating the beauty of a woman.

He sipped at the water she brought him after ordering
food he didn't necessarily want, but he'd eat just to spend
time watching her. He liked the way she moved, flowing
over the stone of the patio, her hips a provocative sway. That
didn't mean he could stop, even for a few minutes, the way
he scanned his surroundings, checking rooftops and streets.
He noticed everything, registered and processed data even
as he kept an eye on his beautiful waitress.

She was keeping an eye on him as well. At first he put it
down to her being good at her job, watching out for her
customers, but he was observing her closely and realized
she barely took her gaze from him. She worked, laughed
softly with people at other tables, took orders and brought
food, but through it all, she always had her eye on him.

His first reaction was to be suspicious again. It wasn't as
if he was good-looking. He was rough and scarred, covered
with tattoos, and looked, according to his brothers, as mean
as hell. A beautiful woman wasn't going to notice a man
like him. She certainly wouldn't look twice—but she was.

"Bella! You need to take your break," a voice called from
inside the restaurant just as she emerged with his bowl of
gumbo.

She glanced over her shoulder, nodded and set the plate

in front of him. "It's stuffy in there. I think they need another overhead fan."

He glanced around. There were no other tables available outside. "Join me. At least you can get off your feet for a few minutes. There's a good breeze coming off the river." His heart actually accelerated. His pulse never changed when bullets were flying, but asking her to sit opposite him and have a conversation was almost terrifying.

She hesitated, and he held his breath, uncertain if he wanted her to sit or to go. She slipped into the chair across from him and gave him a tentative smile.

"I'm Ezekiel Fortunes."

"Bellisia Adams. My friends call me Bella."

He liked that. Her name. It was unusual and sounded Italian to him, not Cajun or French.

"I've seen you before," she admitted with a shy smile. "You brought your three little girls into Baraquin's. They came out eating snowballs. Baraquin's makes the best snowballs in New Orleans."

He sat back in his chair, his muscles loose, one hand coiled around the handle of his fork. He could kill her in seconds and be gone before her body dropped. What the hell? She saw the girls? Noticed them? He was supposed to believe that? Deep inside, everything in him stilled. His heartbeat was as steady as a rock. This was his world. One of death. Of violence. He understood this world.

"They were adorable. Triplets. I think it's my first time ever seeing triplets."

He took a breath. A big mistake. Vanilla and orange inflated his lungs. Of course a woman might notice triplets. They were cute, with their mops of dark curly hair and big eyes. They could melt hearts at twenty paces.

"Not mine. My friend's." He couldn't even put a fucking sentence together. He sounded like a caveman. The next thing that was bound to happen was that he'd start grunting. Flinging her over his shoulder and carrying her off to a cave was looking pretty good to him, especially if he didn't have to talk. "They're his daughters." He made an effort to get his head out of his ass. "They love to go to Baraquin's. The moment they see me, they tug on my pant leg and look at me with their big brown eyes and I'm a sucker." It was the truth, and he was glad to be able to give her truth, especially when she sat across from him, innocent, and he'd thought about killing her to protect the girls.

"I have to confess, I like to go to Baraquin's for their snowballs as well."

"It's popular for that reason." Scintillating conversation. She'd go home and remember it for certain.

She nodded. "A friend told me about it and once I tried the shaved ice, I was hooked—as I suspect the little girls are. You weren't eating one though."

A ghost of a smile hovered. "I have two brothers. If they caught me eating a snowball, I'd never hear the end of it." And it wouldn't all be about the shaved ice either; they'd make dirty jokes. He wasn't about to tell her that.

She laughed. It was a real laugh. Low. Sultry. Smoky even. Her laughter played over his body like the touch of fingers on his cock. He shifted just a little in the chair to give himself a little relief. Great. Now he was thinking with his dick. That wasn't improving things.

"I love that. I don' have any siblings, so I missed out on gettin' teased when I was younger."

He had acute hearing. Her accent was perfect—or nearly so. He'd listened to Nonny, born and bred in the swamps of Louisiana, and Bella sounded close, but there was just a single note off. One. Single. Note. He tried to put that out of his mind. He wanted to stop being himself for one fucking hour and be a man enjoying the company of a woman.

"You grow up here?" he asked casually, and took a bite of the gumbo. It wasn't nearly as good as Nonny's. He kept his gaze on her face. The more he looked at her, the more he thought she was extraordinary. Especially those eyelashes.

So long and thick with their exotic color. He was certain now that the bluish tint was natural.

She nodded, her gaze shifting slightly away from his. "Not right here, but close by. My dad fished. My mom was a nurse. I lost them a few years back and I left. There's something about New Orleans that drew me back."

She was lying. Damn it. She was fucking lying to him. He wasn't going to get his hour pretending to be normal, whatever that was. Still, she could have her reasons. People lied for all kinds of reasons. He might not get his hour, but he was going to touch her skin. The sun was still beating down and she was very fair.

He reached out and ran his fingers over her forearm, and down across the back of her hand. "You're going to burn out here."

She felt like paradise. Softer than he imagined. Like silk, only better. It was strange, but he felt as if he'd absorbed her through the pads of his fingers—as if she sank deep into his bones. His gaze drifted over her. Who the hell was she? Why did he have such a reaction to her? Why was he so damned suspicious, his warning system going off even as his body was telling him to carry the woman off and have his way with her?

She didn't give off the GhostWalker vibe. GhostWalkers nearly always knew when another was close by. They gave off a subtly different energy. He was close to her. Very close. Close enough that her scent was driving him right up the wall, but he didn't feel that GhostWalker power.

He knew. Well, maybe he knew. Bellisia just stopped herself from tucking a stray strand of hair behind his ear. He was gorgeous. Not in a handsome, magazine model type of way, but a real man with muscle and tattoos kind of way. His hair spilled in every direction as if it wasn't to be tamed, clearly a herald of the man he was. She liked that too.

He'd touched her. *Touched* her skin. It felt like a caress. Her entire body reacted to the feel of his fingers on her. A shiver of absolute awareness went down her spine. Her sex clenched. She was acutely aware of her breasts suddenly aching. All because of a single touch. She had it bad for this man, and that was very, very dangerous.

She should get up and leave. It would be smarter and safer. She was very smart, but she was rarely safe, and really, why should she start now? She'd studied him for the last few weeks. Studied his entire team. Most of them were gone at the moment, and she liked how he stayed close to the adorable little girls and the older woman. Nonny, they called her.

She'd never actually seen a real household before. She was drawn back time and again to spy on them. She hated the way it made her feel, the outsider looking in. She wanted that for herself. She hadn't known she did, because she hadn't known it existed, but she liked the laughter and camaraderie. She liked the way the men looked after Nonny, not that they made a big deal of it. Just small things really, but she loved that they did them for her.

Nonny was very respected and well known along the waterways and even in town. Less was said about the men living at the Fontenot home. The swamp was a place where the locals knew one another; they went back generations. That was the reason she'd told Ezekiel she was from a town close by, but not right there. If he made inquiries, there was a reason the locals wouldn't know her.

Without thinking about what she was doing, she picked up the water glass and dribbled water along her forearm to cool the burning sensation. She did the same to the other arm. When she realized what she was doing, her gaze jumped to his.

He frowned slightly. "You really are burning. Don't you use a sunscreen?"

She liked the genuine worry in his voice. That little edge that told her he was not happy that she had even a slight burn. He wasn't focused on her pouring water on her skin—and why should he be? She was just paranoid that he suspected her. But why would he? She was a waitress, doing her job. He'd happened by.

She tried not to stare at him, but she couldn't help herself. She'd watched him for so long she felt like she knew him. She especially liked to see him with the triplets. He told them great stories. She listened, of course. Who wouldn't listen? He was different around the children than he was with other people. For some silly reason, she wished he were different with her as well.

"Bellisia, do you use sunblock?" he persisted.

She doubted if that was a question he asked very many people, and for some reason it pleased her that it mattered to him. She nodded. "It doesn't always help. On the other hand, mosquitoes don' like me, so it evens out."

"I don't like you out in the sun like this. I don't burn, but it looks like it hurts when others do."

"Never? You've never had a burn?"

"Not a sunburn," he qualified.

Instantly she wanted to know more. He was a Ghost-Walker. She knew he was a member of the famed PJs, the pararescue squadron of the GhostWalkers, and that he took his job of protecting everyone around him very seriously. He was a member of the team Violet had sold out to Cheng. She was fairly certain he wasn't a traitor to his country, but she had no way of knowing if anyone else on his team was. Or if the moment she revealed herself, they would try to send her back to Whitney. She would never go back. By now, she was certain there were orders to terminate her on sight.

"You're so lucky. When I was a child, I got them all the time." She had too. She loved the water and rarely was away from it. The longer she swam, the more her skin burned when she got out to run around with the others.

"The triplets don't seem to burn. Although it could be that their great-grandmother slathers them with some concoction she's made from her natural pharmacy. She grows all sorts of plants and uses them for medicine. Quite a few people come to her for help. Wyatt, her son, is a doctor, and that helps because if she doesn't think she can help them, she makes certain he sees them." Another ghost of a smile. "Usually free of charge. Nonny likes to barter for services rendered."

She liked that little hint of a smile. It didn't do much to soften the features of his face, he looked as rough and tough as ever, but it did make him more human. She could stare at his face for the rest of her life. It was that perfect to her. She especially loved the sound of his voice. More and more she found herself in the swamp by the Fontenot compound, although it was insanity to keep going back there. It had been especially crazy to watch Nonny digging up dead black nightshade and then spying on her as the soldiers at Stennis turned her back from accessing the property where she needed to go to get the plant for her natural pharmacy.

Bellisia had dug it for her and then snuck onto the compound to leave it. She'd left a note under the plant warning the team of the dangers. Telling them about Violet's latest treachery. She should have done that and walked away, but she was already too intrigued with Ezekiel, those little girls and Nonny and she'd stayed. She still didn't know about the other members of his team, but she was very intrigued with Ezekiel and felt she *had* to warn him.

"What's a natural pharmacy?" She'd watched Nonny for hours dealing with various people coming to her door and leaving with powders in small bags.

He gave her a look that warned her she'd just treaded far too close to making a mistake. Her question didn't sit too well with him, as if she should already know the answer. She clamped her teeth down on her bottom lip hard. She didn't make mistakes. It was the only way she stayed alive. If she was making them now, it was because she was so enamored with him she couldn't think of anything else.

"Nonny was born and raised in the swamp. She grew up in a time when most people who were sick or injured consulted with the local *traiteur*, or healer. She trained, of course, because according to those living around her, she had the gift. She began transplanting plants from wherever they grew wild to an area of the swamp so she would have them together in one place. According to Nonny, each of these plants can cure or heal depending. She seems to know how to extract the right ingredients because her patients always come back. And doctors consult with her. Pharmacists as well. She's got quite a reputation."

She leaned her chin onto the heel of her hand. "However did you meet such a woman? She sounds so cool."

Nonny *was* cool. She always seemed genuine. Bellisia was desperate to meet her. To quit hiding and actually become part of something. She needed a purpose. She'd lived her entire life with purpose, and, although she loved it, just waitressing wasn't cutting it for her.

"Nonny is extraordinary," Ezekiel said. "She's the best woman I've ever known."

His voice said it all, said more than his words did. He admired and respected Nonny. More, he had affection for her, and Bellisia was certain he didn't have affection for that many people. More than ever she longed to meet Nonny.

"Is she related to you? Your grandmother?" she guessed.

His eyes flicked over her. Not drifted with that small exhilarating expression of interest—it was suspicion. He didn't like to be questioned. She hastily tried to back off, sending him a faint smile and placing both hands on the table to push herself up.

"I'm not good at this. I've always been awkward with getting to know someone. I'll just be quiet now and get back to work."

He put his hand over hers and instantly her veins ran with a thick, hot molasses, moving through her body slowly, scorching every cell along the way. She'd never felt such a sensation. It was both frightening and a little bit thrilling.

The moment he touched her she sank back into the chair. She didn't mean to; she was blowing it being so close to him. She'd stalked him. Like a creeper. She had started out intending to make certain the men on GhostWalker Team Four were worth risking her life and freedom to save, but then she got caught up in their lives.

How could she not? They were loving to one another. Rough, but definitely very affectionate. They were protective of the three little girls and both women. Truthfully, the men were protective of one another. She'd formed friendships with the other girls, but there was only one she truly trusted. She wanted to trust the others and she cared about them, but she didn't have what Ezekiel had with his team and with Nonny. She wanted it. She just didn't know how to get there.

"I'm the one not very good at this," Ezekiel said softly.

His voice moved through her. That sound just tugged at her even when she didn't want it to. She had no business fantasizing about him, or even getting this close to him. It was dangerous for both of them. If he wasn't what she thought . . . If she'd miscalculated and he was an enemy, she'd have to kill him. And she would. She wouldn't want to, but she would.

"Nonny is actually a friend of mine's grandmother. She raised him as well as his brothers. I think she believes she's raising me now."

He sent her the same ghost of a smile that twisted her up inside. He was gorgeous. She even loved the scars on him. That rough five-o'clock shadow. She had no idea what she'd do with him if he were hers, but she still wanted him.

"She really does sound wonderful." There was a wistful note in her voice she couldn't hide and didn't bother to try. She wanted to give him as much truth as possible about her, because most of her was all about deceit.

"She can cook too." His gaze moved from her face to the shops across the way. "She sends me into the Quarter for the damnedest things. Spices. She makes quite a few of her own but then she has to have certain ones that you only find in that spice store over there. And it's always an emergency."

She liked the thread of affection in his voice, and the hint of humor. He really liked Nonny, and that made her soft inside when ordinarily that wasn't her way.

"My friend Zara loves to cook. When we were kids she used to sneak into the kitchen where the cook—her chef—was and beg him to let her cook with him. He always did it. Zara can be very persuasive when she wants something and she loves being in a kitchen." She stumbled over that one. She detested misleading him but she couldn't talk about mess halls and dormitories.

She suddenly realized his hand was still over hers. He hadn't moved it, but his thumb slid along her wrist, back and forth. Mesmerizing. A caress. She felt it all the way to her toes. He was far more dangerous to her than she first thought, because every time he touched her, he left more of his print behind. In her. As if somehow with a touch he'd branded her and it sank deep into her bones.

"Do you cook?"

She shook her head. "I never really had the opportunity to learn. And now I'm waitressing with zero chance of ever being a chef in a restaurant like this or really any other. I'd have to go to a school to learn."

"Nonny taught both Pepper and Cayenne. Pepper is my friend Wyatt's wife. Cayenne belongs to my friend Trap. Pepper seems to take to cooking, although we tease her a lot. My brothers especially. They always act like they might die when she's the cook, but they eat every single bit. No leftovers."

She loved hearing about his family. She didn't remove her hand from beneath his in spite of every instinct telling her to run while she had the chance. "And Cayenne?"

"Let's just say it's a good thing Trap can cook."

She burst out laughing. She couldn't help it. The way he

shook his head as if Cayenne was a hopeless case in the kitchen was hysterical.

"Nonny already has the three girls sitting in the kitchen with her when she's cooking, helping her. I hear her talk about the ingredients just as if they could do the family cooking, and they're only just about to turn two."

"Two?" Bellisia had observed the triplets interacting with various members of the family, and they seemed a lot older than two. They were small, but they talked as if they were seven or eight. Maybe even older than that. She'd put them down as very intelligent four-year-olds.

His thumb stopped moving and his eyes were once again on her face, not blinking. Alert. She'd definitely given her shock away. How to recover? "They were talking to you when you bought them the snowballs and they were using very big words. I guess I don't know much about children because I didn't think two-year-olds had that kind of vocabulary."

"Wyatt, their father, is a genius. The real deal. So is Pepper. I don't know much about children either, but my guess is, those girls come by their intelligence naturally."

His thumb was back, moving over her skin in an absent caress, as if he was unaware he was stroking along her inner wrist.

"You don't have children of your own?"

"Not married. Yet."

"Do you want children?" She couldn't stop herself. She tried to work up the necessary strength to pull her hand away, but this might be her only time. This moment. This fantasy. With this man. She wanted the dream even though she was smart enough to realize it was only that. There was no future for her. Not like Pepper or Cayenne.

She'd seen Pepper. She was gorgeous. Stunning. She'd seen Cayenne, and she was beautiful. She could see why Wyatt Fontenot and Trap had claimed them. Most of the team members were away now, so she hadn't had much time to study them, but the ones left behind guarded the women as if they were treasures, yet still treated them as equals. In fact, sometimes it appeared as if everyone deferred to both Nonny and Pepper.

She wanted equality. She wanted freedom. She wanted this man. He even sang to the three little girls. He did it when no one was around to hear him, but he did it enough that they begged him to sing before bedtime. They clearly loved his stories and his songs. It was soul-destroying to see such a big man, tough and dangerous, being so loving and sweet with toddlers. It got to her every time.

More than him singing to the triplets, which was beautiful, it was his voice. The sound of it. He had a rough edge to his voice, speaking or singing, but so perfectly pitched. She could listen to him forever, and truthfully, she'd fantasized many times about him singing to her. In their bed. She had to fight to keep from blushing, but she managed.

"I think I have to meet your Nonny someday," she said. "If I'm lucky, she'll offer to give me cooking lessons. I'll be able to cross it off my list."

"Your list?" he echoed.

She hadn't meant to give that away, but she was happy he wasn't looking at her suspiciously so she nodded. "I made a list of things I'd like to learn."

"Before you die?"

She winced. The possibility of her dying was a strong one. Whitney would send someone to hunt her. He'd be angry that she got away, but he'd be livid that she didn't give him the information he wanted. He wouldn't think she had the right to be upset just because he'd almost killed her with his virus. Or that he'd held her a virtual prisoner for nearly her entire life. That wouldn't even make sense to him. She'd been an orphan. No one wanted her anyway. No one ever would. That was drilled into her and she believed it. She was . . . different. She'd always be different. Whitney had made her that way.

She ducked her head and pulled her hand out from under his, starting to rise. "I'd better get back to work. Thanks for letting me sit here with you."

"I want to see you again."

Her heart clenched in her chest. Her gaze jumped to his, was caught and held by his strange amber-colored eyes. They appeared almost gold right then, as if they could glow brilliantly if the sun hit him just right. She touched the tip of her tongue to her suddenly dry lips and once again subsided into the chair.

"I'm not good at relationships," she admitted, hedging for time. She needed to think about this. She wanted to be with him. To get to know him. What better way than to agree to see him? But how dangerous to both of them would it be? She needed to calculate the odds of their mutual survival.

"Neither am I."

"I would like to, really, but . . . I don't date. I don't know how."

That ghost of a smile appeared again and turned her insides to hot molasses. She felt a million butterflies take wing in her stomach, and deep in her core, she felt liquid heat and a terrible throbbing as if she could feel her heartbeat right through her sex.

"We won't call it a date then," Ezekiel said. "We'll just get together like this and talk. That can't be too hard for either of us."

His hand was back. That thumb. He had big hands, and the pad of his thumb took in a lot of territory on her sensitive wrist. She hadn't known her wrist *was* sensitive until that moment, but she felt every caressing stroke go right through her until it was hard to breathe with wanting him.

"Bellisia."

Her name in that soft, low voice. The one that sent streaks of fire racing through her body straight to her most feminine core. She was in so much trouble. No one had ever made her feel the way he did. She was in over her head. All that time spying on him, watching him with Nonny and the triplets. With his brothers.

She loved the way he moved. He was light on his feet for such a powerful man. All corded but long muscle so that he could move fast and silently. He went into the swamp, no hesitation, as if he'd been born there. Some nights she'd watch him leap up onto the roof, rifle in hand, ready to protect those he called family. He'd actually crouch low and just make the jump, something she couldn't do. She could climb easily, but he was so fast because he was strong enough to make the leap.

"I'm swamped at work for the next few days, but give me your number. I'll call you when I can get away."

"I don' have a phone."

His eyes darkened to antique gold, not with suspicion, but with something altogether different. Concern. Definite worry.

She wrapped herself in that. No one had ever looked at her that way. "You can get me at work." She couldn't believe she was doing such an insane thing, but she wrote down the number of the little restaurant and handed it to him. Before she could change her mind, Bellisia pulled her hand away and got to her feet. "Your gumbo is cold. I'll get you another bowl."

"That's all right. I still have to get Nonny's spices before the store closes." He dropped bills on the table and lifted a hand.

She watched him walk away, totally mesmerized by how fluid he appeared. How his muscles rippled beneath the tight tee stretched across his chest and back. How the jeans cupped his butt. His body looked powerful. Several women turned to watch him as well and she felt the first stirrings of an emotion she'd never felt before. Jealousy. Pure and simple—jealousy. She didn't want him looking back at them—and he didn't. She knew he saw them because nothing escaped his notice, but he didn't look at the women. Not like he'd looked at her. She hugged that knowledge to herself and would for a very long time.

4

"Gentlemen, let me welcome our colleagues from Indonesia, Kopaska Group 5, to the Navy training facilities here at the John Stennis Space Center in the state of Mississippi," Senior Chief Petty Officer Ben Wallace said. "They are the elite of their navy. We will be assisting them in the rescue."

Stennis Space Center was the second largest space center in the United States with 220 square miles of land. Of that land, there were 140,000 acres that no one resided on and 138 acres where people worked. A wildlife preserve, it had black bear, deer, wild boar and bald eagles as well as a wide variety of other animals.

Stennis had its own zip code, and 5,400 people worked on the site. There was a farmer's market every other week, a bank, a post office, a hair salon, a coffee shop, child care, a full-service car station, a Navy Exchange Station and its own security department.

It also was home to the SWCC—Special Warfare Combat Craft. Ezekiel loved Stennis for that alone. Those were the

soldiers he knew he could count on to bring them safely
home should there be trouble. He knew them by name and
admired every single one of them.

The Nasciats program, training military from other countries, was a good one. Their barracks were next to the barracks for the members of the teams training with them, but
fortunately—or unfortunately—because Ezekiel was a
GhostWalker, he wasn't under the same orders as the other
teams. He could go home at night. He had women and children to protect. Women and children who were lethal and
still a part of the military program.

They were shorthanded during the day. With most of his
team out in the field, that left only four GhostWalkers, and
he needed them helping him train the six-man team joining
with a twelve-man SEAL team from the United States. Cayenne was the security force when they were gone. He tried
to leave at least one man home to help her, but he needed
them now that they'd gone from the war room to the active
field.

Ezekiel nodded to the six Indonesian soldiers, the twelve
SEALs and Draden, Gino and Mordichai, who would be
joining him on the mission.

"Five weeks ago a joint security team under the United
Nations came under fire by a radical Islamic terror cell operating inside of Indonesian borders. During the engage-
ment, three soldiers were taken hostage—two Indonesians
and an American. We're together to train for and undertake
a mission to rescue these men," Senior Chief Petty Officer
Wallace continued.

"We will be aided by the Navy's esteemed Special Boat
Team 22. They will be part of the mission we will deploy
to Indonesia as one team along with four members of an
elite pararescue team who are here to oversee this training.
We know two of the prisoners are in bad shape, and we need
our PJs on this operation. Captain Ezekiel Fortunes Doctor
will be in charge of your training." Wallace gestured toward

him, and Ezekiel nodded again as Wallace stepped back to give him the floor.

"Good morning," Ezekiel greeted. "This is Lieutenant Draden Freeman Doctor, Master Sergeant Gino Mazza and Master Sergeant Mordichai Fortunes. They will be assisting with your training. Expect to be pushed to your limit for the success of this mission. We have determined that the time on target will be limited to no more than three minutes."

He watched the Indonesian soldiers as he laid it out for them. What they were doing was extremely dangerous. He wanted to know that he could count on every man to have his soldiers' backs. He knew their reputation, and they were good men to have at one's back, but he didn't know *them* and he wasn't about to lose any of his men on this mission.

"SBT-22 will be transporting us to and from the objective. We'll have to move about seventy meters from the drop-off and pick-up point to reach the target building. Satellite images have shown the hostages being moved to and from the building, so we know that they will be there."

Keeping his eye on the Indonesian soldiers, the six unknown to him in a combat situation, he continued, "We expect heavy resistance. The latest video the terrorists sent shows the hostages were alive as of last night. However, they plan to execute the hostages in one week. Two of them look to be in such bad shape that we're not certain they'll last that long. Therefore, we have four days until we deploy to Indonesia. This will be cutting it close. Everyone, gather around the sand table."

Ezekiel preferred to use the mini sandbox. He had set up a scale version of their objective. It was easy to change as more intelligence came in the closer they were to the execution of their mission. He waited until they were surrounding the sand table and he knew everyone could easily see.

"This is a to-scale mock-up of our objective, the buildings, guard towers, fences and so on. This is the Musi River that will provide us with our infil and exfil route. We will be staging here at Palembang City on the southernmost point of this island. There are docks already there that we will use. An Indonesian Marine unit is getting things prepared there as we speak."

Again, he kept his eyes on the Indonesian soldiers. Four of them appeared to be paying close attention. The other two exchanged glances and then looked around the room, seemingly more interested in their surroundings than the mission. He caught Gino's eye and glanced toward the two. Gino moved in between them. He wasn't polite about it.

"Nineteen kilometers west is Sri Jaya, that is where we will find our men. This is a small village of mostly innocent people. We will need to make certain we positively identify our targets before we engage them. We are *not* going to see images of dead women and children on CNN. I cannot stress this enough. Anyone encountered with a weapon will be designated Tango and will be put down."

He gestured to the whiteboard he had set up. "On the whiteboard is a diagram of where each man will be and which boat they will be on. You will ride that position every time. We will drill on this until we can load and unload without thinking about it. I want it automatic. Natural. You were born doing it."

The two soldiers he most worried about had gotten with the program and seemed to be paying attention. He breathed a sigh of relief. The Indonesians had a good reputation for being extremely well trained. The training to become a member of their elite forces was one of the most difficult in the world.

"Each man needs to know the job of the person on either side of him so that they can take up his portion of the mission if he's taken out of the fight." He waited until every eye was on him. "Gentlemen. We will not leave a single man behind, including any of ours that may be killed. If one of ours is killed, he comes home. *Everyone* comes home."

He felt his gut tighten as he looked at the two Indonesian

soldiers who hadn't been paying attention earlier. Rather than nod or look determined or even stone-faced, the two exchanged another smirk.

"Does that amuse you?" he challenged them. He didn't care for political bullshit or why he was briefing and training the men for the mission rather than Senior Chief Petty Officer Wallace. He only cared that they succeeded in their objective and brought the hostages home as well as all his men—and that included the two clowns.

The other four Indonesian soldiers stiffened, one turning and saying something in a low whip of a voice to the other two. Both snapped to attention instantly.

"No, sir," the one introduced as Amar Lesmana said.

"Good." Ezekiel would have liked to get rid of both of them on the spot. He had a bad feeling about them, but he was used to the respect his rank and experience gave him. He was a government experiment, classified, and a member of an elite force. No one questioned him and they damn well listened when he spoke— especially if he was the one with the plan to keep them all alive.

"When we disembark the boats, we'll need to move with a purpose to our assigned location. Team Alpha will be a four-man extraction team—Mordichai, Draden, Gino and me—who will move into the building and gain custody of our men. The rest of you will be on security. You will be divided into three six-man teams: Bravo, Charlie and Delta. Bravo team will take up position here."

He indicated on the sand table just where he wanted them. "They are responsible for ensuring the rear entrance to the target here and taking out any squirters that may try to escape. They will effectively have Alpha's six while they are retrieving the HVTs—high-value targets. Charlie will be here, securing the main approach."

Again he indicated the position on the sand table. "Delta will be at the main entrance keeping it secure for the Alpha team. When we have custody of these targets, we will do a quick assessment of their condition and then move to the extraction point for exfil. SBT-22 call sign 'Wolf Pack' will be providing copious amounts of 'whup ass' for us to be able to get to them. Then it will be a luxurious cruise to our staging area where the Marines who held down the fort will be waiting to render any advanced medical aid needed."

He hoped he wouldn't have to be the one rendering it on the boat. He'd done it, operated right in the middle of hell-fire, but it wasn't something he wanted to repeat often.

For the next couple of hours he went over and over the information, drilling it into them so each man knew exactly what he was doing, where he would be and what the men beside him would be doing. Finally, he let them go.

"You have twenty minutes for chow and then we'll start the crawl-through."

Ezekiel watched the men file out. He went over every-thing he'd said, the step by step of how the mission would play out in a perfect world. No mistakes. No accidents. No Murphy's Law. They went over the contingency plans if and when things went "pear-shaped"—which they usually did.

They were ready to take it outside. Ezekiel sighed. They *should* be ready for the first walk-through. He had drilled each team member on every detail until they knew the entire mission inside and out. They knew the number of buildings, the spacing between them, even the color of each. They knew how long each portion of the mission should take. So why was his gut nagging at him? Why did he have such a sense of unease?

Each team member knew where they would go and what responsibility they had in the objective. They had to know everything so if one team member went down, someone else could readily take up the slack. That was especially impor-tant in the chain of command, and he'd made certain they knew everything. If the leader went down, the next in order of command had to step up immediately to fill the job, all the way down the chain. They knew that. It was time to take them into execution phase.

Ezekiel cursed under his breath and stared out the window for a long time, turning the pieces over and over in his mind, trying to figure out what was wrong. Because something was. Something was off.

He wasn't a friendly man. He didn't have to like them, and he didn't give a damn if they liked him. He wasn't there to be a friend; he was there to make certain they came home alive. That, maybe, was the trouble. He didn't like two of the Indonesian soldiers. Usually when he trained others for a mission, he felt some sort of camaraderie with them. They were fighting on the same side. They were brothers in battle. They had certain things in common. He could decide to request two new team members, but there would be a political upheaval, and the two soldiers had toed the line once their commanding officer had snapped them back to attention.

"What's the problem, Zeke?" Gino—Phantom—asked. His voice, as always with Gino, was pitched low. He didn't talk much, and he was the best tracker of all of them, other than Ezekiel. Like Zeke, he was a hunter with an exceptional sense of smell. He moved like a ghost through almost any terrain. Cool, almost black eyes, black shaggy hair, a hint of a shadow on his jaw, wide shoulders and lean without an ounce of fat on him, he was a man most others avoided.

Ezekiel shook his head. "Two of those soldiers have the wrong attitude, Gino. I just plain don't like or trust them. I can't even say why. There's no good reason. I've trained a few foreign soldiers now for specific missions and with all of them I've felt some sense of camaraderie, but these men . . ." He broke off because what could he say? They paid attention. They learned. They knew the mission. They just seemed off to him. Disrespectful. Even to the other Indonesian soldiers. He didn't want his fellow soldiers to go into combat with them.

"Clearly they've seen combat," Gino pointed out, playing the devil's advocate. "They know what they're doing. They know their way around weapons."

"And yet I give them an order and they're slow about responding. They do it, but they're casual about it. They have to look at each other as if they can't be bothered or maybe they're amused by what I'm telling them." He sighed heavily. "More than that, it's just a gut feeling. I don't like what my gut's saying to me."

Gino nodded. Clearly he didn't really want to go into combat with them either. "I'll have Flame run more background checks on them, see if she can turn up anything that doesn't fit."

"They wouldn't be here if they weren't seriously vetted, but I'd appreciate that, Gino. No matter if she finds something or not, if they don't perform any better in the field, then I'm going to have to make a harsh decision that might have political ramifications. Politics don't matter to me, and I'll be damned if I'll send a fellow soldier into combat with one of these jokers if I don't feel they'll have my soldier's back."

He cleared his throat and continued staring out the window. "I met someone yesterday. A woman. A waitress at one of the restaurants in the Quarter. Her name is Bellisia Adams. At least that was what she called herself. The restaurant was Nourriture Joyeuse. I know it isn't much to go on, but ask Flame to see if she can find out anything about her."

"Should we be worried?"

Ezekiel shook his head. "It's personal. I liked her, but I'm busy here. I can't exactly start dating someone right in the middle of this. I just want to know I can find her again if she takes off. It didn't sound like there was anything holding her here."

Gino nodded. "Will do. What's next?"

"Crawl phase."

Gino lifted a hand. "I've got this down, been making the run-through. I'll get on this and check with Cayenne, make certain everything's all right. The other team will show up soon to take over protection for the family."

Ezekiel nodded, turned away and then swung back,

suddenly recognizing the casual disinterest for what it was—
pure bullshit. "Stay away from her, Gino. She's no threat to
us." Even as he said it, he wasn't altogether certain. He
seemed suspicious of everything and everyone lately. Even
a pretty waitress he'd met randomly—and liked.

Gino just looked at him, and Ezekiel swore softly.
"Sometimes, Gino, this life we lead is fucked-up."

"You got that right."

"Their gumbo isn't nearly as good as Nonny's."

"Doesn't surprise me," Gino said, lifting a hand before
he went out the door.

Ezekiel had never minded the physical enhancements as
some of the other GhostWalkers did. They hadn't signed on
for it, but they came out from under the anesthesia with an
entire new set of genes. It was done. It couldn't be taken
back. He could see better, smell better, run faster, disappear
when he had to and hunt the enemy in any terrain. That
made him invaluable to his country. And that was without
psychic enhancements. He was a military secret, and meeting a woman, even randomly, called for her to be checked
out. He didn't have to like it, but he had to do it.

❦

The next phase of training—the crawl phase—consisted of
literally walking them through each part of the mission.
They simulated the boat ride and swim, forming up exactly
as they would when riding in the boat. They simulated getting out of the boat and into the water and then the order
and formation of the swim and walking to the objective.

Once they had repeated the getting in and out of the boat
and the swim, they walked, step by step, where each man
would go and what he'd do while on the objective. Each
soldier acted out what he would do during the assault. Each
man would say, "Bang-bang, I am neutralizing this specified
target," when shooting. If using a grenade, they did the same
thing, indicating what type of grenade was being used. He

kept them at it, repeated the sequences over and over, the soldiers simulating firing at the paper targets.

Ezekiel paid particular attention to the Indonesian soldiers. All performed without hesitation, remembering their exact positions and what they were supposed to be doing. They didn't have a lot of time to rest. He only had four days to drill this into them to keep them alive and to bring the hostages out alive. He took them to the next phase—the walk phase.

They went through everything at a faster pace, firing blanks and using simulated grenades. Dummies were set up, using the exact height and weight of the targets to be rescued. Paper targets were replaced with dummies. He included the boat ride and swim, and he worked them far after the sun had gone down over the swamp and canal. He dismissed them only when they were all exhausted, sending them to the barracks for chow and rest.

They had no time to mess around. Before light they were at it again, first in the briefing room and then the crawl-through phase followed by the walk-through. The Indonesians proved why they were regarded as elite, even the two soldiers Ezekiel had been concerned about. He was fairly certain the other four soldiers from their Kopaska Group had straightened them out.

He took the men through the next phase, the run phase, where everything moved at actual speed. They had live rounds and grenades. There was a mix of paper targets and live people to avoid as they raced to simulate the rescue of the high-value targets. They worked the entire procedure over and over, from boarding the boats to securing the hostages and getting out fast.

When he was completely satisfied that each member of their team knew exactly what he was doing, he introduced various wounds and kills to different players. In each phase the trainers randomly "killed or wounded" members of the team. The members of the team had to adapt to the situation. During each different run, a card was issued to various players with an injury on them. No one knew who would get what or when. The injuries could occur at any time, from boarding the boat to the actual "safe" area.

Ezekiel had them repeat the run over and over, as many times as possible throughout the day. They only had a couple of days left to work together as a team, and he wanted to throw in as many surprises and disasters as possible, making them have to improvise, adapt and overcome each obstacle.

It was hot as hell, the humidity adding to the misery of repetition and constant action. That was a good thing, he told himself. He needed the men to work in an environment exactly like the one they'd be carrying out their mission in. Indonesia had high humidity. He reminded the men often to hydrate. The insect population was having a feast, mosquitoes bingeing on any exposed skin.

He worked them long into the night, and that meant re-supplying the water more than once, but it also meant they were coming together as a team. Each man moved smoothly and efficiently, and they watched one another's backs. Half-way through one of the fastest runs, his stomach cramped and his vision blurred. He blinked several times and found himself staggering.

He took a slow look around him. All around him, the men were breaking their positions, vomiting and staggering around, hanging on to trees to stay upright and some going down, doubling over in what appeared to be agony. The wind blew and fog had begun to creep in. He blinked several times to clear his eyesight, but instead of getting better, it got worse. Alarms went off in his brain, but he couldn't think what to do.

"You okay, Captain Fortunes?" Amar Lesmana bent over him solicitously. "Let me help you." He took Ezekiel's arm.

Ezekiel felt the sting of an insect on his neck. A burn. He slapped at it and hit the back of a hand, rather than the bug he was expecting. "What the hell?" Half turning, he struck the Indonesian soldier hard in the gut, doubling him over. He recognized he was in trouble immediately.

Whatever the man had injected into him was fast-acting. He was losing focus and strength. His legs went out from under him and he found himself on his knees.

Mordichai. That was all he could get out before something hit his head savagely and he saw black.

~

What was wrong with them? They were supposed to be such a hotshot team, men enhanced physically as well as psychically. So, okay, maybe the physical was working, but they didn't seem to have the least bit of psychic talent at all. Bellisia stayed in the water where it was impossible for anyone to detect her presence and watched as the men being trained went down, one by one.

She'd left a note warning them under the plant in the box she'd left on the doorstep for Grace Fontenot. Ezekiel had no business being with those treacherous bastards. Clearly Cheng had gotten to them. The man did business with the terrorists in Indonesia all the time. Everyone knew that, didn't they? Whitney certainly knew it, as did Violet.

Just thinking of the woman made Bellisia furious at herself for not trying to take her out when she had the chance in China. Now, the two traitors were loading Ezekiel's body into a boat. She couldn't tell whether he was alive or dead. She assumed they wanted him alive. That would definitely be Cheng's preference.

She slipped noiselessly under the water, sending out warning vibrations to keep any alligators from thinking she might be a tasty snack. The boat cut through the water heading down the canal, away from Stennis. At the turn, just under a sign proclaiming the dangers of traveling the canal due to laser training, a man crouched in the denser brush on the shore. They stopped the boat and he took over.

"You got my money?" He had a distinct Cajun accent.

"It's in your account. Get us out of here."

She could have told the fisherman he should have made

certain the money was in his account. He was disposable, and as soon as he guided them to where they were going, he was a dead man. It was difficult to blame him; Cheng probably offered him more money than he'd ever seen in his lifetime. Cheng was very good at finding people's weaknesses.

With the local fisherman, born and raised there in the swamp, the boat picked up speed as it raced away from the laser training area heading toward the river. She knew she wouldn't lose them, not even in the dark. She was fast, nearly as fast as the boat, and she could maneuver the shallows faster than they could.

They traveled without lights, under the stars, the local guiding them, and she followed, her heart in her throat. The water was black and she navigated by the sounds of the boat beneath the surface. Sometimes the water was so shallow she crawled through gravel and silt. Sharp sticks tore at her arms and legs. Eventually she began to tire and fell behind, but not far enough that they could actually get away from her.

Her heart nearly stopped when she realized the engine had been cut and the boat drifted up a bayou, with only the aid of long poles. They were taking Ezekiel to a predestined location in the swamp. She had been certain they'd take him out the Gulf of Mexico to a waiting ship. What did that mean? Why would they keep him in the swamp?

She tasted fear and with it came guilt. She'd spent far too long trying to make up her mind about the GhostWalkers. She'd let time slip away from her, and she knew why. She'd followed Ezekiel everywhere, so obsessed with him, watching him like a crazed stalker. She'd loved his stories as much as the triplets had. She had listened with rapt attention to every word, his voice soothing her, making her long for a life she knew she'd never have.

He sang. His voice was incredible. Mesmerizing. She noticed everything about him. Not even the smallest detail escaped her. She should have been watching the others and assessing whether or not they were loyal to one another the way Ezekiel was, but mostly she found herself watching him and sometimes Nonny.

He paid attention to the children, seemingly hanging on to their every word, but he watched his surroundings carefully, alert to any danger around them. She knew he could explode into action if there was the slightest hint of harm to the girls.

Most of the time Bellisia spent in the water, where she felt the safest and most comfortable, where she was nearly undetectable but could be close enough to the boat that she could hear every word. She loved how soft his voice got when he was alone with the girls—or Nonny. She doubted he even knew he changed his entire demeanor.

She'd heard the soldiers at Stennis in the boat turn Nonny away when she wanted her plant, and she'd followed her back to her "pharmacy." There was nearly an acre of pharmaceutical plants near the property where Cayenne and Trap, two of the GhostWalkers, resided. When she knew the exact plant, she'd gone to Stennis, dug it up and left it for Nonny on the doorstep. She'd put a warning note in the box underneath the plant. It hadn't been easy sneaking into the heavily guarded compound, but she liked challenges and she needed to keep her skills honed. She should have emphasized just what the GhostWalkers were up against and that they needed to be far more alert.

The bayou narrowed until it was almost nonexistent, branches sweeping down into the water and brush growing heavily on either side. It was one of the small bayous opened up by the ever-shifting waters. It was extremely shallow—rocks and debris made up the bed, the water running just inches over it. With the branches hanging so low, few would ever think anyone would travel up the narrow waterway.

She got to the edge of the shore where she could see drag marks in the mud where they'd pulled the boat up onto land and into thick brush. Saw grass guarded the entire outer rim. She detested saw grass. She'd found it didn't discriminate when it came to cutting one to pieces. There had to be an opening through it, because if it would cut her, it would cut them.

Bellisia dragged herself out of the water, shivering a little in the cool night air. It was clear, a million stars scattered across the sky, but it was also windy. Somewhere in the distance an alligator bellowed. The swamp was always alive with the droning of insects, but at night it was particularly loud. All different types of frogs vied for attention. Fish jumped in the water after bugs, the splashes loud and carrying a great distance in the stillness of the night.

The boat was hidden in the brush and she took the time to pull it back to the water's edge. Ezekiel didn't look in the best of shape and she would have to transport him out of there. She needed that boat. Just to the right of where they'd hidden the boat was a narrow opening hacked out to allow single file passage. She smelled blood, and with the brightness of stars, she saw dark splashes against the green blades as she followed the trail deeper onto land.

She was slight, but the ground still felt marshy and unstable to her, like a springy sponge under her feet. She could see where the men had sunk much deeper, leaving behind holes filled with water. That wasn't good. Surely the local fisherman had told them it was dangerous and sooner or later the ground beneath them would simply disappear and they'd sink.

She followed them deeper into the interior, silently cursing as her arms and legs were cut from the wicked saw grass. She couldn't imagine what was happening to the much larger men, especially Ezekiel. The trail wound around straggly trees, but it was salt water mixed with river water, and few trees grew. Most looked as if they were postapocalyptic, barren limbs rising like spiny specters, dark and twisted.

A small camp was there, the cabin clearly thrown together, built high in case the water table rose as it did with most camps in the swamp. Clearly this cabin belonged to the fisherman aiding them. It was old and well-used, if sparse. No more than one room with a porch. The door was open, hanging by one hinge only.

She nearly tripped over the fisherman's body. Someone had shot him in the back of the head and left him right there. Her heart accelerated in fear for Ezekiel. Why hadn't they taken him out to the gulf to rendezvous with a ship or freighter? Why take the chance of keeping him in the swamp?

Everyone would be looking. Already, she was certain, they would have locked down Stennis and put helicopters in the air to hunt. Captains of classified teams didn't go missing without a huge search. So what did that mean for Ezekiel?

Hearing the murmur of voices, she sank low, crawling now, dispersing her weight on the spongy ground. She had no choice but to scuttle over top of the dead man, making her way to the cabin. Bright lights were set up, aimed at Ezekiel. He was tied to a cross-pole of some sort, his arms spread wide. He was awake, but his head was down. Blood ran down both arms and legs from hundreds of thin cuts from the saw grass. At least, she thought that at first.

The equipment, a camera and the lights had to have been brought in by boat and then carried through the marsh. The weight of the objects combined with the weight of the men had left several deeper ruts filled with water where they'd carried the heavy items. The ruts ran right up to the stairs of the cabin, and two of them were extremely deep and filled with vile-looking water.

"I want every piece of him. Don't forget the head. Start with small cuts and go to the bigger ones. I don't want him dying for a long time."

Everything in her went still. That was Cheng for certain; she'd recognize his voice anywhere. He always spoke in pleasant tones, when he was the least pleasant person she knew—except for Dr. Whitney.

"I've never let you down," said an unfamiliar voice.

That meant Ezekiel wasn't just with the two soldiers.

They'd rendezvoused with others. They had a satellite link set up with Cheng and he was instructing them on the atrocities he wanted them to commit while recording it all for him.

"We don't have a lot of time. They'll be looking for him." Now the stranger was out in the open. He was tall and thin and looked cadaver-like. Could she kill all three of them fast and take Ezekiel back? Get him out of the saw grass and into the boat? She didn't know whom to trust. She couldn't take him back to Stennis, because any of the other team members could be involved in Cheng's plot to uncover the GhostWalker secrets.

"I want it done right."

They were going to take Ezekiel apart right there with Cheng watching. The samples of blood and tissue as well as body parts would be sent to the laboratory. She still didn't understand why they hadn't taken him out to the gulf. There had to be a ship out there that these men planned to use to escape.

She moved with infinite slowness, inch by inch, out of the brush and over the spongy ground, her body blending in with the black mud and debris.

"Is everyone in place?"

"Of course. They won't see them until it's too late."

She froze. More? There were more of them? Cheng's mercenaries. Why hadn't she smelled them? This was a trap for the others. Cheng knew if one of the GhostWalkers was taken, the others would come for him. Cheng was greedy, willing to sacrifice one GhostWalker so he could lure in several others in the hopes that he'd have plenty to study.

Staring up at the underside of the cabin, she could see little bricks attached to the floorboards and the underside of the stairs. Explosives? Were they going to blow up the cabin after they took apart Ezekiel in the hopes of destroying the evidence?

Silently swearing inventively in several languages, she slipped into the rut that would take her away from the cabin.

She didn't make so much as a ripple in the water. The bad news was it wasn't that deep. She could still go under, although it was the foulest, saltiest, most horrible brackish water she'd ever been in. Still, it was her best bet for moving quickly without detection.

She needed to find out where each of the men was hiding in the swamp and kill them before she tried to rescue Ezekiel. There was no way to escape with more of Cheng's hired mercenaries close by. She lifted her head carefully and studied the terrain. If she were drawing in GhostWalkers, men she knew had enhanced abilities, where would she hide? The brush would have to be thick. Really thick. The men would have to be spread out so that when the GhostWalkers came in to get the bait—Ezekiel—they would be caught between forces.

Bellisia crawled from the rut, staying close to the ground, moving along the thick brush until she saw bruised stalks, some slightly bent away from a narrow animal trail. There were signs of rabbits and muskrats as well as nutria all around. She didn't want to accidentally startle any animal, giving away her position to the men waiting to kill or capture GhostWalkers. To be safe, she sent out a soothing call to the wildlife, announcing her arrival and that she had enemies.

She touched on several varieties of mammals, but none were very close to her. Still, they gave her an indication of where the mercenaries were hiding. Wildlife would avoid them, and the numbers were concentrated a good distance from the camp.

Bellisia used her forearms and toes to propel herself over the surface and along the narrow game trail. It was impossible for one of the men, much larger, to pass through the brush without leaving some trace behind. She followed the bruised and bent stalks until she "felt" the presence of a man.

5

Bellisia smelled blood. There was no sound, but the man hidden in the brush was covered in cuts just as she was from the saw grass. She inched closer, trying to circle around behind him. It wasn't easy moving without disturbing the plants. With her body weight evenly distributed over the marshy surface, she didn't sink into the brackish water oozing up from the unstable surface. She scooted on her belly, using her toes and arms to propel her forward.

One moment she was alone with the constant drone of insects, and the next she was almost on top of him. He lay sprawled out on his belly, the toes of his boots sinking into the mire as he peered through the dense brush with his night goggles. She let her breath out and stayed very still, trying to keep her heart under control.

She was designed to kill, and there were times it was necessary. She didn't have to like it. Knowing this man lay in wait in order to capture or kill Ezekiel's friends while Ezekiel was being tortured just a few yards from him, she realized she really had little choice. If she didn't do what she was designed to do, like it or not, she would always feel responsible for anyone he hurt or killed.

Once the decision was made, she closed her eyes and summoned the venom. Over the last few years she'd gotten much better at controlling it. She was immune to it, but the poison was deadly. The venom mixed with her saliva and one break in the skin was all she needed to deliver it to her victim. It would quickly spread through a human being, blocking signals from the body's nerves and resulting in full body paralysis. Even the lungs were paralyzed. It didn't take long for a human to die with no oxygen getting to the brain.

She spat into her palm and rubbed her fingertips in the venom. She could bite him and deliver the poison much more effectively, but he might get off a yell of warning and she couldn't afford the others to know she was there. She also didn't have time, not with Ezekiel being tortured.

She found a particularly deep-looking cut on his calf and, with the direction of the wind, she brushed her fingers along that cut, making certain a good deal of the venom entered the wound. He turned his head, as she had known he would. She held herself very still, her body blending into the ground and shrubs around her. He blinked. He turned away from her and she scooted back, already dismissing him. He'd be paralyzed in three or four minutes, dead in ten to fifteen, probably less.

Using toes and elbows, she shrank back into the shrubbery and took the narrow trail that led about ten feet from the man she'd just killed. The mercenaries would be spread out. They would surround the cabin. The second man had to be close. She kept moving steadily, working hard not to disturb the shrubbery. Again, it was the scent of blood that tipped her off that she was close to her prey.

As she moved toward him, she caught sight of a small pack attached to the roots of a long-dead cypress tree. Her breath caught in her throat. More explosives. They were attached to the underside of the cabin, and now she'd found others. What were they planning? Enough explosives like this could sink half the marsh. She had to get Ezekiel out of there and fast.

She didn't waste time by hesitating. She'd already made up her mind it was necessary to kill, and she did it quickly, introducing the toxin via an open wound on his thigh. There was less brush to hide in but, even looking right at her, her victim didn't see her.

She took out victims three and four, but it cost her in time. She had to check on Ezekiel. This time she removed weapons from the two men. Knives. Guns. She found more explosives but left them alone. It wasn't her field of expertise and she didn't want to accidentally set them off.

Covered in mud, she took time to slip into the long track of water near the cabin. Her skin instantly felt better, not so tight and drawn. She came up just as a man stepped out of the cabin onto the stairway. His name was Bolan Zhu, and she recognized him as one of Cheng's top aides. She had followed him for four days in Shanghai.

Even there in the marsh, he wore a suit. He had a briefcase in his hand and had turned halfway back to look over his shoulder into the interior. She caught a glimpse of Ezekiel laid out on a makeshift table now, blood running over his ribs and dripping down the sides of the slab of metal. Her stomach lurched. While she'd been killing the mercenaries, they'd already been torturing Ezekiel.

"Wait. I'm doing the spinal tap now."

"I've got what I need to complete phase one, David. You do the tap and finish phase two with him." Zhu tapped his briefcase. "I've got the blood and tissue samples and they have to get back to the lab." He continued down the stairs in spite of the other man's protest. He actually put on speed, striding fast away from the cabin in the opposite direction of the boat.

David, inside the building, cursed loudly, making her wince. He was clearly angry, but more, she heard the note of fear in his voice. He had reason to be afraid. She'd studied Cheng. He protected himself at all times. He rarely had a tie to any operation, and through a satellite hookup, his voice had been heard. That would be unacceptable to him. His trusted aide brought out the blood and tissue samples, leaving the second phase of his operation to a man who was disposable; Cheng would insist on his death.

The charges scattered over the marsh surrounding the hunting camp had to have been placed there to destroy all evidence—as well as any people Cheng had bribed to aid him. The Indonesian soldiers. The local fisherman. David for certain. Who knew if he used the same mercenaries all the time? Even if he did, to him, they were disposable.

The moment David was out of sight, she reached up, caught the closest supporting pole, and began to climb. She could blend into the wood, but she was carrying weapons—something she rarely did—and she couldn't hide them. She climbed fast, aware that David was angry and afraid enough to kill Ezekiel and be done with it. On some level he had to know that if Cheng was so afraid of whoever was coming for Ezekiel, or even Ezekiel himself, that he had his trusted man leave with the blood and tissue samples, then there was a problem.

She gained the porch and crawled across the floorboards to the partially open door. The cabin reeked of blood and death, and her heart seized at the thought that she'd left Ezekiel there long enough for the two men to carve him up. She wanted to lift the gun and shoot both of them right then and there, but it would alert any of the other mercenaries still in the marsh, and she couldn't get Ezekiel out and fight them off while she got him to the boat.

His head was turned toward the door, his dark hair falling in on his forehead. His eyes were open. Clear. Dangerous. David was on the other side of him, bending over him, complaining to the other man in the room.

"That arrogant prick. He left because he's certain the

SEAL team is going to show up. We've got to kill him and get out of here."

"That's not the deal." The other man stepped closer. He had a video camera and clearly was waiting to record whatever David did to Ezekiel.

The thought of what they had in mind turned her stomach. She left the knives and all but one gun by the entrance and crawled inside the small cabin. Ezekiel stared right at her. Aware. She was in full camouflage mode, but something, maybe her movement, had given her away to him. He made no sound. He didn't even blink, but she felt him—his energy—and she didn't understand how the other two men didn't feel it building in the cabin. Building and building. The air in the cabin was thick with an electrical charge. The hair on her head went static with it. Still, the two bickered, not paying the least attention to the man on the table.

He would recognize her. She'd blown her cover big-time, but there was no taking it back—and she wouldn't have wanted to anyway. He was a man worth saving, one of the few she'd met, and the one she thought the most of. He wasn't going to die on that table, and Cheng couldn't have him to dissect. She'd get him out, patch him up and leave the area as fast as possible. Her mind shied away from the idea of leaving. She liked Louisiana. The people. The humidity. The swamp. The bayous. She liked it all. Mostly she liked being close to Ezekiel and Nonny.

She was halfway into the room when David took out a long needle, clearly intending to stick it into Ezekiel's back. She lifted the gun and shot him between the eyes, just as Ezekiel rolled from the table, dropping almost on top of her. The sound of the gunshot reverberated through the close quarters of the cabin.

Ezekiel kept rolling, somersaulting across the room in a blur of speed. He moved so fast she almost couldn't track him. He was on the cameraman in seconds, taking him down to the floor by sweeping his legs out from under him.

As the man went down, Ezekiel yanked the knife from the man's boot and cut the arteries in both legs and then, as he landed hard on the floor, his throat.

"Can you walk?" Bellisia hissed. She was at the door. The others would come running. She knew there were more of them—and then there were the explosives. "We have to go now. Right. Now."

He looked like hell. Covered in blood. She couldn't assess the damage or stop to clean him up. They had to go.

"Everything is wired to blow," she explained, skirting the table to crouch by him, still looking at the door.

Ezekiel didn't ask questions. He made an effort to get to his feet, scooping up weapons as he did. He tucked guns and knives into his belt and boots. "Go. I'll be right on you."

Bellisia spared one quick look at him. He wasn't going to make it on his own. No way. He'd lost too much blood and was still losing it. He was on his feet out of sheer will. She ignored his order, as clear as it was, and dropped back to slip an arm around his waist. He was a big man, but she had tremendous hidden strength. They'd stripped his shirt off in order to get the blood and tissue samples as well as to inflict the knife wounds that were crisscrossing his chest and back. They appeared shallower than she'd first thought, but combined, they created a blood loss no one could afford.

Anchoring the tips of her fingers in his skin, she ignored his hiss of displeasure at her failure to obey. "Just move with me. We have to get out of here now," she reiterated. "We're going to jump together, roll, and then run for it. We'll have to shoot our way out, but whoever is on the other end of the claymores is going to light this place up fast."

He went with her to the door. A shot rang out as they jumped, rolled and sprinted for the boat. Fortunately, the reeds were high enough to cover most of their departure. Unfortunately, they didn't have time for stealth. Bullets hit all around them. Twice he urged her to the ground and bullets flew like angry bees right where both had been.

She didn't ask how he could do that—how he could know. They didn't have time for conversation and, in any case, she knew better than to ask—he wouldn't answer her. Like her, he was enhanced and his gifts were classified. Cheng had wanted him taken apart as fast as possible, looking for that very thing. Answers to the GhostWalkers' secrets. How Whitney had done it. Whitney was elusive, difficult to find. Had she been Cheng, she would have targeted him instead of the very lethal GhostWalkers.

Ezekiel took most of his own weight, but he ran stooped over, and every breath he took, she heard. Air left his lungs in ragged gasps and entered just as labored. If she didn't have the microscopic setae on the ends of her fingers, she never would have been able to hold on to his blood-slick skin. He was covered, looking like something out of a horror movie where they had no budget so they used copious amounts of red paint.

She all but dumped him in the boat, shoved it off shore and slipped into the water, the rope in her hand. "Stay low. Just lie down and I'll get us out of here." She knew she didn't have a hope in hell that he'd obey. The mercenaries were firing at anything that moved in the marsh. They'd realize in just a few moments that they'd made it to the boat.

Once in her favorite environment, she wrapped the rope around her waist and surged forward, away from shore, pulling strongly with her arms and legs. She got the boat out of the reeds fast, still hearing the mercenaries firing. Just as she caught the sides of the small craft and climbed in, an explosion ripped the night apart.

Ezekiel jerked her all the way into the boat, all but throwing her to the bottom, his larger body covering hers as fiery debris rained from the sky. The smell of blood was overwhelming. He was heavy. Very heavy. Dead heavy. Her breath caught in her throat and she pushed at him. He didn't move.

"Ezekiel." She reached up and tried to find his neck to feel for a pulse. For a few horrible moments, she thought he

was dead. Thankfully, it was there, that all-important heartbeat. The relief when she found it made her almost giddy.

She pushed his body off of her and crawled back into the
water. There was no doubt in her mind that whoever had set
off the explosions was going to be picking off any survivors.
She didn't want to start the engine and tip anyone off that
they'd escaped. Towing the boat was easy with the rope tied
around her, but the scent of blood had to be strong and she
didn't want any friendly visits from alligators, although she
did consider them the least of her worries.

It took over two hours to tow the boat upriver and through
a network of canals and then back to the river to the island
where she lived. It was too far to take him back to Nonny
and his friends. Stennis would be crawling with military
personnel and she didn't want to get shot or be discovered.
Whitney had a faction of supporters in the military and he
still carried a tremendous amount of clout. She was *not* going to be delivered back into his hands.

The island was owned by a grizzled veteran of a war no
one wanted. He'd come out of that war scarred, tough and
dangerous. He'd bought up the land around him, brought
electricity to it and sold it for a huge profit. He was good at
speculation with land and turned everything he touched into
a moneymaker. That gave him the ability to live as he
wanted—free.

The island was difficult to breach even by boat due to the
massive cypress trees guarding it, making it impossible to
get too close. Several landing sites were muddy and shallow,
with huge sweeping vines blocking a boat's access. She went
straight to the pier. There were numerous signs warning any
potential visitors that they weren't wanted, and most people
living in the area knew Donny and that he meant business.
His island was off-limits to anyone coming without his permission. He had dogs and weapons and no fear of using
either to protect his privacy.

She had found the island while exploring, using the waterways of course. Donny had several cabins—camps, he called them. More, he had several bathrooms he laughingly called his outhouses. The bathrooms were outside the cabin but completely plumbed. The man did his own building. He ran the electricity and then hooked it up with the local electric company.

He realized someone was living in the camp closest to the water. There were two entrances, both by water. He left food for her on several occasions. She left him fish in return. She'd gotten the job at the restaurant and that gave her the ability to pick him up other types of food occasionally. They both thought it a fair trade.

Eventually, she allowed him to see her and they became friends of sorts—as much as someone like Donny, who was very leery of people, and someone like her, a woman on the run from a very powerful enemy, could be friends. Donny knew she was hiding, but he didn't ask questions about what or who, and she appreciated that trait in him. He simply accepted her.

She needed him now. She doubted if she could get Ezekiel up to the cabin. It was all uphill and steep walking on the narrow trail Donny had carved into his wild habitat. They had a signal Donny had set up in case of an emergency, and she dragged herself up onto the pier, ran to the pole and triggered the alarm, praying he was home.

Ezekiel was still unconscious. He looked pale, almost gray, and he was cold to the touch, his body continually shivering. She was strong, but he was a big man and completely dead weight. She hooked his body with the setae on her fingertips and dragged him from the boat. He sprawled out on the pier. She glanced up toward the cabin. It seemed a long way up.

It took some maneuvering but she managed to get him over her shoulder, and she cautiously stood, taking his full weight. The smell of blood sickened her, and he was slick with it. It took a couple of minutes to anchor him to her when he wanted to slip off due to the amount of blood coating his chest and back. By the time she got him up to the cabin she was sweating, unusual for her, even in the humidity of the swamp.

She put water on to heat, but didn't wait until it was warm to inspect him and the numerous cuts. Some needed stitches to close. All needed to be thoroughly washed and treated. Infections in the swamp were common. The good news was that none of the lacerations were life-threatening. She suspected he was out more due to whatever drug they had injected him with than from any of the wounds.

She bit down hard on her lip. He *had* lost a great deal of blood. She could give him her blood, she knew she would be compatible, but she didn't really know what she was doing in that regard. She cleaned him up as best she could, washing the blood from his body so she could try to see to the worst of the cuts. Considering that she'd been only a few minutes behind them, Cheng's man had worked fast to collect the blood and tissue samples and record the amount of pain Ezekiel's body could stand.

"You all right, Bella?" Donny demanded, sounding out of breath.

She glanced over her shoulder at him. Donny was in his seventies, but he was still a strong, steady man. He held his guns as if he meant business.

"You have blood all over you."

"It's his blood. He was training some men at Stennis. All of them got really sick and were staggering around, vomiting and . . . other things. I saw two men take him away from the others. They injected him with something, put him into a boat and took him to a camp in the marsh. The local helping them is dead, they killed him. They met more men at the local's camp and started taking him apart with a knife. They had mercs in the brush so I was busy with them and they managed to do all this damage to him."

Donny looked her over, one eyebrow raised, clearly surprised at the anxiety she couldn't keep out of her voice.

"There's a first aid kit in the other room, on the top shelf, kid. Bring it here."

"Do you think he's lost too much blood? I don't want him to get brain damage or something." She jumped up, although she feared leaving him, even with Donny.

"Go get the kit. I'm not going to hurt your man."

She didn't even protest his remark. Maybe in a secret fantasy, he was her man. She just knew he was too good of a man to lose to Cheng.

Donny knew his way around a first aid kit. He worked efficiently and very fast, stitching up the three wounds that were very deep, butterfly stitching a dozen more and bandaging the rest. He worked in silence while she stroked Ezekiel's hair back from his forehead.

"In my day, no one wore their hair like that. Not in the military. They'd have received a midnight visit and gotten their head shaved."

She glared at him. "Don't you dare even think about touching his hair, Donny. I love his hair."

"Yeah. I kinda noticed. As soon as we get him fixed up a bit, he has to go back. He's not a pet you can keep."

Donny sounded sarcastic, but she knew him well enough now to know he was teasing her.

"Very funny."

"I'm going to strip him and wash the rest of him. His clothes aren't sanitary, and with all these open cuts he could get a nasty infection. Go shower and change, and for God's sake, wash your hair. You stink of bayou water. There's a T-shirt and sweats in a box just outside the door. I was going to give a few things away to . . ." He trailed off, scowling. "They'll be too short for him, but better than his own clothes."

Donny provided for quite a few of the people living far below poverty level, there in the swamp. He'd put several local children through college and paid for dental as well as vision care for others. To the outside world he was a cranky, dangerous man, considered a little mentally unstable, and who knew? Maybe he was. To his trusted friends, he was a kind, generous man with a soft spot for those in need. She knew he would defend her with his life even though they really barely knew each other.

"They might be coming for him, Donny. Whoever those men were, you see what they're capable of. They blew the marsh up just to cover what they were doing and there were men they'd paid still there. They killed them without thinking twice about it."

"I can take care of your man. No one sets foot on my island without my knowledge."

She hesitated, her hand hovering just above Ezekiel's forehead. Her eyes met Donny's.

He snorted. "You don't count. You're some kind of evolutionary anomaly. I expect your offspring will have gills."

She forced her pretend outraged smile while deep inside she winced. She was never going to have a home and family so it really was a moot point, but if she ever was in a position to have children, he might not be that far off.

By the time she got back, Ezekiel lay under a blanket, his head on the only good pillow in the cabin. She'd bought it at a little boutique and it was embroidered with a silly-looking sea anemone; at least that's what she hoped it was, otherwise it looked like something she might find in an adult toy store. Still, they were practically giving it away and it was a pillow.

Wrapped in a light sweater, she handed the clothes to Donny. "Thank you for helping me, I really appreciate it. You can't stay after he's dressed, it's too dangerous. The minute he's strong enough, I'll take him back to Stennis, and then they'll leave us alone."

They'd only leave her alone if they couldn't find her. She'd blown her chances of ever settling down in Louisiana—and she loved it there. She really liked the people—especially Donny. She wanted to get to know Nonny and her family.

She'd envisioned herself staying there, building something—
a home like Ezekiel had.

"What are you into, girl?" Donny snapped, his faded blue
eyes shrewd. "You think I don't know trouble when I see it?
You're in all kinds of trouble, but this is a safe place for you."

She struggled against an odd feeling welling up. A burn
behind her eyes. A lump in her throat so big she couldn't
swallow, couldn't quite catch her breath. Feeling vulnerable,
she turned her back on him with the excuse that it gave
Donny privacy to pull the sweatpants on Ezekiel. "It *was*
safe, but not so much anymore. Still, I couldn't let him die
like that. Look what they did to him. I think they planned
to torture him even more, but I can't understand why. None
of this makes any sense."

But it was Cheng. Cheng had stayed alive and in business
because he cut all ties if things got out of hand. It made
sense that he wouldn't want the actual GhostWalker, not one
he had no idea if he could control. He'd get whatever data
he could on one and then he'd study it before he made his
move to actually grab one to keep. The mercenaries hadn't
been there to collect other members of his team as she first
thought; it was to protect the project as long as they could,
all the while sending the information to Cheng via satellite.
They'd planned to kill Ezekiel and, if possible, the others
all along.

She pressed her fingers to her pounding temples. She was
exhausted. She wanted to curl up under a blanket and go to
sleep for hours, but she knew that was impossible. She had
to get Ezekiel back to his people as fast as she could.

"He's coming to, Bella," Donny said.

"Then you have to get out of here. He can't see you."

"He's seen me before. He's one of Grace's boys. She's got
more boys than any woman should have to raise. This is one
of them. If they belong to Grace Fontenot, then they're good
people."

"He shouldn't see you. He can't know that you ever saw him tonight. They're training for a mission and . . ." She broke off, turning back to him and putting one hand on his shoulder.

They hadn't got to the touching stage or showing any kind of overt affection yet, and the gesture surprised both of them. She snatched her hand away as if she'd been burned as his eyes flared with surprise. She'd never voluntarily touched a man, not unless she planned on killing him. Not unless she had no choice. Or she was saving his life.

Ezekiel groaned. She gasped and stepped back, pointing toward the stairway. "Please, Donny. You have to go."

"Will you be all right?"

She nodded, uncertain if that was the truth. She just needed to know he was safe, that she hadn't brought down the wrath of a GhostWalker team on him. In her experience, supersoldiers were unpredictable.

Donny reluctantly left. She watched him disappear into the night. He moved like a cat, an old veteran, a man weary of war but ready to fight if the situation called for it. When she turned back, Ezekiel's strange amber eyes were staring at her. For a moment, they glowed at her, the way an animal's eyes did when it could see in the dark. He blinked and the illusion was gone.

"You. I should have known."

"What does that mean?"

He patted the floor. "Sit down. It's too difficult to keep looking up at you."

She hesitated and then sank down beside him. "What did you mean, you 'should have known'?"

He rubbed the bridge of his nose, but even that small gesture seemed to tire him out. "I lost too much blood."

"You need to drink water. I can't give you a transfusion because I don't know how. In any case, we might not be compatible." They would be, but a stranger wouldn't know that, and she had to play her part as best she could.

"You could give me a transfusion. We're compatible." A ripple of a shudder went through his body, but didn't show on his face.

She narrowed her eyes at him. "How would you know that? I didn't tell you my blood type. You don't know the first thing about me."

"I know you're not Cajun and you didn't grow up around here." He closed his eyes. "I'm damned tired. What's your real name?"

"Why would I want to tell you?"

He opened his eyes again and pinned her with his amber stare. He had beautiful eyes and she tried not to notice, just like she was trying not to notice he was in pain but not acknowledging it.

"Seriously? I heard you talking and walked across the square to catch a glimpse of you. Never in my life have I done something like that. I told my friend to find out about you so I wouldn't lose you if you decided to up and leave before I was back from the field. I've never done that either. Tell me your name."

She liked that he'd done those things for her. She didn't like his tone. She'd just saved his life and he wasn't acting grateful in the least. His eyes didn't blink. Not once. He just stared at her until she wanted to give him whatever he asked for. She made a face at him. "Bellisia. My name is Bellisia. Sometimes I'm called Belle or Bella." She hadn't really lied to him. "I told you the truth when we met."

"How is that associated with a flower?"

She frowned. "That's a weird question. It's from the family of Bellis."

"Belladonna?"

She felt color begin to sweep up her neck to her face. She was poisonous, but not from any flower. "No. That's a different flower. Are you feeling up to walking to the boat? I have to get you back."

"I need a transfusion."

"No, you don't. You just need to drink some water and give yourself a few minutes to recover so we can leave." She detested needles. If she gave him a transfusion, she would be too sick to get him back to his people.

"I'm a doctor, I know when I need a transfusion."

"I'm not giving you one. Drink water. The faster I get you back to your people, the better off we're all going to be."

He was very pale, she had to admit. He looked exhausted.

"I'm not trained for that sort of thing," she said. "I wouldn't even be able to find a vein."

"I would."

She swore under her breath and pushed the medical kit at him. "I don't know why I found you attractive. You're kind of a bully." But he wasn't. He was so good with the little girls. All three of them adored him. She had watched him for hours, even watched him rock one of them to sleep on the front porch with Nonny and the triplets' mother, Pepper.

He really was weak, she realized, watching him dig through the large first aid kit Donny kept in most of his camps. He was weak and in pain. She took the kit and found what he needed and handed the needles and the long tubes to him.

"Come closer."

He mesmerized with his voice. She'd noticed that before when she listened to him tell the girls stories. She could listen to his voice forever, and there was a compulsion to do anything he asked.

Bellisia scooted as close as she dared. She felt like she was within the striking distance of a tiger. Her thigh rubbed against his and she flinched. Panic was beginning to rise, but she curbed it. She'd been in tight places before and she'd always managed to handle the situation. It was just that it was . . . *him*. Anyone else she'd be impersonal with, but it was impossible for her not to look at him and be aware of every tiny detail about him.

She felt the bite of a needle and looked away, bile rising

fast. She hated needles. All those times when Whitney had studied her as if she wasn't human. Wasn't a person. He treated her like an insect pinned to a mat. She had sworn to herself she would never be a prisoner again. Never have anyone telling her what to do or sticking needles in her. Worse, it hurt, the needle passing through the rows of double muscles, lighting up nerve endings until the pain was excruciating. Whitney had declared that a flaw and had forced her to endure the bite of needles over and over in the hopes of curing her.

"Are you all right? Did I hurt you?"

Ezekiel's voice was low and soothing. He actually sounded genuinely worried for her. She turned her head to look at him. He was beautiful. Not in the traditional sense of the word, he was too tough-looking for that, too much of a man. There wasn't anything soft about him, but he was gorgeous. His eyes. His hair. The shape of his jaw. His mouth. She had fixated on his mouth more than once. Even his eyelashes, and she hadn't even started on his body.

"Bellisia. Talk to me. Is this hurting you?"

She wanted to scream that it was. That he shouldn't talk to her in that soft, low voice, the one she was certain belonged to a fallen angel. The one that made her soft inside. The one that made her long for things she couldn't have. She shook her head, fighting the nausea. "I have a thing about needles."

"I'm sorry. I wouldn't do this if it wasn't necessary."

"How do you know your blood type and mine match?"

"You really don't know?"

She knew, but how would he know? She shook her head. He hadn't blinked. Those gorgeous eyes were suddenly reminding her of a predator's.

"Whitney always makes certain the men and women he pairs together have compatible blood types so they can work together more efficiently in the field."

Her heart stilled and then began to pound. Of course

Whitney did that. He was God in his mind. He wanted to choose who would give him his supersoldier children. Now she really just might throw up.

"Breathe." His hand came up to the nape of her neck and pushed her head down. "Take a breath. I don't want you fainting on me."

She took in great gulps of air and then indicated she was okay by pushing against his hand. For a man who had just been tortured and needed a blood transfusion, he was surprisingly strong.

"That's not possible. What you just said is not possible." She was close to panicking, and when she panicked, she wanted to get to safety. Safety was water. She glanced at the open porch just a few feet from her. She couldn't dive from where she was, she would have to get down to the pier.

Movement caught her eye. Her hand dropped to the needle in her arm and in one motion, she pulled it out and stood, already starting toward the open half wall that would allow her to escape.

Ezekiel wrapped strong fingers around her ankle and held her in place. She kicked at him, but he seemed ready for that, taking her down hard so the breath left her body in a rush, leaving her lungs burning for air.

Someone was on her, rolling her, a knee to her back, dragging her hands behind her back to secure them with ties of some kind. She turned her head to look at Ezekiel. She'd saved his life, and he repaid her with treachery.

"Bellisia." His voice was soft. Gentle.

She stared at him blankly. Inside, she could hear herself screaming. Raging. It was her own stupidity for trusting anything Peter Whitney had created.

6

Hard hands caught at Bellisia and dragged her into a sitting position. She made no sound, nor did she look away from Ezekiel. If she could get close enough, she might be able to deliver venom into him. It hurt that he'd betrayed her. Maybe there was no relationship to him, but she'd risked her freedom for him. She'd risked *everything*.

She tried to still her mind. She'd been a fool, she could admit that. She had to admit it. She'd built up such a ridiculous fantasy in her head, as if Ezekiel could possibly care for a woman like her. That was the thing—she wasn't a woman. She'd never been one. She'd trained to be a warrior almost from the day she was born and she knew no other life. She could have killed him, but she'd chosen to save him. Damn him for that. Damn her for caring.

"Her arm. She was giving me blood," Ezekiel said. "She's bleeding. Bellisia, my brother Mordichai is going to bandage your arm. Don't do anything aggressive toward him, please."

He sounded so reasonable. So gentle. As if he hadn't just betrayed her. He knew she was going for the water. No one could match her in the water. Once there, she would have been long gone. He'd been the one to stop her—to expose her to these other men. Ezekiel had been hers. She'd claimed him. In her mind, they were friends, more than friends. He was hers to protect and watch over. That's what she'd been doing and he repaid her with treachery.

"She saved my life," Ezekiel added. "I would never have made it out of there without her."

She didn't take her gaze from him, letting him see that wasn't enough. It would never be enough. She sat there on the floor, her heart pounding, hurt beyond belief. She'd never felt such hurt, and none of it was physical.

"Ma'am." Mordichai crouched beside and just behind her. Her wrists were bound together high, just above the small of her back, with strong plastic ties. She tested the strength of them surreptitiously to see if when she was in their boat she might be able to snap them and free herself. She thought it was doable, so she just had to bide her time. "You're bleeding all over the place. I'm just going to wrap a bandage around that. I'll need to put a little pressure on it."

She made no response. These men were Whitney's and they intended to give her back to him. That wasn't going to happen. She would never go back, not alive anyway. If she couldn't escape, then she would be forced to use poison on them. There was no antidote. Not even Whitney had been able to come up with one. She didn't want to kill them— well—maybe Ezekiel. He deserved to die.

Ezekiel had known they were there. He'd known they could find him. His blood, of course. If they were Whitney's creations, there had to have been one or two elite trackers among them. Once his blood was in the air, they would know he hadn't died in the explosion. They just followed the scent of his blood.

"Bellisia, we're going to have to take you back to the compound with us," Ezekiel said softly.

His voice was a weapon. She recognized that now. He

was a hunter. He could soothe wild animals and people alike. His voice was the lure, the snare, and she'd fallen for it. She wished he sounded rough and ugly, that he'd shown his true colors. Luring her into a false sense of safety had been wrong. Talking as if he cared about her feelings, or even about her at all, was even more wrong. She just stared at him, with no expression on her face. She was his prisoner, but she didn't have to talk. She had no intention of engaging with him at all.

"I know what this looks like, but it has nothing to do with Whitney. We have to clear you. We've got a very important mission coming up and we can't take any chances. I've got another couple of days of training and then a couple of days in the field. You'll be made as comfortable as possible in the compound while I'm gone."

She stared at him impassively. He was the enemy. She'd trained to be captured. She also knew their end game— returning her to Whitney—so there was really no reason for her to continue with the pretense of friendship. There would be no other reason to take her prisoner, in spite of what he said.

"Can you walk, Zeke?" Mordichai asked.

Ezekiel nodded. "You'll have to help me get on my feet. I'm still a little dizzy. Bellisia patched me up and we were in the middle of a transfusion when you arrived."

More than once, Bellisia had observed these men teasing each other. They rarely were serious with each other, but now, Mordichai didn't do anything but help his brother to his feet, wrap his arm around his waist and start him toward the door. One of the men, Gino, caught her arm and urged her to her feet. She saw no reason to give him a difficult time because he was actually moving in the direction she wanted to go.

As they walked along the pier toward the boat, drops of water touched her face and hands. Just that light spray sent a ray of hope through her. A fish jumped in the middle of the water. She heard the splash and kept walking, hoping

Gino would loosen his hold on her arm. She was small. That always made big men less cautious. She walked with no resistance, as if defeated, her head down, hair falling around her to add to the illusion she was presenting to them.

"If she makes it to the water, Gino, she'll be long gone. Not one of us is that good in water. She'll just disappear," Ezekiel warned quietly.

She didn't lift her head. Didn't acknowledge that further betrayal. She wanted to kill him in that moment. Ezekiel just kept up his treachery, proving to her that she'd been right to wait, to study them. All along she'd believed these were good men, not like the supersoldiers Whitney surrounded himself with, but these men were even worse. Whitney's soldiers didn't bother to lie and present a decent face to the world. Ezekiel and his team were deceivers.

"She's not going anywhere." Gino's voice was devoid of all expression. He wasn't trying to suck her into a false sense of security. He made it clear that he was all business, and she appreciated that. She understood all business. She'd set aside the fantasy and that's what she'd become. All. Business.

At the pier, the boat was tied up next to the one she'd used to bring Ezekiel there in the first place. She waited without comment while Mordichai helped Ezekiel into the boat. She was next and stepped into the vessel easily, crouching a little in order to get her footing with the sway of the water. Gino attempted to step with her, using his longer legs to ensure she had no pathway to the water. When he had one foot in the boat and one out, she exploded into action, using the power of her legs to propel her upward, catching him under his chin, knocking him off balance.

She kept going right on past him, leaping for the water in spite of her hands being tied. She didn't need hands in her favorite environment. Joy swept through her. Elation. She was actually out of the boat, over the water when hard hands settled around her waist. Fingers bit into flesh and she was hauled backward as she began her descent. She fell into the man who had prevented her escape.

Instantly she knew it was Ezekiel. She turned her head to sink her teeth into his arm. Venom rose fast, mixing with her saliva.

"Shit. Shit, Ezekiel, look out!" Draden yelled the warning.

It was there, waiting. She just had to deliver it. One bite. That was all, and he'd be dead. He *deserved* to be dead. At the last second she turned her head away from him and spat the venom into the water.

She felt their eyes on her. She knew what they saw. Not just the venom floating on the water, but the faint bluish rings that marked her skin and hair when she called up the venom. They were already disappearing. Draden had recognized it far before the others had.

"Thanks, Bellisia," Ezekiel said, his voice as mesmerizing as always. "I appreciate that you didn't kill me. I know this looks bad, but I'm telling you, giving you my word, you have nothing to fear from us."

Her gaze jumped to his, blazing with fire. "If that were true, I wouldn't be your prisoner. I didn't kill you this time, but that doesn't mean I won't the next." She didn't know why she hadn't bitten him. She should have. They would have tried to save him and she might have had another chance at escaping. Right now, they were all on alert.

She let the contempt show in her voice. Any puppet of Whitney's was beneath contempt. She ought to know; she'd been working for the puppet master her entire life. She had discussed the idea of how disgusting it was that they all stayed in spite of their abilities with the other girls she'd been raised with. Her sisters. Late at night when Whitney thought their every move and conversation was recorded. He'd put them in cages and expected that they would stay there. They were all good at getting out of cages, just not escaping.

Fear of the unknown held them. The need for Whitney to acknowledge they were human so they could feel human—feel deserving of living in the world with other human beings. Love for one another and fear that he would hurt those left behind. Whitney was a master at giving them reasons not to escape.

Gino tore off the bottom part of his shirt and wrapped it around her mouth, tying it tightly at the back of her head. He dragged her to the middle of the boat and shoved her down. She didn't look at him. She only watched Ezekiel. She wanted him to know *he* was her target. He would always be her target.

He'd been fast. Faster than she conceived a man could be, especially one of his size. No one was that fast, to stop her midair. She wished she'd seen him in action, instead of being on the receiving end. Had he been a blur? He'd caught her with both hands in spite of blood loss. She still felt the evidence around her waist. His fingers had bit deep, leaving brands behind. Burns that went through skin to bone. He was there now, inside of her, stamped deep, and every finger-print marked his betrayal.

At least no one called her names. Whitney's guards called all the women names. Mostly "bitch." She was feeling bitchy. She turned her head to take one last look at the camp as the boat swung away from the island. She'd been happy there. She didn't have the modern amenities, but she didn't need or even want them. She sat outside at night and just listened to the sound of freedom. It was the most beautiful sound she could imagine. Sometimes Donny would sit with her. He didn't talk much. He heard it too, and he knew what it meant, she could tell.

"There's no need to be rough with her, Gino," Ezekiel said. He sounded tired. Exhausted.

Bellisia couldn't help the little catch in her breath as her gaze jumped to his face. He had lost so much blood, all those cuts, some deep, some not, but they'd taken a toll on him. She didn't want his health or well-being to matter to her, but it did. She acknowledged it to herself, because if she was going to escape, she had to know what she would or wouldn't do to gain her freedom. Clearly, she wasn't willing to kill him.

"She almost killed you, Ezekiel." It was Mordichai who answered. "One bite and you would have been gone."

"The point is, she could have and she didn't," Ezekiel pointed out and slid off the bench seat to sit beside her. He swayed and then caught himself with one hand propped against the side of the boat. "She isn't an enemy. I can understand why we have to take her into custody until this is over, but I don't want anyone to be rough with her. If that happens, make no mistake, you'll answer to me." His words, uttered in that beautiful voice, seemed a little slurred to her ears.

She could see that his word carried weight with the men. She glanced at the others under the cover of her lashes and the darkness. She recognized the others. She'd been watching Ezekiel long enough to identify them. Master Sergeant Gino Mazza. They called him "Phantom," and she understood why. He was utterly silent when he moved, and her best guess was he was the one leading the way to them. Even when she'd observed him around the family, he rarely smiled or talked.

Mordichai, Ezekiel's brother, laughed more than some of the other members of his team. He was a master sergeant as well. Unlike his brother, he wasn't a doctor, but she knew to be in the PJs he had to be good at everything he did. She didn't know much about him, what his skills were, but he had steady hands and eyes that saw everything, even when he was joking around.

Lieutenant Draden Freeman was hands-down gorgeous. Like drop-dead gorgeous. He didn't belong in the military—he belonged on the cover of a magazine. She'd heard him referred to as "Sandman," but she had no idea why. He ran all the time. Day or night. When he wasn't running and he'd taken guard duty at night, he did martial arts, long, complicated katas, sometimes including weapons. He was also a doctor, and she couldn't imagine any woman going to him and not being embarrassed. No one looked good when they were ill, and who wanted to be in his presence when they looked terrible?

The fourth man was one she hadn't seen much of. His name was Rubin Campo, and she knew that he liked birds. He was always looking at them, watching them intently for long periods of time, and he even had a couple that appeared to hunt with him. He was a chief master sergeant and quiet about it.

She noted that no others had come with them. None of the SEALs training at Stennis. No one else who might interfere with whatever they planned on doing with her.

Ezekiel slumped down as if he were too exhausted to hold himself upright. Her heart stuttered. Maybe he really had suffered a great blood loss, so much so that his body was shutting down. She couldn't hold him up because her arms were tied behind her back. She couldn't say anything because Gino had tied his ratty shirt around her mouth.

She glanced at his brother and the other men. None of them seemed to be aware that he was having a problem. The moment he moved close to her, they all should have gone on alert. Arrogant asses. They thought she wasn't a threat because she was a woman? Well, okay, right now she didn't feel threatening toward him, only a little protective, which made *no* sense to her.

Ezekiel moved again, this time dropping his head into her lap. She held her breath. Gino was there instantly, gripping her hair, holding her head away from his friend, while he reached in with two fingers to check Ezekiel's pulse. She wanted to smirk. At least he was smart enough to realize she could inject the venom through the shirt if she wanted to. She didn't. There was something about Ezekiel that made it impossible for her to want to kill him.

"He needs more blood. We interrupted them," Gino said.

He looked down into her eyes. "I'm taking off the gag, but if you try to bite me, or Zeke, I swear, I'll kill you, regardless of what Zeke has to say."

Bellisia waited calmly for him to remove the foul material from her mouth. She thought about spitting at him, but it was so undignified. Instead she tried to moisten the inside of her very dry mouth several times.

"How long were you giving him blood?"

She thought about not answering, but what was the point? She didn't want Ezekiel to die. On the other hand, she didn't want to help them in any way. They were all doctors and medics. They could figure it out. She shrugged. "Minutes. A few. He said he needed blood several times, but I didn't know how to do that for him. I was afraid if I did, I wouldn't be able to get him back home."

Gino exchanged a look with Mordichai. The engine picked up speed and in spite of the darkness of the night, regardless that they weren't running with lights, they sped through the river very fast to get Ezekiel home. She knew, by the direction they took, that they weren't headed to Stennis. That just reinforced her opinion that they had their own agenda, like returning her to Whitney.

"That doesn't make sense," Mordichai said. "He wouldn't know her blood type."

"He would if he thinks Whitney paired her with him," Gino corrected. "He asked me to look into her while he was training. I went to the restaurant where she works. In all honesty, there was nothing to indicate she was a Ghost-Walker, but something about her put me on edge."

Her chin jerked up and she glared at Gino. "You aren't a very nice person, are you? You don't even know how to be nice."

He ignored her. "I didn't get the vibe from her, but then she wasn't using her talents on anyone."

"He needs blood fast," Draden said, making the decision. "What's your blood type, Bellisia?"

She could just lie. Let them think she wasn't compatible. Maybe he'd die right there on the river. Damn him. Damn her. She knew she wouldn't let that happen. She couldn't. She knew she wasn't thinking clearly. Ezekiel Fortunes was her greatest enemy, but she couldn't stand the idea of him dead.

"Bellisia." Draden was already searching for a vein in Ezekiel's arm. "Tell me right now."

"I'm RH-null."

Draden suppressed his reaction. One of shock. The men exchanged long looks and then Draden caught up her arm, looking for veins. She was used to that. She hated needles, but she'd been a pincushion for Whitney.

RH-null meant she was born without any antigens in her blood. None. She was the perfect donor. One that would be sought after by every hospital, every scientist. Everyone. No one knew about her. Whitney had kept her for himself. He'd be pulling out his hair, furious that he lost her.

"She's got venom in her. Could that poison Ezekiel?" Mordichai asked anxiously.

"It's more likely in her saliva," Draden answered absently. "Not her blood."

Talking about her like she wasn't there. Like she couldn't understand what was being said. Worse, like she wasn't human and didn't matter in the least. Clearly her feelings didn't matter. She wasn't anything to them but a blood donor for their friend. They treated her with the same disdain Whitney did.

She detested giving blood. She hated the needle in her arm. She hated the way it hooked two people together. She was always dizzy and nauseous afterward. Draden didn't hesitate, hitting her vein with the boat skipping over the water and in the darkness.

A gift he had, no doubt. Night vision, probably. Or maybe he saw through skin to veins. It didn't matter. She was back in the laboratory, the sweaty techs leaning over her, sticking needles in her. They were careful of her teeth, much more careful than Draden or Mordichai, both men leaning over her. She had only to turn her head either way and sink her teeth into them. They should be afraid. There was no way they'd forgotten. They were just discussing her ability to kill.

She glanced at Gino. He hadn't forgotten. Rubin drove the boat at top speed, slowing only when they hit shallower waters. Mordichai and Draden worked on Ezekiel, paying no attention to her or anything else. Gino was the man who was the most lethal right then. The most dangerous to her. He never took his eyes from her. If she made a move to bite any of them, he would kill her. She had no doubt.

She was too tired to bite anyone. Exhausted. She wanted to think accepting defeat for the moment was all about physical exhaustion, but really, she couldn't get over the hurt of Ezekiel's betrayal. She wanted to curl up into a ball and disappear. She was good at camouflage, but disappearing on the small boat with a needle stuck in her arm hooking her to Ezekiel was asking too much of even her.

"We don't want to hurt you," Gino said.

That was the last thing she expected from him. He was quiet. Watchful. A man standing apart. He kept himself from feeling anything for her deliberately—so he could kill her if it became necessary. He was telling the truth. He didn't want to hurt her. Of course they didn't. Whitney wasn't going to barter or give favors for a dead body. She knew Whitney so well now. He could make the decision to kill her. He liked having that power. He certainly wouldn't like anyone taking that decision from him.

She lay back in the boat, uncaring of the smell and dampness of it. Her skin wanted to absorb every bit of water; no droplet was too small. She stared up at the night sky. It was dark. No stars. Clouds were heavy and threatening. She hoped they'd be so heavy they'd burst and pour down on them. She needed the comfort of the rain on her skin.

Her lashes glided down. The fierce hurt that felt as if it had shattered her receded just enough to be bearable. She let the sound of the boat's engine and the slap of the bottom of it hitting the surface lull her into a state of drifting. She thought about Ezekiel in the boat, a lazy day of taking the triplets down a bayou. She'd been in the water, and it wasn't the cleanest. It was still and dark, but she didn't care because she was moving along with the boat.

She'd attached herself to the side and floated as he told wild tales of adventure to the little girls. She loved his imagination. She especially loved that the girls were always included as characters in his story. They were the heroines and they always prevailed against all odds. The sound of the girls' laughter and the deep affection in Ezekiel's voice when he talked to them had been what made her fall so hard for him.

Right then, her body tied to his, she could acknowledge that she had been a bigger idiot than she'd ever want to admit to anyone. She couldn't see other men. There was only Ezekiel. He was extraordinary. Every time he took the children out, he made it fun for them. He was teaching them about the ever-changing waterways and the landmarks. He taught them about tolerance and caring through his stories. His lessons were practical ones—who could name the birds and plants the fastest. How many? Who could spot the animals on land or the alligator in the water.

Life for Ezekiel's children would be an adventure. He would teach them survival skills, but the lessons would be filled with fun and laughter. She'd only known discipline. Rigorous training. She watched the way he touched the children, little caressing strokes down their hair. Hugs. A kiss on their forehead or top of their head.

Once, one of the girls had gotten angry and bitten her sister. She'd been horrified the moment the deed was done and had backed away, her expression so terrified Bellisia had almost broken cover to go to her and comfort her. It had been Ezekiel who had lifted the child in his arms, cradled her close and murmured soft, gentle words to her while the others took the triplet with the teeth marks on her arm quickly inside.

Bellisia had seen those looks the adults had exchanged. She knew immediately those little girls had a venomous bite, just as she had. Her venom was easily controlled. She didn't think the triplets could do the same with theirs.

Ezekiel had been so calm and reassuring. No one had yelled at the child. No one had hit her, or made her feel worse than she already felt. Clearly she was intelligent and knew her sister was in danger from that momentary loss of control of her temper. She'd probably never make that mistake again.

Her arm burned, bringing her out of her semi-drifting state. They were heading toward the Fontenot compound, and it was a distance from Donny's island and the marsh where Ezekiel had been taken. They must have called Stennis to call off the search for Ezekiel, yet they were bringing him home rather than to the military barracks or the hospital she knew Stennis had available.

Draden removed the needle from her arm, applying pressure to stop the bleeding. "You'll feel dizzy. Don't try to sit up too soon." He held a water bottle to her lips. "Drink. You need it."

Her arms hurt from being forced behind her back for so long. She was feeling needles and pins and knew her limbs were close to going completely numb. She felt very sick and was afraid she might throw up in front of them. She took the drink because her body cried out for water, but she didn't look at him. His hands were too gentle. His voice too solicitous. She wanted nothing from any of them, especially false concern.

She preferred Gino to the others. At least he didn't pretend to be anything but what he was—a cold killing machine.

"More?" Draden offered.

She could have downed the entire bottle, but she shook her head, not liking him so close to her, afraid she'd give in to the one moment of loss of control as that little girl with the dark, shining hair had. Her stomach lurched. Her arms were completely numb now, a dead, heavy weight that made her feel even sicker.

She tried to move fast, to get to the side of the boat. Gino caught her shoulder in a hard grip and she vomited on his shoes. She might have actually enjoyed the irony of it, but once she started, she couldn't stop, her stomach heaving over and over, cramping and protesting. She knew from experience it was a reaction to the needle. She hated them that much. Giving blood always made her sick. Always.

Whitney hated that. He thought it a defect. She wasn't perfect because she puked every time he forced her to donate blood. The more she'd gotten sick, the more he'd taken her blood until it had become a vicious circle.

Mordichai bunched her hair in his fist to keep it from pooling in the mostly bile on Gino's shoes and in the bottom of the boat. "Draden, what's wrong?"

"I'm not certain. I've got antinausea meds in the bag. I'll give her a shot and see if that helps."

She shook her head violently, unable to talk through the gagging. She hated that weakness in front of them. It made her feel more vulnerable than ever. She even hated the fact that she'd thrown up on tough man's shoes. If the earth opened up and swallowed her, she'd be all right with that. But she was close to the edge of the boat. Very close.

Tough man Gino had let go of her shoulder. She clearly wasn't faking her reaction, so none of them considered that she might leap over the edge of the boat into the water while she was vomiting so violently.

"The medicine will help settle your stomach," Draden said, moving close to her with a needle in his hand.

That fine metal entering her skin, slipping in between her cells. Each time it bit into the set of muscles running beneath her skin, she felt an exquisite pain that ran through every cell and every nerve she had. It was as if that needle connected the cells and nerves in some way, bringing every-thing in her body to fiery life, a pain so deep and ugly she could barely breathe through it.

How did one explain that to others? No one else seemed to have the same problem. The site of the needle entrance always swelled, but worse, deep inside, she could feel the swelling there as well, beneath the skin in those muscles that allowed her to change the texture of her skin. To cam-ouflage herself. She moved her body away from the needle and a couple of inches closer to the side of the boat, not even having to feign her fears.

"Is it the needle?" Draden asked.

She nodded her head vigorously. She'd endured the fire spreading to every nerve while giving Ezekiel blood by put-ting herself in a state of near hypnosis.

"It causes this severe of a reaction every time?"

She shook her head. Not every time. Just most of the time. The gagging was getting worse. Her stomach cramped hor-ribly. She couldn't use her hands to press against the terrible churning. She shifted uncomfortably, gaining another two inches. She didn't make the mistake of glancing toward the water. She kept her head down, trying to take in air between each session of what now was the dry heaves.

The boat slowed. They were close to the pier. She had been close to the Fontenot compound dozens of times. Right there in the water watching all of them and they never knew—or suspected. She exploded into action, coming up right in between all three men, leaping to cover the few inches left to go overboard. Her scalp screamed in pain. A cry escaped as she went backward, falling hard without the use of her hands. Mordichai still had her by her hair. Tears burned behind her eyes, but she kept fighting.

She rolled and kicked hard, knowing this was her last real chance to escape. They would take her somewhere away from the water. They'd lock her in a cell and she'd be at their mercy, waiting for Whitney to show. She had no hands to use against them, but she still fought viciously, thrashing, using her head as a weapon, her feet and even her shoulders.

Mordichai never once let go of her hair. If anything, he tightened his hold. She felt like her scalp might detach at any time. Gino caught one leg and pinned it and then waited patiently, timing her kick at him so he could get a hold of her other leg.

Ezekiel crawled to her. "Settle, baby. Just settle." His voice was a soft croon. "No one wants to hurt you. Just be still. Be calm."

Could she hate him? She wanted to hate him. He deserved to be hated. He used that voice, the beautiful one, the one he talked to the triplets with. All the while his hand massaged her scalp, ignoring the fact that his brother still held her immobile that way.

"Come on, sweetheart, just relax. Stop fighting them. I'm right here with you. I'm not going to let anything happen to you."

The boat docked. On some level she was aware that Gino had tied her legs to her hands, leaving her like a roped calf, but that didn't stop her from thrashing around like a crazy person. She couldn't stop. Stopping meant admitting defeat, and she refused to believe she was caught again. That she'd made it so easy for Whitney to reacquire her. She'd always thought once she was out, she'd be able to elude him. It just took staying near water. Staying close to an escape route.

It was right there. Scant inches from her. The river. The water. Her haven. Why she didn't bite Ezekiel she would never know, but it honestly never occurred to her. In the end, he pillowed her head in his lap, stroking caresses over her hair and down her face, following the line of cheekbones and jaw with a gentle finger, just as he'd done with the little triplet who had bitten her sister in anger.

"That's it, sweetheart, just relax. I've got you. I swear to you. I give you my word, nothing bad is going to happen to you. Just be calm for me."

She had to face the fact that there was no getting into the water. No escape. These men were too fast and there were too many of them. She forced her body under control. Her face was wet and she hoped it wasn't with tears; she hoped the rain had started, but she couldn't tell, she couldn't be bothered to look up at the sky. She kept her face turned away from Ezekiel and her eyes closed tight even as she drew in great gulps of air and managed to stop her body from fighting them.

"I'm sorry, Zeke," Mordichai whispered as if she might have gone to sleep. "I wasn't trying to hurt her."

Ezekiel didn't reply. He just wrapped his arms around her. Tight. For some odd reason that comforted her, the tight cocoon of his arms. She knew how the triplets felt, safe and secure. She also knew it was an illusion. She wasn't safe with him or anyone else. There would always be a bounty on her head. Whitney was a billionaire, one of the wealthiest men in the world. More, he had powerful friends.

She lay quietly, enduring the pain of the position of her arms and legs. Enduring the pain in her heart was worse and much more difficult. But she was a highly trained operative and no one, not even these men, could take that away from her.

It was Gino who lifted her up into his arms, cradling her close against his chest, his hands surprisingly gentle. She didn't lift her lashes, but she knew his scent. His body. The way he moved. She absorbed those things in the way her body absorbed water. Ezekiel was helped by his brother and Draden. She didn't need to see that to know; it was more instinctive.

She knew how many steps it took to go up to the house, and they didn't go that way. She didn't get the house. She wasn't going to be introduced to Nonny or the triplets or even the triplets' mother. She was going to be locked away, the dirty little secret kept from the women.

Doors creaked. Groaned. Big ones. The garage then. She smelled chemicals and nearly lost her composure. A laboratory. It took all she had not to inject Gino with the venom already beginning to pool in her saliva. She knew the faint blue rings were showing on her skin when he spoke. It said a lot about him that he didn't toss her away from him. She knew she wouldn't be able to hold out much longer; fear was overcoming her ability to think straight. Panic set in. She couldn't stand being an experiment again.

"I know this looks bad," Gino said. "I can tell you know where you are, but it's the only place we have that you can't escape from. Wyatt and Trap use this as a lab to try to find antidotes for . . . poisons."

That saved him when maybe nothing else could have. Of course they would search for antidotes for whatever venom the triplets injected when they bit anyone. They would have to. She turned her face away from him just to be certain she stayed in control.

She stayed that way while he cut the ties binding her and gently massaged her arms and legs until blood flowed freely. Then he left her there. Alone. In the dark. In a cage.

7

Bellisia stood up the moment she was alone and began to systematically examine the cell she was locked in. They'd left the lights off, and there was a small cot with a blanket. The night was warm and humid, but she found herself shivering. Desperately trying to keep her mind blank, she paced the length of her cell, counting the steps, feeling the flooring. It was definitely concrete. No way to escape under that. She kept pacing, counting each step forward and then across.

Reaching up with her hands, uncaring that a camera might be trained on her, she used the microscopic setae to climb to the top of the cell. With great care, she explored every wall, running her fingers through any crack she found. When all four walls were examined, she clung to the ceiling and did the same thing. Searching. Scrutinizing. Missing nothing. Inch by inch. Foot by foot.

She was patient. She relied only on herself, she always had. The idea that she'd been caught because of a fantasy was humiliating. Worse, she hadn't defended herself. She hadn't been afraid they would kill her, and she knew all of them would have if she'd injected venom into any of them. It wasn't fear that had stopped her, and that humiliated her even more.

She'd been trussed up and dumped on the floor of the boat as if she were nothing more than garbage. It was no different than she'd always been treated, but it hurt far more. She expected that sort of treatment from Whitney, but she'd convinced herself Ezekiel was different. He knew she wasn't part of Cheng's attack on him. He *knew*. Still, he'd forced her to become a prisoner, preventing her escape.

Patiently she continued her exploration of the cell. There was a small bathroom, crude, hidden by a partial wall. How many prisoners had they had? Gino had said they used this laboratory for researching antidotes. If that was the case, why the cell? What would they put in a cage that needed a bathroom? She began her exploration of that small space, paying particular attention to the plumbing. There had to be pipes that led outside.

The piping was very small. Even if she tore them loose from the wall, she doubted if she could make her body small enough to fit inside them. She needed the comfort of water so she ran her arms under the faucet, letting her skin absorb the moisture, giving her some relief. When she was stressed, more than ever, she wanted that connection.

The door to the laboratory opened and she swung around, her heart accelerating. Adrenaline poured into her body. She felt the venom rising and knew her skin was dotted with blue rings. Someone had come in alone and hadn't turned on the lights. That didn't bode well for her. She shrank to the back of the cage, making herself as small a target as possible.

His scent reached her first. Ezekiel's warm spice mixed with blood. The lacerations didn't like him moving around so much.

"You shouldn't be up," she reprimanded before she could stop herself.

"I couldn't stand the thought of you being out here all alone. I'm either going to spend the night locked in the cell with you or we're going to strike a deal." Ezekiel's voice was mesmerizing. A beautiful tone that sank into her skin the same way the water did.

He walked right up to the cell. She could see the keys in his hand in spite of the darkness in the room.

She moistened her dry lips with the tip of her tongue. "I'm pretty upset with you right now." She meant it as a warning, but she didn't know if she were secretly trying to convince herself she really would inject him with venom if he came near her.

"I'm well aware of that. I know you think I deserve it, that I betrayed you, but if you give me the chance to talk things out with you, you'll understand why I had to keep you with me."

"I'm not with you. I'm in a cage. Locked up like some animal." She rubbed at her wrists. They ached. Gino hadn't been gentle when he put the ties on her. She hated what her voice gave away. The note of hurt that just emerged when she didn't want it to.

"Deal, or I spend the night in the cage?" he prompted.

Could she rush him and slip past before he got the door closed? She doubted it. He was fast. Really, really fast. She didn't have a halfway venom. She couldn't just incapacitate him. If she bit him, he would die. She sighed.

"Tell me your deal." At least she would listen. She had all the time in the world. She drew her knees up to her chest and peered at him from across the cell.

"Come here."

She leaned her chin on the heel of her hand. "Why?"

"Because I asked. Nicely."

"That was nice?"

"It's about as nice as I get."

"Don't start off lying to me. I've heard you. When you were with the girls. I followed you when you took them exploring. The stories, the singing. I heard it all." She didn't care if she was condemning herself in his eyes. Just admitting to him that she followed him day after day made her vulnerable.

"Why did you follow us?" His voice was deceptively mild.

"I took a job for Whitney. You know him. Your buddy. He probably told you all this, so I don't know why I should." Bitterness ate her. That way led to mistakes. She couldn't feel bitter or angry, she had to make things impersonal again.

"Peter Whitney is no friend of ours. I know you're not going to believe that, I'll have to prove it to you, but for the sake of disclosure, keep talking. What job did you take for Whitney?"

"He sent me to China. He was worried that a U.S. senator was trading secrets for dark money for a campaign that was important to her. Cheng has money. Lots of it. He's a businessman in China with ties to nearly every terrorist cell around the world. No one has ever been able to bring him down. He wants the GhostWalkers' secrets to sell to the highest bidders. My guess is, that's where your blood and tissue samples were sent."

Ezekiel remained silent, just watching her. It was eerie to look across the room into the disconcerting, shiny eyes of a hunter. He was that and more. He didn't blink, staring at her the way a predator might. She thought of herself as lethal. She knew that she was, but the man on the other side of the bars made her very glad the bars were in place. ·

She sighed. "I was undercover for days and then she came. I had the information and started out of there, but Cheng locked the place down while she left. Someone must have found the wig I left behind and I was detained inside the building unexpectedly."

He was perfectly still. She was good. She could hold a position for long periods of time, blending in with her surroundings, but he was out in the open. Exposed. A big man. Because he didn't so much as move a muscle, he became harder and harder to see. Silence stretched out between them. She sighed. She might as well tell him everything. It wasn't as if she had a lot to lose.

"Whitney injected me with a virus specific to me. If I didn't get out when I was supposed to, the virus would kill me. That was how he ensured I would return to the fold after each mission."

That revelation caused a stir. The slightest of movements.

"Bastard." His voice was low.

"When I was finally able to leave, and it was difficult, I was pretty beat-up and already running a high fever. For someone like me, a fever can be deadly. I made it to the van where the men waited. Instead of giving me the antidote right away, Whitney wanted them to get the information from me. I feigned unconsciousness, and when they gave me the injection, I didn't move. Whitney told them to get me water. They opened the van doors and I blew past them and jumped into the river. Once there . . ."

"It was impossible to find you."

"That's right."

"Why did you come here all the way from China?" Once again his tone was mild, but she knew how it looked. She had followed him. There were three little girls, all obviously loved, but Whitney must have engineered them somehow. She could be a threat to him. None of the GhostWalkers would tolerate a threat to those girls, and she liked them better for that.

"The senator told Cheng that a GhostWalker team made their home near Stennis and often trained soldiers from other countries for joint missions. I knew Cheng would try to get to one of you. I wanted to make certain you weren't with Whitney, or like his other supersoldiers, before I broke my promises to myself and disappeared for good." Her chin went up. "So I watched you. I followed Nonny and fell for her. Who wouldn't? She's lovely. Perfect. And then you with the girls. The way you are with them."

"If you were so certain we were in danger, why didn't you warn us?"

"I did. I dug up the plant Nonny wanted and I left the note under the plant where I knew she'd find it."

"You left a note?" He sounded skeptical.

"Ask her. She had to have found it by now."

"I will. So Cheng is told by a U.S. senator that my team trains foreign soldiers here and he arranged for a terrorist cell to attack UN workers and take them hostage just to get at us? That's insane."

"Cheng's insane, and in his world, it's so easy. He deals with terrorists all the time. All he had to do was reach out and ask a favor. Believe me, any one of the cells would be happy to have Cheng owe them a favor. They grab the workers, make certain one or two are injured and need medical aid and just as predicted, you are training at Stennis to rescue the hostages. They snatch you, take what they need— Cheng's cautious. He's not going to bring one alive to his lab until he knows what you can and can't do. Besides, if he doesn't have to actually deal with a live person, but can just sell the information, it's much easier, cheaper and less of a danger to him."

She rubbed her chin with her palm, a small sigh escaping. "I didn't get that at first. I thought he was luring your team members in to grab them, but he was blowing everyone up. Once they got everything they needed from you, they were going to kill you, so I had to get you out of there."

He didn't have to believe her, but she'd told him the truth. He would never know how difficult it was for her to tell anyone the truth, let alone him. She'd made up her mind to die tonight, or escape. Either way, she'd be gone and it wouldn't matter that she'd given him the facts. Maybe she'd whitewashed the details, but he didn't need to know how the hooks had bitten into her skin, that she still bore the scars on her back and thigh.

She lifted her chin and let him see her eyes. "And after I saved your worthless ass, you betrayed me. I could have escaped. You knew I had no part in what Cheng did, you knew I got you out of there, and you still put me in a cage."

"I had no choice."

"There's always a choice. Go away, Ezekiel. You mattered to me. I don't know why I let you in, but I did. I'll take the blame for that. You didn't give me any kind of false promises, but still, I don't forgive you for betraying me."

"Those hostages are going to lose their lives in a few days. No one knew about this. We've kept it under wraps, but you were there watching us. You followed the boat to the marsh. You took me to that island rather than back to Stennis."

"Yes, I watched you train. I felt like I was watching over you. I couldn't believe after the note I wrote to Nonny you still went through with it. It had to have put you on alert. You had to realize that Cheng did business with that very terrorist cell. You knew it had to be a setup, yet you still went through with it. That made you a hero, but it also meant someone needed to watch your back. I *chose* to do that. It was my decision, so again, I can't blame you for my own stupidity. Of course I followed the boat. They injected you with something and you were dead or unconscious. Everyone was so sick they weren't paying attention when the two soldiers walked you right into the swamp and out of sight. As for taking you to the island, that was my sacrifice. I knew I'd have to give up my home—which I love, by the way—but it was closer and you needed medical attention. I didn't know how bad your wounds were."

Suddenly she wanted to weep. She didn't cry. Whitney had drilled that into them from the time they were babies, but still, there was burning behind her eyes and a terrible lump in her throat. She detested Ezekiel all the more for that.

"Go away and leave me alone. I don't want to know your deal anymore and I don't want you in here with me. You may trust me, but I don't altogether trust myself right now." She laid her cheek on her knees and looked at him from under her lashes, weary of the entire conversation.

"The deal is this. You give me your word of honor that you'll stay with Nonny, Pepper and the girls and help protect them while we're gone, and I'll let you out of here. You'll come up to the main house and live there until I can get back. But I'll need your word."

She lifted her head, shocked that he would even consider such a thing. She couldn't believe he really meant it. "Are you crazy? What are your friends going to say? They can't be on board with this plan." Her skin hurt. Her arms and legs. As if the skin had shrunk and was pulled tight over muscle and bone.

"I don't give a damn what they have to say. This is between the two of us."

She held her breath, thinking it over, examining the offer from every side, looking for hidden traps. "Why did you keep me from escaping?"

"We couldn't compromise the mission. If it was known that you overheard and saw exactly what we were going to do and you're an unknown element, they might make the decision to pull our team. The hostages would die. No one would risk an entire team of SEALs, GhostWalkers and Indonesian elite."

She hated it, but his reasoning made sense. She was a soldier and she understood that what he was doing was important.

"Will they believe you, that I'm harmless?"

"You're anything but harmless."

She liked that he knew that about her. "Will they believe that I'm no threat to the mission?"

"You'll be under wraps here at the compound. They don't have to know you were in the water at Stennis watching everything we did and said."

That was huge. *Huge*. Enormous. She knew the Ghost-Walkers went their own way a lot of the time and made their own decisions. Like all the women at Whitney's training facility, she'd soaked up the stories of them, but she hadn't known they were so independent.

"What will happen when you come back?"

"We'll talk. I want you to stay. I have my own personal reasons for wanting you here that have nothing to do with GhostWalkers, Whitney or anyone else. Come here."

She was much more inclined to go to him, even though he was sounding a little bossy. She thought over all the times he'd been with the girls and Nonny, the times she thought him wonderful and perfect. He'd sounded bossy then as well, but she wasn't the one on the receiving end.

"You know . . ." She got up and dusted off the seat of her pants. "I just got my first taste of freedom a few weeks ago and now you're using that bossy tone with me. I'm not certain I like it."

"I'll grow on you."

She noticed he didn't apologize or attempt to lie and say he wouldn't do it again. She sighed and walked across the small cell to stand in front of him.

"Tell me how the venom works."

She shrugged. "I can call it up at will."

"So if I kissed you, I wouldn't be poisoned?"

She tipped her head to one side and studied his face, her heart racing. "Not unless I wanted you to be poisoned."

"I'll risk it." He crooked his little finger at her.

"Maybe that wouldn't be a good idea. I'm still kind of upset with you." She took a step back instead of toward him. She didn't have the first idea how to kiss a man. She had full confidence in herself as a soldier, a warrior, even an assassin, but as a woman? Kissing him sounded far more frightening than remaining in the cell.

For the first time a faint smile softened the hard edge of his mouth and revealed his straight, white teeth. The effect was startling. It sent heat spiraling through her body, and rushing through her veins so that her blood pooled low. She didn't faint or anything, but she felt a little weak in the knees. She couldn't understand why he affected her that way when she'd been around men all of her life and found most of them disgusting. Certainly none of them had ever elicited a physical response from her.

She thought him gorgeous and heroic even in the face of him keeping her from escaping. He'd done it for all the right reasons—reasons she had to admit as a soldier made sense to her.

"Baby, stop fucking around and come over here." He pointed to the spot right in front of him. "I dream about kissing you. I can barely think about anything else."

She doubted that, but she loved hearing him say it. She hadn't gotten that far in her dreams. She wanted the home and family, but she didn't know the least thing about being physical with a man. She'd kept as far from that subject as possible because Whitney had his beloved breeding program and was always selecting one of her fellow soldiers to partner with one of his supersoldiers to try to have a baby. She wanted no part of his latest madness.

She moved the scant foot separating them until she was right up to the bars. He pushed the key into the lock, turned it and then deftly keyed a code in. He pulled the door open and stood in front of her, blocking the way to freedom with his body. He was quite a bit larger than her, taller and wider, his shoulders nearly making two of her.

She licked her lips, finding it difficult to breathe. "I've never done this," she blurted, half hoping that would drive him off. Who wanted someone totally inexperienced?

His smile widened. Very gently he wrapped his palm around the nape of her neck and pulled her closer to him. Right up against him. Both hands framed her face and held her still for him. "Do you think that matters to me?"

She blinked up at him. Up close he was even more dangerous than she'd first thought him. "It should."

"Why?"

"Won't you feel cheated when it isn't very good?"

"Who says it won't be any good?"

He sounded amused. His amber eyes had gone a really intriguing shade of gold. His thumb swept her cheekbone, sending more heat through her body. Electricity seemed to arc between them. If he felt it, he didn't show it, but she did, the little strikes shocking on her nerve endings.

"It's bound to be terrible, since I don't know what I'm doing."

"I know exactly what I'm doing. You're in good hands, baby."

Now butterflies took wing. Hundreds of them. No, thousands of them. Her stomach did a slow, rolling somersault. She knew he was teasing her, but coming from him it was sensual. Sexy.

She wanted the kiss from him, but she knew it was far too much for her to handle. She shook her head, her gaze held captive by his. "It's not a good idea."

His smile reached his eyes, turning the gold molten, so that just looking at him had her breath catching in her throat.

"It's not an idea, sweetheart, it's a necessity. I must not have explained that very well to you." He bent his head toward hers. Her breath left her lungs in a long, ragged rush. She felt the press of his lips against her forehead. A brush. Then his mouth was on her left eyelid. "Are you going to forgive me?" He kissed her right eyelid.

She pressed one hand to her stomach, a mass of nerves. The touch of his lips felt . . . exquisite. Perfect. Better than anything she'd imagined. Her brain short-circuited.

He trailed kisses from her eye to her right cheekbone, following that path so that everywhere his lips touched she felt little darts of fire. "Will you, Bellisia? Will you forgive me?" His voice slid over her skin like a caress and slipped under her guard as it always did.

She tried to find her voice. Words. Anything to deter him. Kissing her would be the last thing he'd do with her, she was certain of that. She hadn't even read about kissing the way some of the other girls had. There had been one night when a couple of the girls had been clowning around and practiced with each other. They both burst out laughing and made faces. She didn't want Ezekiel Fortunes ever laughing at her.

His lips slid down from her cheekbone to the corner of her mouth. Barely touched there, but she felt it all the way through her skin to her insides. His tongue traced along the seam of her mouth and then he licked her lips. She gasped. Her hands curled into two tight fists, both bunching his shirt so the material was soft against her palm.

Everything about him was a contrast. His skin was warm and soft, yet his muscles were so hard he felt like stone. His hands were huge, shaping her face with just his palms, leaving his fingers to move over her skin, teasing behind her ear and over her pounding pulse so gently when he could have crushed her.

"Baby, you have to say the words to me so I know you mean it. I need your forgiveness. There's no way for me to close my eyes and rest if I don't have that from you. I'll have to stay up all night convincing you I would never hurt you or allow anyone else to harm you."

He alternated brushing his lips over hers and licking at her lips with the tip of his tongue. His mouth was warm and satin soft, but firm and very persistent. His tongue was hot and damp, teasing her senses until she would have given him anything if she could talk. She nodded her head, because of course she could forgive him. She understood.

There was relief in knowing he detested Whitney as much as she did. He didn't have to state it. He'd said "bastard." In that tone. That said it all.

His mouth was gentle on hers, kissing her until she was

reeling with the strange, exhilarating feeling. "Say it now, baby, right now. Whisper the words into my mouth so I can keep your forgiveness inside me forever."

He was the devil tempting her. She couldn't help herself. She wanted to give him the moon. Saying what was already true was no hardship if she could catch her breath. Her lips parted. She drew in a breath. "I forgive you."

The moment she said the words to him, his mouth was on hers, his tongue sliding into her mouth, exploring, stroking little caresses along her tongue until she thought she might go insane with wanting to kiss him all night. Sensations poured into her body. Crashed through her nerve endings. Awakened things she hadn't known existed inside her.

He kissed her over and over. Gently. Almost reverently. All the while his hands cupped her face, fingers stroking those amazing caresses behind her ears and into her scalp that only added to the dizziness she was swept up in. Her mouth followed his. Survival skills were something she excelled at. She learned fast, she always had, and kissing was something that suddenly was extremely necessary to her survival.

When he finally lifted his head, just inches from hers, she chased his mouth, feeling almost bereft without his lips on hers.

"Sweetheart, if we don't stop, this is going to get out of hand, and that's not a good idea until we know each other better. I don't want you disappearing on me now that I've found you. Let's get into the house."

He stepped back because right in that moment she was incapable of moving. She touched her lips with shaking fingers. "That was . . ."

"Perfect," he finished for her. "Perfect for now. I promise to do better when we're where we need to be."

Reluctantly he let his hand fall from her face, only to trace a finger from her shoulder to her wrist. He picked up her limp, trembling hand and put it in his palm. Her entire hand, fingers and all, fit right there. If it got any better, she wasn't certain she could handle it.

"You ready to go inside? We only have tonight, Bellisia. Tomorrow morning, I have to be at Stennis at zero six hundred. When I get back, we'll have a great deal more time. I want to convince you not to take off. To throw in with us and help keep Ginger, Thym and Cannelle safe while they grow up."

A faint smile made its way to her mouth. She felt it under the pads of her fingers. Her lips were still tingling, still feeling him. It felt like a brand on her.

"You've got to give me something, sweetheart." He threaded his fingers through hers, and then brought their linked hands to his chest. "We good right now?"

"Ask me." She managed to get the two words out. She doubted she could be much more coherent than that.

"Ask you what?"

"For my word." She liked that he was willing to take her word. That he thought she was an honorable person. That he was willing to believe her to the extent he was.

"Bellisia, will you give me your word of honor that you'll stay with Nonny at the Fontenot compound and help guard the girls, Pepper and Nonny while I'm away?"

She nodded her head but replied aloud. Solemnly. "Yes. I'll stay."

"I wasn't finished."

She lifted her chin, frowning at him. "You weren't?" When he shook his head, she couldn't help being a little wary. "There's more?"

"There's more. And it's important. Maybe the most important part of all."

She regarded him steadily. "Lay it on me."

"I need your word of honor that once you hear I'm back, and you will, probably long before you see me, that you won't go off with some new man who has been flirting outrageously with you."

"Okay. I can do that. I don't think I'm ready to run off with another man."

"Good. I'd hate to scare you by causing bloodshed to some unknowing male, but there's more. I'm not finished."

She tried tugging at her hand halfheartedly. She was acutely aware of him and the teasing only intensified her feelings for him. "How can there be more? Obeying your orders. Kissing. Giving my word. Steep price to pay for leaving my very fancy real estate. I had my own private bathroom."

"Uh. No. That's the bathroom for the laboratory. You'd have to share."

She rolled her eyes. "What's the rest?"

"You can't leave when you hear I'm on my way back or even that I am back, not until we have a chance to spend a little time together."

"You drive a hard bargain. I don't know, I just might have to go back into the cage. You're not my favorite person."

"You forgave me."

"I did, but you lost my job for me. I liked waitressing. It had its perks. You know, like being able to actually eat real food."

"I'll get your job back for you," he promised, his thumb sliding over her jaw in a caress that sent a shiver of acute awareness down her spine. "Or at least find you another one you'll love and where you'll be able to eat real food."

"How can you do that?"

"I'm charming when I need to be."

She believed that. "I don't find you all that charming."

"You're lying your pretty little ass off, baby."

"Now I know I'm going back in the cage. You're arrogant on top of everything else."

He shook his head. "Not arrogant. *Confident*. You admittedly don't have a lot of experience, so you need a confident man to guide you in these perilous times."

She arched an eyebrow. "'Perilous times'? 'Confident' man?"

He nodded solemnly as he took a step toward the door.

Her arm was locked to his side, her hand to his chest. He moved slowly, but he definitely took her with him. "I need your word, sweetheart, that you won't run off on me, not before I have a chance to talk you into staying with me after the mission is completed."

She took a breath. A long one. She felt as if her mind was at war. One side was pure panic, full flight mode. The other side wanted to spend as much time with Ezekiel as possible. She had never played or teased or been teased by a man before. She knew it was much more than that. She was having fun because it was Ezekiel, not some random man. For some unknown reason, she liked being around him.

"All right. I'll stay until you're back home from your mission," she conceded. "But you'd better be prepared to get my job back for me."

He grinned down at her, and immediately her heart stuttered in reaction.

"Nonny knows everyone. I get Nonny on my side, you'll have your job back." He eased her toward the door.

"Isn't that cheating?"

Bellisia realized she was hanging back, reluctant to go with him. This was her chance to meet Nonny and the three little girls. She could meet their mother. It would be the opportunity of a lifetime to be able to question them without any of the men present. Why was she so hesitant to go with him into the house?

"What's wrong, sweetheart? No one in that house will hurt you. The children are highly intelligent and very sweet. It will be fun for you."

She tried to analyze exactly what was wrong and came up with the reason she was dragging her feet. "I don't know the first thing about talking to children. I've never had a grandmother or even really talked to someone I . . ." She trailed off. How to explain her feelings about Nonny? She didn't have the words.

"Someone you admire? I understand completely. The first

time I ever saw Nonny, she was sitting on her front porch in her rocking chair. She had a shotgun close to one hand and a pipe in the other. She didn't ask us questions, she just accepted us because we were Wyatt's friends. Wyatt is one of her grandsons and he'd brought us back with him. I have two brothers, Malichai and Mordichai. They've never known a lot of love in their lives. They're good men, but sometimes a little rough around the edges."

"Like you."

"No, babe, not like me." He shook his head as he pulled the door open and drew her through into the night. "They're good men," he reiterated.

She could hear the soothing sound of the river lapping at the pier. At the bank. She turned her head toward the sound. In spite of the darkness, to her, the water was shiny, radiating a brilliance that beckoned to her. She loved the sound of water, even needed it, but his tone overrode the continual pull of the water on her body.

"Ezekiel, you're a good man. I've seen you with the triplets, and you were unbelievably gentle."

"Don't." His voice was low. A whip. "Don't see me as something I'm not. Growing up, I didn't have time to learn the nicer things. How to be polite and civilized, I grew up fighting for every scrap of food I could get for my brothers. You have no idea what I'm like inside. What I've done or am willing to do for my family."

She took a step and turned so she blocked his path to the house. All the while a part of her felt the pull of the water. The droplets in the air no one else ever felt, cool on her skin. Her skin felt dry and tight, stretched over her muscles, aching and even painful in spots, but even with that, the call of the water wasn't stronger than her need to get him to see himself the way she saw him.

"I never learned the niceties either, Ezekiel. And I don't have a family to fight for, but if I did, there wouldn't be much I wouldn't do for them."

"I'm ruthless. Brutal, even."

"I saw that when you stopped me from escaping. I felt hurt and betrayed and angry at you."

"You didn't inject me with venom and you could have any number of times. You didn't inject any of the others either." There was a question in his tone.

She shrugged. "I hadn't fully made up my mind about you or your team members. I didn't know for certain if you were working with Whitney or not."

"You believed it. I saw it on your face and you still didn't kill me when you had the chance."

She glared at him. "I'm trying to say something here. You're a good man whether or not you believe it. You had good motivation for stopping my escape. Saving hostages comes before hurt feelings."

He swept his thumb along her lips, tracing the bow. "I'm sorry I hurt you, Bellisia."

"What the *fuck* are you doing, Ezekiel?" Gino's voice came out of the night. He strode toward them, his eyes glowing like that of a predatory cat. Every step betrayed his anger. "She goes back in that cell right now."

Bellisia's first thought was to make a run for it. Her body coiled tight in preparation, yet appeared relaxed. One strong jerk should break Ezekiel's hold on her. Everyone underestimated her strength. She would sprint for the water and be gone.

Ezekiel transferred her from his right side to his left, even closer to the water, but away from Gino. He tucked her beneath his shoulder, his entire demeanor protective.

Behind Gino came Mordichai, Draden and Rubin, all looking grim.

8

Bellisia found herself noting every single detail around her. A slight breeze stirred, came off the river and rushed the house. It swirled on the front porch and then moved on as if playing. A fish jumped not more than two feet from the pier. There were rustlings at the edges of the swamp as if mice scurried there. The scent of anger mixed with concern, with worry. The clouds rolling over her head and the layer of dirt under her feet.

Mostly it was Ezekiel who penetrated her defenses. Heat poured off of him. She glanced up at his face and his features were impassive, but she felt the coiling tension building in him, power so strong it was frightening. His hand, holding her close to him, was gentle. He drew her beneath his shoulder protectively.

That gesture nearly stopped her heart. No one in her entire life had ever offered her protection. Not once. Not even when she was a child. She'd seen the way Ezekiel held the triplets, so gently, his entire demeanor one of steadfast protection, and right then, in that perfect moment, he'd done the same for her—only far more intimately.

The way he held her to him was definitely all about her being a woman and him being a man. She knew he had a protective instinct; she'd seen it many times watching him with the girls, Nonny, Pepper and even his teammates. But this was different. This was solely about her and his willingness to stand between her and the people he clearly loved. That was huge. That took her breath away and drove out every thought of escape. If he could put his career and his relationships on the line for her, then she owed it to him—and to herself—not to leap into the water.

This was a moment in time she would never forget. She wanted it etched into her very skin and branded in her bones. She never forgot something once she saw it, and she knew this would always be her favorite and most important memory.

"She's coming with me to the house. She's no threat to anyone in that house, or to the mission."

Gino swore aloud, his fierce tone, although low, making Bellisia wince. The others surrounded them.

"Zeke, even if she's pure as driven snow, word gets out, you know they'll call things off. If they know you were hurt, they'll call them off. You have to be able to stand in front of the colonel, look him in the eye and tell him you're physically fit for duty and there's no threat whatsoever to any man going on that mission." Draden stepped closer. "You can't say either with absolute certainty."

"That's bullshit. Step back, all of you."

Energy crackled around them. Power was amassing in Ezekiel, and coming off him in waves. She doubted if he would be able to contain it much longer. Taking a deep breath, she stepped in front of him, her free hand going to his chest, a slim hope that she could stop him before something terrible happened.

"They're right, Ezekiel. As much as I hate to admit it,

they're right. The most important thing right now is the hostages. I can sit in a cage for a few days while you get it done. We can sort things out later." She couldn't believe she was making the offer. She'd been in a cell of one kind or another, a prisoner of Whitney's, and it was the last thing she wanted. Ever.

She realized why she hadn't bitten him or any of his friends. It wasn't because she knew for certain they weren't Whitney's men. She didn't know that. It was Ezekiel. He was already imprinted in her somewhere deep. The men were his. Under his protection. She didn't want to kill him or them—so she'd given them another chance—a chance she didn't believe they deserved at the time.

Ezekiel framed her face with both hands and bent his head toward her. His features were gentle. Almost tender. Taking her breath away. "And what happens if I don't get back, baby?" His voice turned her heart over. "That's a real possibility every time I go out. What happens to you if you're sitting in a cell unable to protect yourself?"

As if at a great distance she heard Mordichai gasp. Gino swore softly.

"I'll manage. Come on." She tugged at his shirt, trying to get him to move back in the direction of the laboratory. She hated that she was putting him at odds with his team members. Most of all, she didn't want to see what would happen if all that energy building inside of Ezekiel was let loose. Did they know? Why provoke him if they did? She knew that power was enormous. Lethal. Once it rose to the surface, how did he get rid of it?

"I'll get her out," Mordichai said, his voice almost as gentle as his brother's. "I see what she is to you. You have to know I'd protect her."

"And what happens if you don't come back either?" Ezekiel raised his head and all hint of softness was gone.

Bellisia stroked her hand over his chest, rubbed in little soothing circles trying to keep the dark energy pulsing in his body from spilling out. His skin was hot right through the material of his shirt. She felt him coiled tight inside, like a spring about to snap. She didn't want to be anywhere in the vicinity if he did let go.

"Zeke," Gino said, conceding with a sigh. "We get it. All of us."

The wind stirred again, and this time it brought the scent of spice and smoke. "Ezekiel." The female voice was authoritative without being the least bit abrasive. "You bring that child to me this instant."

The moment he heard the voice, Ezekiel leaned his head down even more and took ownership of Bellisia's mouth. His lips coaxed hers and she opened her mouth, helpless to do anything but give him everything he wanted. Even with his teammates looking on.

His mouth was scorching hot and turned aggressive immediately until every trace of gentleness was gone and she felt his nature rising toward hers. Power mixed with possession poured into her. It was dark and ugly and very, very scary. Terrifying even. Yet she couldn't pull away. At the same time, there was something beautiful and real about the way his mouth moved over hers, and his tongue stroked caresses all the while she absorbed that very dangerous energy.

How could she be safe taking in all that power and need for action and dominance? He short-circuited her brain every single time he kissed her, but it was there, working at the back of her mind, and the moment he lifted his head, his peculiar gold eyes searching hers, she knew.

With a small cry, she tried to tear herself out of his hold, but he was fast and strong. Her instincts for self-preservation were so strong she actually lunged toward him, venom rising, the faint blue rings moving up under her skin, but at the last moment she turned her face away from him and spat out the venom.

"He paired us." It was an accusation, although she knew

he couldn't have known either. She had wanted her attraction to Ezekiel to be real, to have one thing in her life that hadn't been tainted by Whitney. Just one.

Whitney had found a way, using pheromones, to program his male soldiers with his female soldiers. His vision had been a two-person team that could work together in the field. The couple had to be compatible psychically and physically, their gifts complementing each other. Whitney had abandoned his plan, finding he didn't want to give up the female soldiers he'd used for his experiments, he wanted babies to work with. When they were away from him, he lost control of his creations.

"I should have known. I couldn't kill you when I had the chance." She whispered the admission, her eyes meeting his.

Ezekiel stepped closer to her, one arm a bar across her back, pulling her body tightly against his so that she felt the hard length of him, the urgency of his need. "He can pair us physically, Bellisia, but no way can he do so emotionally. That's where he goes wrong. He doesn't have emotions. He's a cold bastard who can cut up children without batting an eyelash. He doesn't feel, so he doesn't understand feelings. Maybe I went looking for you because the wind was coming my way and I caught your scent. Hell, all I remember is looking across the square and seeing you. I can describe every single detail of that moment. He couldn't possibly make that happen."

She moistened her dry lips. She desperately needed water, but she needed his reassurance more. At the same time, it was all too much to take in. Whitney's pairing them. The hidden weapon inside of him. So dark and scary. The energy Ezekiel was capable of manipulating was dangerous.

The water lapped at the pier, calling to her. Night owls chimed in. Not too far away, an alligator slid from the bank into the water.

"Do they know about you?" She tilted her chin at him, challenging him. What government in their right minds would let him go walking around if they knew?

He shook his head and pressed his mouth against her ear. "Only you know. I took that chance and put my life in your hands because you were putting your life in mine. It was only fair."

His lips brushed her ear with every word—sweet, hot strokes that she swore involved his tongue. Each brush sent shivers down her spine. "That cage is looking more inviting by the minute."

"Ezekiel. Bring that child to me," Nonny persisted.

The creak of her chair indicated she had stood up. Soft footfalls on the porch and the sound of her pipe hitting the bannister told Bellisia the woman stood at the top of the stairs.

"She's not a child, Nonny," Ezekiel said. "And I'm working on convincing her."

There was a small silence. "Son, if you haven't got her convinced by now, you're not half the man I think you are. Bring your woman to me."

"Zeke, she means business," Mordichai warned. He sounded a little nervous.

Bellisia risked a glance his way and realized the Ghost-Walkers were still surrounding them. She'd all but forgotten they were there. It was their stillness. She could imagine insects and lizards crawling right over them, not realizing they were human. They'd also gone from combative and hostile to protective. She didn't know what had caused the difference, but even Gino was on board. They were clearly guarding the couple rather than guarding the compound against her.

"Don't get him in trouble with Nonny," Rubin advised.

"Cut through the bullshit," Gino added. "You aren't going to turn him down, because someone has to look after the lug. I don't know what you know about him that we don't, but it sounds like you're meant for each other. Just get over there to Nonny before she decides to quit cooking for us."

Bellisia shook her head, a little bit stunned. The big, badass GhostWalkers were afraid of an eighty-year-old woman—or more precisely, their stomachs were. "I have to decide in two seconds? How did you go from 'lock her up now, you're insane to be with her' to 'Bellisia, just accept the man and get on with it'?" What had caused their sudden about-face? They were all in with her relationship with Eze-kiel now that they knew Whitney had paired them.

"They think with their stomachs," Ezekiel said, glaring at them. "Don't push her around like that."

"It's more than our stomachs, ma'am." Mordichai pushed a hand through his hair, somewhere between agitation, amusement and absolute seriousness. "Although I'll admit that may have a small amount to do with it. It's Zeke. That's all I can say. It's Zeke."

Ezekiel pressed Bellisia closer to him, keeping her small body sheltered by his. She was scared. So much had hap-pened so fast. And she was exhausted. She knew Ezekiel had to be as well. She couldn't imagine how much longer he could stay on his feet or even what was keeping him upright. He had to have a will of iron.

He swayed, and she tilted her chin to look up at his face, examining the lines of strain there.

"You're frowning, baby. I find it very sexy when you frown and that's not a good thing right now."

"Ezekiel, you need to lie down." Her hand tightened in his shirt as she took a better grip on him.

"You have more compassion in your little finger than I do in my entire body. I couldn't help testing my theory."

"Your theory? You mean almost falling on your face to see what I'd do?"

He nodded, his eyes going to a beautiful Florentine gold. "You have no idea what you are to me, do you?"

She couldn't hide the fine tremor that went through her, so light she hoped he didn't catch it. She wasn't nearly as confident as she was trying to make him believe. "No, but then right now, I think you've been a little oxygen-deprived, so who knows what you're thinking."

"Being a smart man, I'm not going to let you find out just what that is, sweetheart. You already have me tied up in knots. I can't afford for you to ever figure out that you'll always have the upper hand."

Mordichai groaned. Gino shook his head. Rubin made a sound like a dying dog. Ezekiel took a step toward the porch and Nonny. "I've got to get you to the verandah and Nonny before these clowns have you running. That woman up there is going to be my greatest advocate and ally. You just remember that she's wise and these men are just wiseasses."

She would have laughed if she hadn't been so nervous. The men were pretty funny together.

"Zeke, a call came in from Stennis just a few minutes ago," Gino said, his voice low. She could have sworn he projected it straight at Ezekiel so the wind couldn't carry the sound anywhere but where he directed it. "That's why we all were looking for you and found you out of bed. Indonesia sent a warning that two of their soldiers were found dead, two who were supposed to have come here to train. There was evidence to show that someone had made molds of their faces."

"What about the other four soldiers? How could they not know?" Ezekiel continued to move Bellisia toward the house. She'd been far less nervous surrounded by the GhostWalkers. The closer they were to the porch and Nonny, the more she trembled no matter how hard she tried to control it.

"Baby," he whispered softly. "It's going to be okay." He paused for a moment, wrapping his arms around her and holding her close. "She's going to like you."

How did he know? Nonny was the most important one there. She knew Ezekiel would never admit it, but he considered her his mother and grandmother all rolled into one. She heard it in his voice when he spoke of her. She saw it in his body language whenever he was close to her. She knew nothing of his life, but she would bet her next paycheck that Ezekiel's own mother wasn't alive.

"The Indonesians were suspicious something was wrong. Their teammates were acting strange and kept to themselves, very unlike either man. They contacted their superiors and an investigation ensued," Gino continued. "That's when the bodies were found. We were told immediately."

"But too late," Mordichai said. "You could have been killed."

"Fortunately, Bellisia followed us." Ezekiel tugged at her when her feet stopped moving forward.

They were very close to the house. A few more feet and he'd have her up the stairs and in Nonny's company. That would be the defining moment. Nonny would either like her or not. If she didn't . . .

"You probably could have escaped on your own," she objected, trying to stall for time as well as give him his due. "I saw you were awake and planning something."

"I would have taken out the two in the cabin, but I wouldn't have been able to get out of the marsh. I was too weak. I'm a doctor, so I knew my physical condition was extremely compromised. My mind had become a little fuzzy and I was dizzy and nauseous. I wouldn't have been able to make it through the mercenaries or get out before the explosives had been set off, not without you."

He hadn't stopped moving, and he had her all the way up the steps. Then they were standing in front of Nonny. She pressed a hand to her churning stomach. She was *not* going to throw up on Nonny's shoes.

"Bellisia, this is Grace Fontenot, Wyatt's grandmother. She's graciously allowed all of us to stay here. Grace, this is Bellisia Adams. Her friends call her Bella."

He sounded so proud, as if he was introducing someone very special to his grandmother. She tried to smile but she just couldn't. She'd never had a mother or grandmother either. She didn't know what having that would be like. She only knew what she'd witnessed these past few weeks watching them all. Nonny was extraordinary with all of them. She was well loved and deservedly so. Bellisia desperately wanted the woman to like her, to look at her the way she did the men and Pepper, Cayenne and the three little girls. As family. Family had a meaning now and it was all wrapped up in this woman.

The faded blue eyes moved over her slowly with great care. Bellisia felt as if those eyes saw right into her, saw every bad thing she'd ever done as a child—and she'd done plenty. She'd been one of the defiant ones. She doubted if Whitney would have kept her if she hadn't been so good at her job. It wasn't as if he had very many like her. In fact, to her knowledge she was the only one with her gifts.

She'd been healthy, so he'd performed several experiments on her, and her body hadn't rejected the things he'd done genetically. He had put extra guards on her dormitory because she was very, very good at escaping. She liked to see how close to his personal sleeping quarters she could get before she got caught. When he finally realized what she was doing, he'd begun putting her in a cell at night. She trained hard and liked the physical training, but she also stirred up trouble, talking about subjects that he'd forbidden to the other girls.

She bit her lip, thinking this woman probably knew when her grandsons had told her lies. She doubted if anything could get by Nonny. *I can kill people when I bite them.* She nearly blurted her secret out loud. That was how compelling Nonny was. How magic. You just wanted to confess every single bad thing about yourself. She kept biting her lip harder and harder, feeling a little faint.

"Call me Nonny, child. You're the one who brought me the black nightshade." She made it a statement. "Thank you for that. More, thank you for the warnin' that someone might be lookin' to kidnap or harm one of my grandson's friends. They're family to me now and I don' take kindly to anyone hurtin' them."

"You found the note?" Ezekiel asked. "She told me she left you a warning."

"Just today, underneath the plant. I haven't had time to transplant it, but it was droopin' in that box, so I put it in somethin' a little friendlier."

"I'd like to see that note, Nonny," Rubin said. "We'll need to keep it for evidence of Bellisia's innocence if we need to prove anything to anyone."

"This is a family matter." Nonny swept them all with her regal expression. "It stays in the family."

"We still have to see the note," Rubin insisted gently.

"I'll get it for you in the mornin'," Nonny complied.

"You're right about family, Nonny," Gino decreed.

"Ezekiel, you sit down in that rocker before you fall down." Nonny and Mordichai gave the order simultaneously.

"I know you'd like to talk with Bellisia, but I have to get some sleep, Nonny," Ezekiel said. "I have to get up early tomorrow and go to work. I'd like Bellisia to stay here with you and Pepper and the girls. It would be a huge favor to me."

"No need to call it a favor. She's yours. I can see it plain as day. That makes her mine." She looked around at the men sitting on the bannister and porch stairs. "Ours. Ezekiel is goin' to do whatever needs doin' and his woman will stay with me right where she belongs. We could use another warrior just in case someone makes their play for the triplets. No one is goin' to take my grandchildren. I'll take good care of your Bella, Ezekiel, although I suspect she doesn't need that."

Bellisia wanted to say she did. She wanted to say she needed care and knowledge, the kind that could build a family, but she only bit her lip harder, afraid if she opened her mouth she'd make a fool of herself. Ezekiel's arms slipped around her chest, right below her breasts. He locked his hands there and pulled her back against him. He felt solid. Warm. Protective.

He bent his head so that his mouth was against her ear. "Stop biting your lip. You're going to draw blood soon."

Color swept up her neck to her face. She could only hope the darkness covered her blush as she closed her lips tightly, wincing a little, certain she may have actually bitten down hard enough to make her lip bleed. Great. She wanted to impress Nonny, not act like a terrified child. It didn't help that she was always so acutely aware of Ezekiel. His scent enveloped her. She felt every breath he took.

She didn't belong here. It was so far out of her comfort zone she didn't even know how to act. She was a woman trained for violence, for the shadows, not to stand so close to something bright and warm and beautiful. His arm pressed deeper into her skin as if he knew what she was thinking.

"Good night, everyone. We're heading to my room."

Nonny tried to look scandalized. "Don' you do anythin' I'll have to get the shotgun out for, Ezekiel."

"Unfortunately, Nonny, I'm not in the best of shape right now or I wouldn't be able to make that promise, but," he added hastily as her face darkened and her brows came together, "I give you my word as a gentleman Bellisia is safe with me."

Mordichai and Rubin made some noise that indicated they thought Ezekiel was hilarious. Bellisia found herself smiling as Ezekiel stepped in front of her, retaining possession of her hand so he could lead the way.

She wanted to see the house, but it was dark and silent. Ezekiel moved fast and unerringly through the hallway and down past a number of doors. He stopped in front of one toward the very end of the hall, opened it and stepped back to wave her through. She still couldn't believe she was there. Inside that home. A part of her was close to panicking. She'd never been inside anyone's home. She didn't know how to think or act.

"You're shaking, baby. There's no need for that. You're safe here."

She hoped everyone else was safe there as well. He let go of her hand, and she thought about clinging, but had far too much pride for that. She watched him sink down onto the bed, bending to unlace his boots. His face was nearly gray, but his hands were steady.

Bellisia crouched down. "Let me." She didn't tell him he looked like hell. She pushed his hands away and pulled at the cords to loosen the ties. Her own hands were shaking and she willed herself to be calm. She didn't like not being in control, but she had no idea what Ezekiel expected of her.

"Sweetheart, there's no need to be nervous. Nonny gave you her approval, and no one would dare upset you or try to take you back to the cage." He dropped a hand in her hair, burying his fingers deep and massaging her scalp.

She took a breath and gave him honesty. "I'm not worried anyone is going to demand I go back to the cell. I just have never been inside a civilian's home. I was raised in barracks. I trained from the time I was a small child, not much older than the triplets. The stories you tell the girls? I never heard anything like that in my life. At night when you, Nonny and Pepper hold them on the front porch and rock them? I not only haven't had that; I never saw it. Until I watched the three of you with those little girls, I didn't know anyone could be so kind. This is all new to me. Having any kind of feelings for a man is new." She admitted the last in a very low voice.

He caught her chin and gently raised her face until she was looking into his eyes. "You're safe with me, Bellisia. You always will be, and I don't mean just physically."

She knew what he meant, she just couldn't conceive of it, not in regard to her. "Why? I know Whitney paired us, but that's all about sex. And just for the record, I'm not going to be any better at sex than I am at kissing. I don't know the first thing about it." There was a hint of defiance in her voice, and that made her a little ashamed.

"Have I indicated in any way that I didn't like your kisses? Not to say that if you feel the need for practice, I'm more than willing." He bent his head to brush his mouth over hers. "But I've got to lie down."

She tugged his boots off and put a hand on his chest. Up high, where the least of the lacerations were. Pushing gently until he lowered himself to the mattress, she eased his legs onto the bed. Then she didn't know what to do. She felt a little helpless, looking around trying to figure out what she was supposed to do.

"Come here, Bellisia." Ezekiel patted the bed beside him. "Lie down next to me."

Her heart stuttered and then picked up the pace until it was galloping. She'd never done that before either. Gingerly she sat on the edge of the bed so she could remove her own shoes. Somehow taking off her shoes seemed intimate and made her feel very vulnerable. "This relationship thing is scarier than going alone into Cheng's laboratory. Believe me, his security is very tight, so that's saying something."

"Is it possible Whitney has formed some kind of an alliance with Cheng?" Ezekiel reached up, took her arm and tugged her down until she was lying on her back beside him. That wasn't good enough for him. He rolled her over to her side and tucked her in close to him.

"No way. Cheng sells arms to terrorists. Whitney's capable of using a terrorist cell to get what he wants, but he would never arm them, nor would he do any real business such as trading secrets. He's a monster and a sociopath, but he's also a patriot. He sent me to Cheng because he was afraid Violet was forming some kind of alliance with him—and she was. She needs money for the campaign. She plans to become vice president first. Maurice Stuart has named her as his running mate. Once he's elected president, she plans to have Stuart assassinated so that she becomes president. Cheng can provide the money for her, but his price is a GhostWalker, or at least the body of one."

"Why didn't they put me on a freighter? They could have gone right out to the gulf."

"But everyone was going to be searching for you, and they couldn't afford to get caught with you. They don't know your capabilities." She relaxed into his warmth. Now that they were discussing work, the tension ebbed out of her. "If you studied Cheng at all, you'd realize just how cautious he is. He would never risk an unknown with the capabilities the GhostWalkers are reputed to have in one of his laboratories before he knew for certain he could control that kind of power."

He made a sound as if he was half drifting already. She put her arm around his waist. She couldn't help it. She wanted to be closer to him. He'd be leaving in the morning and she would have to have enough faith in him to keep an open mind about any kind of a relationship. They barely knew each other. And what kind of relationship was he after? She assumed, because she wanted a family, that he was thinking along the lines of something permanent, but she knew from all the gossip in the barracks that most men didn't settle down with one woman. They wanted variety. At least most of Whitney's supersoldiers seemed to confirm that.

"Violet can't be president, Bellisia. She hates the Ghost-Walker program. I think mainly because it's Whitney's baby and she despises him with every cell in her body, but I think another part of her wants to be the only one with psychic and genetic gifts," Ezekiel said. "Did you know Whitney paired her with him?"

"I suspected as much, but her actions don't appear to make that so."

"That's the rumor. If it's true, it just goes to show Whitney can't control our emotions. He might be able to make us lust after each other, but he can't make me feel like this. Like I do about you."

"You don't know me."

"I know you. I knew you the minute I looked at you and knew you were the one. When a man has searched as long as I have, believing he didn't have a shot at finding anyone who would take him as he is, that man recognizes the right woman, the *only* woman, and he isn't willing to walk away."

"You're crazy. Do you have any idea how lethal I am?"

"Yes." He sounded proud. "It turns me on, baby, knowing I'm always going to be living on the edge of danger."

"That just makes you crazier than I thought you were."

He laughed softly, and in the dark of the room, it sounded a little like music to her. Outside crickets and frogs created their own music, but she thought his laughter trumped their symphony. She had to be honest with him though. "I don't belong here, Ezekiel. As much as I love the fantasy of it, I don't fit in anywhere and I never will. Whitney saw to that."

He threaded his fingers through hers and pulled her hand over his heart. "You still aren't getting it, baby. I don't belong here. I don't fit anywhere. None of the GhostWalkers do. Why? Because Whitney screwed all of us. The psychic enhancements were bad enough, but we signed on for those. The genetic enhancements were a surprise." He turned his head. "You belong with us. With me."

She didn't want to feel hope rising. Hope was something she'd learned not to trust. She couldn't look away from him, but she couldn't respond either. She didn't dare.

He brought their joined hands to his mouth, his teeth scraping gently at the pads of her fingers. "When I was a boy, just heading into my teens, hormones running wild and my strength growing, I was already taking care of Mordichai and Malichai. We were street rats, living in an abandoned building. I insisted we all go to school. They were so fucking smart, honey. Like you wouldn't believe. I had to fake papers and parents and addresses."

"Parents? What happened to yours?"

"Our mother was a crack whore. She sold herself for money for her drugs. Got hooked right after Malichai was born. Our father was killed in a shootout with a rival gang and she just went to hell after that. One day I heard a man talking to her about selling us on the street to some of his friends. She turned him down, but I knew it was a matter of time, that she'd get desperate enough. And she did."

Her heart actually hurt for him. No wonder he was such a protector. He'd been looking after his brothers for a long, long time.

"I took them and ran, never looked back. They trusted me to get them food and to keep them warm—which I did. There's only a couple of ways for a boy to earn money on the streets. I could be a runner for drugs—something I wanted no part of. I could sell my body, which I wanted no part of, or I could fight. I could use my fists to get us cash. There's always underground street fighting."

"I heard of it, but don't know much about it."

"It's pretty brutal, not a lot of rules. On my thirteenth birthday, I promised the boys we'd get a cake. That meant shoplifting one. Not so easy. Cakes aren't exactly a good size or shape to steal."

"I can imagine."

He sucked her finger into his mouth, and her body went hot. Electric. He used his teeth again and then kissed the spot that stung. "I told the boys to wait, that I'd be back in a few minutes and we'd get the cake. I hadn't started fighting yet, not really. Just took a couple of easy bouts, but I knew I'd have to commit. I got halfway down the block and went back because I'd forgotten to tell the boys to put out the fire we'd started. I wanted it good and out before we left. The place was drafty and a good wind could get the ashes stirred up."

She tightened her fingers around his, realizing he was giving her something important.

"Malichai just couldn't wait for me. He'd rushed off to go look at the cakes, to try to find the 'right' one. He was only eight at the time. Mordichai was writing me a note because he wasn't about to let Malichai go off by himself. It wasn't safe."

She took a breath, her eyes on his face. The night was dark, but she could see the outline of his face. He stared up at the ceiling, but his hand held hers almost tight enough to crush her fingers. She didn't pull away.

"He was in an alley and there were two of them. Boys quite a bit older than me. I'd heard of them. Seen them around a time or two. Bullies. Liked to hurt others. Set fire to a couple of homeless camps in the alleys. They were kicking the crap out of Malichai. Had him down on the ground and he was bleeding, but he wasn't crying."

He rubbed her knuckles along his shadowed jaw. She felt the dark bristles against her skin. The sensation was sensual in spite of what he was telling her—or maybe because of it. He was giving her a part of him she knew instinctively he'd never given anyone else.

"That was the first time I felt it inside me. Really felt it and identified it for what it was. A dark energy that rose when I was angry. Before that day, it was always my temper. I knew I had a bad one and I had to keep it tamped down around the boys, but then it was rage coiling inside me like a fist. I could call it up at will, and I could defeat any enemy, even two seasoned fighters. It was dark and ugly but it served me well. I felt the power running through me and went after them. I nearly killed both of them."

He turned his head toward her. "Baby, look at me." His voice was pitched very, very low.

She obeyed him. His eyes were pure gold, glittering at her like a cat's in the dark. She held her breath.

"When Whitney enhanced me, he boosted that part of me as well. It's there inside, a deep well, and it gets out every now and then. All that dark energy looking to fight. Looking to hurt." He touched his mouth to her knuckles. "Or find you. You took it away. I didn't have to hit something until my fists were bloody. I didn't have to hurt anyone. You kissed me and you took that away."

That was huge for him. She could see why. She'd felt that buildup of power in him and realized he was capable of destroying everything around him—a bomb going off. "Did Whitney realize what he'd done?"

"He doesn't know. How could he? Not even my brothers

know. They just think I have a really bad temper when pro-
voked." He pried open her fingers one at a time and then
pressed a kiss to the center of her palm. "That's why it's so
important to me that you wait for me, Bellisia. I know you're
scared and probably confused. I know you don't have any
reason to trust me, but I'm asking you all the same to wait for
me. Here with Nonny and the girls. The people who matter
to me. That should tell you how important you are to me."

He gave her so much of himself, made himself utterly
vulnerable, laying his emotions on the line for her, so much
so that she was completely lost in him, willing to give him
whatever he wanted.

9

Bellisia woke to the sound of giggling. She stayed very still, assessing her surroundings. She was in Ezekiel's bed. He was gone, but she wasn't alone. She smelled baby powder and shampoo. Very carefully she opened her eyes and peered at the three little identical girls from behind the veil of her lashes.

"You're awake!" The one closest to her wore a long, ruffled dress with a blue sash. "I'm Ginger. These are my sisters, Thym"— she indicated an identical child with the same dress but with a green sash—"and Cannelle. Everyone calls her Elle." She wore the ruffled dress with a pink sash.

"Good morning." She sat up carefully. Cannelle and Thym looked a little more hesitant than Ginger, and she didn't want to alarm them. "How did you know I was awake?"

"Your heartbeat," Ginger said. "Why are you in Uncle Zeke's bed?"

"I'm Bellisia. Your uncle asked me to wait here with your Nonny until he got back. He's going to be gone for a few days."

Cannelle nudged Ginger. Ginger shook her head, and her sister glared and nodded vigorously, all the while studiously avoiding Bellisia's gaze. Clearly the girls could communicate telepathically.

"You can ask me whatever it is you want to know," she said, trying out a tentative smile.

Ginger sighed. "It's so rude. Mom said not to ask personal questions, and asking you if Uncle Zeke kissed you is rude."

"Then ask her if she's Uncle Zeke's girlfriend," Thym chimed in.

Bellisia sighed. This wasn't going to be easy. She felt like she was walking through a minefield. These girls adored their uncle and they might not take kindly to a woman in his life. "I did kiss him," she conceded. She wasn't touching the girlfriend question.

"Nonny said if we came in here bothering you, she was going to tan our hides," Ginger said. "Although I don't think she understands what tanning a hide is. I asked mommy to look it up for me and we don't have hides to tan."

Cannelle rolled her eyes. "I told you it wasn't like that but you don't ever listen."

"I listen most of the time," Ginger protested. "Are we bothering you?"

"Do all two-year-olds talk like the three of you? I didn't think they even understood that many words, let alone knew idioms."

The three exchanged long looks, once again communicating. Of course it was Ginger asking the question. "What is an idiom?"

Great. She didn't know the first thing about children or their capabilities of understanding. "Well, an idiom would be a phrase or word you can't take literally. There are tons of them. *Tons* would be an idiom because words obviously don't weigh a ton. *Tan your hide* might mean *spank you*. *Bought the farm* could be used to mean *dying*, not actually purchasing property."

The girls wore identical frowns on their faces. "Say more," Cannelle pleaded, clearly wanting to understand.

"Going with the theme of dying, *kicked the bucket* could mean that as well. *Piece of cake* can mean something is easy, as in talking with you three is a piece of cake."

The frowns faded, to be replaced by three identical smiles. "Tell us more," Thym urged.

Bellisia had to think hard to come up with a few more. It wasn't as if she went through life using idioms as a rule. "Let me see, there's *break a leg*, that's a rather famous one, and some people say it to mean *good luck. Let the cat out of the bag* doesn't mean someone actually put the poor cat in the bag, it means *to tell a secret.*"

The girls broke into giggles again. "Nonny has breakfast ready."

"Well, if I said, *don't bite off more than you can chew*, I wouldn't be referring to breakfast and what you can eat, but I'd be saying not to take on a chore or task that's too big for you." She was still dressed in the clothes she'd been wearing from the night before. "Can you show me where another bathroom is?" Bellisia asked, needing to get the girls out of the bedroom, since she was not sure if Ezekiel had any weapons hidden.

All three heads nodded simultaneously. They slid off the bed and started toward the door. Ginger looked back over her shoulder. "When we bite, we hurt people. Really, really bad."

She delivered her warning in a grave, ominous tone, clearly wanting to scare her. Bellisia's eyebrow shot up. "You do? Biting does hurt," she said solemnly, all agreeable. Little Ginger was throwing down the gauntlet now that they were on the move.

Ginger scowled at her as if she wasn't quite bright. Bellisia continued to smile as she followed the girls out of Ezekiel's room and down the hall. Cannelle and Thym had stopped outside a door.

"Thanks, girls. I'll meet you in the kitchen. Tell Nonny I'll be right there."

"Don't forget to wash your hands," Ginger said.

"Thank you for the reminder," Bellisia said, and firmly closed the door on three little faces.

What she wanted to do was fill the bathtub with water and climb in it, but she hastily took care of her morning business, going so far as to brush her teeth with her finger. She hoped she could use the telephone and let Donny know she was all right. Maybe he could bring a few of her things over for her. She didn't know if returning to the island would be a good idea, even for a couple of hours, not if Ezekiel thought someone might be coming for the three girls.

She stared at herself in the mirror, barely recognizing herself. She looked different. Her eyes were enormous, very, very blue and ringed with her fair, bluish lashes. Her hair was a pale blond, a blue sheen running through it. She remembered the feel of Ezekiel's fingers in it and couldn't help smiling.

He'd fallen asleep with her tucked close to him, his arm a band around her. She'd lain next to him, awake in spite of her exhaustion, listening to him breathing, knowing she was going to stay no matter what the danger was. She could fit in anywhere, be what Whitney had designed her to be, or she could try to be Bellisia, whoever that was.

He wanted her to give his family the real thing. She was the rebel. The troublemaker. She was the one who stood up for the other women and nine times out of ten ended up in solitary. She took pride in her abilities and training. She'd worked hard to be good at what she did, and she'd do the same in whatever she did next. She took a deep breath and tried to comb her hair into some semblance of order with her fingers. She needed her things. She couldn't just run around in the same clothes day and night. No toothbrush. No hairbrush. There were such things as the niceties of hygiene.

She made her way down the hall toward the sound of

laughter coming from the kitchen. The walls were lined with photographs. Boys. Plants. The bayou. The swamp. She paused to study one of the oldest. It was clearly Nonny in her younger days, and looking down at her was a very handsome man. She was looking up at him with a faint smile on her face, but it was the way they looked at each other that caught and held her attention. It was one of the most intimate things she'd ever seen and yet they weren't even touching each other.

She wanted that. She hadn't known it could be real, but the evidence was right in front of her. She loved being what she was, what she could do, even the good she knew she'd done with her various assignments, but this was personal. This was something that touched her where nothing else ever had.

"Bellisia?" Nonny had come a few steps into the hallway. "Are you all right?"

Her tone was gentle. Caring. Warm. All the things Bellisia associated with Ezekiel. Was it possible to miss a man when she barely knew him? When he'd only been gone a short period of time? Remembering the way Nonny and her husband had looked at each other, she believed it possible.

"Yes. It's just that . . ." She trailed off, sweeping her hand to encompass the house. "I've never done this before. I don't go into homes."

Nonny smiled at her and stepped back to indicate that she go into the kitchen before her. "Then you'll fit right in. My daughter-in-law, Pepper, had never been in a home before, and certainly Cayenne, Trap's wife, hadn't either. My three granddaughters were equally without knowledge of homes until Pepper brought them here."

Bellisia stepped into the kitchen and inhaled. Even the scents were unbelievable, the way she'd pictured a home should smell. Cinnamon. Sugar. Spices. The room was large, the table long and beautifully carved. Pots and pans hung from a rack over a center island that should have been messy after preparing a meal, but was spotless.

A woman stood up gracefully. She was breathtakingly beautiful. Her hair was very thick and dark with strange patterns woven through like diamonds and was braided into a thick rope. Her eyes were gorgeous, a distinct shade of blue violet. "I'm Pepper, Bellisia. Welcome to our home." She spoke with a French accent, her tone low and sensual, even to Bellisia's ears. "Apparently you've already met my girls. Ginger, Thym and Cannelle couldn't wait to see who was sleeping in their uncle Zeke's bed." She did her best to look disapprovingly at her daughters, but only succeeded in looking proud of them.

"Yes, they were nice enough to tell me breakfast was ready." She couldn't believe how nervous she was. It was silly. Pepper and Cayenne had been prisoners of Whitney just as she had been. They were enhanced psychically as well as physically. They were sisters, just as the women she'd been raised with had been. Not by blood, but in every other way. They just . . . fit . . . here, whereas she had no idea what she was doing.

"We're so happy to have you join us," Cayenne added, skirting around the table to join Pepper and Bellisia. "I'm Cayenne. Trap is my husband. I don't know if you've met the team members yet." She sounded as if it was a foregone conclusion that Bellisia would.

Pepper was ultra-feminine. Soft. It was difficult to see her as lethal or a warrior at all, yet she had to be in order to have been enhanced by Whitney. Cayenne looked very small and fragile, and very young. She was slight with dark black hair, so dark and shiny it almost looked a midnight blue, although down the back of it ran a red hourglass. It was hidden until she moved and then it burst to life beneath the lights in the kitchen. Although she looked young, she also gave the impression to Bellisia that she was someone to contend with.

Bellisia looked young, small and defenseless. She was anything but defenseless, so she recognized a warrior when she saw one. She identified more with Cayenne, and that made her feel as if she had a chance with Ezekiel. If Cayenne could transform herself into someone who fit there in that home, it was possible Bellisia could.

"Please call me Bella. Everyone does. Well, with the exception of Ezekiel."

Nonny waved them all to the table. The triplets were in chairs with booster seats. All three were making short work of strawberry waffles and what looked like homemade whipped cream.

"Where did you meet Zeke?" Cayenne asked, her voice casual.

Bellisia wasn't deceived. This was going to be an inter-rogation. She was very, very good at interrogations. She'd been through enough of them. She took the chair Nonny indicated, not surprised in the least that it was directly across from Cayenne.

"I worked as a waitress in New Orleans. Jackson Square. He was shopping, he told me he was getting spices for Nonny, and he sat at one of my tables. He asked me to sit down with him when I had a break so I did." She rubbed the pad of her thumb over the center of her palm where he'd kissed her. Her fingers closed around the center as if she could capture that feeling forever. "He's very compelling when he wants something."

"Yes, he is," Cayenne agreed.

"Help yourself to food," Nonny said. "There's no need to be shy."

It was a good thing Bellisia had decided to learn to wait-ress. The food provided in the barracks had been nutritious, but definitely not like what she'd seen at the restaurant where she'd worked, or spread out across Nonny's table. There were the waffles, but also a very traditional Cajun casserole of eggs, grated cheese, salt, butter and Worcestershire sauce. As if that wasn't enough, there was a platter of bayou crab cakes. Someone had cut up fresh berries and put them in a bowl to eat with the waffles and whipped cream. In order to blend in, Bellisia had learned to do her homework, and food was one of the identifiable markers for New Orleans. She could name all of it and even knew the ingredients, but she hadn't tasted it.

"Aren't you hungry?" Nonny asked, nudging her plate.

"Yes. I haven't eaten in over twenty-four hours." She'd been too busy watching the men train. She'd been in the water the entire time. Her body had loved it, but her stomach—not so much. The others had food on their plates, but she wasn't certain how to proceed. "I've never done this before." She thought it better to tell the truth. Ezekiel wanted her to be with these people—the ones he considered family. They might as well know the truth about her.

"Eat breakfast?" Pepper said, frowning.

All three little girls stopped laughing with one another and went eerily silent, forks with waffle bites hovering in the air. As usual it was left to Ginger to do the talking. "Never?"

"Not in a house. A home, with other people around. I grew up differently." She sounded casual because she felt casual about it. That was a fact. She'd been sold to Whitney as an infant and experimented on almost from birth. She'd been trained as a soldier and then an assassin. She was a highly skilled operative and she'd performed numerous successful missions. She wasn't ashamed of that, only anxious that she didn't offend anyone without Ezekiel present to guide her a little.

Nonny smiled at her. "Just choose the food you like and put it on your plate. If it isn' close to you, just ask for it. We don' stand on ceremony in the kitchen. I like my girls to eat up, keep their strength up." She looked at all three girls and instantly they began eating.

Determined, Bellisia took a little of each dish. Donny often left spicy food, mostly fish and shrimp that he'd caught, for her to eat. She enjoyed it, but she learned to go easy since she was new to the varieties of New Orleans cuisine.

"Thanks for savin' Ezekiel," Nonny said. "He's a good boy, tough as nails. I was upset that I didn't get your warnin' in time to stop him from goin'."

Again silence reigned. The triplets exchanged long looks. "What happened to Uncle Zeke?" Ginger asked, a little quiver in her voice. Her chin wobbled. "Mama?" She looked toward Pepper.

"Do you remember when I told you we always have to be careful because there are some very bad people who want to find us and take us away? That's why we have guards and dogs and we have to look after one another," Pepper said softly. "Uncle Zeke was busy trying to help some people who really need it and the bad people had infiltrated the team he was working with."

Bellisia kept her eyes on the three little girls absorbing news that was far too mature for them, but that they clearly understood. She watched them while taking her first bite of the casserole. It took a minute to process all the flavors. It was good. She definitely could eat it.

The triplets' faces dropped and tears shone bright in their eyes. "But Uncle Zeke is . . . special. Tough. No one can take Uncle Zeke. He's like Daddy." Ginger again voiced what all of them were thinking. It stood to reason that if Uncle Zeke wasn't safe, neither was their father.

"The bad men made everyone sick and then pretended to help Zeke, but instead they injected him with drugs that made him unconscious. They took him to the marsh, to one of the camps there," Pepper explained, clearly having been given all the details by one of the other GhostWalkers.

Cayenne leaned across the table toward the girls. "I know that scares you, that someone as tough as Uncle Zeke could be taken by our enemies, but the reason we're always together and tell one another where we're going is because someone will come and get us, just like Bella helped Uncle Zeke."

"Actually," Bellisia said, mostly for the triplets, "I'm not as certain as he is that he couldn't have gotten out of there without my help. He was awake and already out of his bonds when I managed to get to him. They had several mercs positioned around the cabin and it took a while to work my way through them. By that time, he was groggy and . . ." She paused, searching for the right word to describe Ezekiel cut to pieces. "Hurt." She settled on that as the least scary word for the triplets. "He was hurt but ready for action."

There was a brief silent interchange between the three girls while she calmly ate her food. She could see why the team was so obsessed with Nonny's food. It was delicious and maybe a little addicting.

"How hurt?" Ginger asked suspiciously.

That brought her a flashback of her first sight of Ezekiel lying on the table, covered in blood. Blood dripped from the table onto the floor in a steady rhythm. Suddenly she wasn't so hungry and she put her fork down and pushed her plate slightly away from her.

Ezekiel was a big man and strong. He looked—and felt—invincible. He wouldn't have made it out of there before the charges had been set off. He'd lost too much blood and was too weak. She'd nearly lost him. All of them had. She hadn't allowed herself to think about that. She'd fallen so hard for him in the weeks that she'd followed him, stalking him like some crazed woman. A great pressure suddenly squeezed hard on her chest. Behind her eyes tears burned.

"Obviously he wasn't hurt that bad, Ginger," Nonny said. "He came home, didn't he? He's still carryin' out his work because he left before dawn this mornin'. He'll be coming back in a few days, and he's asked us to look after Bella for him. He's countin' on us."

Nonny reached out casually and put a hand on Bellisia's shoulder. It was light. Caring. That gentle touch made her want to cry for real. The girls comforted one another on those nights in the barracks when things had been rough and particularly awful. Having Nonny comfort her was— extraordinary.

A crackle sounded and beside her Nonny went still. "Incoming." Rubin's voice was terse and came from a speaker somewhere in the kitchen. "Cayenne, move it."

Cayenne instantly was up and gone. Nonny rose without a word and went down the hall, Bellisia trailing after her while Pepper took the three girls in the opposite direction. The girls were obviously well versed in security precautions. They didn't protest or argue in any way as their mother shepherded them toward safety.

Nonny picked up a shotgun that was set right beside the door before opening it. Bellisia didn't like her exposed that way, but she stayed back, out of sight, ready to spring into action, trusting that wherever Cayenne had gone, she was protecting Nonny.

"Donny. What a surprise," Nonny greeted their visitor. "What brings you out this way?"

Bellisia sagged against the wall with relief. Of course Donny would come for her. He was considered a little crazy by the local population, but those who knew him were aware he was loyal to his friends, and if you were in his inner circle, he was protective. He'd allowed her to live on his island. That made her his. It also made her very aware that the compound needed more guards.

"I believe one of my kids is here, Grace. I've come to bring her home."

"You look loaded for bear."

"I am."

Bellisia hugged herself tightly. In a few short weeks, her life had changed dramatically. Those two quiet words, "I am," said it all. Donny was prepared to go to war with GhostWalkers for her. Whitney had raised her from the time she was an infant and he'd planted a virus in her that would kill her if she were a few hours late returning from a mission. Donny had known her a few weeks and he was ready to fight trained soldiers. He lived and worked in the swamp. He knew the Fontenot family and he was a veteran. He'd served his time in the military and he recognized dangerous men. Still, he'd come for her.

Bellisia moved up beside Nonny, unable to keep the smile from her face. "Donny, I can't believe you came looking for me."

"Armed to the teeth," Nonny added.

He shrugged, in no way perturbed by Nonny's assessment. It was the truth. He was dressed for war. He hadn't even bothered to pretend that he was there for anything else. He had guns, knives, grenades and a vest filled with ammunition right out in the open.

"Didn't want anyone to mistake this for a friendly visit. They came and took my girl last night. She was exhausted and she hauled that soldier's ass into a boat, all the way to my island, got him up on land and took care of him. Even donated blood. They hauled her away hog-tied, Grace." He stepped closer and reached out to catch Bellisia's hands. He turned them over and held them up to the light. "You see those bruises? They weren't gentle about it either."

She'd never heard that particular hardness in his tone. Donny was a law unto himself. He wouldn't think twice about shooting a trespasser, but he took in stray children, gave them work and put them through school. He had a dog he sounded gruff with, but the dog was taken to a vet regularly and Donny went over him every day looking for parasites or signs of trouble. Now, he sounded as if he *wanted* to go to war.

Nonny reached out and gently removed Bellisia's hands from Donny's grip. "I've got something for these bruises, child. You should have told me."

Ezekiel hadn't seen them either and she knew instinctively he would find them abhorrent. She shrugged. "His friends weren't taking any chances, Donny, and they shouldn't. They're soldiers. Bad things happened, and I was a question mark. A stranger they didn't know or trust. Their friend was hurt. At least they didn't shoot first and ask questions later." She sent him a faint grin, referring to one of the numerous signs he had up around the island to warn people off.

Nonny stepped outside the screen and raised a hand to her hair. It took a moment for Bellisia to realize she'd signaled to Cayenne and Rubin that their visitor was a friend. "Come in, Donny. Sit a spell."

"Prefer outside, Grace."

She nodded and waved her hand toward one of the three rocking chairs on the front porch. Hand carved, the rockers were beautiful. Donny nodded and took the one that afforded the best view of the river and surrounding trees at the edge of the swamp. Grace sank into her favorite, leaving Bellisia the third chair.

"Had some visitors." This time Donny looked directly at Bellisia. "That's why I was late getting here this morning."

Everything in her stilled with the exception of her heart. That slammed painfully hard in her chest and then began to gallop. She knew what was coming.

"Two men. Big. Something off about them. One showed me a picture of you, said he'd tracked you to a local restaurant in the square and one of the waitresses said you knew me—that you'd talked about me."

Her big mouth. She hadn't said she'd lived with him, but in attempting friendly conversation, she had admitted she'd met him. The waitress had been regaling her with tales of the locals and she'd mentioned Donny and that he was out of his mind. "Batshit crazy," she'd called him. Bellisia couldn't help but defend him. She'd said she'd met him and he seemed very nice.

Donny hadn't taken his eyes off her face as he took his phone out of the inside pocket of his jacket. "This one said he was your husband. Said you were bipolar and sometimes ran off. He always tracked you down and took you home."

He passed the phone to her. "That's Gerald Perkins, and he's probably with his partner, Adam Cox. I'm not married to either of them. In fact, I'm not married." She handed the phone back to Donny.

"You're running from them." Donny made it a statement.

"Yes. What did you tell them?"

"Said I'd met you a time or two, but didn't have a clue where you lived. Thought you were too fancy for the swamp, said I pegged you for a townie."

"Do you think they believed you?"

"Don't care. They'd better not try to come on my island."

She knew Donny was a hard-ass, but Whitney's super-soldiers would wipe the floor with him. "You can't fight them."

"Bullet kills them same as me," he stated.

She shook her head. "It doesn't always though. A bullet won't kill them. Some of these men have armor under their skin. Seriously, Donny, don't try to go to war with them. If they come on the island, use one of your many ways to get out. Don't be seen. Dump anything of mine into the river, and get rid of all the evidence that I was ever there."

"I packed your things and already got rid of the evidence. Brought your clothes and personals to you. Knew you might have to run again. Brought money and supplies." He sounded gruffer than ever.

How could he care after only a few short weeks, when Whitney had been around her for her entire life and was willing to kill her if she was late? It made no sense to her, but that warm feeling inside of her began to grow stronger. There were good people in the world after all, and she'd been lucky enough to find some of them.

"That was so kind of you, Donny."

"That's me, kid, I'm all about the kind."

"Would you care for some coffee or breakfast?" Nonny asked.

"Coffee works. I scouted around before I came in. You got one man here and a bunch of women. Think I'll sit a spell and wait for your reinforcements to arrive. They are coming, aren't they, Grace?" He looked to Nonny.

"Rubin said we got word that a few of the boys are back and will be comin' home soon. I don' know what that trans-lates to in time, but thank you, we could use your skills."

Great. More of Ezekiel's friends no doubt, but she was grateful they were coming. She would have to leave as soon as they got there so she could lead Whitney's men away from Pepper, Nonny and the triplets. She had the feeling Cayenne could take care of herself. Still, Bellisia didn't want anyone hurt on her behalf. She tapped her thigh with her fingers, her mind protesting. She'd given Ezekiel her word, but she'd also promised him she'd take care of Nonny and the others. That meant leading the supersoldiers away from the Fontenot compound.

"That was fast, them finding me." How had they tracked her? She'd stayed near the water. She knew the tracking device Whitney chipped all of them with was too deep in her for her to get out by herself, but water messed with it. She'd been careful to stay in the river or a bathtub for long periods of time. She worked, but she had chosen a restaurant near the river where she could go on her breaks.

She looked at Nonny. "I promised Ezekiel I wouldn't leave without seeing him first, but if I stay here, eventually those men will come here looking for me."

Nonny shrugged. "It won't be the first time. If they come, they'll run into a parcel of trouble. You made your man a promise, Bella, and you can't go back on your word. That wouldn't be right."

"It wouldn't be right to put everyone he cares about in jeopardy either," she pointed out.

"You leave, they'll come all the same," Donny said. "You told that man you'd wait, you best be waiting. He's not the kind of man you want to lie to."

Cayenne walked up, went straight to Donny and touched her foot to his in a weird gesture of affection. "What's with the firepower, chief?"

"I came to straighten your spidery ass out, woman. Where's that man of yours? He's the only one that can keep you in line."

"Chief?" Bellisia echoed.

"Chief cook and bottle washer," Cayenne said. "He baby-sits for Pepper occasionally."

Donny bristled, puffing out his chest. "You're going to be in a world of hurt, woman, you keep that up. I don't baby-sit." He leaned over as if he might spit, looked at Nonny and changed his mind. "I *instruct* those little girls on plants and animals in the swamp. Just because they like my company more than they like yours, you don't have to be so snarky."

The two sounded like they were at war, but clearly they were friends. It occurred to Bellisia that Cayenne was every bit as wary around people as Donny was.

"I'm telling them you're here," Cayenne said. "We'll see about all the instructing you do."

"They'll be jumping all over me, and I'm here to protect your spidery ass."

"You can't keep calling me 'spidery.'"

"I can as long as you have that red in your hair. Why women have to go putting God knows what kind of junk in their hair, I'll never know."

Cayenne stuck her nose in the air and swung around to show Bellisia the hourglass in her thick mane of beautiful black hair—an hourglass that was natural, not dyed as Donny so clearly believed. "You like?"

"I have to admit, it's pretty cool," Bellisia agreed.

Donny scowled. "And people think I'm crazy. Where's Pepper? At least she's got some sense in her, marrying a Fontenot. You married Trap. Got crazy hair and a crazy husband. What the hell are you doing with that man?"

"He's *amazing* in the sack, Donny. Ah. Mazing," Cayenne taunted.

Donny rolled his eyes. "Stop talking. In fact, go away. I'm going to take my supplies and go lie up on the roof until your men come home. I hope your ah-mazing man spends a lot of time on spanking your ass."

"Oh." Cayenne fanned herself. "He does. Hurts so good."

"Cayenne." Nonny said her name. A warning.

"Sorry, Nonny." Cayenne blew her a kiss. "I'll behave myself. I just can't help it, especially when he calls my man crazy."

"He is crazy," Donny argued.

"Like a fox," Nonny said. "He's one of the smartest men on the planet."

Donny sighed and pushed the duffel bag at his feet closer to Bellisia. "There's your belongings. These men hunting you disappear, you come home. And if Ezekiel really wants you, he can come talk to me." Without another word he sauntered off in the direction of the side of the house where he knew they kept a ladder.

"Wow," Cayenne said, awed. "He's so amazing. He's already treating you like a daughter."

"What did that mean? About Ezekiel going to talk to him?"

"It's a tradition for a man to ask for her father's permission when he wants to marry a woman," Nonny explained.

"Whoa." Bellisia straightened up from getting the duffel bag. She pulled it onto her lap and held it in front of her like a shield. "No one has mentioned marriage. He barely knows me. There are things that would make him run for the hills if he knew them about me. Everyone is jumping to conclusions just because he asked me to wait for him."

"Wait *here* for him," Nonny corrected. "We're his family. By bringing you here openly, he's telling his team members and us that you're family as well. These men make up their minds fast and then act on it."

Bellisia tucked a stray strand of hair behind her ear. She was desperate to be in the water. She wanted to run a bath and sink down into the soothing liquid that would keep her from feeling like a dried-out prune. It would also slow Whitney's men down if they were still able to use the chip in her to track her.

"You said he barely knew you. What do you think of him?" Cayenne asked curiously.

If she answered, she'd look like a stalker, but these people were Ezekiel's family; she didn't want to start off by lying to them. "I carried out a mission for Whitney and I over-heard some things that led me to believe a member of Eze-kiel's team—or maybe several members—might be in danger from a man living in China. Cheng is very powerful and has tentacles all over the world. He doesn't appear to be in league with Whitney, if anything just the opposite. Whitney almost killed me, and I'd had it with him, so I escaped and came here to assess the situation."

"Assess the situation?" Cayenne echoed, not looking too happy with her.

"The only men I'd ever been around had been Whitney's supersoldiers, and I have to tell you, they aren't good men. I had to find out if these men were worth saving. I parked myself in the water right over there." She pointed to a spot a little way from the pier. "I could see the house and keep it under surveillance. When Ezekiel took the girls out in the boat, I'd follow. I realized he was a good man, and I wrote the note to Nonny."

Cayenne nodded. "It's horrible to come out of what's virtually a prison and try to figure out how to maneuver in the real world. Who to trust, who not to trust."

"Exactly." She stood up. "If you don't mind, I'd like to take a bath. If you leave the kitchen, I'll do cleanup since I didn't do any of the cooking."

"Can you cook?"

Bellisia frowned. "Um. Not without harming someone. But I'll try."

"You'll have to get in on Nonny's cooking classes. We're slowly getting better."

Bellisia contemplated learning to cook while submerged in the bathtub. That sounded like a good idea.

10

Ezekiel looked around him. The C-17 was cavernous in spite of holding the two boats with the gear for two boat crews, as well as all the men strapped inside. He knew these men now. All of them. Some of them were friends. Several members of the boat crew had been to the Fontenot compound for their crazy crab or shrimp feeds. He'd served on several occasions with nine of the twelve SEALs. There were the men from his squadron, his brother Mordichai, Gino and Draden. Now, having trained with the others, the two new SEALs brought in to replace the fake soldiers from the Kopaska Group and the remaining four Indonesian soldiers, he knew he was going into the situation as prepared as possible with good men.

He felt responsible for them, the way he always did. He accepted that about himself. He would always feel responsible for the men he went into combat with. They mattered, and he would get them home. Every. Single. One. That was always the vow he made to himself and tonight was no different.

He glanced at his watch. He'd slept on the way, the roar of the powerful engines not bothering him in the least. He could sleep anywhere, anytime, when the possibility presented itself. He'd learned that valuable lesson on the streets a long time ago, and serving in the GhostWalker PJ squadron had only strengthened that trait in him.

The men varied in their reactions, spending the time in several ways. Some, like Ezekiel, slept while they could. Others joked with one another, relieving the tension that built before dropping out of the dark sky into a hot zone. He found that although it was all familiar to him, this time was different. It was different because for the first time he had someone to go home to.

He'd never considered what having a woman would mean to a man like him. She made him vulnerable in ways he didn't want to think about. He barely knew her, but it didn't seem to matter. She was his. He knew her the moment he sat down at that table where she was working. She wasn't anything like he expected her to be. He'd always looked at tall women. Women he thought were strong. He wanted a woman at his side, a partner, like Nonny had been with her husband.

Bellisia was extremely slight. In spite of her size, she was lethal as hell, had confidence in herself and would protect their children as fiercely as he would. He liked those traits. Admired them. He hadn't expected that he would think about her night and day. That she would creep into his thoughts during the down times of his training or at night when he lay in bed. Or now, just before he would make the jump onto foreign soil.

He glanced at his watch; it was 20:40. They were to jump at 21:00. He stood, signaling to the others that they were twenty minutes from jumping. The cargo doors of the plane were already beginning to open and the wind howled through the interior. He looked at his men, all grim-faced now. They were faces of warriors, where only a few minutes earlier they'd been joking around with one another or simply sleeping. Like Ezekiel, those who had been napping woke completely alert.

The boats were pulled out of the plane by their drag chutes that would open the mains. The boat crews followed their boats closely. The SEALs and Kopaska warriors went next, one right after the other, no hesitation. They were then followed by Gino, Mordichai, Draden and last, he was out, floating in the dark sky. He always found peace there.

Initially, facing the unknown in the dark, there was always that trepidation, a fear that gripped his insides and sent adrenaline rushing through his body like a freight train. Staring down over water or forest in the dark, knowing men were somewhere hiding with guns ready to kill him, gave him that rush. This time he would be parachuting onto an island on the Musi River.

Part of Palembang City is on an island in the Musi River nineteen kilometers from Sri Jaya. An Indonesian Marine unit had set up the staging area in an abandoned building on the southernmost point of the island near some old docks. His men assembled their gear while the crews refueled the boats with swift efficiency.

"This is it, gentlemen. In a few minutes we'll be embarking on the mission we've trained so hard for. In spite of the setbacks, all of us are ready for this. We will be victorious and bring our comrades out safely."

He got a couple *hooya*s; they were all listening. He wanted them listening because every word he said was important and couldn't be drilled in enough. "Everyone needs to check that their gear is functioning properly. Test radios, NODs and strobes. Everyone will wear their IR strobes. They are what will identify us from the enemy when the boat team moves to extract us. The last thing we want is a fratricide incident."

They'd checked their equipment prior to stowing it in the boats, and it had been checked before they ever set off, but checking gear multiple times often meant the difference between life and death, and he was bringing them all home.

"Make no mistake, gentlemen, these men are Islamic radicals. They consider it a blessing to die for their cause. Let's accommodate them. Number-one priority is the hostages. We want to get in and get out without detection if possible, so when you're accommodating them, do it as quietly as possible."

That got a ripple of laughter, and a couple of the SEALs nudged each other. "Don't worry, Slick, you die on this one, I'll take good care of your girlfriend for ya." Another ripple of laughter went around as Slick flipped his buddy off.

Ezekiel waited a heartbeat or two until the laughter died down. Humor was a good way to deflect the intensity of what they were about to do. "Boat teams, get your gear ready. It is 01:00, we leave in ten. The rest of you, finalize your gear and be formed up on the dock with your game faces on."

"*Hooya*, Captain."

They moved into the boats as they'd practiced over and over until they could do it in their sleep. No one spoke as the SWCC crew took them along the river. The boat crews were all business now. It was their job to protect the men going in to rescue the hostages, and they were elite when it came to doing so.

Ezekiel had been to Indonesia several times. The Musi River's source was deep in the Bukit Barisan Mountains. The water rushed down to the plains where two converging rivers, the Ogam and Konering, fed the Musi so that it widened into a large river right at Palembang. He liked Indonesia and its people. He didn't like that the terrorist cells were growing into the population, infesting the young and putting most of the good-natured, hardworking people at risk.

The weather was very close to the weather in Louisiana, and the humidity didn't bother his fellow PJs or him. SEALs trained in every kind of environment and they weren't bothered by the heavy humidity either. It was a fairly clear night, no clouds, which wasn't in their favor, but that didn't matter. It was particularly dark, however, just the way he liked it. The GhostWalkers believed in their creed. *The night is ours.*

Ezekiel glanced around him at the faces of his team. He had become used to running missions with his own squadron. They tended to keep to themselves. It was far easier using their abilities without an audience, but he knew these men now, what they were made of and that they'd get the job done.

The boats took them within a kilometer of the village. They entered the water, using snorkels to breathe as they swam through the river until they were at the very edge of the village. Very cautiously they slipped from the water. Gino and Draden hid snorkels, fins and masks in the bushes while the others remained in place, waiting for the signal.

Mordichai called the SWCC crew. "Wolf Pack, Wolf Pack, this is Liberator."

"Liberator, this is Wolf Pack."

"Wolf Pack, Liberator is on the objective."

"Wolf Pack copies, Liberator is on the objective."

Gino and Draden split and began moving in a circle. It was easier to use their skills without an audience. Gino scented the air using his acute sense of smell. Immediately he picked up on the location of the outer guards. There were two on his side set apart at fifteen-foot intervals. There was one in the tower overlooking the river. He could even scent the two guards on Draden's side. So five altogether. He knew there would be more, but these five were the direct threat to his team.

He moved through the brush unerringly, his feet never snapping so much as a twig, but he was fast, coming up behind the first guard, covering his mouth while he slit his throat. He caught the rifle cradled in the man's arm and lowered it to the ground along with the body. Then he moved the fifteen feet to repeat the action with the second guard. He knew Draden would be doing the same.

Gino went up the side of the tower, blending into the structure as he climbed. He barely used his toes to propel him up, using mostly upper body strength. At one point the guard made the short walk around the top of the tower. He muttered into his radio, reporting, and slumped down, drinking water. That gave Gino his opportunity. The guard's back was against the wall. As he leaned over stretching, Gino came up over him and drove his knife deep into the back of the guard's neck, severing the spine and killing him instantly. Gino activated his infrared strobe for two seconds signaling Ezekiel it was clear. He then climbed down, moving quickly to join his teammates.

"They're expecting trouble," Gino reported tersely.

It didn't change anything, and they'd expected it after the attack on Ezekiel, but it made getting in and out without a firefight tougher—probably impossible.

The SEALs nodded, but didn't respond. The two Kopaska soldiers looked at each other with far too much satisfaction for Ezekiel's liking. He couldn't blame them for wanting to take out the entire nest, but this was an extraction. Getting out the hostages was the main objective of their mission.

The men had already broken into three six-man teams as well as the PJs four-man team as practiced during training. Bravo team had four SEALs and two of the Indonesian soldiers. They were responsible for ensuring security at the front of the target building. They moved silently toward their destination while Charlie team, consisting of four SEALs and the other two Indonesian soldiers, spread out to keep the way secure going back to the water. Delta team, consisting of six SEALs, kept the rear entrance secure for the Alpha team to get in and out with the high-value targets.

Gino and Ezekiel took lead, moving in after Bravo team signaled them forward. Two bodies lay rolled to one side and a third was just at the entrance. There were yet three more enemy waiting beyond the door. Gino, Ezekiel, Draden

and Mordichai stacked up, prepping for entry, one man behind the other. When they were ready, Mordichai, the last
man, tapped Draden, the man in front of him, on the shoulder until the signal reached Gino, the front of the line.

Gino kicked the door and then stepped to the opposite
side. Ezekiel tossed a flash bang grenade through the door.
The grenade detonating signaled the entry. As each man
cleared the door they alternated to which side they would
go. Gino went right, Ezekiel left, Draden right, Mordichai
left as they entered the room. All four engaged the roomful
of targets as they did so. In less than four seconds they
eliminated every hostile in the room. Gino signaled they
were ready to move to the next room.

Gino and Ezekiel both had unique gifts that allowed them
to smell the enemy, but it was Gino's gift in such situations
that always astonished Ezekiel. The man seemed to be able
to see through walls.

*Two ahead. They're hiding to the left of the door. Both
lying flat, weapons ready. No hostages in that room, but
don't want them at our backs. You call it,* Gino whispered
in their heads.

Take them out quietly, Ezekiel ordered and signaled to
the others to stay still.

Gino and Draden moved up the wall and across the ceiling like a couple of spiders. Neither was a particularly small
man, but it was difficult to see them in the dark of the room
as they crossed into the next room where the two terrorists
lay in wait. The two GhostWalkers slid down the wall behind
the enemy. In seconds it was over and they signaled to Ezekiel and Mordichai that it was all clear.

Ezekiel scented blood and infection ahead and to his
right. He indicated the direction to Gino. Gino shook his
head and indicated the room veering off to their left. He
held up three fingers. Ezekiel understood. Three enemies
lying in wait.

Tell me what's in the room with the hostages.

Gino switched his attention for just a moment. *Four guards. They've got knives to the throats of the hostages.*

Ezekiel swore. Hell. They knew it wasn't going to be easy. He indicated the room veering off to their left. The four GhostWalkers approached silently in formation. They stood to the side of the door. Gino exploded into a kick, taking the thin door from its frame as Ezekiel tossed in the flash bang. The enemy began firing blindly, but all four GhostWalkers had already chosen their targets and shot them.

Fuck. Draden spat the word as they turned toward the room with the hostages. So far they hadn't been in the building longer than a minute forty-five seconds.

You hit?

A scratch. Just kissed my arm.

You're getting slow, Sandman, Ezekiel said, pausing to look him over as they approached the room where the scent of blood was strongest. He slapped a bandage on Draden's arm to stop the blood flow.

What's the plan, Zeke? Gino asked.

Four of us, four of them. I say we just shoot the fuckers and be done with it. Gino, tell us exactly where they are.

Gino pulled the image of the room into his mind. *Bed is in center of room. All three hostages are sitting on the bed; one is slumped over. All four bad guys are behind the bed. They have guns on the bed but knives to their throats. Stupid.* He gave exact positions and as long as no one moved, they were golden.

They used the same entry, tossing the flash bang and following it in. They were expert marksmen and they each hit their target. Two to the chest and one to the head. One man's hand jumped, and the hostage, one of the Indonesians, yelped, but all four enemies fell backward, knives clattering to the floor.

Ezekiel was on the hostages immediately, bandaging what he could and evaluating them for travel. The American and one Indonesian looked in bad shape. The American would need immediate attention. The third Indonesian was far more alert and clearly he'd been trying to help the other two. All three had been tortured. The smell of infection, urine and feces was potent in the room. There were rats everywhere and a bucket in the corner that they had been using as a toilet. Ezekiel was gentle as he prepared them for travel.

"We'll get you out of here. It's gonna hurt, but we'll get you to the boat and then give you medical attention."

He glanced over the American's head, his eyes meeting Draden's. It didn't look good. Aside from looking as if he'd been beaten and dragged, he had a knife wound and clearly a punctured lung. He was fighting for air. They needed to get a vein before every vein collapsed, but they didn't have the luxury of doing that until they were in the boat. Draden was the best he knew when it came to collapsing veins and getting a needle in when helicopters or boats were pitching wildly, or a firefight was on top of them. Already, outside, the sound of gunfire was constant and growing intense.

Ezekiel, Mordichai and Draden each took a hostage, hoisting them over their shoulders while Gino led the way through the house to the rear entry where they were going to bring out the hostages. Gunfire erupted around the corner of the building when Gino stepped out. He dropped to his belly and fired off three quick rounds. Delta team was already on it, clearing the way for them.

The three teams collapsed in on themselves, keeping the GhostWalkers with the hostages in the center as they ran for the river. Around them, the enemy closed in, trying to surround them. The SEALs and Kopaska returned fire as they moved to wait for the boats.

Brad Henderson went down, one of the SEALs Ezekiel had worked with more than once, his leg going out from under him. The bullet spun him around and he swore as a second bullet hit. He went down on his side. He was a good man and a fighter. He struggled to rise, blood pouring from his thigh and buttocks, pain on his face. He kept laying down a hail of bullets, providing cover fire as the others settled into a defensible position, waiting for the boats to get to them. Two of his buddies turned back, one spraying the nest of the enemy with his M240L machine gun as the other one dragged Brad to his feet and got them moving again.

Mordichai applied a tourniquet to Henderson's leg and slapped a bandage on his butt while Ezekiel called for extraction.

"Wolf Pack, this is Liberator. We are heavily engaged. Need extraction."

"Liberator, this is Wolf Pack. Make sure everyone is marked. We are inbound."

"Roger, Wolf Pack is inbound."

He took one moment to ensure his men had complied. In the heat of battle he didn't want anyone forgetting to make certain their strobes were engaged. They covered the hostages but continued to engage the enemy. The terrorists outnumbered them, but they'd hit hard and fast, getting in so quickly and retrieving the hostages, the SEALs and Kopaska warriors doing their jobs, thinning the ranks of the enemy and providing a route back to the extraction site. Circling the hostages, they faced every direction, bullets coming in from everywhere while they picked their targets and did as much damage as possible.

They could hear the roar of the eight hundred horsepower–driven boats as they thundered up the river coming to their aid. As the SWCC crew got to the extraction site, Ezekiel yelled for everyone to get down and tossed the red smoke that would tell the crew exactly where to bring in the boats.

"Wolf Pack, this is Liberator. Bring the rain!"

With that the boat crews opened up with everything they had. Each boat carried two 7.62MM mini-guns that fired six thousand rounds per minute as well as two MK19 40MM grenade launchers that could fire forty rounds per minute.

It was deafening and awe inspiring. After one minute the crew of the first boat stopped firing in order to allow the men to board.

Ezekiel and the other GhostWalkers lifted the hostages and made a run for the boat. Behind him, just as in training, the six SEALs hustled into the boat as fast as humanly possible. Every second they delayed meant a delay for the others to get aboard the other boat.

The moment they were in place, the crew changed positions. The second boat that had continued firing stopped and nosed into the bank, allowing its passengers to load while the other boat took up firing to cover them. Ezekiel had been extracted from a hot zone several times by the SWCC crews, but it never failed to amaze and awe him, the skills the crew had and the sheer efficiency with which they worked. They were all business, moving together like a well-oiled machine. The guns thundered all around them, the bank with its trees and shrubs disappearing in a haze of smoke.

When they were all loaded, the boat crews now launched smoke grenades, and as they sped away the .50 caliber machine gunners on the back of the boats opened up. The craft raced away at over forty MPH, bouncing everyone around while the GhostWalker PJs began treating the wounded.

"Draden, I need you," Ezekiel called. There was no way, in the moving boat, bottom slapping hard on the surface of the water as they roared away, he could get a collapsing vein on the American. Draden was the only chance the man had. Even Draden's skills were being challenged as he worked to place an IV into the hostage they hadn't been able to treat while on location.

Ezekiel and Mordichai worked on the other two hostages. One of the Indonesians was in nearly as bad a shape as the American and Ezekiel had to fight to get a vein, but he managed in spite of the wildly bouncing boat. While Ezekiel was getting the vein, Mordichai was stripping off the filthy shirt to get to the seeping wounds on the man's chest. Ezekiel flinched when he saw the infection. Not only saw it, but smelled it in spite of the open air they were in.

Gino put quick-clot and a bandage on the bullet wounds to Brad Henderson's thigh and buttocks. "You doing okay?" It wasn't a through and through and the bullet would have to be dug out. Just not there on the boat. They'd wait until they were in the air.

Despite his sickly color, Henderson gave him a thumbs-up. His two buddies stayed to either side of him, protecting him, even as their weapons were ready to help defend the boat should it be necessary. Henderson was going to get razzed big-time about getting shot in the ass, but right at that moment, his friends were all about protecting the hostages as well as their buddy.

"Captain," Draden called, "need you now."

Ezekiel switched places immediately, leaving the Indonesian to Mordichai. The American was having trouble breathing, his chest heaving as he tried to draw in air. Ezekiel put a calming hand on the patient and made the call to the Indonesian Marines at the staging area.

"Safe Haven, Safe Haven, this is Liberator. We're coming in with three wounded. All three are in bad condition, but we have one needing immediate assistance. We'll need the room." He gave the condition of each hostage and the injured SEAL and then orders to have what he needed waiting for him.

"Safe Haven understands. Liberator, are you coming in hot?"

Ezekiel glanced over his shoulder. There was no boat in pursuit close, but in the far distance a couple appeared to be coming toward them.

"Negative, Safe Haven. Liberator is not engaged at this time. Believe we will have company very soon."

The big guns were silent, the crew saving ammunition while the enemy boats were too far away, but they were ready and it showed on their faces.

"Prep him for surgery the moment we get into the warehouse," Ezekiel said to Draden. "We'll get him stable and then take him with us. Either that or I'll have to stay behind." That was the last thing he wanted to do, but he wasn't leaving the hostage behind where someone could possibly get to him in a hospital. The man had suffered enough. He was American and Ezekiel had the job of bringing him home.

Draden glanced over his shoulder at the pursuing boats. The Marines would hold any terrorists off the docks, and the SWCC crews would use their boats to help, but staying and trying to work on their patient for any length of time would endanger everyone. They had no choice if they were going to save the man.

The moment the boats arrived at the staging area docks, the Indonesian Marines were there with stretchers in hand. Ezekiel and Draden ran with a stretcher toward the old broken-down warehouse to the right of the dock on the edge of the island.

Other Marines stood by to help guard the docks while one boat unloaded and the other watched the river, weapons ready. The SEALs and Kopaska soldiers spread out to help the Indonesian Marines defend the area from the terrorists coming toward them in their boats. The SWCC boats hurriedly left the dock to get into a better position to defend against the enemy.

Draden was a good anesthesiologist—the best as far as Ezekiel was concerned. Right now, Ezekiel was certain the American had a collapsed lung and was fighting to keep air moving through the other lung. Putting in a chest tube without anesthesia would hurt like hell. His patient was very lucky Draden was with them.

They ran alongside the gurney to the dilapidated warehouse. "We'll get you home in one piece," he assured the hostage. "I'm going to have to put in a tube so you can breathe. I won't lie, it's going to hurt, but once I have it in, we can transport you, get you to the carrier and I can take care of the problem."

The man nodded, his gaze clinging to Ezekiel as if he was his last hope—and he was. That was the scary part. Ezekiel never let himself think about failing or making mistakes. In his case, if he didn't get the job done, someone died. He knew while he was caring for his patient, Mordichai and Gino were seeing to the wounded SEAL and the Indonesians had taken possession of the other two hostages. The Marines had set up the room as best they could with the equipment they had.

"Captain, I've got both lidocaine and ketamine in my trauma backpack," Draden informed Ezekiel. All of the PJs carried their trauma backpacks with their basic equipment of needles, IV catheters and chest tubes.

"In high doses, ketamine works as an anesthetic. It doesn't suppress the respiratory system, but it can cause hallucinations, vivid nightmare-like dreams. For a short period of time it can produce increased salivation, increased heart rate and elevated blood pressure, but I think this is best for him."

"Do it." Ezekiel didn't hesitate. He'd rather work with Draden as an anesthesiologist than anyone else. He trusted him with his patient's life just as he did with his own.

Draden was already using the vein to get his patient under as fast as possible.

"The knife wound is deep." Ezekiel felt as grim as his voice. Outside the firefight continued as the Marines, SEALs and SWCCs kept the enemy off of them in order to give the American hostage a chance to live.

Ezekiel applied an occlusive dressing—an air- and watertight seal—to the wound. Made with a waxy coating, it provided a seal other bandages couldn't. The dressing would keep additional air from being sucked in through the wound. His movements were fast and efficient, his hands rock steady. He'd done this many times out in the open, bullets hitting around him, without Draden to put the patient under. It was very, very painful, but without the lifesaving technique, he knew the patient wouldn't last until they could get to a hospital.

He used an eighteen gauge IV catheter for the decompression, placing it in the intercostal space between the second and third ribs along the mid costal line—halfway between the sternum and side. He removed the needle, leaving the catheter. Instantly there was a hissing sound as the pleural space was decompressed. It was temporary but very necessary.

They placed the patient in a supine position with his arm up so his hand was above his head. Identifying the fourth and fifth ribs, they quickly prepped the area. Ezekiel glanced at Draden, who nodded. He was barely keeping the patient under. It would hurt, but not like in the field without him.

Ezekiel made the incision quickly and inserted the curved clamp into the muscle tissue to spread the fibers and then used his own finger to develop a track. Once he hit the rib, he angled the clamp just over the rib to continue the dissection. He found the pleural, inserted his finger and explored for adhesions. Attaching a large bore 36F chest tube onto the clamp, he passed it along the track to the pleural cavity. He had to stitch very carefully to ensure it was held in place. He used a Heimlich valve—a one-way valve—to stop air from coming in through the tube when the man inhaled.

Ezekiel reexamined his patient to make certain everything was working properly, nodded to Draden and the waiting Marines and hurried out to release the Kopaska soldiers to accompany their countrymen home so they could get back to their home base and take the wounded hostages to the hospital. As he did so, the SEALs let loose with an AT-4 rocket, blowing the enemy boat out of the water.

It sounded like thunder, and then the night was lit up with orange and red flames, a shower of flaming debris falling into the river. The SWCC boats returned to the dock and the SEALs and GhostWalkers once more took up their positions, this time with their wounded hostage.

The boat crews headed off with all of them, making the fifteen-mile trip out to the ocean to rendezvous with two Chinook helicopters. The GhostWalkers took their two patients up first, and the SEALs followed them, climbing what looked like a precarious swaying ladder up into the helicopters.

The boat crew rigged special lifting harnesses to their vessels while the helicopters hovered over them. When they descended to just a few feet above the boats, the crewmen attached the harnesses to the hooks on the bottom of the aircraft. The helicopters lifted the boats from the water for the thirty-minute flight to the waiting amphibious assault ship USS *Makin Island*.

There were several operating rooms aboard the ship, and the American was taken to one while the SEAL was immediately taken to the other. Ezekiel did surgery on the American, while Draden took care of the SEAL. Both patients were then airlifted to a tertiary hospital while Ezekiel and the other soldiers were put on a plane back to Stennis.

Only when they were heading home did Ezekiel allow himself to relax. He'd come full circle. He leaned his head back and closed his eyes, weariness in every bone and muscle in his body, yet sleep was elusive. As a rule, he could sleep anywhere, anytime. He'd learned to do that over the years of adrenaline and gunfire, but now, his mind was filled with Bellisia. He couldn't think about anything else. If he was being entirely truthful with himself, he was maybe a little obsessed. If any of his brothers had brought home a woman and claimed she was the one in such a short time, he would have laughed his head off, after he beat the shit out of him and hopefully some sense into him. Then Ezekiel would have told him he was a complete idiot.

He'd never expected to have a woman of his own or a chance at a family. He loved what he did. He belonged with the GhostWalkers. He saved lives and he helped his brothers. He was good with that, but truthfully, he was lonely. Somewhere inside where he'd never looked, he had wanted more for himself. He wanted a woman to walk with him. To look at him with love in her eyes. To do the little things like rock a child on the front porch, raise her head and smile at him over dinner, hold his hand when they walked somewhere together.

It sounded a little pathetic to him, and he was grateful the others couldn't read his mind. He'd never thought about holding a woman's hand. Bellisia was small. Delicate even. She looked fragile, but he knew she wasn't. Still, her physical body was small and fragile. How the hell would that work? He wasn't a small man and at his best he was still rough. He'd learned life on the streets, fighting with his fists for food and a space in abandoned buildings for his brothers to rest. To call home. That hadn't left a lot of room for gentle.

What if she hadn't stayed? There really wasn't a good reason for her to stay. His mind kept looping back to that no matter how hard he tried to stay focused on the here and now. *Be present.* What was the use of getting upset over something that was outside his control? It was just that if she was gone, she was gone for good. He'd never find her.

He sighed. He had to quit thinking about her or he was going to drive himself crazy. "Draden, let me take a look at your arm."

"It's nothing, Zeke. A burn."

"I still have to check it." Rather than make Draden come to him, and to forestall any arguments, he forced his exhausted body to get up and move.

"What the hell kind of name is *Draden* anyway?" Mordichai asked.

Ezekiel knew he was distracting the man with an all-too-familiar argument.

"Don't start with me, you Bible-thumping baboon." Draden glared at Mordichai while Ezekiel stripped away the bloody sleeve.

"One doesn't thump a Bible, one *reads* it," Mordichai declared piously.

"I'll bet you never read the damn thing *ever*," Draden said, clearly trying not to pull his arm away when Ezekiel wiped away the blood to get to the wound.

"He read it. I made both my brothers read it." Ezekiel poured antiseptic into the long wound where the bullet had torn a chunk of skin from Draden's bicep.

Draden erupted into a storm of swearing, and he was very inventive at it. He scowled at Ezekiel. "You do that again I'm laying you out, captain or not."

"Don't be such a baby," Gino said, opening one eye. "You got kissed. You didn't hear that SEAL crying his little head off."

"Do you know what the name 'Draden' means?" Mordichai asked, clearly gleeful for the opening. "Sweet little Draden loves to be cuddled when he's not feeling well. You want to come and give him a cuddle, Phantom? Might make him stop whining like a girl."

Draden turned his scowl on Mordichai. "Shut the hell up, you cretin. I'm telling Cayenne you said 'whine like a girl.' She'll deliver the bite of paralysis, wind your worthless ass in a cocoon of webs and hang you upside down from the nearest tree."

"Oh shit, she would," Mordichai said. "She'd totally do that and just leave me there. I take that part back."

"You can't take it back. You said it, now you own it."

Ezekiel sewed up what he could. Draden would have a hell of a scar. He'd kept going, never missing a beat, never complaining, getting his job done, including taking care of their patients, and he'd lost a great deal of muscle when the bullet plowed through his arm. It was a little more than a kiss. Draden had been damned lucky.

He felt pride in his "brother" GhostWalker. In all of them. In the SEALs and SWCC crew. The Indonesian soldiers who had served with them. Each one of them had walked into a situation knowing it was probably a trap, and they'd still gone. They'd still risked their lives to bring out hostages who would have been dead in two more days. The American wouldn't have lasted through the night. He still might not. At least he had a fair chance. Ezekiel had blasted him with antibiotics.

He staggered back to his seat and looked at his fellow GhostWalkers. They had stayed alive after their enhancements by watching one another's backs. That was the way it had to be. Each was a multimillion-dollar weapon, and supposedly top secret. Secrets had a way of leaking out. Violet was the largest leak they had.

He sighed as he sank into the uncomfortable seat. *Senator Violet Smythe. She's one of us. Enhanced psychically and probably physically as well. If we don't stop her, she really will get to be president and she'll wipe us all out. What the hell are we going to do about her?* He used telepathic communication to keep the SEALs traveling with them from overhearing.

We've got to take the bitch out, Gino said, not bothering to open his eyes. *We should have done it when she went after Pepper and the girls.*

There was a question mark, Mordichai pointed out.

There isn't now.

She's a United States senator, Draden said.

She's an enemy and she has to go, Gino insisted. *If we don't kill her, she'll eventually kill every member of all four teams, their wives and children. Hell, my guess is she'll even kill Lily Whitney just to be a bitch. We don't have a choice if we want to survive. Personally, I don't mind doing the job myself.*

There it was. Ezekiel had to agree with Gino's assessment. Senator Violet Smythe had to die.

11

Colonel Joe Spagnola, Doctor, the squadron leader for the GhostWalker PJs, returned on Bellisia's second day. He came with one other man, Diego Campo, Rubin's brother. She had noticed how good-looking Draden Freeman was, what woman wouldn't? He was a gorgeous man, looking as if he'd stepped off the cover of a magazine. Joe Spagnola could give him a run for his money. The man was beautiful, like a model. Well over six feet, with olive skin and dark hair, she pegged him as Italian American.

Colonel Spagnola was not very happy to be informed of the things that had transpired while he was gone. It was far too late to pull Ezekiel out of the field. The hostages were in poor shape and if not pulled out before the deadline, they would be killed. He was definitely furious, but he controlled his anger, questioning Rubin over and over until he was satisfied he had every detail, and then he turned his cool, dark eyes on her.

Joe especially didn't like that the two Indonesian imposters had been in on the training for at least one day before they made their move. It was very possible that they were in league with the terrorists and the mission was compromised before it had begun. The latest information coming out of the village was that the enemy hadn't geared up any more than usual for a possible assault.

Bellisia knew the inevitable was coming. The women had treated her with kindness and respect. This was the man responsible for his team members, and he wouldn't be too happy knowing she'd been spying on them, even if she did save Ezekiel's life.

"I'd like a word," Joe said, the moment after Rubin filled him in. His tone was mild enough, but it was a clear order.

Bellisia gazed longingly for the river. She hadn't said *where* she would wait for Ezekiel. Joe turned and led her away from the others, back into the laboratory. This time she wasn't put in a cage, but rather escorted to the office. Rubin's brother, Diego, brought up the rear so she was effectively sandwiched between the two. She was fairly certain they were both fast. With every step that took her away from the river, her hopes of escaping them dwindled.

Joe waved her to a chair. "You're one of the women Whitney took from the orphanage." He made it a statement.

She nodded and waited. She'd learned a few things from being in Nonny's home. Pepper usually disappeared when there were males around if her husband wasn't present. She didn't go out of the house without him, except very rarely. She had been created to be an assassin and could lure men with her voice. Sometimes the need for sex was overwhelming as the chemicals in her body flooded her system, and then she really hid until her husband came home, but they worked it out.

If Pepper could endure the cycles she had to go through in order to be with Wyatt, Bellisia could get through another interrogation. Ezekiel was worth it. She couldn't help feeling nervous and maybe, if she was being strictly honest with herself, scared. This man carried authority easily. He looked tough as nails. He couldn't exactly order Ezekiel to get rid of her, but his veto would be strong with the members of his squadron and, she suspected, the Fontenot family.

"Would you like to tell me in your own words how you came to be here?"

Her heart stuttered for a moment. His tone was so mild. So deceitful. He wasn't feeling mild. He wanted to pound someone into the ground. Self-preservation rose swift and fast. There was no way to stop the venom from rising to protect her. With it came the faint telltale blue rings on her skin and hair. Fortunately, they were very faint, but a man like Joe Spagnola wouldn't fail to notice them.

He leaned back in his chair and studied her face. "Do you feel threatened?"

Her chin went up. "Yes. You want me to feel threatened."

"I'm sorry if I gave you that impression. If I believed you were a threat to my men, I would have either thrown you back in a cage until I was certain, or I would have pulled out my gun and shot you on the spot."

If that was designed to make her feel better, it didn't. She had no doubt that he was very capable of shooting her the instant he thought she presented a threat. She lowered her blue-tinged lashes, not taking her gaze from him, but making certain of Diego's position in the room. They'd closed the office door. The door to the laboratory had been closed as well. No locks had been engaged. She'd counted the steps from the house to the river and from the laboratory to the river a hundred times over the last two days.

Realizing she had to say something, she made a face at him. "So glad you decided not to shoot me. I didn't know that was an option." So screw him. If he didn't believe she was a threat, what was she doing in here, other than being intimidated?

"Sarcasm. You can't be too scared."

"I'm scared, but you're not my commanding officer. I don't have to do a damn thing you tell me. I've been through an interrogation and it was determined I'm not a threat to anyone, so this is rather irritating."

"Who is your commanding officer?"

Sniping at him didn't faze him in the least. His expression didn't change. He looked like a tiger, watching prey. She resisted the urge to rub at the blue rings on her arm. She hated that he could see them, hated that he knew she was nervous. The bad news was, knowing she was enhanced, he wouldn't see a slight woman, very small and fragile-looking. He would know she had weapons. The blue rings would clue him in that she was lethal and very, very strong.

"I don't have a commanding officer. I escaped Whitney and, although I know he's looking for me and I can't stay here long, I gave my word to Ezekiel that I wouldn't leave until he returned. And I won't. If you prefer, I can go back to Donny's island and stay there until he's back."

"I don't want you to do that. It wouldn't be safe for Donny. He'd fight on your behalf, and anyone Whitney sends after you would be capable of crushing the man."

"I'll keep Donny safe."

Behind her, Diego stirred. She kept her eyes on Joe, but shifted just enough in her chair that she had a better view of Diego. He was average height, and a slighter build than Joe, but all muscle. He clearly was of Mexican American descent with his thick dark hair and even darker eyes. He had a knife strapped to his side like most of the men, but she noticed when he moved even slightly, his light jacket opened and there were throwing knives in loops on the inside of his coat—an airport security nightmare. She detested that he was behind her.

She judged she had about five steps to the window. Could she get her sweater off fast enough to protect her face and hands while going through it? Probably.

"The glass is bulletproof. No matter how strong you are, you wouldn't get through it first try and we'd be on you," Joe cautioned.

She smirked. "That wouldn't be such a good idea."

"Lethal venom every time? Or can you control it like Cayenne and Pepper?"

Bellisia didn't know why, but the fact that she couldn't control the amount of venom going into her victim made her feel inferior. Damn him. He was doing it deliberately. "What is your point?"

"My point is, I don't know anything about you or this situation. Ezekiel is not only under my command, which means I'm responsible for him, but he's my friend. I need to know what happened. How you got here. What you're like. Give me something, Bellisia, anything at all. Hell, I don't even know your last name."

Was she making him an adversary because she was so sick of answering to men? Whitney treated all the women like his slaves. He had power of life and death over them, and he'd killed more than one with his crazy experiments. They worked hard to keep from being put in his insane breeding program or worse, more experiments. He wanted everything perfected so his male soldiers had the best of his science.

She took a breath. "Okay. I'm sorry. That makes sense. We don't have last names. None of us. We make them up. I was called Bellis and my "sisters," meaning the other women at the compound where I was raised, began referring to me as Bellisia, an Italian version. I liked it because they love me and I matter to them. So when I escaped, I went by Bellisia, and I added Adams because one of the super-soldiers is named Adam and he's a bit of a badass."

Gerald and Adam were most often assigned to her as her handlers on the outside. She didn't want to kill either of them, but if they kept coming at her, she might not have a choice. She knew Whitney wanted to pair one of them with her eventually. Maybe both. He might have already done it. She figured Whitney hoped she would develop feelings for one or both of them. She had, just not in the way he wanted.

"Whitney thinks women are weak. He uses us for his experiments and to perfect his enhancements before he gives them to any of you. We're disposable, you're not. He became suspicious that Violet Smythe was selling out the Ghost-Walker program to Cheng for money so that her running mate could get the presidency. That's her ultimate goal, to become president. Whitney sent me undercover to Cheng's when he heard that she was doing some kind of diplomatic tour and one of the stops would be China."

"Unusual." He steepled his fingers together and nodded for her to continue.

"I infiltrated Cheng's laboratory. Whitney always has the best paperwork. Cheng's security didn't even raise an eyebrow. I fit right in." She put her hands in her lap to keep him from seeing her clench her fists. Whitney's betrayal still infuriated her. "He injected me with a virus specific to my DNA. I had a certain time to complete the assignment or the virus began to work. By the way, just so you know how he treats his operatives, the virus was fatal."

Joe glanced up to meet Diego's eyes. Something burned right behind the cool, but he blinked and the emotion was gone. "Keep going."

"Whitney apparently paired Violet with him, so he couldn't conceive of the fact that she'd actually betray him by selling his life's work to an enemy, but he couldn't take the chance. I was really there to disprove the rumor. She came and met with Cheng."

Joe's eyes flickered. Heat this time. Anger maybe. "You saw her? You actually saw her yourself?"

"I not only saw her, I heard her selling out her country. More, she sold out this specific squadron. Apparently you all consort with insects and snakes, and she doesn't like bugs or snakes. She was willing to sell all the GhostWalkers down the river for her own purposes."

"Do you have a recording of this conversation?"

She shook her head. "You'll have to take my word for it."

"Your word is good enough. I can hear a lie. You aren't lying."

"You aren't as shocked as I was," Bellisia observed. "But you're very upset by her betrayal. She has a certain reputation."

He sighed. "True, but I held out a small bit of hope that she was redeemable."

"She's a sociopath. No conscience whatsoever. Violet is willing to sell out her sisters, the women raised with her. She wants to be the only female GhostWalker, and she wants power." Bellisia shook her head. "Her voice is compelling. She weaves some kind of spell with her pitch. Don't fall for it."

"It doesn't work on me," Joe said.

Bellisia studied his completely expressionless face. That wasn't good. Whitney was very careful when he paired his couples to make certain one didn't have a distinct advantage over the other. In her case, because her venom was fatal, Ezekiel was certain he was immune to it, but she wasn't willing to take the chance to find out. If Joe wasn't susceptible, that could mean he was paired with Violet. She hoped not. Intellectually she knew it was just physical attraction, but it was powerful and with it seemed to come an emotional attachment.

"What did you hear?"

"Cheng wanted Whitney's files, but she said she couldn't get those for him, but she could deliver a GhostWalker. She really detests anyone with insect or reptile DNA. It repulses her, and according to her, cheapens all of you superior beings."

His eyes flickered with heat again. "Let's get this straight. The GhostWalkers, and my squadron specifically, do not believe anyone with insect or reptile DNA cheapens us."

There she was, doing it again, sneering at the male soldiers, lumping them all together. She hadn't even realized she had an issue, but apparently growing up in Whitney's company and having him cram it down their throats that women were inferior to men in every way upset her.

"I'm sorry. Sometimes I let my mouth run away with me. Violet sold out this team and told him they were here in Louisiana. Cheng locked the laboratory down while Violet left, and that meant I was trapped there."

She shuddered and ran her fingers along her arm, feeling the tearing of her skin when the hook ripped at her. Joe's gaze followed her fingers, noting the long thin scar running along her forearm. His eyes narrowed and grew darker, making her shiver.

"Cheng's mercenaries searched the building and found my disguise. The alarm went up and I crawled into a water tank up on the roof. They had hooks and kept throwing them in the water. I got tagged a couple of times, but in the end, they couldn't find me."

Joe let out his breath. "How long were you delayed there?"

"Long enough that the virus took hold. I needed the antidote immediately. I climbed down the side of the building and my handler Gerald was waiting. He picked me up and ran with me to the van. Whitney didn't care that I was dying. He only cared that they got the information. I faked how bad off I was and they injected me. I pretended not to come around, and my body temperature was soaring, so Whitney told them to get me water. My other handler Adam opened the van doors and jumped out. I launched myself out of there and made it to the water."

"Tell me your abilities."

She lifted her chin. "Why?"

"Obviously Ezekiel is claiming you as his. You seem to feel the same way or you never would have given him your word that you'd stay."

"We barely know each other."

"You know him. Zeke isn't that hard to read. He's a good man. Protector. Off the charts protective, but lethal as hell. I think you're the same way. You're a good match for him. I can't see you doing whatever he tells you, but you're not going to argue with him just so you can get your way. That means you'll be living here with us. I need to know every asset we have."

"I can get in and out of very small places. I blend in easily wherever I am. Not just camouflage, but any environment or culture. Anything I see or read, I retain. Word for word. So no need for a recording. I can pick up languages fast and easily use the correct accents." She hesitated and then shook her head.

He didn't press. "Tell me the rest. Obviously you made your way here."

"It wasn't hard to get money or an ID. I knew, once I was out of water, Whitney would track me. He would know the moment I got on a plane. It was difficult finding you here at first because I didn't know any names and I didn't have a place to start. Then someone mentioned the Fontenots and all the building going on, that it looked as if fortresses were going up. They also mentioned a lot of the Fontenots' friends were buying up the land all around them and putting up places. Did I mention they said 'hot' friends? That was enough to guide me right here."

"Why didn't you just come forward, say who you were and warn us that someone might be coming this way to hurt one or more of us?"

She shrugged and looked him right in the eye. "I didn't know you. Any of you. For all I knew, you took orders from Whitney. Quite a few of his men are really awful. That is a very mild way of describing them. I was on the run, and I'm sure he'd pay a great deal of money for me, or even news of me. I had to know before I took a chance."

He nodded. "I will admit that sounds reasonable. I wouldn't be so eager to put myself in harm's way again if I just managed to escape Whitney."

"I found Donny's island. I'd been swimming around in the river and it looked remote and difficult to get to from anywhere other than his main pier. There were No Trespassing signs everywhere, but I knew as long as I stayed near the river, I would be okay, so I moved into one of his cabins. It was right near the water's edge, above it of course, but there was an open porch and I felt safe there."

"Donny's a bit strange, Bellisia. A good man, but you don't want to cross him. You're lucky he decided not to shoot you."

"He left me food and some blankets. I was really happy for both and left him a note saying I would pay him back as soon as I could. Then I found a job in New Orleans at a restaurant there. When I returned, Donny had written me a note saying not to bother paying him back, just get some supplies for myself with the money. He continued to leave food on and off, and I knew he was keeping an eye on me. Whenever I didn't have a shift to work, I was here, in the water, watching everyone. When I saw those three little girls, my heart nearly stopped. I was so afraid for them."

She had been. She'd been terrified that Whitney had an experiment going. Even when she first saw Nonny, she hadn't believed what she was seeing.

"We protect them from Whitney—or anyone else wanting to do them harm. They were scheduled for termination when we first found out about them. Cayenne was as well. When we went in to get them, Trap allowed Cayenne to escape. Apparently Cayenne was considered too dangerous, and no one could handle the girls. They're off the chart smart. And they have tempers, so right now, their little teeth are a problem."

She nodded. "Talking with them is like talking to someone much, much older."

"They grasp complicated concepts."

"Not so much idioms," she said. "I have to say I'm a little worried about staying here. Now that you're here, maybe I should find an abandoned camp. Whitney's men will be back here soon and I still have a chip in me. I tried taking it out once, when I first escaped, but nearly bled to death."

"I can take it out," Joe said. "I'm a surgeon. We've got a

scanner so we'll be able to pinpoint its exact location. Once we have the chip we can take it far from here, lead them away from us. And, honey, seriously? You don't think I'm up to handling a couple of Whitney's new boys? Don't let my looks fool you."

It was the first time she even caught a glimpse of humor in him. She let herself smile. "Well, okay then. The sooner you take out the chip, the sooner I'll feel as if I'm not putting everyone in jeopardy. You do realize, Gerald and Adam will take one look at you men and realize what you are."

"Not me. I don't give off enough energy. You don't either, by the way. You must have been part of the experiment to see if he could stop GhostWalkers from identifying one another."

"If I am, I wasn't told."

Joe stood up and waved her toward the door. "Diego, can you scan while I prep? Hop up on the table in the little room off to your right. Is Gerald the one claiming to be your husband?"

When the others had filled him in about everything that had happened in his absence, they weren't joking around; they'd left nothing out. She walked in front of him, following the silent Diego out. She was excited that she might actually be free of the last part of Whitney. That horrible chip that meant he knew where she was, unless she stayed in the water.

"So Donny says."

Diego opened the door to the room and she got up on the table. Nerves took over. She hated to be examined. She'd spent far too much of her life on tables with eyes staring at her, with needles poking her and blood being drawn.

"What's your blood type?" Diego asked as he gestured for her to lie down so he could pass the scanner over her body.

Well maybe they hadn't been as thorough in their information as she thought. Her gaze jumped to his face. She wanted to see his expression when she told him. "RH-null." She didn't even smirk, that was how disciplined she was.

Diego's eyes widened and his movements jerked to a stop, the scanner hovering over her. "What did you just say?"

"RH-null."

"Oh. My. God. There's like forty known people on the entire planet with your blood type. You're like blood royalty." He glanced over his shoulder and raised his voice. "Are you listening, Joe? She's RH-null."

"I heard." Joe couldn't quite keep the suppressed excitement out of his voice. "You're a gold mine. What the hell was he doing sending you out on dangerous missions?"

Instantly she started to sit up. "Should he have used me for more experiments than he already did? Is that what you think I'm good for?"

"No, honey. Settle down. Has anyone told you before that you have a hair-trigger temper? I'm warning Zeke that his woman is like a little powder keg ready to blow at any little thing."

"Right here, Joe, along her ribs. It isn't just floating around. He embedded it on purpose. And there's a second one." Diego hovered the scanner over her left side. "This looks trickier, Doc. She may need to be put out for this."

Two? She had two chips in her? Even if she'd managed to get the first one, she never would have known about the second. "Put out? As in anesthesia?"

Diego grinned at her. "Don't be a little pu— um . . . chicken. I'm trained for this."

Bellisia thought quickly. "Does Cayenne faint easily? At the sight of blood?"

Both men burst out laughing. "Cayenne doesn't faint at anything."

"I'd like her to be here. And I want to talk to her before I agree to go under." She'd rather leave, break her word to Ezekiel, than put herself in a position of trusting someone and then regretting it.

"I'll call her in," Diego said and stepped out of the room.

"Whitney does like people with high IQs," Joe commented. "Pepper and Cayenne both are brilliant. Cayenne has to be to keep up with Trap, and same thing with Pepper and Wyatt. He paired them and that can't be a coincidence. Do you suppose that's his gift?"

"He has more than one," Bellisia said. "He does make mistakes though, because he's so arrogant. His ego is so large it never occurs to him that one of us might outsmart him. He doesn't make sense half the time. He allows us to plan missions. He trained us to carry them out, yet he doesn't think we're smart enough to figure out ways to escape."

"Because most of the time, you don't."

There was a question in there. She heard it in his voice. "When one of us leaves, the others are punished. Sometimes it's severe. There were ten of us in the compound. Three died. One was killed on a mission and two were killed during an experiment. Whitney acts as if they were heroines choosing to die for the greater good. The rest of us, Scarlet, Blue, Cat, Amaryllis, Shylah and Zara, talked hundreds of times about escaping, but the threat to one of us was unthinkable. Never seeing them or talking with them is difficult."

"But you still did it." He reached a hand out.

She took the offer, slowly sitting up. "Yes. We had all talked about it the night before I left to go to China. We're pretty valuable to him. We knew he wouldn't kill us unless it was the only option. We made a pact that if given the opportunity to escape, we'd take it."

"So I get the name Bellisia, as a flower. Zara?"

"Means 'desert blossom.'"

"And Shylah?"

"Quite a few of us called her Shyshy and the other half called her Lahlah. We put it together and now all of us call her Shylah, just not in front of Whitney. He named her Peony and said it was the name of a shy flower. Can you imagine being called Peony? We all just started with Shy and then"— she shrugged—"it kind of went from there. I guess he could have numbered us. He really likes numbers. It's his thing."

"What do you mean by that?"

"He practically talks in numbers. His codes are complex because he loves numbers, and he likes making up codes and then adding to them. Makes it really hard to figure out what he's doing next. It takes time to break down his codes. His private office is always guarded. We have to go in at night. Zara, Shylah and I can get in and out without too much trouble because of our size. They're built like me."

"Are you saying you can break his code?"

"Not just me. It takes three of us. Usually. When we're together, we're really fast at it. Well," she hedged, wanting to be strictly truthful. "Fast for actually breaking code. It takes days, sometimes weeks, depending upon how complex. Keeps our minds working though, and he doesn't have a clue, because Shy is great with computers."

"We've got two other women like that. Flame, her name is officially Iris, and she's married to Raoul Fontenot. He's part of the GhostWalker Army Ranger Unit. Jaimie is married to a GhostWalker Marine, Mack McKinley. Both are very good on the computer, especially Jaimie, but I think they use programs to help crack codes."

"We don't have much else to do but train and screw with Whitney. I told you he had a weakness, right? His arrogance." She walked over to the window and stared longingly at the water. Her skin felt too tight. "He also has a thing for rare flowers. Who knew, right? He's moved us a couple of times, and he always brings certain plants with him. He has a greenhouse every place we've gone." She turned to look at him over her shoulder. "If I use that bathroom, will you lock me in?"

"No."

She took a breath. Her skin felt like it was cracking. It actually hurt. She'd taken a long bath that morning. The night before she'd filled the old, very deep claw-foot tub four times before she finally got out. She'd fallen asleep twice and only woke up when the water was very cold.

"I just need to run water over my skin. Sometimes when I'm stressed my skin is painful. One of my weaknesses. Whitney hates that and thinks I'm flawed. He detests that I can't stop that sensation when it doesn't show on my skin, and he really detests the fact that I can't control the amount of venom, just as you pointed out. I don't think it's a matter of control so much as the type of venom."

Bellisia crossed the room to the cage and stood just outside of it summoning up her courage. Diego was already on his way to get Cayenne. If Bellisia was wrong about trusting Joe—which she didn't entirely—then hopefully Cayenne would get her out.

"You belong to Ezekiel, honey," Joe said quietly. "He made that very, very clear to everyone. Zeke isn't a man anyone— man or woman—wants to cross. He'll protect you, Bellisia. More, he'll kill for you. That man is relentless. He's a born hunter and enhanced, there's only a couple equal to him, and I'm being generous. We've got Gino, so I know someone else is that good, but seriously, Zeke would hunt me down and kill me, friend or not, if I harmed you in any way."

She had that impression from Ezekiel. She saw a flash of that, just for a moment at the restaurant when she'd told him that she'd seen him with the little girls. She'd been on a fishing expedition, trying to find out if Pepper was his wife and the triplets his children. She didn't think so, but she wanted to be certain. When she told him she'd seen him with the triplets, his eyes had gone scary hard. She knew she'd made a mistake, one that could possibly be fatal. She'd hastily added seeing him at the store getting snowballs for the girls. Anyone might have seen him there.

She stepped into the cage, half expecting the door to slam closed on her, but she didn't so much as glance over her shoulder at him. She walked with her head up as she went into the small bathroom. She left the door open and simply turned on the water, letting it run over her arms.

The relief was tremendous. She hadn't realized just how

stressed she was, or how tight her skin felt until she felt the water pouring over it. It was cool and wet and she absorbed it fast.

"That's amazing," Joe said from behind her. "You look almost luminous, yet at the same time, you're disappearing right into the sink. If it wasn't for your clothes, I'm not certain I could spot you if I didn't know you were there. That must come in handy."

"In the water, I'm gone. I've never had anyone find me when I didn't want to be found in water. Even a pool. The hooks did a number on me though. I still have faint lines on my arm, thigh and back where they nailed me."

"That had to have put blood in the water."

She shrugged and reluctantly turned off the tap. She didn't bother to dry off her arms; they would absorb the water and it felt so refreshing to have the drops beading on her skin. "I didn't let it. That took a lot of control, and I think because I was under so much stress, that allowed the virus to work faster."

She went back to the examination room and hopped up on the table. The table gave her a little more height.

"How the hell can you control bleeding, especially underwater and at more than one site at once?"

Colonel Joe Spagnola was looking at her with respect. It was the first time he'd really shown emotion. He hadn't even commented too much on her unusual blood. She couldn't help but feel good about that.

"The same way I change the texture of my skin. I have a set of muscles that help change the surface shape and make me look different. It's difficult to do or hold for any length of time. I had to train for years in order to be able to actually will the muscles to comply with what I needed."

"That's extraordinary. Does Ezekiel know?"

She shook her head, feeling as if she'd done something wrong. Conversations with others were difficult, like walking through a minefield. She hadn't had time to talk to

Ezekiel, and now she felt as if she might have made a mistake. He should know everything about her first.

Cayenne walked in, Diego trailing behind her. "What's up, Bella?"

Bellisia liked that Cayenne didn't look to either man first. Cayenne made her own alliances, and acted on her own judgment. She wasn't in the least intimidated by the men. Bellisia was more comfortable with her there. She slid off the table. Both men towered over her, but with Cayenne in the room, even without water close, she felt empowered.

"If you don't mind, I'd like to talk to Cayenne for just a minute. Alone."

Joe cocked an eyebrow at her but he shrugged and indicated for Diego to go out. He followed and politely shut the door.

"I've got two chips in me. They appear to be embedded in my ribs on either side. Joe says he can go in and take them out but I'd have to be put under anesthesia. I'm a little uncomfortable with that. I don't know them. They just arrived, and I'm still pretty nervous around men. If I don't have it done, I'll have to leave before Ezekiel returns."

Cayenne shook her head. "Don't do that. Just let them take the chips out. Joe's a good doctor. They fly all over the world, sometimes performing surgery with bullets flying all around them. He's got a steady hand."

"It isn't that. I'm just . . . uncertain he'll do what he says. I've been experimented on so many times. I just want you to . . ." She trailed off again. She couldn't very well ask another woman—one she'd only just met—to kill someone on her behalf if he was really an enemy. Why should she trust that Cayenne would really do it?

Cayenne touched her shoulder. Just touched her with gentle fingers, a brush, no more. Bellisia realized Cayenne didn't touch others very often. It felt like the sealing of their friendship.

"They're afraid of me with good reason," Cayenne said.

"I'm beginning to care for them, but like you, I'm not so good with men. I'm not much better with women, but Nonny, Pepper and the girls are teaching me. I'll get there and if you stay with us, you will too. I know you can trust Joe and Diego, but if you feel better with me watching out for you, I promise, I will."

That had to be good enough. She had to trust someone if she was really going to have any kind of a life. She trusted Ezekiel and Nonny. They claimed these people as their family, so she had to make that leap of faith once again. She nodded and, before she could change her mind, yanked open the door and told them she was ready.

12

Ezekiel detested paperwork. He would much rather go into a hot zone and pull out a dozen SEALs with mortars flying than sit at a desk and do reports. He preferred when Joe Spagnola was with them on a mission and it was his job to fill out one million pieces of paper that no one ever looked at. Okay, maybe that was going too far. Major General Tennessee Milton looked at anything that had to do with the GhostWalkers. All orders came directly from him, and he definitely looked at the paperwork. Ezekiel knew that for a fact because he'd been called to the man's office on more than one occasion for more detailed information.

He sighed as he continued working, bent over the desk, hearing the hideous teasing from the GhostWalkers emerging through the door. He wished he didn't have such acute hearing, although if he was being strictly honest with himself, he could turn it down, but he *needed* to hear every word his about-to-die brother and his friends were saying. He'd had them call the moment they were finished with their probably only two-page report, to find out if Bellisia was still there at the Fontenot compound. What they told him instead was that Joe was there. Of all people, *Joe*. It just had to be him.

An overly loud pounding came on the door, making him wince. "Stop daydreaming about getting laid and do your damn work, Hunter," Draden called, using the nickname given to him a long time ago.

The eruption of loud, taunting laughter had him gritting his teeth. "Get the hell home and check on my girl," he yelled back. Murder wasn't good enough for any of them right now. Slow torture would work. He could get behind that.

"Your girl's pretty cute," Mordichai said. "I think I'll tell her you got your ass kicked again, and she'll realize you may be pretty, but you're not worth too much. I'll be right there to comfort her."

That was it. Ezekiel had already skipped the part where he'd gone into the field with stitches on his body. He'd taken Lily Whitney's concoction that promoted healing, and also used the second-generation Zenith drug she'd modified from her insane father's first-generation drug. He hadn't bothered to tell his fellow GhostWalkers about that, and he wasn't about to tell the major general. He was the doctor. He knew what would keep him on his feet through an intense mission. Swimming through the river might not have been the best idea, but the rest of it . . . He handled it.

He had actually written the report, minus the details about his capture, torture and rescue. What the hell was he supposed to say? Bellisia was a big part of that, and Major General Milton wouldn't be satisfied with a paper report. He'd most likely show up and give her the once-over—if she was still there. She had to be. He couldn't imagine Mordichai, or the others for that matter, giving him a bad time if they knew she was gone.

He added a couple of lines, glossing over what happened, knowing the old man was going to call him out for it, but whatever, he was going home. For the first time ever in his life, he had a reason to want to go home. He filed the report and then stepped out of the office and slugged his brother hard, doubling him over. Draden and Gino burst out laughing, but wisely ran for their lives.

"What was that for?" Mordichai demanded innocently. "Sheesh, Zeke, you've got a hell of a temper, always did. Bet your little octo-pussy . . ."

"*Don't* say it. Don't ever let me hear you or anyone else call her that." Ezekiel went from playing to pissed in record time. "I swear, Mordichai," he threatened, advancing on his brother.

Mordichai held up his hands in surrender. "Sorry, bro, that was in poor taste. I'll tell the guys James Bond jokes are off the table."

"You do that. You think she hasn't heard it all before? Whitney has his supersoldiers running around wanting these women to accept them as partners whether the women want them or not. Those men aren't going to be nice about it."

Mordichai cleared his throat. "Speaking of Whitney's supersoldiers, I talked to Joe and apparently Donny had a couple of visitors out at the island. Two of Whitney's for certain. They showed him a picture of Bellisia and one calling himself Gerald claimed she was his wife. Joe took two tracking chips out of her a couple of days ago. It was a bit of surgery; the bastard had embedded them along her ribs on either side. He said it was a nasty little operation getting them out."

Ezekiel swore under his breath. Of course Whitney would chip the women. He'd want to know where they were every second. He hadn't been there for Bellisia when she needed him. The surgery had to have hurt. Was that what men like him went through, out on a mission when things went to shit back home and his woman had to take care of it by herself? Without him. It was bad enough that Joe had to show up and had most likely interrogated her. He groaned, thinking about that.

Joe was a good-looking bastard, but deceptive as a snake. One moment he was charming and the next he struck hard and fast, confusing his enemies. Ezekiel followed his brother and the others out to the truck. He should have been there for that as well. He wouldn't have allowed it. Joe could posture all he wanted, but in the end, what was he going to do? What could he do?

The GhostWalkers were considered military. They served their country, but they had been wronged in a government-sanctioned program that had cost the Earth. No one wanted them walking around as civilians, but what were they going to do with them? Force them to stay in the program? No, they had to sweet-talk them, handle them carefully. That meant GhostWalkers had their own code, and they followed it to the letter. But it didn't include interrogating another man's woman.

"Getting hot in here, bro," Mordichai said under his breath, a whisper of sound.

Gino probably heard, but Ezekiel doubted if Draden had. "He shouldn't have talked to her without me being there, Mordichai," he said. "Not only was it disrespectful, but she belongs to me. She's my choice. And as far as he's concerned, she's a civilian."

Gino cleared his throat. "She came at a bad time. Cheng, if that's the man behind all this, orchestrated the terrorists—and we know he has a connection to that particular cell—to take hostages. Then he has two elite soldiers murdered and his men take their places with the soldiers' faces. Who can do that? This plan wasn't just thrown together, Zeke. If Cheng is really behind this . . ."

"Bellisia isn't lying." He resisted the urge to turn around and smash Gino in the face, but that dark ugliness in him spread. The temperature in the truck raised a degree.

"I know she wasn't lying. She convinced all of us, but Joe wasn't there and it's his job to make damn sure we're all safe when we see action."

"She saved my life. She didn't have to do that. Her repayment has been nothing but interrogations, locked in a cell, betrayal . . . *Hell*." He raked his hand through his hair, wanting to hit someone. He needed that outlet now, the powerful energy building up until he almost couldn't control it. Whenever it got to that point, he usually fought someone, or at least pounded a heavy bag. It wasn't safe sitting in a truck with his friends.

He took a deep breath and let it out, powering down the window to stare at the swamp as they hurtled past. Mordichai drove like a maniac. Right now, it wasn't fast enough. "I keep wondering if circumstances were the other way around and I'd saved her life at the risk of my own and I was treated the way she was, just what my reaction would be. I wouldn't stay. I would be so pissed I'd want to come back and hunt down every single one of the fuckers who treated me like shit. I'd probably do it too."

"That's because you're one mean son-of-a-bitch, Zeke," Draden said. "Does she know you have that side to you?"

"Probably thinks he's all cute and cuddly," Gino sneered, obviously trying to lighten the mood in the truck.

Ezekiel knew better. He'd seen her face, her eyes, when he'd caught hold of her twice, refusing to let her escape into the river. In her mind he'd betrayed her. In his mind he'd kept his woman from running from him. He wanted to believe he'd done it for all the right reasons—to save those hostages. The truth was something else altogether. He'd found her. His woman. He knew if she got into that water he'd never see her again. He couldn't allow that.

"I am cute and cuddly with her," he mused, "not so much with the rest of you. Right now I want to beat someone up, so please, keep up your bullshit."

The cabin of the truck went suspiciously quiet. Ezekiel leaned back against the high-backed seat with a satisfied smirk. He was still furious with Joe. Still worried about Bellisia's surgery. What did they even know about her physical makeup? Nothing. Joe just operated on her for the good of those at the compound. He should have done tests. She could have bled to death right there on the operating table, or reacted to the anesthesia.

"Come on, Zeke, pull it together," Mordichai hissed. "I haven't seen you like this for years. We're going to roast in here if you don't calm the fuck down."

The truck was barely stopped before Ezekiel had the door open and he'd flung himself out. It was pitch-dark, very late, the entire household in bed with the exception of the guards. He strode into the house, not even looking back at the others. They'd be smirking and he was afraid of what he might do if he saw them.

It didn't matter that he was out of control and acting like he was a teenager, he *had* to see her. By the time he hit the end of the hallway and turned toward the newer wing where his room was, he was sprinting. He opened the door to his bedroom and stepped inside, his gaze going straight to the bed.

He didn't see her, and his heart stuttered in his chest. He took the four steps to the side of the bed and touched the covers. She was slight; maybe it would be difficult to see her. He even ran his hand over the sheets and blanket to see if he could have missed her. She was good at camouflage. It was possible. But she wasn't there.

He nearly hit the floor. He'd been running on adrenaline practically since he'd been captured. All of a sudden his body just wanted to shut down. She was gone. He sank down on the edge of the bed and scrubbed both hands over his face. Emotion welled up like he'd never experienced. Deep. Shocking. Terrifying almost. He didn't feel like this. Not. Ever. Not even when he heard his own mother bickering back and forth at what price she'd sell her sons to a pedophile for the night. He hadn't hurt like this. Ached inside.

Her scent was everywhere. Clean and fresh with a faint hint of vanilla and orange. He picked up the pillow and held it to his nose, breathing her in. Where would she go? She'd given him her word. The boys would have told him if Joe had run her off. Could there have been complications with the surgery? Maybe she was in the hospital room. They would know better than to take her to an actual hospital with Whitney on her trail.

Joe was going to get a rude wake-up call right then in the middle of the night. Ezekiel decided to hit the bathroom first. Take care of business and then go beat the crap out of Joe. He opened the door to the room and stopped abruptly. The scent of vanilla and orange was stronger here, not as elusive.

The room was dark but he heard the faint lap of water and everything in him stilled. His breath left his lungs in a rush of heat. She was there. He hadn't seen her, but he felt her. She had to be in the big, claw-footed tub he hadn't had any use for but Nonny had insisted should take up room in his private bath. He closed his eyes and took a deep breath, pulling Bellisia's scent deep into his lungs.

Grace Fontenot really did have the second sight. She'd made him go into New Orleans on a bullshit errand and he'd met Bellisia. Bellisia had saved his life and was definitely his woman. Now, he had this oversized monstrosity of a tub he hadn't wanted but gave in because it was Nonny's house, and his Bellisia needed it. That made him thankful for it.

He took the few steps that would take him to her side. He put his hand out. He was actually trembling. It was ridiculous that he could be such a fucking baby, but he couldn't help himself. Gripping the edge of the tub, he crouched low and peered down at her. She was immersed in water, other than her face. Her eyes were open, those beautiful eyes that were so blue and framed with long, thick exotic lashes.

"Hey, baby," he said softly.

"Hey, yourself."

She sat up, clearly forgetting she wasn't wearing a stitch. For being so small, she definitely had breasts, two little handfuls just for him. His mouth watered. He couldn't help himself, he had to touch her. Her skin was the softest thing he'd ever felt in his life, even wet. Silk or satin, he couldn't decide which. He drew a finger from her collarbone to the swell of her breast, then caressed the swelling curve with the pads of his fingers.

"I thought about you even when I shouldn't have been."

"I thought about you too," she whispered, not flinching under his touch.

"Mordichai said you had surgery."

"Whitney put a couple of chips in me, and they weren't easy to get to. Joe took them out so I wouldn't have to leave."

He hadn't thought about that. Maybe he wouldn't kill Joe after all. "Did it hurt?"

"After. I woke up and felt like someone had scraped my bones with a serrated knife."

Okay, killing was back on the table. He bent down and brushed her lips with his. He had no idea where gentle came from because he hadn't learned it from his mother or on the street. He was a rough man with rough ways, and Bellisia was so small and delicate that right at that moment, looking at her, feeling how fine her bones were, he was afraid if he actually fucked her, he'd hurt her. Bad. Really bad. He wasn't small and he didn't know how to have sex all sweet and romantic. He tended to pound into a woman, hard and fast and satisfying. He'd break her in half.

His cock was so hard he was a little afraid he might shatter. Kissing her didn't help, but he couldn't stop. He knelt down and got serious because she tasted so damn good he had to have more. He locked his arm around her back and half lifted her against him, uncaring that she was soaking wet and now he was as well.

His lips brushed hers, back and forth, demanding entry. His tongue teased the seam of her mouth. And then she opened for him and he was lost. He was swept away into a place of sheer feeling. He'd kissed a lot of girls, although he'd never been into kissing, that was just to get where he was going. He was all about getting inside and getting off. He didn't have relationships, but he always made certain the woman knew the score and both walked away clean.

He'd never wanted to do this. Kissing. Exploring her mouth. Savoring her taste. Claiming her with just his mouth. His fingers bunched in all that wet, thick silk, and he held her there for him to feast on. He took his time with her, not because he was a good guy trying to be gentle, but because this was what she needed and he found he needed it as well. Just kissing her was paradise.

It didn't matter that she tentatively followed his lead. No, he *loved* that. He loved that his was the only mouth she'd ever willingly kissed. He loved that she'd chosen him. It was a huge risk for her. It had been from the very beginning. She could have escaped Whitney and kept going, never looking back. She didn't have to warn the GhostWalkers Cheng was after them and Violet had sold them down the river. She'd risked her freedom to come to Louisiana and warn them. Then she'd saved him. She didn't have to do that either. Then she'd stayed for him.

He cupped her face in his palms. Held her so he could look down at her eyes. Liquid blue, like the deepest sea. A little dazed. He brushed kisses over her eyelids and then followed the line with his lips to the corner of her mouth.

"I'm getting you wet." Her voice was breathless.

"Are you?" he murmured and reached down to tug at the chain to pull the plug and empty the tub. He swung her up in his arms, cradling her against his chest while water dripped on the floor and soaked his shirt and jeans.

She put her arms around his neck, threading her fingers together at his nape. "Yes. And now you're making a big mess."

"Am I?" He took her mouth again. She had a beautiful mouth and he spent a little time just memorizing the shape and feel of it before delving into that heat.

She kissed him back, giving herself up to him. Giving

him everything. He shifted her a little to catch up a couple of towels and heard her breath hitch. Instantly he lifted his head. "Surgery still hurts."

She shrugged. "A little. No big deal."

"I might have to murder Joe. Was he really mean to you? He can be rough."

"Not as bad as it could have been. I wanted to stay. Nonny has been so wonderful to me. I even had my first cooking lesson. I've been watching the cooking channel. Pepper showed it to me." She nuzzled his throat as he took her back into the bedroom. "Did everyone make it home, Ezekiel?"

"One wounded, but he'll be fine. Got the hostages out. One of the Indonesians was in bad shape. We turned him over to the medics there. The American wouldn't have lasted more than a few more hours. We operated on him and he was taken to a hospital. It will take a while for him to heal." His voice turned grim.

She rubbed his shoulder. "You got him out of there. That's what counts."

He set her on her feet and wrapped her in one of the no-nonsense towels Nonny had for the household. She didn't spend a fortune on nice towels. Ezekiel had never noticed or cared until right at that moment. Who would have thought it would matter what kind of towel he dried Bellisia off with, but it did.

"What about you? Are the lacerations healing?"

"I slapped some second-generation Zenith on them before I left and took a couple of the pills. I'm healing fast. Did Joe give you the drug?"

She nodded. "And antibiotics. I didn't take the antibiotics. I knew I wouldn't need them."

"Babe." His tone was sheer reprimand, but seriously? "Woman, you spend half your life in water. It isn't always clean."

She laughed softly and the sound was low and sexy, playing over his body until he couldn't breathe with wanting her. "Joe actually tried ordering me to stay out of the water. I

didn't go swimming in the river just to keep him from having
a heart attack." She looked him over. "Ezekiel, you're soaking
wet. You need to get out of those clothes."

His heart jumped. She hadn't made it sound like an invitation, but he wasn't going to make the mistake of hesitating just in case she had meant it that way. He began shucking
his clothes fast, and she stepped closer to the bed and lifted
the sheet.

"Wait, sweetheart," he said softly.

She turned to look up at him with her large, sea blue eyes,
making his heart pound. "What is it? I'm actually dry already. I dry off fast."

"Don't get in bed yet. I want to look at you."

She raised an eyebrow, but she didn't slide under the
sheet. Instead she dropped it and turned to face him boldly.
He loved that. She took a step toward him, and when he did
a little spin with his finger, she turned slowly for him. She
had a perfect little body. Perfect for him. Those breasts, the
flared hips that would cradle his body so nicely.

"I need to braid my hair. It won't dry like that, but I can't
have it all over the place."

She moved toward the bed again, her hands going back
to divide her hair in three sections. The action lifted her
breasts. A single drop of water ran along the slope to her
nipple. Without thinking he leaned down and licked it off.
She went utterly still, her gaze fixed on his face, hands still
behind her, hair in her fists.

He cupped her breast and drew the soft, inviting mound
into the heat of his mouth. She gasped and let her hair fall
in a long pale waterfall down her back. "Ezekiel. That feels
like fire running straight from my breast to my sex. More.
I want more."

He could do that. Give her more. He was all about the
more. Just her talking in that breathless sultry voice sent his
blood streaking with fire, and that fire went straight to his
cock. The thick shaft, as hard as a steel spike, rubbed along

her rib cage, up high, almost to her breasts. She hadn't run when she saw his cock, and that was a good sign. He dragged her closer, his mouth working, tongue teasing her nipple, flicking and dancing, then suckling and scraping with his teeth until her breath was coming in ragged little pants.

He used his hand on her other breast, first cupping and kneading gently then tugging and rolling her nipple. He took his time, savoring the taste of her skin, the feel of it, so soft against the roughness of his. He experimented a little, wanting to be gentle, knowing eventually he would fail and needing to know how much she could take. He bit down a little harder and tugged rougher.

Bellisia cried out softly, a needy moan, and then her hands moved down his chest to find his cock. The breath slammed out of his lungs. She stroked him. Rubbed the broad, sensitive head and skimmed her fingers down the shaft with the very pads of her fingers. It was the sexiest thing he'd ever felt. As if thousands of tiny little soft fingers caressed him as she stroked.

"That feels good, Bellisia," he encouraged, wanting her to do a little exploring of her own.

"It feels amazing. Really soft, but extremely hard at the same time. The bad news is, there is no way you're going to fit."

So she had been looking. "I'll fit." He stroked his tongue over her breast again and then kissed her mouth when she turned her face up to his. So solemn. So certain. He was really going to be happy proving her wrong.

Her fingers kept petting him, almost as if he was a beast she had to tame. He caught her hand and wrapped her fist around him, squeezing hard. "I like it rough, baby. You want to get me very wet and then you slide your hand like this."

"How do I get you wet?" She looked around a little helplessly.

He grinned at her. "Your mouth. Use your mouth."

She smiled up at him. "Of course. I panicked for a minute.

We had sex education, of course, but not the particulars of the rest of it."

Before he could reply, she bent her head and licked up his shaft as if she were licking a candy cane. Then her mouth closed over him and he nearly came apart. The sensation was so amazing, he felt his balls growing hot and tight. The muscles in his thighs shuddered and danced with desire. She didn't have any hesitation or embarrassment. She wasn't shy about trying anything new with him. She sucked hard, and then used her tongue. A jackhammer drilled at his head. Blood thundered and roared in his ears.

"Tell me," she ordered.

He grinned as he held her head to him, careful not to push her head down over him and take control. He liked her bossiness. That meant she'd talk to him about what she liked and wanted. In the meantime, he'd let her explore until he couldn't take it anymore, because nothing in his life had ever felt so damned good.

Bellisia was decisive when she wanted something and she wasn't afraid to go after it. She'd made up her mind while she waited in the house with his scent surrounding her night and day that she was going to make Ezekiel Fortunes her man. She could live in the swamp close to Nonny, Pepper and Cayenne and be happy. She didn't have a single clue what she was doing, but she was determined.

"Do any damn thing you want, baby, just don't bite."

Her eyebrow went up. "Um, Ezekiel? You might want to rethink that statement. It gives me a lot of room and I have a very vivid imagination. You went into combat, and I was worried every single minute you were gone." She rubbed her thumb over the soft, velvety head, smearing the fluid around, using the setae to stroke caresses over what clearly was an extraordinarily sensitive part of him. She knew he liked that because he shuddered every time she did it.

"Just one moment, sweetheart, and you can do all the exploring you want."

He turned and walked back to the bathroom, his body moving in the fluid, sexy way he had, all rippling muscle. She liked the way he reminded her of water when he moved. It was as if he flowed over a surface so silently he was unheard and he left no trace of himself behind. That appealed to her as everything about him did.

She'd had plenty of time to think about him while he was gone on his mission. He could have been killed and she'd never have had the chance to know—this. Being with him intimately. Most others always got the warrior, but she got the man. And she wanted him. She wasn't stupid; she knew with Whitney breathing down her neck, she was a danger to the people Ezekiel loved and she might have to leave, to lead Whitney away from them, but in the meantime, she was going to be intimate with the man she'd chosen. Whitney wasn't going to take that away from her.

She might not have started out with confidence, but once she made up her mind that Ezekiel Fortunes was the man for her, she used her time wisely waiting for him to come back to her. She had open, frank discussions with Pepper, Cayenne and Nonny. All three women were fountains of information, but clearly a few of the details had been left out.

Nonny gave her the best advice. *Trust your man, Bella. If he's the right man, he'll want your pleasure and will help you get there. Talk to him. Communicate. Let him know what you like and don't like. Ask him what he likes. Sex is important. Sacred between the two of you. You want it to be the best it can be always for your partner, and trust that he wants it to be the best for you.*

So she was talking to her man. Asking for guidance, because Bellisia liked to be the best at whatever she chose to do and she was going to be awesome at pleasing her man.

He came back into the room, a blow-dryer in hand. It was the last thing she expected and the sight of it in his hands made her laugh.

"Who knew my badass GhostWalker used a blow-dryer?"

He bent down to plug it in and then stood at the end of the bed, pointing to the spot in front of him. "Woman, when I'm walking around naked, you don't laugh. Not for any reason. Worshipping is acceptable; laughter, absolutely not."

"Do your brothers know?" She couldn't help infusing the unspoken threat of blackmail.

She made the mistake of not being out of his reach, and he caught her arm and tugged her to stand between his legs facing him.

"Talk like that could get you in trouble." He switched on the dryer and pushed her head down so that her hair fell upside down toward the floor. At once his fingers began to move over her scalp, separating strands as he played the warm air over her hair. "You might want to use your mouth for something else so you don't get into trouble."

She already was cupping his heavy sac, rolling his balls gently and stroking the setae on her fingertips along the velvety surfaces. "I don't know. What exactly would trouble get me? I always like to weigh every decision with facts."

She had always teased her "sisters" and they'd reciprocated. It had been a part of her life from the time she'd grown up. Not in front of Whitney. Whitney believed if they had time for fun, that meant they had time for more training. She liked that Ezekiel teased her. She especially liked that his breath hissed out between his teeth just at the caressing motion of her fingertips. She added her tongue, tracing the velvet, absorbing the texture and feel of him as delicately as she did any new food before she ever tasted it.

His fingers tightened in her hair, bunching the wet strands into a fist. She hesitated. "If I'm not doing something right, please tell me," she reiterated.

His fist let go and he smoothed out her hair. "Sweetheart, anything you do is right. You don't have to do anything at all if you prefer not to. We're just exploring here. If you don't enjoy it, or find it pleasurable, we don't do it. It's that simple. In fact, Bellisia, I missed the hell out of you and thought about little else than getting home to you, so whatever time you give me will be enough for me."

She heard both the sincerity and the edge of desperation in his voice. He was telling her he would be willing to just talk, but that wasn't enough for her. She wanted to know what true intimacy was with him. If she never had another night with him, she was going to have this one.

The more she touched him, the harder his shaft was, the thicker and longer it grew. She knew all about sex for procreation, but she had missed out on the exploring/fun part. She wanted that. She wanted to be unafraid of anything in life, especially something that should be fun.

"Not for me," she whispered. "I want you, Ezekiel. I made up my mind that it's you. I'm not asking forever, I know you can't give that to me, but I want this night."

Instantly, he shut off the dryer and tossed it aside. Catching her face in his hands he forced her head up. "Baby. What the hell is that? You know I can't give you forever? Are you planning on seducing me and then leaving?"

She frowned up at him. "Seducing a man is much harder than I thought it would be." She must be doing something wrong. The books made it sound simple, and talking to Cayenne and Pepper had convinced her she would have no problems.

"Trust me, sweetheart," he said, his voice grim. "You seduced me."

An expression she couldn't read but didn't bode well for her came over his face. He lifted her in his arms and tossed her into the middle of the bed. She landed with a squeak of shock, sprawled out on her back. Before she could move, he came down over top of her, pinning her to the mattress. He knocked the breath out of her, and he was very heavy.

His body settled over hers, his hips pushing her thighs apart. Her heart stuttered hard in her chest. She was grateful for the change in positions, but was nervous as well. She'd been the one in control before; now, just that quickly, the tables had been turned on her. She moistened her lips and took a much-needed gulp of air.

Her skin absorbed the feel of him. His texture. His muscles. Bone. The ridges and planes. There was no stopping herself from touching him. She needed to feel him. Skin to skin. She could barely breathe with wanting him. She began to caress him with her fingertips, sliding her fingers down and up the perfect slope of his back, brushing over every nerve ending with the fine setae, feeling every shuddering answer in his body.

He propped himself up on his elbows, taking some of the weight off of her, his hands once more framing her face. "Bellisia, look at me."

"I am looking," she defended. How could she *not* look at his chest? His arms? Who had muscles like that? Her hands slid from his back to his front.

His breath hissed out and her gaze jumped to his. "I want to see your eyes while we talk, Bellisia, because we're damned well *not* having a one-night stand. What the hell are you thinking?"

She leaned up to lick at his nipple and then subsided when he growled. "I was thinking I wanted you to be the man I have sex with. I'm practical, Ezckiel. I always have been. I've thought this through. If I stay here, Whitney isn't going to back off and leave me alone. He'll come after me. He's already sent two of his men. I don't want to kill them and he knows it." She was a little distracted by his mesmerizing body.

His muscles tensed under her exploring fingers. "What the hell does that mean?" He pulled back even more, and this time, when her gaze jumped to his, she could easily see that roiling dark entity in him rising like a storm.

She bit down on her lip to keep from swearing aloud. She'd just given away something very important, and he wouldn't like what she said no matter how she explained it.

"Bellisia. Start. Talking."

Now he was scaring her just a little bit, and she was very hard to scare. It wasn't that she thought he'd hurt her exactly, it was that she was certain he would hunt down Gerald and Adam immediately. Ezekiel Fortunes was a hunter and he would find his prey and kill them.

She tried to push at his chest. When he didn't seem to notice, she used her enhanced strength, shoving again. That earned her a dark scowl.

"What happened to seduction, babe? I thought that's what you had in mind."

"Well you aren't exactly cooperating, are you?" she snapped. Better to have a fight and distract him than have to answer questions she didn't want to answer.

He blinked and instantly her gaze followed the downward path of his dark lashes. He had a lot of lashes. Long and thick and probably the only feminine feature he possessed. He was rock hard. Every muscle, every distinct line and bone in his body was purely masculine. Up close she could see the laugh lines around his eyes. His jaw was definitely all man, covered in the five-o'clock shadow that seemed to be perpetually there no matter what time it was.

Those long beautiful lashes rose and she knew she was in trouble.

13

Outside, the sky lit up as lightning split the night in two. Thunder crashed, a loud roar that shook the house. Rain slashed at the window, beating at it in a steady rhythm. Ezekiel's gaze drifted over Bellisia's face. She was beautiful. So delicate. Almost ethereal. Sexy as hell with that expression on her face. She thought she was going to get out of answering his questions by fighting with him. He bent his head and took possession of her mouth. She tasted like a warm summer's day. Fresh and clean and all his.

His mood matched the wild storm that had come in fast, as the weather often did in the bayou. She made him absolutely crazy. He'd never experienced the emotions she brought out in him. She was going to lead him in a terrible dance, but he didn't care. She was worth it.

He kissed her over and over, losing himself in her, giving up a little more of his control with each kiss. He explored every inch of her mouth, teased her tongue into dueling with his, stealing her breath and giving her his. His hands moved over her body. Her skin was extraordinary, so soft he knew he could spend hours just feeling it under his fingertips.

He cupped her breast and ran the pad of his thumb over her nipple. Her breath hissed out in a little rush. She was sensitive. That didn't surprise him with her soft skin and the way she felt every brush of his fingers. He kissed his way along her stubborn little chin and down her throat. He found her pulse point, licked it and then drew her soft skin into his mouth and suckled, wanting to leave his mark.

There could be only a couple of reasons why his woman wouldn't be willing to kill men Whitney sent to bring her back. He didn't like either of them and he wasn't taking any chances with her. He'd claimed her. He knew she was the one. *Knew* it with every breath he drew.

Her hands were driving him crazy. His head felt like maybe someone with a jackhammer was having at him. She'd done that with her fingertips, stroking his cock, sending fire racing through his bloodstream. He was fairly certain every drop of blood in his body was centered in his groin. He needed to stay in control and it wasn't helping that her hands were back to caressing him.

She wasn't slowing him down, matching the fire roaring in his belly. He hadn't had a woman in a long while and just that alone was going to put him off his usual control, but her hands . . . He was going to lose it if he wasn't careful.

He caught both her wrists in one hand for his own sanity. She couldn't touch him, not yet. Not when every brush of her fingertips drove him wild. He stretched her arms over her head and pinned them there while his other hand went to her left breast. His mouth was thoroughly occupied with her right. So soft. She had a faint taste on her skin he couldn't quite identify, but it was as addicting as her kisses.

He took his time exploring, needing her to be just as out of control as he was. The storm increased in strength, adding fuel to the fire already burning in him. She'd ignited it when she'd put her mouth on his cock, her soft, velvet tongue stroking along his shaft, her fingertips dancing along with her tongue. The combination had nearly brought him to his knees, and he would have exploded right then if she hadn't been so certain she was going to walk away after their one night together.

He used the edge of his teeth, testing her response to rough. He liked rough. He was that kind of man and he wanted her to like it as well. He brought her in that direction slowly, keeping it gentle, but every now and then, using his teeth and fingers to see if she liked the sensation. He followed up his teeth with a soothing tongue until she moaned his name.

"Ezekiel. I need my hands. I have to touch you."

Her voice, that breathless little moaning pant, sent him right out of the stratosphere. He kissed his way down her rib cage to her belly button and spent some time lavishing attention on that.

"Can't give you your hands, baby," he told her between kisses and licks over her delicious skin. "You're driving me crazy already and I have to make this good for you."

"It's good. I'm good."

He smiled against her flat stomach. "I plan on making it a whole hell of a lot better, sweetheart. You have to be ready for me."

"I'm ready."

She sounded so breathless, almost desperate, and he raised his head to look at her. She was so damn beautiful with her face flushed and her eyes glowing a beautiful blue. He loved the sweep of those blue-tinged lashes, thick crescents that framed her eyes.

"You will be." He made it a decree and released her wrists, sending up a little prayer that he could hold on.

Ezekiel hooked her knees with his arms and lifted her hips as he bent his head to kiss his way up her inner thigh. Her muscles jumped and she cried out, a little half sob, her fingers gripping his shoulders as he swiped his tongue across her entrance. That faint elusive taste was present, but even more addicting than ever. Orange? Vanilla? What did it matter? He needed more.

He lifted his head and smiled down at her. "Like saltwater taffy, only better. Vanilla and orange, just what I like." It was no wonder she always had that scent. Something inside her produced that taste—his very own supply.

He devoured her, forgetting to be gentle, lapping at the cream spilling from her body, using his tongue and fingers greedily. She tried hard to be silent, her body writhing in his hands, hips bucking, her fingers digging into his shoulder for an anchor. He should have been more careful, but he was lost in the taste of her. Drunk on her. Feeling decidedly primitive.

He used one finger to stretch her. She was tight and scorching hot. His cock jerked and pulsed in anticipation. He was definitely going to have to take his time. He kissed her inner thigh again. "Take a breath for me. Relax, Bellisia. We want to do this right. I don't want you to feel pain." He used his thumb on her clit, circling gently to arouse her more.

"It's so much. The sensations, I can't believe how that feels."

"It gets better, I promise, but you have to let me take care of you. Relax for me," he coaxed. He wasn't certain how much longer he could hold out. Very carefully he pushed a second finger into her, listening to her breath catch. "That's it, baby, just like that." He scissored his fingers open but was met with tight resistance. She was slick though, and he felt her inner muscles grip him hard.

He replaced his fingers with his mouth, this time deliberately driving her up as high as he dared. Her head tossed from side to side on the pillows. She buried her fists in his hair as if she might pull his head away from her. He curved his finger inside her, finding the sweet little spot that would send her over the edge. She tumbled with a shattered cry, her muscles clamping down as she flew.

He moved over top of her, lodging the head of his cock into her, inching in slowly while he watched her face. Her eyes widened and she shook her head.

"It burns."

"I'm stretching you. You're small, babe. I'm not. We'll get there and it will feel good." He could feel her muscles still rippling from the aftershocks of her orgasm. The pulsing and squeezing on his shaft and sensitive head nearly were his undoing. He paused, taking a breath for himself. For her. "So fucking tight, Bellisia. And hotter than hell." He inched forward, feeling the way her muscles resisted but gave way for his invasion.

Flames streaked up his cock and spread like a wildfire out of control, roaring in his belly and flicking at his thighs with hot licks. He actually had to clench his teeth the burn was so good, but he was beginning to lose her. Panic was on her face, and she began to writhe under him, shoving at his chest with her hands.

"You're too big, Ezekiel. It isn't going to work."

Fighting the need to surge into her and bury himself deep, he stopped moving again. "Wait, sweetheart. Relax for me. Breathe. You're holding your breath. Give your body time to adjust. It will." He used his voice unashamedly. He could pitch his voice low, almost a hypnotic tone, and he did so now. As a rule, he was careful using that tone with his friends, although not the triplets or his brothers. He'd discovered that particular pitch when he was young and his brothers were scared. It always worked, and it did so now. Her gaze clung to his, but she nodded several times and took in air.

"That's it, baby. Keep breathing for me." He bent forward and took her mouth, needing her to stay completely with him, focused on him. One hand slid to her breast when he lifted his head, the other took his finger to her clit. "Feel your body relaxing around mine." He drew her nipple into his mouth, teasing with his tongue until he felt hot liquid gathering, surrounding his cock. "I love the way you taste. You smell like vanilla and orange and you taste the same. I could spend hours eating you up."

It was the truth and he knew she heard the sincerity and liked it. She liked the way he talked to her. He slipped in more and met her barrier. His teeth bit down gently on her nipple, she gasped and he surged forward, taking her innocence and burying himself deep.

"Ezekiel!" His name was a soft, panicked cry.

"It's done, sweetheart. Just give yourself a few seconds to relax." He tried to breathe through the scorching heat. She was strangling his cock, her channel squeezing him so tightly he couldn't breathe. He had to move soon or he was just going to go up in flames, but he wanted her to feel pleasure. That mattered to him, and that meant being careful even though he needed to pound into her.

It took a little longer than he'd hoped, but eventually her body relaxed around his and the panic in her eyes receded. He began to move again, the first two strokes slow and careful, watching every expression on her face for signs of discomfort. Then her fingers flexed on his hips and he felt the pressure to move a little harder and deeper. He obliged before she could change her mind.

Holding her hips still, he surged into her with a fast, deep stroke, watched the heat flush her skin, turning her rosy. That was all he needed and he let himself lose control by degrees, surging into her again and again, letting the fire consume him.

"Fucking paradise, sweetheart," he managed to get out between clenched teeth. His breath came in ragged pants, matching hers. He was grateful for the good shape he had to stay in as a PJ. It gave him stamina in spite of his need to empty himself in her. He didn't want it to ever end.

He pushed her up higher than he intended. She said his name, that single word, the way she'd done before when she was scared and needing reassurance.

"Let go for me," he whispered. "Just let it take you." He angled her body a little differently so he could hit that sweet spot as well as her clit with every stroke.

She gasped and dug her fingers into his hips as the orgasm took her like a tsunami. He tried to hold out, but her release was far too strong, sweeping him with her, her body clamping down like a vise, her muscles dragging over him, gripping and milking with enough force to pull his boiling seed up like a rocket. Jet after jet splashed into her, coating the walls of her channel, adding to the heat and ripples, and then he collapsed over her, burying his face in her neck, fighting for air. It was only then that he remembered what he'd never once forgotten—that all-important condom.

That knowledge wasn't enough to make him move. He stayed in her, buried deep, as he waited for his breathing to catch up with his racing brain. She was incredible. He lay there, letting her take his weight while he fought for breath. He knew he was too heavy for her, but he loved feeling her under him, all that soft skin, all that belonged just to him. She didn't protest, just held him, breathing shallowly. He realized she could breathe that way for a long, long time, the way she did underwater. Smiling against her neck, he took advantage and gave her a strawberry.

Her lashes fluttered. "What are you doing?"

"Marking you so everyone knows you're mine."

"That's a little primitive."

"I'm feeling primitive, baby." He pushed up a little on his elbows, but stayed buried deep, refusing to leave his sanctuary. "You need to tell me why you don't want to kill the two men Whitney sent after you, specifically the one claiming to be your husband."

Her wide eyes blinked up at him. A hint of color swept up her neck, adding to her already flushed skin. He pushed back the wealth of hair tumbling around her face. In just that short time he'd forgotten the feeling of silk. She surrounded him with a silken clasp, still holding him tight. He doubted if he would go soft, not when her body was so hot and still calling to his. He leaned down and kissed her before she could start coming up with a line of certain bullshit. He kissed her until she was kissing him back just as feverishly. Only then did he lift his head and brush his knuckles along her cheek.

"Tell me, baby. I can keep this up all night and I will. I love being in you." He began a slow glide, watching desire heat her eyes. "He isn't your husband, is he? Because if he is, you might find yourself a widow before the next sunset."

Her lashes fluttered again and she shook her head. "He isn't my husband." She gasped as his cock thickened, pushing against the tight walls of her channel, stretching her all over again. "He was one of the few good ones. Whitney has a small army of supersoldiers. They're all rejects from the psychological or physical or even psychic programs. Men who didn't quite make the cut."

He was well aware of that, although he had never heard the term "small army" before. "I didn't know there were any good ones. What does 'good ones' actually mean? And be specific."

"I can't think when you're moving like that." Her voice was breathless.

He didn't want her thinking, only feeling and telling him the truth, not thinking too much before she answered his questions. "I can't stop moving, so you'll have to find a way to talk to me. I need the answers, baby."

Bellisia sighed and lifted her hips to match his slow, languid rhythm at the urging of his hands. "Gerald and Adam both were from one of the Marine units, the Marine Recon unit. Gerald had the psychic ability and psychological profile, but he had been shot one too many times to pass the rigorous physical. Whitney has that in place to make certain his GhostWalkers can be genetically enhanced. Adam was able to pass the physical and psych evals, but not the psychic one. He has some small talent, and Whitney did enhance it, but it isn't as strong as the doctor wants for his GhostWalker program."

He leaned down and rewarded her with a kiss on her throat and then he nudged her face to one side with his jaw so he could scrape his teeth over her pulse point. He loved how that sent hot liquid bathing his cock. She would be able to get off on his rough when she was a little more experienced. He was growing harder with each slide into her body, but he kept moving slowly.

"Explain 'good.'"

She had to catch her breath, and her hands went to his hips in an effort to get him moving. When that didn't work, she sent him a little frown but forced herself to keep giving him what he wanted.

"'Good' is a conscience. They were careful with all of us, unlike his other soldiers. Respectful. They went out of their way to protect us when they could. If they had to take us to the most hated room in the compound, the one Whitney used for his science experiments, they were extremely nice about it. They often risked his wrath by sticking up for us, telling him that was enough or he was going to permanently harm us. That always stopped Whitney."

He didn't want to hear anything good about either man, but he'd asked for the explanation. He might have to kill them. Chances were extremely high that he would have no choice. They sounded like men he could respect. "Still, Whitney sent them to bring you back, and I'm certain that's what they mean to do."

"I'm certain Whitney paired them to me," she blurted out. "I've never been attracted to either of them, not ever, and I don't think they were attracted to me either. But right before I escaped them in Shanghai, I heard Whitney tell them to bring me to Italy, where he's been sending women for breeding. Whitney felt that if he paired us, we wouldn't want to be away from each other. He talked about it all the time. He doesn't get that one can be physically attracted without any emotional attachment."

He closed his eyes and rested his forehead against hers, pausing all movement. He stayed buried deep inside her, surrounded by that living silk as it grasped him in a tight, searing fist. "If you can't kill them, sweetheart," he said softly, "you do have an emotional connection."

"I do have an emotional connection, but not like you think," she admitted. She wrapped her arms around his waist. "I didn't say I couldn't kill them, Ezekiel, only that I didn't want to have to. Would it be difficult? Yes. It would haunt me, knowing they're both good men, but if it was your life, or the triplets'? Nonny's? I would kill them."

Her voice held such complete conviction it shocked him.

"I didn't think it was possible to kill someone you were paired with. Look at Violet and Whitney. She went into a hangar where her brain-dead husband was and shot him in the head. She came out with Whitney, and witnesses swore she was all over him.

"Violet hates him. I think she hates him for a number of reasons, but first and foremost because he began using reptiles and insects in his enhancement of the other women even though he paired them with GhostWalkers. She doesn't have those kinds of enhancements, so in her mind, we all have to go. She has to be the best, the one with the most power and the one sought after."

"She's a treacherous bitch. She left women in Whitney's compound to be used as broodmares so he has more babies to experiment on." Ezekiel felt the familiar rising of darkness in him, that need for violence.

"That she is, and she wants to be the only one. In order to do that, she has to be in a position to shut Whitney down and have him hunted until he's dead. She's already gathering her own army."

Her fingertips began a slow, mesmerizing brush over his

buttocks, tracing his muscle on the way up and sliding caresses over it on the way down. The feeling sent streaks of fire straight to his groin. Blood roared in his ears. His veins felt on fire. Just her fingertips, and he was lost in her all over again. Her fingertips and the scorching-hot fist surrounding him with silken fingers so tight he thought she was strangling him.

"You're certain?" He could barely get the words out. Somehow she'd managed to turn the tables on him and distract him from his very important interrogation. No man wanted to know his woman was physically attracted to other men. He might have to kill them just for that.

"Absolutely certain. She's visited Whitney on several occasions with them. Whitney provided them for her, thinking, I believe, that they would stay loyal to him, but he's forgotten just how powerful her voice is. Those soldiers were eating out of her hand."

"If she wants him dead, why didn't she kill him right then?" Her fingertips were driving him crazy. She was going to kill him with the sensations she created. Need grew in spite of his resolve to let her rest. He needed his brain right now, but his body wasn't listening.

"How could she? Whitney had begun to suspect that she was opposing him and he always had someone with a gun pointing at her head. He makes people disappear, she knows that." She raised her head a few inches and kissed his throat. Her lips followed a path down his chest and then she licked at his left nipple.

"Baby, this is important." He didn't sound quite as desperate as he felt. They needed to talk about Violet, but mostly he wanted to talk about Gerald and Adam. "What exactly was Violet doing with Cheng?" There was no stopping his cock from growing thicker or harder thanks to her scorching heat. He moved a little faster, plunging into her, reaching for the ultimate ride that had sent him into another stratosphere.

"Selling out the United States, the GhostWalker program

and your squadron in particular. It became clear to me why she chose this one once I met the triplets and Cayenne and Pepper. They are everything she despises. She'll come after all of them again. More than anything, more than hitting at you or Whitney, she'll strike against the children and women." Her breath left her lungs in a heated rush and her hands were back at his buttocks, this time urging him on.

She had to be sore. He was large. It was her first time, but even that knowledge couldn't stop him, not with her fingertips sliding over his muscle, doing a dance that sent streaks of fire spreading through every cell in his body.

He couldn't talk, couldn't do anything but sate the wild craving she'd set up in him. She was fast becoming his greatest obsession. He lost himself again; the vicious darkness in him, the need for violence was just as consumed by her fire as his body was. The storm was out of control. Wild. Sheer magic. He was gone, taking her the way he needed, the way her fingers playing on his skin demanded.

He'd never lost himself completely before. She did that, took away every horrible place he'd hidden his brothers, every fight he'd been in to make money to feed them or to protect them from the bigger bullies and pedophiles cruising the streets looking for boys too young and small to protect themselves. She took away the battles and the blood and the many times he'd shot and killed human beings when he'd taken an oath to save them.

Her soft cries and ragged little pants filled his ears like music. He buried himself in her body, over and over, feeling the tight clasp of her sheath. Hot and silky, a fist milking him, he never wanted it to end. Then she said his name. *Ezekiel.* Just that. And he knew she was there. Her body clamped down on his, a hot vise, so perfect he had never conceived it possible, the force taking him in that way she had, throwing him into a place he wanted to stay for a long, long time.

He buried his face in her neck, giving her his full weight,

absorbing the way her body, all silky soft, imprinted on his. He rested there, waiting for her to push him off. He was far too heavy and had no business squashing her, but he couldn't help himself, taking the time to just feel peace.

Reluctantly, he pushed up on his elbows and was shocked to see tears in her eyes. Time seemed to stop. His heart jerked hard in his chest. "Oh, God, baby, did I hurt you?" He'd been rough. Really rough. He should have taken more care with her.

She shook her head, but it didn't dislodge the tears clinging to her long eyelashes or the ones swimming in that wild blue sea.

"I'm sorry, sweetheart, I just lost control. You're so fucking tight and . . ." What did a man say to his woman when he'd been so damned selfish he'd forgotten it was only her second time? And her first time had only been half an hour before?

"I'm definitely sore, Ezekiel," she admitted, "but in a good way. I might not be able to walk properly for a couple of days, and I think I'll feel you inside me for a very long time, but I like that."

His heart clenched. Damn but he was falling hard. "Why are you crying?"

She moistened her lips with the tip of her tongue. "It's just so beautiful. I didn't know it would feel like that, or I would feel this way about you."

He framed her face with his hands. "There's no going back from this, Bellisia." His thumbs brushed at the tears in her eyes. "I want this perfectly clear between us. I gave myself to you. All of me. Maybe I wasn't as gentle as I should have been, but that was the real me. I just put my heart in your hands, baby. Don't crush it. I've never given it to another woman and I won't again."

"Ezekiel, what about Whitney? The threat to the children, Pepper and Nonny? If I stay . . ."

"You're staying. We settled that, otherwise you wouldn't

be lying under me with my cock still inside you. You want to be with me as much as I want to be with you." He used his voice unashamedly. Fuck being nice. She wasn't going anywhere.

Bellisia laughed softly. "Sugar, I think you had better learn right now that, although I totally love your voice, I'm not susceptible to it like most people. I'm not to Violet's voice either. That's why Whitney always had me watching her. You don't need to use your voice on me. I want to stay. I gave you my promise I'd wait for you because I *wanted* to be with you."

"Then stop thinking about leaving. You're my woman, and that means we—meaning my family; Nonny, Pepper, the triplets, Cayenne and all the men—will figure out together what we're going to do about any threat coming this way. Whitney and Violet both have sent soldiers. We sent them back in body bags. You get me, baby? Say you get me."

She nodded, the expression in her sea blue eyes soft and loving as her gaze moved over his face. "I get you, Ezekiel. I'm not going anywhere. Well, except the bathtub again. I need to soak for an hour or so. I'm sorry, but I do better in water when I'm a little sore."

Ezekiel brushed a kiss across her lips and then slowly eased out of her. She winced a little, obviously trying to keep that small movement from him, but of course he caught it. He saw everything she did, the slightest expression, every gesture. He was a hunter and there was little he missed. His mind recorded everything around him and played it back to him down to the slightest detail.

"Mordichai, Malichai and I each bought property butting up to the Fontenot land. We're building homes. In ours, we'll need a very large Jacuzzi, large enough for both of us to sleep in, because I'm not sleeping alone."

She blinked up at him, her lashes catching his attention. Thick and curled up slightly at the tips, they framed her incredible eyes with a bluish tinge. He bent and kissed her again because he had to, and then rolled off of her.

"I like water, Ezekiel. I need it."

He laughed softly. "I get that, baby. Did you think I was making a joke? You need to spend time in the water, then I'm there too."

"I don't actually *sleep* in water," she protested, and then she frowned. "Well, it has happened, if I'm being strictly honest, but I don't need to. I like a bed just like everyone else."

He shook his head. "I'm going to start the water for your bath. *Don't* go to sleep." He could see her lashes already drifting down. He wanted to continue their discussion about the man claiming to be her husband—the one she didn't want to kill even though he was sniffing around, prepared to bring her back to Whitney.

He padded on bare feet into the bathroom and turned on the taps, checking the temperature before he went back to her. Bellisia lay on her side, propped up on one hand, watching him. The sheet had been pulled up to her waist, allowing him to see the marks of his possession on her breasts and neck. She'd have them on the insides of her thighs as well. He'd been like a teenager and he should be a little ashamed of himself, but instead he grinned at her.

"What?"

"You look like you're mine."

"I am yours."

The satisfied grin faded from his face. "You need to remember that at all times, sweetheart."

"I think I have enough evidence all over my body to remind me if my brain suddenly short-circuits and I forget."

His eyebrow shot up. "Sass already. Clearly I didn't tire you out enough. Next time I'll be going for pure exhaustion." She made him want to laugh. He couldn't remember a time when he'd just wanted to laugh for no reason other than he was happy.

"I think you did a thorough job of it, Ezekiel. I don't think I can move, not even to make it into the bath, and I'm longing to be in the water."

"Is that your subtle way of asking me to carry you?"

"If it isn't too much trouble." She threw off the sheet and rolled to the side of the bed.

He was right, there were strawberries up the inside of one thigh and down the other. He couldn't help the smirk as he lifted her into his arms. "You don't weigh very much."

"I think it's my skeletal structure. I'm bendable."

"Don't say things like that when I have sex on the brain."

"Don't you always have sex on the brain?"

"Well, yeah. Now that you say that, we can talk about how bendable you are. There's a lot of room for positions. We'll have to try them all."

She laughed, the sound wreaking havoc with his breathing.

"Kiss me, Bellisia." He made it an order, sobering. He'd never expected a woman of his own, not one he was certain would be a true partner. She didn't need him to take care of her, but he was going to do just that anyway. He loved that she was strong and he wouldn't have to worry too much when he was away. Okay, he'd worry, but deep down he'd know she could handle anything that came up.

She didn't hesitate. She lifted her face to his, at the same time wrapping one arm around his neck and drawing his head down. Her lips were cool and soft. He realized her skin was. All silk, his woman, but her mouth was nearly as hot as her sweet little channel and tasted of vanilla and orange. He let her have control, her tongue exploring his mouth, sliding almost shyly along his, when he didn't think his woman was shy. He loved that too, the hint of vulnerability she didn't show to others. That was his alone and he was going to take care of it.

When she pulled back to look at him, he saw the beginnings of what he needed from her. It was there in her eyes. Love. That humbled him. She might not know it yet, but he could see it was there. He put her in the water, climbed in behind her and pulled her body between his legs so she could rest against his chest. The moment her body rested against his, he felt the energy running through her, almost a trembling.

Looking down, even though he still hadn't turned on lights, he could see the way the water lapped at her skin, which seemed to drink it in, absorbing the moisture as if she was a sponge.

"So tell me what you think we're going to do with your friend Adam and the man claiming to be your husband, Gerald."

She turned her head to glare at him over her shoulder. "Don't say it like that. You're going to be awful about Gerald, aren't you?"

"Yes." He saw no point in denying it. "The other one too. They came here to retrieve you for their master. You can say how wonderful they are all you want, but the fact remains, they want to take you back to him, and I'm not going to let that happen."

"They'll come around and everyone can just say I'm not here and eventually they'll move on. Joe told me they were taking the two chips Whitney put in me to another part of the bayou so that will lead them away from here."

"They'll buy that for about two minutes, Bellisia, and you know it." He poured soap into his hands and began to massage her shoulders and arms with it. "They'll know we're GhostWalkers and they'll know we're hiding you."

"Even if you kill them, Whitney will send others."

"Maybe. Maybe not. Sometimes he backs off." He rinsed off her shoulders and back.

She sighed and reached out to capture water in her cupped hand and then watch it slowly fall into the tub. "I just want you to talk to them first, Ezekiel. I don't think they'd endanger anyone else here . . ."

"Anyone else?" He wanted to shake her. "I'm not risking you."

"It isn't your risk, it's mine."

He caught her shoulders and gave her a little shake. "Seriously, Bellisia? What do you think we're doing here? This is permanent. You. Me. We're going to build a life together. Be a family. *Have* a family. At least that's what I'm planning. I thought you were on the same page."

"I am on the same page, Ezekiel. I'm as committed as you are to trying a life with you. Because I don't want to start off that life by killing two good men doesn't make me less committed, it makes me sane."

His breath hissed out between his teeth. He hated that she actually made sense. Maybe he was a little bloodthirsty when it came to Gerald and Adam. "What do you think we should do, baby? Invite them to one of Nonny's dinners?"

She was silent a moment, turning his sarcastic suggestion over and over in her mind. He sighed. "Sweetheart, I was kidding."

She pressed her body back into his. "Maybe you were, but that might be just what we need to do. We could recruit them. They don't like Whitney any more than we do."

"Are you crazy? Even if they did decide to join us, how would we know if they were really committed to being part of us or playing the role to be a spy for Whitney?"

"How did you know I was telling you the truth? Your people certainly interrogated me."

He ran his hands up the sides of her rib cage. She felt small and delicate, a woman's softer body, so intriguing, so beautiful. He cupped her breasts and then touched his marks on the slight curves. She had a point. "Arguing with you is going to be a fucking waste of time, isn't it?"

She laughed, and the sound slid into his body, an arrow aimed right at his heart. "Yes. You may as well get used to it, honey."

14

~

"You have to devein the shrimp. There is actually shrimp in the gumbo, Bella," Nonny said. "We're doing a shrimp gumbo so it's necessary to use shrimp."

Pepper and Cayenne burst out laughing. Even the triplets, all three girls in their identical aprons standing on chairs, laughed as well.

Bellisia tried scowling at them, but it was funny so she couldn't stop the smile as she followed Nonny's instructions. She didn't eat seafood as a rule. It wasn't because of the octopus DNA; it was more because she craved it and she never gave in to that sort of thing—until Ezekiel.

She tried to stifle a yawn, her third one in the last fifteen minutes, but she was unsuccessful. She'd been with him two weeks now, and they'd fallen into a routine she really liked, other than the fact that she was always tired. Ezekiel woke her three, sometimes four times a night. Well, twice a night, but he never went to bed without sex and it was the first thing they did when they woke. Sometimes he woke her with his mouth on her already, sometimes they had shower sex. He was very inventive and she had the feeling they'd only begun to scratch the surface of his creativity.

"If you yawn again," Nonny said, "I'm going to box that man's ears."

Pepper and Cayenne nearly fell on the floor laughing. Bellisia turned bright red, and the triplets looked at one another.

"Box whose ears?" Ginger asked.

"What do you mean, box his ears?" Thym chimed in.

"I want to box someone's ears," Cannelle said.

"It means," Nonny explained, "that Uncle Ezekiel is keeping Bella up all night making her too tired for her cooking lessons and I'm going to smack his ears."

"That would hurt," Ginger said, covering her ears.

"I don't want you to do that to Uncle Ezekiel," Thym protested.

"I don't think Nonny would really do that," Cannelle said, her voice uncertain. "Would you, Nonny?"

"No, baby, I wouldn't box his ears, only threaten him with it," Nonny explained gently. "I'm really teasing Bella just a little bit. Now everyone help prepare the shrimp. We'll need two pounds."

The triplets watched the women and then tried to help. Bellisia noticed that no one stopped them; in fact, several times Nonny patiently explained how deveining was done, which was a good thing, as she'd never done it before.

"Brown the sausage in the skillet. I use about a pound most times, this time I did about a pound and a half, as we have several of the boys home." Nonny took the large cast-iron Dutch oven and set it on the stove. "Use medium-high heat, otherwise you'll burn the roux for sure. You have to watch what you're doing and continually whisk. If you get black specks, we have to start over. Use about a cup of good vegetable oil. When it's hot enough, stir in a cup of flour a bit at a time, whisking the entire time. Bella, you come try this." Even as she ordered Bellisia, she continued stirring to ensure the roux didn't burn.

"I killed it the first time," Pepper confided. "Seriously killed it. The entire pot turned black."

It was a little difficult to get close enough to the stove to take the whisk from Nonny with the three little girls dragging their stools over to peer into the Dutch oven, but she took her cue from Nonny and didn't protest. Clearly Nonny believed in allowing children to learn no matter how difficult their presence made things.

Bellisia was a good mimic and if she watched someone do something, she could repeat the action exactly, so it was easy to catch on to the motion of whisking the flour in the oil.

Cayenne made a face at her. "You're such a show-off."

Nonny snapped a tea towel at Cayenne, catching her on her bottom. The triplets erupted into gales of laughter when she yelped. "That's perfect, Bella. Pay no mind to Cayenne. She set my kitchen on fire."

The three girls nearly fell off their stools laughing, and Cayenne wrapped them in webs to prevent them from hitting the floor. "You little demons, I'm going to hang you upside down from a tree somewhere and let the spiders eat you for dinner."

Bellisia nearly dropped the whisk into the golden brown roux. She'd heard that Cayenne could produce spiderwebs, but she'd never seen her do it. The action had been smooth and fast, just a quick lift of her hands.

"It's okay, Bella," Ginger assured as she removed the webs. "Cayenne always says that, but she never does it." The other two girls nodded solemnly, clearly not wanting Bellisia upset as they removed the webs as well.

"It's ready," Nonny declared, not losing sight of what they were doing. "Add in the two cups of chopped onions, one cup each of chopped celery and bell pepper. I like to put in green onions, so Ginger sliced two cups of green onions to add as well. Thank you, Ginger, they're perfect."

Bellisia loved that Nonny praised the girls. Ginger looked pleased and the other two girls smiled at their sister, clearly proud of her.

"I chopped the garlic," Thym said. "Didn't I, Nonny? A fourth of a cup."

"You did, baby, and the garlic is perfect. Bella, please add that as well. Stir in the sausage while Pepper fries a half pound of chopped bacon for us. Make certain once it's cooked you drain it on paper towels the way we drained the sausage."

"I'm getting good at frying bacon, Bella," Pepper said, "but it took me a little while. Malichai and Mordichai tease me all the time because I burned so many things."

"The only way to learn is by doin', right, Nonny?" Ginger asked.

Bellisia smiled at the voice and accent. The girls were fast developing Nonny's mannerisms and that was a good thing. In Bellisia's mind there wasn't a better role model. She was teaching all three women how to raise children in a loving environment so they could thrive.

"That's right, Ginger. Cayenne, we need the claw crab-meat. We're adding in about a pound and a half of crab altogether. Cannelle helped with the claw meat, washing and preparing it. Thank you, honey, you did it just right."

That was the other thing that Nonny always did—she thanked the girls, acknowledging everything they did. She made outrageous threats, but she never raised her voice to the girls. Nonny was always patient with them and with the men going in and out of her kitchen grabbing food and teasing her with kisses to her cheeks.

"Pepper, add the bacon to the mixture. Bella, keep stirring. We'll cook this a little bit longer. Cayenne, do you have the shellfish stock ready? Three quarts of it? It should be very hot."

"Yes, ma'am," Cayenne said.

"In a minute you're going to start ladling the stock into

the pot. Bella, keep stirring constantly. I make my own stock and I can give you that recipe later. Don't stop, Bella, or it will be ruined," Nonny cautioned.

Bellisia stirred the hot stock into the mixture carefully, afraid she might ruin their meal, but she managed to keep clumps from forming. She couldn't help but smile when Nonny gave her approval. "Now we just reduce the heat to a low boil and set the timer for thirty minutes. We can take some strawberry lemonade out onto the porch before we finish it off and enjoy the evenin'. When we come back, we'll add spices. Bella, I'll have you fold in the lump crab and shrimp carefully. Sometimes I add oysters, but not this time." She nudged Bellisia. "There's far too much activity goin' on in the bedroom already to take a chance with oysters."

Another round of laughter went up. Pepper and Cayenne each lifted a little girl from the stools where they were standing, so Bellisia followed suit, catching Cannelle in her arms, swinging her around and setting her on her feet. Cannelle clung to her while the room spun and then followed her sisters out to the front porch.

Bellisia noted the porch seemed to be a favorite gathering place. Every night they rocked the girls before bedtime. Sometimes they told stories, sometimes they sang songs. They even played games, anything to spend time together. The men weren't shy about joining in. Ezekiel and his brother worked on Ezekiel's house with a few of the men during the day, but he was always there in the early evening, his arms around Bellisia, nuzzling her neck until Nonny threatened him and his fellow GhostWalkers howled with laughter. Even Donny came over once and joined in the evening's entertainment.

Bellisia loved that the children were never excluded. The adults didn't shield them from the dangers in the swamps, in fact, just the opposite; time and again, an adult took them out to show them plants or animals or traps. Even Donny talked to them about how to survive.

"Bellisia, did you know that moms have babies?" Ginger asked as she sat down on the porch stair.

"No, Ginger," Thym corrected, "girls have babies and they become moms."

"That's what I meant, Thym." Ginger glared at her sister. "It's rude to interrupt, right, Mommy?"

"I wasn't interrupting. I waited until you finished talking," Thym defended.

"The *point*," Ginger said, still glaring, "is that I want to know if Bella is going to have a baby."

Bellisia nearly spit a mouthful of lemonade out.

"Would Uncle Ezekiel be the father?" Cannelle asked.

Pepper and Cayenne nudged each other. "He'd better be," Pepper said. "If he isn't, Bella would have some explaining to do." The two women burst into laughter.

"I'm not having a baby right now," Bellisia explained. "Your uncle and I have just begun a relationship. It would be too soon . . ." She frowned, trailing off. They hadn't exactly been good about protection. She hadn't thought about protection. It wasn't like Whitney issued birth control pills. The women were locked in the dorms at night. Only the women taken to Italy to the program he ran there had to worry about pregnancies. It was something she needed to talk to Ezekiel about immediately. How could they both have forgotten something so important? She hadn't even considered the consequences, not even with the evidence of the triplets right in front of her.

"What's wrong, Bella?" Nonny asked, her voice low as she knocked ashes from her beloved pipe. Her husband had carved the pipe years earlier, and she was never without it. Her tobacco was a mixture of spices that Bellisia knew she would remember her entire life. It smelled like comfort.

"Nothing really. There's just so much to learn. When I was inside, my life wasn't my own. I couldn't make decisions for myself at all, everything was decided for me. It's so strange to be able to actually take charge of my life, but there are so many things I don't know to do, or forget that I should do."

Cannelle slipped her hand in Bellisia's and turned her face up, very solemn, all eyes and seriousness. "I'll help you, Bella. When we first came to Daddy's house, we didn't know how to do anything at all, but Nonny helped Mommy and my sisters and me. I can help you." She frowned and looked down at Bellisia's feet. "I would always forget shoes and socks. We always went barefoot, but Nonny says that's not good in the swamp. I'll help you remember about shoes."

Bellisia hugged her. "Thank you, honey. I really appreciate it. It's hard to remember everything, isn't it?"

All three girls nodded. They looked at one another and then at Pepper. "Can we go play in the playground Uncle Ezekiel, Uncle Mordichai and Uncle Malichai built for us, Mommy?" Ginger, the spokeswoman, asked.

"Of course. But stay in the playground area or come right back here," Pepper said. "It's going to be dark soon, so you come in when I call you."

The yard was set up to the left of the house, in plain sight of the porch. Bellisia could see swings and slides and a little playhouse, a replica of the Fontenot house, complete with a porch. "Ezekiel built that?"

Pepper nodded. "He loves the girls. He acts all gruff and tough in front of us, but he's very gentle with them. They crawl all over him and he never protests. He also sneaks them to one of the local grocers and gets them snowballs. He thinks I don't know, but it's rather obvious when they come back with blue or red tongues and smears of color all over their faces."

Cayenne burst out laughing. "He's such a tough guy."

"He sings to them," Bellisia said. "I think that's when I fell for him, listening to him sing to the girls. His wonderful stories and then his songs."

"He doesn't think we know that either," Pepper said. She ducked her head and then sent Nonny a quick, guilty look.

"When I first came here with Ginger, and Wyatt and the others rescued Thym and Cannelle, I had a difficult time trusting all of them with the children. I was so used to everyone wanting them dead."

"Never apologize for loving your children and looking after them," Nonny said.

Pepper sent her a quick, appreciative smile. "I followed Ezekiel and any of the others when they took the girls out of my sight. I learned, over time, that I could relax and let the others help me with them. Believe me, I need help with them. They're so smart, and what one doesn't think of, the others do."

"Even Trap is pretty good with them," Cayenne said. "And I never thought he'd ever be good with children. The girls love him though and they seem to understand him."

"Why wouldn't Trap like children?" Bellisia asked, puzzled. The triplets were a handful, but they were sweet and funny.

"He has difficulty reading people and he doesn't get social cues," Cayenne explained. "He's extremely intelligent, but he has something called Asperger's syndrome. It's a neurobiological disorder."

Pepper nodded. "It's on the higher end of the autism spectrum. Their IQs can be normal but typically are extremely high, yet they have trouble with social and communication skills."

Bellisia raised an eyebrow at Cayenne. "Is that hard to live with?"

Cayenne laughed softly and shook her head. "Not for me. Trap tends to communicate in the bedroom if he's upset or frustrated. That works for me. And I love him. Really, really love him. I have a tendency to think things over before I react, so we work. When he's not getting it, I have no problem telling him exactly what I want or need or what I'm feeling. I've learned, with him, that's best. The girls seemed to get it right off that he needs that."

"So when I meet him, I need to be prepared to be ruth-lessly honest with him."

Cayenne nodded. "Subtleties are lost on him. Com-pletely."

"Trap's a good man," Nonny declared and lit up her pipe. "Bellisia, run along into the kitchen and fold in the lump crab and shrimp. Turn the heat down a little more and we'll be all set for dinner later tonight when the men are ready for it."

Bellisia nodded and hurried back into the house. She had fallen in love with the Fontenot home and the people oc-cupying it. They were close, all of them, even the Ghost-Walker team. Nonny treated them all like her sons and daughters. She loved the feeling and wished the other women she'd grown up with were able to be there and feel the way Nonny made such a home for everyone.

Very carefully she folded in the crab and then the shrimp, taking her time, afraid she might mess up dinner. If she did, she knew Nonny and the women would just simply start over again, but the men would tease her unmercifully in the way they did both Pepper and Cayenne.

It was impossible not to love Pepper or the triplets. Pepper was—sweet. Her enhancements were extremely difficult to bear, but she handled them with grace. She had a bright, easy energy that shied away from violence. She'd confided to Bellisia that if she had to hurt or kill someone, her brain reacted with a bleed, much like an aneurism that might actu-ally kill her. She'd always had terrible, debilitating mi-graines if she was in a combat situation, but Wyatt and Trap had discovered her brain couldn't take the psychic overload. In some ways it had made her feel better about not being able to handle fighting—that there was an actual reason.

Cayenne and the men protected her in the way they did the triplets, not because Pepper asked for it, but because she needed it. She was always willing to stand with her family to protect the children and Nonny, but they wanted her used only as a last resort.

Several times Bellisia had noticed Pepper pressing her hand to her stomach and turning her face away as they were preparing the ingredients for dinner. In the end Pepper stayed at the sink, washing the dishes for the most part, stepping in occasionally to participate in the conversation and laughter, but she clearly wasn't feeling good.

Bellisia had asked her what was wrong, and she just shrugged and admitted that sometimes the smell of fish and seafood made her feel sick, but she wasn't about to tell Nonny that. Living around the bayous or swamps meant preparing and eating a lot of fish.

Bellisia caught the scent of spice and wood and turned her head quickly to see Ezekiel sneaking up on her. He wrapped his arms around her waist and buried his head in her neck.

"I love coming home to you." His teeth scraped back and forth and then he drew her skin into his mouth.

"Don't you dare put another mark on me, Ezekiel," she cautioned, not really caring if he did, but protesting anyway. She tipped her neck farther to one side, giving him better access. "Nonny gives me the hardest time."

Ezekiel took his time, enjoying the taste of her skin. The kitchen smelled like home and comfort, his woman smelled like his own personal piece of paradise. She tasted that way too. Vanilla and orange. The scent clung to her, the taste was on her skin and deep inside her, spilling out for him every morning or evening, or if he suddenly decided he just had to have her. Like now.

"I thought about you the entire time I was working," he confided, bunching her hair into his hand to get it off her nape. "Laying out the rooms and what we'd do in every one of them." He kissed his way along the back of her neck and down one shoulder. "I have to tell you, baby, mapping out a house on blueprints is very different when you're building the house for the person in your life who matters most."

He meant that. Having Bellisia had changed his entire

world. He hadn't realized he'd wanted a woman of his own so much until she'd shown up practically on his doorstep. He nuzzled her neck again just to inhale her scent and taste her skin.

"You say the sweetest things to me," Bellisia said. "I have to wash these dishes really quick. Nonny says it's better to clean as you go so you don't end up with a huge mess at the end of the evening when you're tired."

"Nonny's word is gold," he said, not in the least distracted from his task of seducing her. He doubted there would ever come a time when he didn't want to be inside her. Just thinking about her got him hard.

We have company coming, Zeke. Look alive. The warning came from his brother. *I'm up on the roof. Gino's in the trees.*

"Company, Bellisia," Ezekiel announced, all business. And if it was that fucking asshole Gerald coming to take her back with him, he'd already picked out a nice place to bury his body.

He was on the move, heading for the front porch, striding through the house fast with Bellisia right behind him. "Girls." He raised his voice as he stepped out onto the porch. "Come to me now." He wasn't kidding around and the triplets recognized his tone and the command signaling trouble. Pepper stood up and caught the railing, watching the girls anxiously.

"Nonny, keep your shotgun with you. You and Pepper take the girls to the safe room. You'll be first line of defense, Pepper second, if they penetrate."

"Who?" Cayenne asked.

"We don't know yet, but it could be the two sniffing around trying to find a trail to Bellisia." He should have gone hunting. He and Gino would have found the two men and taken them out quietly, but he'd respected Bellisia's wishes. He found he wanted to please her, make her happy, but he realized there were some things he couldn't do for her. He had a need to protect his own. He'd always been that way, the dark rage rising like a tidal wave sending him into a cold place where he did whatever needed doing to protect the people he loved.

No one other than Donny had reported two strangers asking questions other than at her work. She'd had to quit, of course, which she'd done reluctantly, but Ezekiel wasn't taking any chances. There were too many civilians, and he couldn't protect her out in the open like that. He knew the men hadn't left the area. There was no way they would. Joe had gotten service records on them. Both men had exceptional careers. They'd served countless missions and were decorated numerous times.

"Bellisia, into the river. Now. You don't come out until I give you the all clear. If it's a firefight, do you have a weapon?"

"Always. I always carry a Glock, the ammo's sealed. It will survive the water. I have a knife, and I'm good, although after seeing Draden and Gino fooling around with one, maybe not so much. I also hid an assault rifle in the bank, completely sealed in a watertight case."

"You're golden then, baby. If we're attacked . . ." She had to know there would be no protecting Gerald and Adam if they came looking.

She hooked her arm around his neck, pulling his head down to hers. Her lips brushed his, as she whispered a soft promise. "I'll kill them, Ezekiel. This is my family now. All of you come first for me."

Before he could catch her up in his arms the way he wanted, she was gone, running lightly down the stairs and across the yard. As she ran, her skin and hair seemed to disappear, blending in with her surroundings. Then she dove off the pier and vanished completely in the water.

He could breathe easier then. He knew she was safe in the river. No one could get to her in the water, and she was a weapon no one would expect. She hadn't so much as trembled. She was like Cayenne, a complete warrior and one he could count on.

Five men dressed in suits with Senator Violet Smythe. Looks like trouble, Mordichai reported. *I've got them covered from the roof.*

Covered from the trees. That was Gino.

I'm in position just to the south of them, Draden said.

We're circling to come in behind them, Diego said. *Gino, Draden, do you see us? Don't want you hitting Rubin or me accidentally.*

I see you, Gino reported.

Eyes on you, Draden said.

Ezekiel was pleased with the layout. Even if Violet and her mercenaries were aware seven GhostWalkers were home as well as Cayenne and Pepper, they couldn't be certain about Bellisia. They would have the advantage no matter what.

"Cayenne, can you get up onto the porch roof just above where they'll come up the stairs? You could drop a net over them or cast one if you needed to. I don't want you seen, and you'll need enough cover if there's a firefight." Cayenne was deadly accurate with her webs and lethal with her bite if needed.

"No problem. I've been up there several times for recon. They won't see me," she reassured.

He caught her shoulder as she reached up to make the climb. "Trap won't survive it if something happens to you. You're his entire world." He didn't have to ask her to help. Cayenne would give her life protecting Nonny, the triplets and Pepper, but he still wanted to caution her. She had never been a team player and took chances. Trap had worked with her on that, and hopefully he'd gotten through to her that she couldn't risk herself in a fight. She sent him a small grin, nodded and was up the side of the porch and on the overhang in seconds. That was all he was going to get from her, but he hoped it would be enough.

All in all, they worked together in under three minutes, getting the civilians under cover and placing his team in the best positions possible. There would be a rifle on every one of Violet's mercenaries.

Their team leader walked up very slowly, his expression unreadable. "It's definitely the senator, Ezekiel. Violet. She's got five men with her, presumably all mercenaries, although she's got them dressed in monkey suits. They aren't Secret Service. She's a vice president–elect and should have them guarding her, but she's come with her own men."

Ezekiel gave Joe a small, grim smile. "Could mean she came without anyone knowing. Not good for her."

Joe shook his head. "Let's hear what she has to say."

Ezekiel studied his teammate's face. Joe Spagnola was a man everyone could count on. He never left anyone behind in the field no matter how bad the circumstances. Once, he'd carried a wounded man on his back, running down a steep slope, gunfire all around him, trusting Ezekiel to protect him. Ezekiel had, but when Joe got the wounded Ranger to safety, they discovered he'd been hit at the same time. He'd run on sheer iron will. That was Joe.

Something was wrong. "You have a reason for not taking her out?"

"Like her being a United States senator and a vice president–elect?"

Joe sounded sarcastic, but Ezekiel wasn't buying it. There was a hollow note in Joe's voice, something off-key. He just nodded and stepped back, allowing his team leader to take the reins.

Violet was a beautiful woman and she knew it. A powerful presence, tall with a good figure, she walked between five big men, but all eyes would always be drawn to her. She wore a form-fitting red jacket over a white blouse and black trousers. The red suited her, adding a vibrancy that might not have been there. Ezekiel couldn't fault her on her confidence. She walked right up to them, coming from the road where they'd parked their vehicle down from the Fontenot property.

He had to wonder why they'd done that. Why not just drive up in the big SUV with its tinted windows? She'd look just as powerful. So why the walk, especially in her fancy boots with the heel? Had she hoped to surprise them? Something wasn't right. He didn't like anything that didn't make sense.

Something's off. They walked in, but parked the car down from the property. Why would she do that?

Joe glanced at him sharply, but didn't reply. That bothered Ezekiel as well. Joe never missed anything. Ezekiel had the feeling he hadn't even noticed or thought about how she'd arrived, and that made even less sense.

I'm on it, Zeke, Gino said.

I could take her out right now, Mordichai informed them. *I have a perfect shot. Just say the word.* He didn't sound like his usual dispassionate self. Clearly he was holding a grudge against the woman who had sold them out to Cheng.

Do not take the shot, Joe commanded.

She's the reason those hostages were taken in Indonesia. She's the reason my brother was tortured.

Ezekiel allowed himself a small sigh of relief. At least the others were acting as usual.

I don't need a reminder of her sins, Joe snapped.

That was a *serious* red flag. This time Ezekiel didn't look at Joe, afraid his expression would give him away.

"Senator Smythe," Joe greeted as the group stopped just short of the stairs. "You should have called ahead. We could have arranged security for you."

The men with her bristled but she shot them a quelling look and no one spoke. "I didn't want anyone to know I've come," Violet replied softly, looking almost demure. Her voice was sinful, a definite sweet-sounding deception. "I needed to speak with you."

"You should have called me. I would have come to you. Do you have any idea how dangerous it is for you to dodge your security? They aren't going to be happy with you."

She indicated the men surrounding her. "I brought my own. In any case, the Secret Service agent assigned to me thinks I'm safely in my home. No one knows I slipped my leash."

"Violet." Joe shook his head. "Someone always knows."

A shadow crossed her face and her head jerked up. "What does that mean?"

"It means you can't run off anytime you feel like it, and nothing you do is secret."

Ezekiel held his breath. If Joe sold out Bellisia, by admitting to Violet they knew she'd gone to Cheng, he had no idea what he'd do. Take out his gun and shoot both Violet and Joe? He shifted slightly to give himself a little cover from her five bodyguards. His team would open up on them and he had no doubt Bellisia had them in her sights as well. What the hell was going on with Joe?

"I'm sorry, Joe." Violet's voice dropped to a hushed whisper. Intimate. Beguiling. That was her gift. She could persuade a roomful of hardened senators to vote just the way she wanted them to. She could convince leaders of nations to do as she wished.

Ezekiel felt his heart jerk in his chest. Clearly, Joe and Violet knew each other outside of the rare times the team had encounters with her. His heart sank. *Who is she to you?* he had to ask, but he already knew. Joe would never act like he was, protective and almost gentle with her. He took another step back, putting himself in the shadows.

Joe didn't answer, nor did he look at Ezekiel, although he had to have sensed the movement behind him. "Violet, what are you doing here?" His voice was weary, filled with a kind of anguish he didn't try to cover.

She stepped closer, put one booted foot on the stairs. "I want you to come head my private security. You can have anything you want. Recruit your own people, within reason." Her voice had dropped an octave so that it played over a man's senses, making him want to give her anything she asked for. She moved up the stairs until she could put a hand on Joe's chest, looking up at him with pleading eyes. "Just

not those insects or vipers. We have to get rid of them, Joe.
You can do that for me, can't you?"

She turned her head to smile at Ezekiel. "You would be
welcome. Just help Joe get rid of the insects." She gave a
delicate little shudder. "I find them so frightening. Such
abominations. They crawl around killing people with a bite.
They aren't human. Whitney should never have conducted
such horrendous experiments." She sounded totally reasonable, her voice persuasive. "We can't allow those women to
be let loose on the world." She lowered her voice as if telling
them a secret. "They have children. Vipers. And they could
have more. You know what ants do? And cockroaches?
There are millions of them, billions. We can't have that."

Ezekiel looked right past the woman who had sold out her
country to the five men behind her. They clearly were completely enamored with her. More, they believed her declara-
tions. *If she makes speeches like this when she's in the White
House, we'll all be in trouble.* It was true. Fanaticism had a
smell to it, and Violet and her bodyguards reeked of it.

"Joe." Now Violet stepped right up onto the porch. Joe
didn't take a step back so she was pressed against him
tightly. She cupped the side of his jaw. "I need you to do this
one little thing for me. Wipe out this nest and then come
work for me. I need your protection. I do, my love. No one
is strong enough to stand up to me the way you do. Only
you, Joe. Please. I really need you with me."

Ezekiel closed his eyes. It was clear that Joe and Violet
knew each other and had an intimate relationship. Violet's
psychic gift of that beautiful, persuasive voice didn't work
on Ezekiel, but he had no idea if it worked on Joe. He
couldn't warn the others, but his fingers closed around the
butt of his gun.

Activity at the car, Draden reported. *Three more of her
beefy mercs just rolled out and slipped into the trees. Another vehicle came in on the southern entrance. At least six
men there, might be more. They came out fast. I caught a*

glimpse of what I think is a third on the other side of the
road leading to Trap's. This is a setup.

Don't see a fourth vehicle, but more men creeping in
from the swamp, Gino announced.

Violet had come prepared to wipe out Pepper, Cayenne
and the triplets if Joe didn't do it for her. Ezekiel could see
her waiting, certain of her power over the men.

Joe sighed and cupped her face in his hands. "Why didn't
you kill Whitney? You've had the chance so many times,
Violet. Why is it you never do it?" His voice was gentle, his
thumbs tender as they moved gently over her cheeks.

15

~

Violet stood very still, looking up into Joe's face. She opened her mouth twice and then closed it, shaking her head. Clearly the question was the last thing she expected. It took her by surprise and she clearly didn't know how to answer.

"Joe."

Ezekiel winced at the pure sensuality, the intimacy in that softly whispered name. Violet sounded as if the two were alone in a bedroom, not there surrounded by others who might overhear.

Her bodyguards looked at one another, one, a burly man with lots of muscle, scowling. He stepped right up to the porch stairs, one hand inside his jacket. Ezekiel drew out his weapon very slowly and held it in his hand, ready to fire, but hiding it low across his body.

Joe shook his head, ignoring the fact that Violet's bodyguard was clearly a threat. Ezekiel would bet his last dollar that the man shared the senator's bed. He was posturing, exhibiting signs of jealousy. Violet never spared him a single glance. Her gaze was eating Joe up, for him alone, as if she was so enamored with him she couldn't see anyone but him. If Ezekiel had been susceptible to her voice, he would have believed everything he was hearing and seeing.

Joe's hands slid almost lovingly up her arms. "No, Violet. This time, give me a real answer. Why haven't you killed Whitney? You say you think he's lost his mind. You say it often enough that everyone in your employ believes you. Hell, *I* believe you, but you don't kill him. No one else gets close to you. You could do it and you know it."

She shook her head. "I can't, Joe. I've tried. I want to. I want someone to do it, but I can't do it myself."

"You don't want someone else to do it," he said patiently. "If you did, you would have told me where to find him and asked me to do it for you."

"No. Never. I would never risk you."

"Even if that was true, Violet, you would have given one of the GhostWalker teams his location and let us kill him, but you didn't. You know we could get in and out without being caught. You let him pack up the women he's holding prisoner . . ."

For the first time, Violet's mask of sweet sensuality slipped. She looked almost ugly, just for a moment. "They aren't prisoners," she spat. She took a breath and once again looked almost hauntingly beautiful. "Love, don't believe that. Don't believe anything those women say. They want sympathy and try to get it from you and the other men, but don't listen to them. They aren't prisoners any more than I am. They work for the government just like you do. Just like him." She gestured toward Ezekiel.

Joe refused to be distracted. "Why didn't you kill him, Violet?"

"You have to understand." Her voice went to a low, musical plea. "To be in a situation where I can do good, good for the entire world, not just for a few women who are unhappy with their lot, I have to be in a certain position. I'm almost there. I need his money. His connections. Until I can replace that money and the connections . . ."

There it was. Violet craved power and she was willing to sell her fellow sister GhostWalkers, the men in the program and anyone else in her way to get what she wanted. She wanted the presidency. Ezekiel believed that once in power, the president would die and Violet would take over. Her plan was very, very close to working. He could only hope that Joe would believe the evidence from the woman's own mouth.

"I want you with me. Do it, right now, Joe. Walk into that house and kill those hideous creatures and come home with me."

Joe shook his head. "That's never going to happen, Violet." Something in her eyes made him start to pull back, his hands sliding from her arms up toward her throat.

They're trying to get into the house from the back. Mordichai's rifle barked. Once. Twice.

Violet gasped, her hands reaching toward Joe's face, the blade of a knife she'd concealed up her sleeve flashing as she slashed it across his cheek, down his chest and then slammed it into his gut. She leapt back and kicked the hilt viciously, driving it deep as she threw herself sideways off the stairs. When she kicked him, she angled the kick so his body would stagger back into Ezekiel. Clearly she'd planned out every move in her mind, carrying it out over and over until it was time to put her plan into action.

The bodyguard on the stair drew his gun, stepping back to try to cover Violet's escape. Cayenne dropped a net of webs over him as he fired at Ezekiel. Joe lunged across his teammate as his body fell toward the floor, taking the bullet meant for Zeke and knocking him down as well.

Ezekiel fired as he was falling, killing the guard behind the one wrapped in webs. Two rifles shot simultaneously and two more of Violet's guards went down. Cayenne's webs spun the first guard up so tight he appeared to be a mummy

on the ground. The sack rose up in the air, so that he hung
macabrely, swinging back and forth like a bad Halloween
decoration. His finger on the trigger, the guard fired wildly
and without direction. He couldn't move, couldn't turn his
head and couldn't see anything. Mordichai's rifle spoke
again and the guard went slack, his automatic silenced as it
fell from his hands into the web.

Ezekiel rolled out from under Joe's dead weight, cursing
Violet, trying to get a decent chance at a shot. She was
halfway to the river, running low. Three more men cut between Zeke and Violet, protecting her as she ran. His bullet
hit one, spinning him around as he threw his body in front
of the fleeing woman. Mordichai took out one of the men
and Diego shot the other.

The last bodyguard gained the porch with a leap, his gun
dead center on Ezekiel's chest. The whine of several bullets
sounded like angry bees swarming, and the big man was
flung into the porch railing, his body jerking. Ezekiel recognized the sound of a Glock firing. His woman, watching
his back. He turned to look down at Joe, for the first time
seeing the terrible wounds to his body.

*Shit. Shit. Draden. Get here any way you can. Right the
fuck now. OR room in the house. Pepper, set up for surgery.
I'll need you or Nonny. Mordichai, Gino, I'm taking him in
now. Keep them off of me.* He kept his voice as calm as
possible when Joe was dying right in front of him. He
crouched low and put his mouth against Joe's ear. "Don't
you fuckin' die on me. We need you. You understand me?
You fight. Don't give Whitney the satisfaction." He lifted
him as gently as possible. Waiting. Counting heartbeats.

Go. Go. Mordichai and Gino began firing, taking out
targets in the front, giving Ezekiel the moments needed to
carry Joe into the house and for Draden to race in after him.
They rushed down the hallway straight to the small operating room Wyatt Fontenot had set up a couple of years earlier.

Pepper and Nonny were there already, Pepper scrubbed and began to lay out the medical instruments.

"We've got blood stored for him," Ezekiel snapped over his shoulder as he laid Joe on the table and ripped open his shirt. "Get it now, Pepper. Hurry."

Nonny was there, removing boots and cutting off blood-stained jeans. "I've got this. Go scrub."

Draden had equipment set up in minutes, getting veins, and helping to prep his team leader for surgery.

~

We're three men down, Mordichai announced. *Violet's mercs are everywhere. Gino, you take the ones in the woods coming in to the left side of the house. I don't have a visual on them.*

They were three men down just that fast. The enemy had several teams moving in and that meant four GhostWalkers, Cayenne and the unknown Bellisia had to keep them off the house.

On it. Gino never had much to say. He was a hunter and he felt right at home in the swamp.

I'm more effective in the trees, Cayenne said.

Negative. I need you here, Mordichai insisted. *I think the teams closing in on either side of the house and in front are distractions to allow others to slip inside from the back. I know there are three more back there.* He'd taken out three, but the other three had managed to get into positions he couldn't see from his location and they could gain the house from the back entrance. *Cayenne. I don't have eyes on the targets. Can you get to the back of the house?*

Moving now. Cayenne was up and running in a low crouch over the rooftop. She blew past Mordichai's position and across the roof to the other side. She dropped down onto the ground, landing in a crouch, and rolled to her left. Bullets spat on the ground where she landed, but she was already in the thicker brush.

You have three targets, Cayenne. I can't cover you. We've got men pouring in from the north and south.

I'm good, Cayenne assured grimly—and she was. She was engineered to be an assassin. Silent and deadly she crept through the brush. She was small in order to get into those places the bigger men couldn't fit. More, they wouldn't think anyone else could. She kept her breathing very shallow, barely there, as she moved along the ground, using toes and fingers to pull her body forward.

Nonny, Pepper and the three little girls had become family to her over the last few weeks with her new husband. Cayenne knew both Nonny and Pepper would defend the children with their last breaths, but Nonny was in her eighties and Pepper's body was too fragile from the enhancements. Whitney and one of the scientists he'd employed had removed so many filters from Pepper's brain that anytime she was around violence, she got brain bleeds. No one had counted on their perfect assassin having such a flaw. Cayenne wasn't about to let the enemy close to Pepper and force her to have to defend the girls. Right now, she was certain both women were occupied helping Ezekiel and Draden save Joe.

She smelled sweat just off to her left. A twig snapped just feet away. She lay very still and waited, letting him come close to her. Another snap and his boot came into view. She looped a web around his ankle, loose, so he wouldn't notice, and continued to loop until she had a strong, unbreakable rope. He took a step and then a second. The second step tripped him and he went down hard, throwing his hands out in front of him to break his fall.

She was on him in seconds, delivering the fatal bite and then scooting back into the brush before he knew what happened. He had no idea he was already dead and that every thrash of his body, every wild pump of his heart only speeded up the inevitable. He didn't realize he'd been bitten. Over time she'd learned exactly how to deliver the venom with no more than what felt like a small pinch or sting.

One down.

The second soldier was at the window to one of the back bedrooms. He was trying to lift it without making noise while the third soldier guarded his back. Cayenne broke cover to the left of them, scurrying around the side of the house with blurring speed, leapt and was up on the roof in seconds. Silently, she crept across the roof until she was just above them.

The third soldier sensed movement, but by the time he'd turned his head toward the brush, she was already above his head. Cayenne didn't fool herself into thinking it was going to be easy. She had to get her net just right and spin fast. She dropped it over both of them, but just as it fell, the guard at the window leaned into the house. The web completely enmeshed the third soldier, and she jerked hard on the silken lines, spinning him fast, encasing him tighter and tighter so that he spun in the air as she raised him.

The soldier leaning into the window pulled back when he saw his buddy yanked upward and then he dove inside. Cayenne flung silk at his ankle, a loop that she pulled tight and wrapped over and over. Her silk was strong, stronger even than normal spider silk, stronger than Kevlar, and she was well versed in using it. She spent hours every day spinning beautiful artwork and practicing using it as a weapon. All that practice didn't let her down. She used the enshrouded body of the soldier to climb down, keeping the cocoon between her and her prey.

She kept looping the ankle with more and more silk before she yanked hard and dropped into a crouch on the ground. The leg of the soldier emerged. He stuck his gun out of the window and fired blindly over and over, striking the body of his friend so that droplets of blood ran down the silk shroud, turning it red, and the man's hoarse screams abruptly ceased.

Cayenne stayed beneath the window, but continued to manipulate the silk by just reading the vibrations alone. She kept adding silk and yanking on it, tightening it and dragging the soldier's leg farther out the window. He planted his other foot hard against the wall in an effort to keep from being drawn outside. The gunfire ceased and she felt him sawing at the silk with a knife, cutting desperately through the strands as fast as he could.

She kept tension on the threads as she slowly stood up into a crouch. She had to deliver the venom into his skin. He wore boots, so she needed to inflict the bite above the boot without getting shot. She had to be fast. She took a breath and moved into him, throwing silk at his face as she injected the venom into him. She felt the sharp burn of a blade slicing through her shoulder and down her arm and then she dropped away, breathing through the fiery pain.

He'd gotten her good. She was losing blood. A lot of it. *Need stitches. It's a bad cut. I'm coming into the house through the back window in Wyatt's old room. No one shoot me.* She dove through the window, ignoring the man lying on the floor, eyes wide open, gasping for breath. The toxin was already doing its job, shutting down his nervous system so that he couldn't move and soon wouldn't be able to breathe.

"I'm all you've got," Nonny said, the shotgun in her hands aimed at the soldier on the floor. "Ezekiel, Draden and Pepper are fighting to keep Joe alive. Let me see."

～

Rubin and Diego Campo had hunted together almost from the time they were toddlers. They weren't twins, but they could have been. They were both just a quarter of an inch shy of six feet. They had wide shoulders and lean bodies, both all muscle. Their brown hair was in a perpetual state of needing to be cut, and both had firm jaws that always had a faint shadow and very dark, nearly black eyes.

Ten months apart, they grew up hunting and fishing for food in the Appalachian Mountains. Their father died in a fall from a horse, their main form of transportation, when they were seven, leaving their mother with nine children and little else other than their land.

Already showing astonishing promise, the two boys discovered a spring up above their house when they were out hunting rabbit. By the time they were eight they'd figured out how to bring that water, using gravity, to their cabin and for the first time, they had running water in the house.

That same spring, the two oldest boys left, looking for work at only fourteen and fifteen. They never returned. Rubin and Diego had no idea what happened to them. They were nine years old when Mary left to marry a man on the small farm next to them. She was only sixteen and died in childbirth nine months later. Their mother didn't smile again after that.

They were ten when they figured out how to make a generator. It was the first time their mother ever had electricity and hot water. The next summer, several men hiked the Appalachian Trail and camped just past their land. Lucy, their twelve-year-old sister, was night fishing with the eight-year-old, Jayne. They didn't come home. Rubin and Diego went looking for them. They found Lucy's body half in and half out of the stream, her clothes ripped off of her and blood under her fingernails. Their little sister Jayne lay beside her, her head bleeding from where someone had struck a terrible blow. Her clothes were torn off as well. She was drooling and not making any sense and when she saw her brothers, she screamed and screamed.

Rubin took Jayne home and collected their rifles while Diego stayed to look for tracks. They left their sister's body to be seen to by their mother and two older sisters, Ruby and Star, the thirteen-year-old twins. They caught up with the four men the second night and shot two of them. They didn't waste bullets because they couldn't afford it. Two shots, two dead. The other men hid, but early the next morning, they were dead as well. The boys didn't bother to bury the bodies. The vultures could have them. They were many miles from their run-down shack, and by the time someone did find the bodies, there would be no tracks leading back to them.

The flu hit the winter they were thirteen. Ruby, their mother and Jayne all came down with it. They buried Jayne first. Three days later Ruby died. Their mother never spoke a single word after that. She sat in a chair and rocked back and forth, humming songs and refusing to eat no matter how much Star coaxed her.

They came home from hunting to find Star sobbing and their mother's body swinging from a rope right in the middle of their miserable cabin. They were only fourteen. It was left to them to cut her down and bury her alongside her husband and children.

They woke the next morning to find a note from their sister explaining that she couldn't stay. She'd gone to the nuns in the next town over. Rubin and Diego packed what little they had and hopped the train leading out of the mountains. They rode the rails for days, staying hidden until they got off in a big city thinking they could find work. It was a terrible mistake. There were no jobs and no home. They couldn't hunt or fish. Everyone they loved left them. Not a single person cared whether they lived or died. And then they'd run into Ezekiel Fortunes.

Crouching low in the trees, they listened to the whisper of the ground. They could track anything. Find anything. Both could make a bomb out of almost anything and take one apart even faster. Rubin signaled to his brother and the two split, Rubin moving around to get in front of the house. He slung his rifle over his shoulder, reached up and jumped for a branch a good five feet over his head. He pulled himself up and climbed a little higher until he found the perfect branch.

Gunfire broke out here and there. It was easy to tell the GhostWalkers from Violet's mercenaries. The Ghost-Walkers only shot when they had a target in sight. One single shot and it was a kill. The mercenaries sprayed the swamp and surrounding area with automatic weapons when the wind blew and they heard noises. They'd been told the GhostWalkers wouldn't be seen and they were experiencing that phenomenon.

Diego began his move, coming up behind the six men spread out and stealthily working their way through the grove of trees to the side of the house. The brush was thick here and old cypress roots jutted up all over the ground as the impressive trees rose high and thick. Moss hung in long veils, shrouds of grayish green, from the numerous limbs twisting toward the sky.

He came up behind one of the men, his knife sinking into the kidney and then across the throat. He dropped the body and was gone just as his brother's rifle spoke. A second member of Violet's team went down. Instantly the remaining four went back-to-back, spraying the forest around them with bullets. Rubin was safe, high up in the tree, calmly sighting in on another. He squeezed the trigger and his target went down. The moment the forest went quiet, Diego shot his second enemy and rolled.

Diego had already chosen his next man and he moved around forward, trying to get behind him, using his toes and elbows to propel him through the thick brush. The two remaining enemy fired into the forest again, a concentrated volley, laying down a river of bullets all along the path where Diego had been. One clipped his leg, and another hit his arm. He heard the sound of his brother's rifle and another body dropped. The remaining mercenary turned away from the house and began to run toward Diego, in the direction of his vehicle. Diego shot him through the heart and then crawled his way to a tree. He sat there waiting for his brother.

Gino Mazza sank down onto his belly and put his ear to the ground, listening to what the earth had to say. He raised his head and inhaled deeply through his nose, taking in the smells all around him. He was a hunter. An elite hunter. There were few in the world who could match his skills and even fewer who could escape him. He was two inches under six feet and all muscle. He had very dark hair, nearly black, and some said his eyes matched his hair, just as dark. He rarely smiled, although Wyatt's three little girls had been known to make him laugh upon occasion.

He'd been born into an extremely wealthy family and somewhere in some bank he had enough money to buy and sell a small country. By now, he was certain, a large country. He'd inherited from his grandparents on his father's side, then his grandparents on his mother's side, then his mother and lastly, his father. They were good people, all of them. Kind. Generous. Loving. Devoted to Gino. All the money in the world hadn't saved them from the kidnappers who had come to their residence during the celebration of Gino's twelfth birthday. His family had fought back and they had been killed. They stood in front of him, refusing to give in to the demands, even as one by one they were executed. Gino carried the scars from the bullets that had torn his world apart. He'd been shot three times and left for dead. Fire had been set to the mansion.

It had been his friend Joe Spagnola who had rushed into a burning building and pulled out his bloody, nearly dead body. Joe's family had taken him in. They were very different from Gino's family. They had money, but they also had high fences and guard dogs. Men with guns patrolling their grounds. Joe was sent to the best schools and Gino went with him. They were also required to learn everything martial arts, boxing and street fighting along with every weapon Joe's father could conceive of.

➥ It had been Joe's father who had tracked down the kidnappers. They'd died hard and it had taken them a long time to do so. Gino had watched and learned. He'd learned a lot about the business Joe's father was in, and then they were

sent away to college. Joe's father had served in the Marines
with Sergeant Major Theodore Griffen and encouraged both
his son and Gino to do the same. Both did, although they
chose the Air Force and the medical field. They both qualified for the GhostWalker program and Joe joined, Gino following right behind him.

Gino found the first man signaling to his buddy to stop
just to the right of the Fontenot home. They were close to
it, closer than Gino would like. No one was getting into that
house where the women were. Where Joe had been taken
for surgery. The mercenary closest to the house nodded,
unslung a bag and dropped it quietly to the ground. He
passed several grenades to his partner and pulled out a block
of C-4. Things were getting serious.

He rose up and threw a knife. It was small, the blade
barely two inches, but perfectly weighted and accurate. The
knife hit the jugular of the man with the grenades, sank
deep, and Gino threw the second one. It was a one-two
throw, one he'd practiced thousands of times. It was rare for
him to miss, and he didn't now. Both men went down, and
Gino was on them to finish them before either could pull a
pin on the grenades, or worse, retaliate with the explosive.

Mordichai fired his weapon and Gino heard the thud
behind him as one of the mercenaries fell. Gino kept moving
forward. The most important thing in his world right then
was to keep these men off the house. He followed the scent
of sweat to the next three mercenaries. They were back in
the trees waiting for the explosion they were certain would
come. They were ten feet apart, down on one knee, automat-
ics aimed toward the house. He was relatively certain the
three were supposed to be guarding the backs of the explosive team, and yet they didn't even know they were down.

He was a ghost, earning him the nickname Phantom, and
he utilized his ability to move in silence, coming up behind
the first of the three. He took them out one by one and not
once did one of them see it coming. He slid back into the

forest and began a sweep for any strays as occasionally he heard the bark of Mordichai's rifle.

～

Bellisia hit the river and swam quickly to the bank where she'd stashed a rifle but she didn't pull it free. She had her Glock on her. Staying low, she watched Violet approach the house with her five bodyguards. It sucked not being able to hear what was being said, but Violet's body language spoke volumes. She was all over the GhostWalker team leader, Joe Spagnola, and his body language was clearly protective. They had a relationship. Bellisia had missed that when she'd been investigating Violet, and she'd watched her for a while. The woman had several lovers, including one or more of her bodyguards.

Ezekiel hadn't relaxed, and he could hear every word being said. He slipped back into the shadows just as she felt the vibration of a swamp boat in the water. They weren't running the engine full out. In fact, it was barely chugging along. She could tell it was a swamp boat by the way it moved through the water. For a moment she was indecisive, needing to stay right where she was to protect the others. If the craft coming toward the Fontenot pier held more enemies, they needed to know.

Just as she began to duck beneath the water to swim toward the moving craft, shots rang out, Mordichai firing twice in rapid succession. She turned back, stroking hard to propel herself back to the bank, all the while watching in horror as Violet slashed Joe to ribbons. It was the last thing any of them, Bellisia included, expected.

Violet might order a hit. She might bring a dozen teams to wipe out the female GhostWalkers and their children, she might even stand by impassively and watch one of them being tortured, but her record was spotlessly clean. If she'd ever harmed another person, hands on, it wasn't recorded anywhere, and Bellisia, for all her research, had never come across such a thing.

Whitney had given Bellisia access to Violet's training. Like all the girls he had acquired as orphans, she had studied how to fight. She had weapons training and extensive hand-to-hand, but she hadn't excelled in either. She'd been paired with Edward Freeman, a young up-and-coming politician whose father had gone to school with Whitney. Both wanted the presidency for Edward. She had seemed devoted to him, but even then, the two of them were always surrounded by bodyguards. She had never had to actually fight off the assassins—another GhostWalker team had done that.

Violet leapt off the porch and Bellisia lifted the Glock as the senator ran toward the river in a crouch. One of the bodyguards fired at Ezekiel, but Joe threw his body in front of him and the two went down, Ezekiel firing at the guard. The firefight erupted in seconds, and she had a choice of shooting Violet or another bodyguard threatening Ezekiel's life. She chose saving Ezekiel. She pulled the trigger and the guard went down. Two more men got in the way of her shot, running with Violet. Bullets flung them back and away. Violet didn't even so much as glance at them as she dove into the river.

Bellisia waited to make certain that no one else threatened Ezekiel. She saw him clearly giving orders. She wasn't telepathic, but she could feel the energy when the others talked. One or two of them were strong and could build a bridge to the others. She wasn't a part of that yet. Still, she could feel it in her brain like a fluttering of annoying wings, and in her ears, the buzzing of bees. Then he was lifting Joe and kicking at the front door. Draden ran out from under cover. Mordichai fired and she did as well to keep three men off of him as he sprinted for the relative safety of the house. She hit one man, Mordichai the other two.

She had no doubt the team could take care of whatever Violet had unleashed on them. In the meantime, she had one goal. She tossed the Glock onto the bank and turned and dove under the water. Violet had a head start, but she was fast and she had a good idea where Violet was heading. Sure enough, the vibrations of the boat became stronger and the engine picked up speed. It was coming toward the pier, still around the bend.

Bellisia streaked through the water as fast as possible. She'd been in the river several times and knew where every snag was. That knowledge aided her as she took every opportunity to try to find the boat before Violet was in it and gone. It made sense that the boat would head out on the river to Lake Borgne. Once out of the immediate area, Violet could take whatever plane she'd used to return home and sneak in as if she'd never left. Her Secret Service agent would attest to the fact that he'd put her in her house and she'd never left. It was imperative that Bellisia catch the boat before it took off for the lake.

She rounded the corner and saw two men leaning down, helping Violet into the swamp boat. She put on a burst of speed just as they dragged her inside and she fell gasping for breath.

"Go. Go," Violet ordered. "Get me out of here." There was suppressed fury in her voice.

Bellisia caught at the side of the craft just below the water line and attached herself as the powerful motor revved up and the boat spun around, spraying water into the air. She began to climb slowly, one hand sticking while she inched upward with the other. It was difficult, even with her strength. The boat was going so fast it slammed the surface hard, making it bounce. Several times they had to slow to get their bearings. She took advantage, peering over the edge. She was behind the man driving. The others looked forward toward their destination.

She slipped over the edge into the boat, her body taking on the color and texture of the wet floorboards. Violet sat on the padded bench seat, her body leaning forward, silently urging the craft to greater speeds. They were a good way from Lake Borgne. Bellisia moved behind the man driving and then around him, inch by slow inch. No one looked her way, but she wasn't taking any chances.

"Are we being followed?" Violet shouted over the roar of the motor.

The man sitting on the other side of the seat shook his head. "I don't think so. The last report was, quite a few of them were trying to save Spagnola. You must have done a number on him."

Bellisia saw Violet's fingers curl into a fist. The glint of a blade lay along her wrist just inside the sleeve of her jacket. She carried two blades and her training on knives had been extensive, but she had been a poor student. She'd slashed Joe's face, not his jugular. She'd cut across his chest and shoved the blade in his gut. But she could have cut the arteries in his legs or done much more damage as fast as she'd been. She had forgotten her training—or she wanted Ezekiel and Draden to be taken out of the fight.

Violet's reasoning didn't matter to Bellisia. Making her body as small as possible, she slipped under the overhang of the seat and continued her forward movement until she was right under Violet. The hem of the senator's trousers hiked up just enough to show skin above her short ankle boots. Bellisia had to do this right—deliver the venom without Violet becoming aware she did so. The injection had to be painless or at least so easy Violet wouldn't recognize she'd been bitten.

The man just across from Violet spoke into his radio over and over. "I can't raise anyone. For a minute I thought someone screamed."

The driver laughed. "Maybe they managed to kill those little vipers."

The distraction worked. Violet turned in her seat to face the others. As she did so, Bellisia allowed the venom to rise. She scratched Violet's ankle deep enough that it drew blood, but shallow enough that it was no more than a brief sting and then gone. Violet jerked her ankle but didn't look down.

"I hope so, Nate. I can't stand the thought of more snakes or spiders running around. They were supposed to be terminated, the entire bunch of them. The orders were given but never carried out. We should have dropped a bomb on that house." She ground out the words, pouring hatred into them.

Bellisia spat into her hand and allowed the venom to drip into the open wound. She waited a moment to be certain enough entered the tiny laceration to kill. She attached herself to the bottom of the seat and waited.

"They'll get them, Senator," the driver assured. "We hit them when they weren't expecting it and very few of them were there to protect the hideous creatures."

"It was a shame to have to sacrifice Joe Spagnola, but he refused over and over to listen to any of us. I tried. All of us did." She didn't sound sad, only annoyed that he hadn't done as she wanted. Clearly Violet was used to her voice paving the way for everyone to do as she desired. "I knew I'd have to kill him sooner or later. He just refused to see reason."

Violet shook her hands and moved her legs restlessly. She coughed. "My hands are going numb. So are my legs."

"It's the cold, Senator. I should have thought to bring a blanket for you," Nate said solicitously.

Violet waved his suggestion away, but brought her hand up to her throat, still shaking the other one. Nate moved up toward the front of the boat. Bellisia was close enough to Violet to hear the soft gasp as breathing and swallowing became difficult. She lay down abruptly, stretching out along the seat. Bellisia waited, but neither man seemed to notice that Violet was in distress. Violet tried to speak; Bellisia could hear her, but over the roar of the engine, the men couldn't. A good five minutes went by. Violet's head lolled to one side as paralysis set in.

"I want you to know that this was for all my sisters," Bellisia whispered softly, her mouth close to Violet's ear, although she was well hidden beneath the seat.

Violet tried to move, but nothing happened. She lay with her eyes open and her breathing shallow, almost nonexistent.

"It won't be much longer before you're dead. If there is one person in this world other than Whitney who I know needs to die, it's you, Violet. You could have saved us, but you left us to Whitney and his knives and needles. His cancer and hideous experiments. You hated what some of us were, but you didn't save us from him. No one can save you now. Even if they discover you, it will be too late. You're dead, and we killed you. Your sisters."

Bellisia allowed a little more time to pass. The boat bumped along. The senator's body flopped on the seat, but the men kept their eyes forward. It was night now and they were running fast through the river out to the gulf. They didn't want to be seen. It was imperative that the senator get back to her home before her absence was discovered.

The boat came about hard and Violet's body fell with a hard thump to the floor of the boat, her face turned right toward Bellisia. Deliberately, Bellisia allowed herself to be seen. Violet couldn't move or speak. She gurgled, her body struggling to get air, but it was impossible.

"You sold everyone out and now look at you. A mass of garbage and no one cares. Not. One. Single. Person. You lie there and die, Violet. I'm going back to a life with Ezekiel."

Bellisia crawled right over her legs and back behind the driver. Violet's body was flung against the side of the boat at the next violent pitch. Nate yelled and the boat slowed then stopped altogether. Nate and the driver both made their way to Violet. Her pupils were fixed and dilated. Both men swore.

Nate began CPR, but there was no response. Within ten minutes, both men were convinced the senator was dead. Bellisia was convinced as well. The heartbeat continued until extreme asphyxia had set in. Bellisia had dosed her with as much venom as possible, making certain they wouldn't discover her in time to save her.

Satisfied, Bellisia crawled to the very edge of the boat and began to make her way over the side into the cold waters of Lake Borgne. It was going to be a long, tiring swim home. She was numb from being in one position for so long, and when the boat lurched suddenly as both men moved away from the body, she had to fling out a hand to save herself from falling back into the boat.

"What the hell?" Nate burst out. "What is that?" He lunged and got a grip on her ankle, his knife in his other fist.

Alarmed, she kicked out and launched herself over the edge. The knife came down again and again and a volley of bullets hit the side of the boat and water as she slipped under.

16

Bellisia dropped to the bottom of the river as quickly as possible. Bullets spat into the water around her, and the knife came far too close, shaving skin on her arm. She swam a distance from the craft, moving like a rocket in the water, but deep so there was no way to see her. Once away from the boat, she surfaced. In the dark, and unless they shone their spotlight right on her, she knew she couldn't be seen.

"Fucking mutant. She killed the senator and we're going to be blamed," the driver said.

Nate shook his head. "This just plays right into what she's been telling the committee about Whitney. He's creating lethal little freaks. Let's just get to the plane. We'll load the senator's body and get out of here fast."

He stared out over the water, one hand on Violet's chest as if he could feel her heart beating. She doubted it. They would have to stay with CPR to keep her going if she was still alive and they'd given up. By the time they got to the island in the middle of Lake Borgne Violet would be long gone from the world. The lake was more of a saltwater bay for the gulf, and Bellisia thrived in salt water.

She waited to see if they were really heading for the island and then she went under the water and swam toward land. She couldn't allow them to get to the committee. The last thing the GhostWalkers needed was for the world to know about the triplets, Pepper, Cayenne and her sisters still in Whitney's hands, not what he'd done to them. Like Violet and those she talked to, many would condemn what they were afraid of.

She would have to reduce the odds fast. She was an assassin, yes, but she used stealth and was rarely seen. Usually when she was seen it was already far too late. These men would be on the lookout for her, or at least they'd be nervous and more alert. She waited in the tide pool, lifting her head just enough to watch the driver bring the boat close to shore. Nate would get out and drag the boat up onto land. That would be her best chance to get him. She swam to the back of the boat as the driver slowed the engine and then turned it off altogether.

"I'm not looking forward to getting out of the boat, Darrin," Nate said.

The driver shone his light all around them, turning in a semicircle to try to take in as much of the water as possible. "I don't see anything. The sooner we get out of here, the better."

Nate sighed, put one hand on the side of the boat and jumped over the side. He caught the front of the boat and began to drag it up onto the land. Darrin continued to shine all over the water at Nate's feet and then up onto the land itself. Bellisia floated just under the surface of the water, her body the same color. Nate stepped from the water to the land and she struck, delivering the venom with the gentlest of bites. She knew he barely felt it, that small prick in his calf. She swam away from him back to the tide pool, where she climbed out of the water and settled into the brush, waiting for the venom to take effect.

The moment the boat was on land, the two men lifted

Violet's body and began to carry her fast toward the small plane sitting silently in the distance. Nate coughed. Staggered. He dropped Violet's feet and pressed his hands to his chest. As he did, Bellisia came out of the brush, hoping to cross the short barrier of grasses before Darrin noticed her. She wasn't so lucky. Darrin's head whipped around, looking for her the moment Nate staggered and then went down to his knees. He dropped Violet onto the ground and pulled his gun.

Bellisia was already on him, knocking the gun aside. He punched her hard in the stomach, doubling her over, flinging her body backward. He followed her up, kicking at her repeatedly. The blows robbed her of breath. Her first thought was to try to make it to the water and get away; her second was just to survive.

Darrin was vicious in his attack, punching and kicking, giving her no chance to recover enough to inflict any damage of her own. She stopped fighting and lay curled up in a little ball, trying to breathe while she called up the venom. Beneath her skin, blue rings showed.

Darrin spat at her in complete contempt and then drew his knife. "I'm going to carve you up into little pieces."

He crouched beside her and she struck fast, biting down on his thigh. As she pulled away, he slammed the knife into her, his eyes wild with fear and hatred. He withdrew it and tried stabbing her again. Bellisia rolled away from him, her body on fire. It felt as if every bone in her body had been smashed. As she rolled, she left behind a long trail of blood. She was so exhausted and hurting from the beating that she couldn't even shut down the bleeding using the muscles lying just beneath her skin.

Darrin swore savagely, slamming his knife into the ground repeatedly as he tried to follow her and cut her again. It took four minutes for the venom to begin to affect him, and it was the longest four minutes of Bellisia's life. She kept rolling away from him every time he got close, but he kept at her, determined to kill her. When he coughed, his throat constricting, his eyes went wide in alarm. Even though she'd managed to bite him, the bite hadn't hurt and he had dismissed it as nothing. It hadn't occurred to him that in that brief moment, she could inject enough venom to kill over twenty human beings, let alone one.

"You bitch. You did something to me." He went to his knees, glancing at Nate, who was facedown in the dirt. Both of his hands went to his chest.

Bellisia didn't waste breath on an answer. She was in bad shape and a good distance from home. She had to find a place to hide in case any of Violet's mercenary teams knew about the plane and came looking. She couldn't leave any trace behind. There was blood on the ground, but that couldn't be helped. All that mattered was getting to the water.

She dragged her body away from him, unable to get to her feet or even get her knees under her. The water seemed a long way away, but she pulled her body to the tide pool and slipped in, ignoring Darrin's curses. He wasn't following and that was all that mattered.

The water was cool on her skin, but burned in the knife wound. She found a small crevice and slipped into it. Just her face was out of the water but she could easily slide under if she needed to for protection. Battered and bruised, afraid to look at the severity of the stab wound, she sent out a silent plea to Ezekiel.

Find me. I hurt everywhere, and this time, I'm not certain I'll make it.

There was no swimming home. There was no way to contact him and let him know she was alive. There was only her beloved water, lapping at her skin and soaking into the wound that burned like hell. She forced herself to squeeze off the blood seeping into the water and it was one of the most difficult things she'd ever done. She knew she wouldn't be able to hold out very long.

Find me, Ezekiel. I need you. She'd never counted on anyone. Not ever. Whitney had drilled that into her.

She carried out her missions alone. She was responsible for her life. It wasn't as if she'd never been in a bad situation before, but this time she had Ezekiel and there was something about him that just made her feel safe and protected. She couldn't imagine that he wouldn't come.

She knew most people couldn't find her in the tide pool, even if they searched for her. She had made herself very small, curling into a crevice no one would believe would be possible for a human being to get into, but she had faith in him.

Ezekiel.

She whispered his name and held him to her. The scent of him. The solidness of him. He was a big man, his body hard with no give in it, just like he was. Strong. Dependable. Protective. He was a good man and he was hers. He would come for her. She knew that without a shadow of a doubt.

―

"Where the hell is she?" Ezekiel said. He paced along the pier, looking out over the Morgan River, Mordichai beside him. "Nothing can have happened to her. I refuse to believe that."

"Nothing happened to her," Mordichai reassured. The problem was, he sounded as worried as his brother, and that wasn't reassuring in the least. "You're exhausted, Zeke. Come inside and try to get a few hours of sleep."

Ezekiel ignored the suggestion. "She fired the Glock. That's the last I heard or saw of her." His gaze swept the other two men standing with him—Gino and Mordichai. "Did any of you see her? See anything? Mordichai, you were on the roof." Was that accusation in his voice? Damn, he was really losing it. He felt guilty as hell. Bellisia was his to protect.

"We were all busy, Ezekiel. There was a firefight going on." Mordichai's voice was very quiet, a warning in itself.

Ezekiel took a deep breath and just listened to the night. The constant drone of insects, frogs calling to one another and the occasional bellow of an alligator told him any

intruders were long gone. He stood looking out over the
water as if any moment she'd surface laughing. She loved
the water. If she was anywhere near it, she was safe. He had
to think that way or he'd lose his fucking mind.

"I know, Mordichai." He shoved both hands through his
hair. "She's got to be all right. I keep thinking about what
Violet did to Joe, and how much hatred she has for the
triplets and Pepper. She'd despise Bellisia."

"We're different," Gino said. "All of us. Violet as well. She
hates herself so she's striking out at everyone around her."

"Those women didn't ask for what Whitney did to them.
They had no choice," Mordichai added. "None of us did,
really. We had no idea he would alter us in any way other
than psychically."

"We have to think about this logically," Gino said. "After
Violet carved up Joe, she headed for the river. That's Bellisia's territory. Once your woman knew you were safe,
Ezekiel, she would have gone after the primary target. Violet
had just slashed Joe up. She gave you up to Cheng. She
betrayed all the women she was raised with as well as any
others like her. Bellisia wouldn't just let that go, so we know
she had to have gone after Violet."

"If she'd gotten Violet, we would have seen the body and
she would have been right here," Ezekiel said.

"We found the Glock on the bank. She had to have gone
after Violet," Mordichai pointed out. "There's no other explanation, otherwise she would have kept the guns with her."

Gino paced along the bank, inhaling through his nose,
trying to pick up a scent. He joined them on the pier. "Joe's
still alive. That's a good thing. You said if he makes it
through the next few hours he'll live." He raised a hand to
his neck and massaged the sore muscles there. "Diego's
sleeping. Rubin's watching over him. Cayenne's fine. The
girls are sleeping. The dead bodies are gone."

"She's not back," Ezekiel reiterated. "Don't give me a list
of the pros. Nothing's good unless she's back."

Gino's eyes met Mordichai's. "I heard a boat. A swamp boat, by the sound of it. I can maybe track her if we get into the water now. It's harder over water, the scent dissipates faster, but I've done it. I followed you that night Cheng's men took you."

"Let's go then." Ezekiel stepped into the boat and waited. Mordichai and Gino followed, Gino casting off.

"Logically, if Violet had a boat waiting to get her out of here, she would have headed for the gulf. She'd have a plane waiting to take her back. She said the Secret Service agent assigned to her had no idea she'd left the house," Ezekiel said.

"Joe hears lies," Mordichai said. "I don't understand why he tried so hard to pull her back to the GhostWalker program. He had to know Violet was a lost cause."

"Joe is a white knight," Gino said. "His father used to give him a bad time about it. He was the white knight and I was the dark knight. He wanted to save the world and I was okay with blowing it up."

"He waited too long," Ezekiel said. "I think he wanted to give her enough rope so she'd hang herself beyond any doubt." He shook his head as he started the engine. "Can you catch Bellisia's scent at all, Gino?"

"I know she ducked under the water. Take the boat around the bend and then idle for a few minutes. Let me see what I can pick up."

She had to be alive. He couldn't think any other way. He'd just found her and he'd known immediately she was the one. He'd just *known*. It didn't matter how ridiculous it was, he couldn't do without her. He'd fought hours for Joe, keeping him alive against impossible odds, and then there was Cayenne and Diego to look after. He was exhausted, but there was no going to sleep, no lying in a bed without her in it.

They swept around the bend and he immediately throttled down to see if Gino could pick up her scent.

"I've got them. Violet's in the boat for certain. Two men." Gino crooked his finger at Ezekiel, and he responded by quartering the area slowly. Gino inhaled through his nose and then nodded. "She was here. She's on the boat as well." He nodded toward the West Pearl River. "They headed in that direction."

Ezekiel's heart stuttered. Had Violet and her men captured Bellisia? He couldn't imagine it. There was no way they would have seen her in the water. She had to have gotten aboard on her own. He pressed his fist to his chest to try to stop the pain spreading like a fire through lungs that couldn't breathe. "She's going to try to kill Violet."

"Zeke," Mordichai said softly. "She's trained for this. She went alone into Cheng's laboratory. We looked into him. The security is better than Fort Knox's and she penetrated it and carried out her mission."

"She's not alone anymore, damn it. She had no right to risk herself. She should have talked to me . . ." He forced himself to stop talking, knowing he sounded like an idiot. In the middle of a firefight she was supposed to halt the action and have a little sidebar with him, asking his permission to go after Violet?

He took them out fast onto the Morgan River, using his night vision to guide him and his running lights to warn off any other craft on the water.

"She's got guts," Gino said, shouting to be heard over the engine.

Ezekiel glanced at him. Gino's face was grim, but he was leaning down toward the water, gripping the side of the boat while his legs absorbed the slap as they blasted through the river as fast as he dared.

"The women in my family, my grandmothers and my mother, were much like her. Small, so you discount her strength, but she stands. No matter what, she stands with you," Gino continued.

"Like Nonny," Mordichai added, giving Bellisia the highest compliment he could possibly pay her.

Ezekiel swallowed bile. He didn't want them paying

tribute to Bellisia as if it was her eulogy. "She's alive." Because, damn it, he refused to believe for one moment that she was gone. "She doesn't understand the word 'failure.' She'll keep going no matter what it takes, or how long."

"Ezekiel, let's figure the route they would take to get the senator out of here fast," Mordichai said. "There are options, but they'll have the best one for her. Stop the boat and let's work it out so we're not just running around like chickens without heads."

His brother was right. It wouldn't be difficult to figure out the way they would take the senator to safety. He slowed and then allowed the engine to idle while they figured the fastest route possible.

"They'll take the West Pearl to Lake Borgne," Ezekiel said. "It's the fastest route to get to the gulf. Lake Borgne is more of a lagoon now. Coastal erosion has made it more of an estuary for the gulf than an actual lake. There is an island large enough to land a small plane."

"I say we go there," Mordichai said.

"How long will it take?" Gino asked.

"I've taken the girls out that way several times. Safely, about an hour. I don't intend for us to be safe. I'll try to cut that time down significantly," Ezekiel warned.

"I was considering that if Bellisia gets the job done, she'd have to swim home," Gino said. "That won't be an easy task at night."

"For most people, no, but for her, a piece of cake. She's at home in the water, and she's a little rocket. She would have been home by now if she was all right." Ezekiel was certain he was right. She would have come back to him if she could have.

"Stop worrying so damned much. Remember, you've run that same route many times and you can do it fast. They couldn't go as fast, not at night. They'll be looking to navigate in the dark, using instruments. They'll be far slower."

"It's been hours. I was doing surgery on Joe, and then

Diego and Cayenne. Too much time has gone by. Whatever transpired already happened. She's waiting for me. She needs me."

"We'll get to her. Just breathe, Ezekiel. We'll find her."

Ezekiel hoped like hell Gino was right. He rubbed the bridge of his nose, thinking about how he hadn't cared about building a house for himself until Bellisia had come into his life. Suddenly, every room took on meaning. He'd never thought he would have children of his own, but now that mattered to him. He wanted a baby to happen before Nonny decided she could lay it all down and rest.

He liked coming into Nonny's kitchen and finding Bellisia stirring the shrimp and crabmeat into the gumbo for dinner. He hadn't had a chance to ask her about her cooking lesson with Nonny or whether she had had fun with Pepper and Cayenne. He knew the gumbo was good because after he'd spent hours in surgery, Nonny had given him a bowl of it along with home-baked bread. That was Nonny, seeing to the practical things, even after a major firefight. He'd had to talk to the triplets. They were understandably upset that they couldn't see Joe or Bellisia. They'd demanded to see Cayenne and then Diego. Rubin had let them into the room in spite of Ezekiel's orders to stay out. He knew they would have just snuck in on their own, and truthfully, he really couldn't get upset with them.

He glanced at his brother. Mordichai and Malichai weren't that much younger than he was, but he remembered them both when they were barely able to talk. He'd fallen hard for his little brothers. The moment his mother had put that first tiny infant in his arms, he'd felt protective and proud. The following year, when Malichai was born, he'd felt the same way. He'd never stopped feeling that way, no matter how hard it was. Rubin and Diego joined them along with a couple of other boys and they made their own family and their own way until all of them joined the service.

Ezekiel revved up the engine once more and they began

flying along the West Pearl River toward Lake Borgne, his
heart beating a little out of control. He had no idea that
finding a woman—the right woman—could tie a man up in
knots so fast. His woman would have come home if she
could have. He didn't question that. He knew it with absolute
certainty. She'd either been taken by Violet and her men and
was a prisoner, or she was injured. He couldn't allow himself
to think about another alternative. She couldn't be dead. His
life wouldn't be worth much without her.

Several times Gino held up his hand and Ezekiel slowed
the boat and idled the engine so they both could test the air
for scent. Gino would nod and they'd head once more in the
direction of Lake Borgne. A land bridge, now a brackish
marsh, separated Lake Borgne from the other lakes. The
water was no longer fresh but salt water. He kept reassuring
himself that Bellisia liked salt water. She often put salts in
her bathwater.

Gino's head suddenly snapped up, alerting Ezekiel, who
immediately slowed the boat. Gino lifted his face toward
the wind, shook his head and lowered his hand palm down.
Ezekiel allowed the motor to idle and let the craft drift in
the river. Gino was silent, turning his head in every direction. He pointed to the small island. Ezekiel swung the
wheel around and took the boat slowly toward that very tiny
land mass.

"There's a plane," Mordichai said. "If they have her, they
haven't left yet."

The plane sat in the dark, parked on a strip of land that
was bare other than grass. There appeared to be no signs of
life anywhere.

Let us find her. Let us find her. He found himself repeat-
ing the mantra over and over as he had dozens of times
throughout the night.

"Gino?" He waited, needing his friend to assure him
Bellisia was alive.

"She came this way, that's all I can tell you."

He couldn't blame Gino. The man was tracking her, but the trail was faint. Very faint. Ezekiel had an acute sense of smell and he could track prey with unbelievable skill, but he was nowhere near as good as Gino. Still, that didn't stop him from catching the faint trace of blood when he drew in air through his nose.

Everything in him stilled. Emotion drained out of him, leaving him with nothing but that dark entity rising fast, taking him over. Around them, the water churned. The boat rocked.

"Gino?"

"It's her blood," Gino confirmed. "That doesn't mean anything, Zeke. She could have cut herself on a rock. Let's just get there before we decide to panic."

Mordichai shot Ezekiel a shocked look. Ezekiel was stone—the rock everyone counted on. He didn't panic, not ever. The idea was ludicrous. But Ezekiel knew better. Little jackhammers tripped in his head. His blood was a roar of thunder in his ears. His mind was pure chaos. Just the idea of her hurt was enough to send him over the edge, when nothing else in his life had ever done so.

As Ezekiel drove the boat right up to the shore beside another boat, Mordichai jumped out to drag theirs partway on land while Gino and Ezekiel covered him. They spread out, moving toward the plane. Violet's body lay in a heap on the ground, as if carelessly dropped. Her face was covered in mud and leaves.

Ezekiel felt for a pulse on Violet's neck. "She's dead. Body's cold."

A few feet away lay another man, obviously one of her mercenaries. He lay facedown. Mordichai lifted his head by his hair. "Any of you see him before?"

Gino and Ezekiel shook their heads. Mordichai dropped the head back into the mud and checked for a pulse. "He's long gone."

They moved on, spreading out to look for signs.

Ezekiel used his night vision to read the ground. There was a fight—a vicious one. One man lay on the ground, faceup, his eyes wide, staring up at the night sky in horror. In one fist was a bloody knife. Ezekiel's heart stuttered. His breath caught in his lungs. Beside him, Mordichai crouched down to check for a pulse.

"Take the knife," Gino advised, his voice grim. "We don't want anyone to get cute and take DNA samples. We have to leave them here for someone to find. We'll call it in and have one of our other teams find them. That will give us time to clean up any sign of Bellisia being here."

There were dark stains on the ground. Ezekiel barely listened to Gino as he followed the stains back down to the water. He looked over the gently lapping waves as they hit the shore. Where was she? Bellisia wouldn't drown, not even if she was wounded, and judging by the amount of blood, the knife had cut deep.

Mordichai and Gino came up on either side of him. "She went back into the water."

"She'd be home by now if she could have gotten there," Ezekiel said. There was no inflection whatsoever in his voice. "She's injured. Knife wound, judging by the knife in his hand and the blood all over the ground."

"She can handle herself," Mordichai said.

"Two big men and Violet," Gino echoed. "Your woman is tough."

She was tough, all right, but she was injured and holed up somewhere waiting for him.

"She'll come home," Mordichai added. "We know she's alive."

Ezekiel shot him a look that told his brother he'd better shut the fuck up. No way was Ezekiel leaving without Bellisia. "She's here and we're going to find her."

"It's a damn big lake," Gino pointed out. When Ezekiel flicked him a glare, he held his hands up in surrender. "Just sayin', bro."

"Her instinct is going to be to find somewhere in the water she can hide but still breathe. She's small and she can make herself even smaller," Ezekiel said. "Think in terms of an octopus. Where would be the places one might hide, but close to the surface? She has to breathe. If she's injured, she wouldn't want to have to keep swimming up from the bottom, or even hold herself on the bottom. That would be too tiring."

"So shallow," Mordichai acknowledged, walking along the shore.

"Blue-ringed octopi like to hang out in tide pools," Ezekiel added, not really paying attention to the other two men. His entire being concentrated on one thing only—finding Bellisia.

She knew she was leaking blood and she hadn't been able to stop it. That worried him. Anyone following that blood trail would know exactly where she entered the water. She wouldn't want to lead them to her hiding spot, so no way was she in open, deeper water. He paced slowly along the shore, keeping his eye out for the shallower tide pools. Even if the water had receded, he knew he wouldn't easily spot her.

Where are you, baby? I'm not going home without you.

Ezekiel shoved both hands through his hair, his gaze quartering the water. She was here. Close. He could feel her now. He willed her to surface, to show herself to him. Gino cast for sign in one direction, Mordichai the other, but he stayed still, working it out in his head. He'd told the others she could make herself very small. Not as small as a blue-ringed octopus, but still, very, very small.

She'd need to be close to the surface so she could breathe without effort, but she'd stay in the water when possible. She was injured, and she'd want to be where she knew she could escape fast.

I'm closer, baby, coming closer every minute. Can you feel me? I'm so close. Just hang in there a little longer.

He walked along the shore to the right of the blood trail

where there were a series of tide pools. The shallow water lapped gently over rocks. His night vision allowed him to see into the water. The rocks created little pools and hideaways, but there was nowhere Bellisia could hide and not be seen. He kept walking, trying to visualize her path.

The next set of tide pools was several feet past the first one. The rocks were a little larger. The water was definitely heavy with salt. His heart stuttered wildly. This was the one. She was there, he could feel her. He just had to locate her hiding place.

Ezekiel crouched down beside the water and peered at each individual rock. There was a small overhang, but the space was empty. He shook his head and glared at the pool.

"No luck over here, Zeke," Mordichai called.

"She's here." Ezekiel indicated the tide pool. "I just can't find her."

Both men hurried over. Mordichai frowned. "You sure? This one has larger rocks, but it's small compared to the others."

"She's here," he repeated. "I feel her close." He stepped into the pool and crouched down, uncaring that he was getting soaked. "Don't touch anything. If she's as hurt as I think she is, she'll be in defense mode. She'll fight back. If you see anything at all, no matter how small, that she might fit into, call it out and I'll do the checking." He wasn't risking his brother or Gino. He knew Bellisia would defend herself. Anyone coming too close to her was at risk. The evidence of how lethal she was lay on the island.

"Move to your left, Zeke," Gino said. "There's a crack. It runs along the rock. I can't see how large it is, but there's something drifting in the water that moves with the waves. It's fine like seaweed, but it's anchored because the waves don't take it out."

Ezekiel swept his hand through the water to his left as he moved forward to examine the crack. Hair brushed across his wrist. Long strands of blond hair moving with the rhythm of the water. She was there. "Bellisia." He whispered her name and closed his eyes for a moment, his heart hammering out his thanks.

"It's her. She's in this crevice. I don't see how she got herself in there, and I have to figure a way to get her out without her thinking I'm attacking her."

He peered closer. He couldn't see her, but she had to be partially out of the crack in order to breathe. Her body blended with the water. Her hair, a pale yellowish red, looked almost like seaweed, blending as well. How Gino had spotted those strands moving in the tide pool when they looked so much a part of her surroundings, Ezekiel would never know.

"Come on, baby," he said softly. "I'm here to take you home." He bunched the strands of hair in his palm and followed them back to her scalp. Her head was just a foot from him. A scant twelve inches. He tugged gently.

Her eyes opened and he was looking right into all that sea blue.

"Come here to me," he said again and added a second tug. His heart pounded hard, telling him she was in trouble. She blinked and recognition was there. Relief. Something else. Something wild and beautiful and all his. He held out his arms.

Bellisia moved slowly. That worried him. She eased out of the crevice, unfolding her body, reaching for him. He closed his arms around her and lifted her, cradling her against his chest.

"I've got you, sweetheart. I've got you now." He started across the beach for his boat, Mordichai and Gino pacing beside him. Bellisia shivered constantly. He could feel blood soaking into his shirt. He knew it was blood and not water because it was warm.

"I'll need a clot bandage," he snapped as he took her into the boat and laid her on the bench seat.

His heart contracted. She was black and blue and swollen. There were shallow defensive wounds on her arms and a long thin slice down one leg, several lacerations, but the worst injury was the knife wound just under her heart.

"Ezekiel." She breathed his name, her eyes drifting lovingly over his face. "I knew you'd come for me." Both of her hands pressed tightly against the wound.

"I will always come for you," he assured. Very gently he took her wrists. "You have to let me see."

Reluctantly she lifted her hands. "I closed it off so I wouldn't bleed out."

"Fuck." He took a breath and forced ice into his veins. He was a doctor, for God's sake. He couldn't panic because this was Bellisia, but he'd be doing surgery the moment he got home. "Baby, I know you're tired, but I need you to close off this wound one more time, just until we get home. Mordichai is going to get us there fast, and then I'll take care of you."

She moistened her lips. Shook her head. "I'm tired."

"I know you are. I know it's hard, but just a little longer. For me. That's all I'm asking, just a little bit longer." He pressed the clot bandage to the wound, knowing that wasn't going to stop the bleeding internally. Her muscles had to do that. He lifted her back into his arms, felt her wince and cursed again under his breath. She wouldn't have survived if she hadn't been able to manipulate the muscles surrounding the gash.

Blood bubbled up, dark and frightening—too much for such a small woman—and she was already drifting away from him, her lashes veiling her eyes and her head turned slightly away.

He wasn't going to lose her. Not now, not when he finally had her. He hadn't lost Joe and he damn well wasn't losing her.

"Bellisia, I'm not fucking around, lock down that wound now." He used the no-nonsense voice he'd taken with patients at death's door, ones who wanted to just drift away. More often than not, that voice would force them to rally.

A small brief smile curved her mouth. "Are you talking to me the way you do to your soldiers?"

His hand was on her rib cage, fingers splayed wide just under her heart. He felt the tightening of her muscles, that hard squeeze that cut off the blood. He signaled Mordichai to get moving. *Fast.* Faster than he'd taken them there. Mordichai nodded, indicating he knew the urgency of the situation.

"Gino, call back to the house. Tell Draden to set up the operating room again. I'll need Pepper to assist."

Gino nodded and complied.

Ezekiel looked down at her face. "Don't you die on me."

"Is that an order?"

"Absolutely it's an order. I've decided I can't do without you. Ever. I think I'll keep you tied to me."

She snuggled into him, her lashes drifting down. "That's not going to work so well when they call you for a mission."

"Then I'll make certain I have fifteen guards around you at all times." He was only half joking. "You're a pain in the ass, Bellisia. A total pain."

"Don't make me laugh." A frown crossed her face. "It hurts, Ezekiel."

"I know it does, sweetheart. I'll make it better in just a few minutes."

"Thank you."

"For what?"

"For coming to get me. I knew you would. That's all I thought about. I just had to hang on until you got there."

He brushed kisses over her forehead, tasting the salt water from the lake. Tasting Bellisia beneath it. "I'm right here, baby, and I'm not going anywhere."

17

Four days. Five nights. Bellisia barely ate when Ezekiel brought her food. Sometimes she ran a fever. He checked the lacerations several times and the one deep wound so close to her heart. That had been a near miss. If she hadn't had the muscles running just beneath her skin to clamp off the artery, she'd be dead. As it was, he'd spent a hell of a long time repairing the damage. She was a GhostWalker, healing faster than humanly possible, but she looked a mess and slept so much that it deeply worried him.

During the day he kept watch over her, filling the tub and gently putting her in it, on his lap so she could sleep if she wanted with the water surrounding her. That eased the soreness, so he did it several times a day. Sometimes, at her request, he dumped sea salt into the water. She curled into him and slept right there while he held her. He left her only when he saw to the other patients. Mordichai and Gino had taken his guard shifts, and Draden did most of the follow-up work with Cayenne and Diego.

He talked with her, little things, nothing to do with work, just about her, what she liked. She seemed overly concerned with the gumbo she'd helped make and wondered several times if anyone had eaten it. He assured her every time she asked that it was good. She didn't talk much and she smiled occasionally, trying to reassure him, but she'd just go back to sleep.

Nights he spent painting thin wood he'd set on the walls of the room, leaving the windows wide open and the fan running. He painted a mural of the sea with a tiny blue-ringed octopus inside a large shell in the tide pool. He had Pepper, Cayenne and his brother purchasing large seashells from one of the stores in town. He put blown glass starfish on the walls and a huge wooden sea turtle. One side of the room looked like a cave with silvery veins glowing, the starfish clinging and lit-up jellyfish in glass in various colors. He filled the room with beautiful flowers, the most exotic he could find close to home.

Sometimes he sang to her, softly, so no one else would hear, but he held her and rocked her in the rocking chair Nonny let him borrow from the porch. Just sang silly songs, ones that, if she'd been awake, would tell her how he felt. Soft. Romantic. Loving. He wrapped himself around her. Every now and then he got a smile, but mostly, if she was awake, she just listened to him.

Ezekiel had gone through another long night, and if she didn't pull out of it soon, he was going to have to do something. What? He had no idea, but he needed her to wake up. He propped himself up on one elbow and stared down at the woman in his bed. He had tucked Bellisia close to him a few hours earlier and she was still there, tight against his body. She didn't ever seem to move in her sleep unless she woke and wanted to take a long bath. She hadn't even done that, she was so exhausted. She was beaten all to hell, but she'd held her own against two men and Violet.

He ran his finger alongside the shallow knife wound, a defensive wound. They'd taken the senator's body to the island where a small plane was waiting. She'd followed them. They'd seen her and they would bring back an army against her. All they had to do was testify that she'd killed a senator and it wouldn't matter what Violet had come to do. She'd used herself as bait to draw them close enough so she could inject venom into their bodies.

He'd seen the news reports. Senator Smythe was being mourned. She and two bodyguards who clearly had tried to save her—there was evidence of CPR on the senator's body—were bitten by a creature not native to the waters. There was speculation that they had found a tiny octopus hiding in a crevice, never thinking the creature at five to eight inches could be poisonous. All three were dead. It was a terrible tragedy. There was speculation that the octopus, found primarily in waters from Japan to Australia, had been trafficked and dumped.

He pulled the light blanket back to look at her body. There were still bruises on her. A lot of them. His heart contracted and he bent his head to brush his lips across a particularly nasty one on her hip. She'd been kicked. Hard. He wanted to go kill the bastards all over again. He hoped to hell it had taken them a long time to die. A really long time.

"You're growling again."

Bellisia's soft voice brushed over him like the tips of her fingers. He loved when she stroked her fingertips over his body. Now, her voice gave him that same reaction and she hadn't even physically touched him.

"Are you going to wake up?" He brushed a kiss over each eyelid because he had to kiss her and she was still beaten up. There was a faint bruise on the side of her mouth and he kissed that as well. Gently. A whisper, no more, just enough to let her know what she meant to him and how afraid for her he'd been.

"I'm awake now. I've been awake on and off for the last few days but it hurt to move. For some reason, when I'm injured, my body just wants to sleep. I heal faster that way."

It was the most she'd said in a week. Mostly their talks were her responding with yes or no. This felt so much better. He almost felt like he could breathe again.

"Is Joe alive?" Her voice was soft with compassion.

He sighed. "He's alive, sweetheart. We wouldn't let him die, no matter how much he wanted to."

"He was paired with her, wasn't he? That's why he kept trying to save her."

"That, and it's his nature. Joe is the man who is going to run right into the middle of the worst firefight and pull the wounded out. He's the man going into the burning building. Whitney knew that about his character. Joe would fight to his last breath for one of us, and he considered Violet a GhostWalker. It wasn't only about pairing them. You can get around physical attraction, but overcoming who you are at your fundamental core is something else."

"There had to be a part of him that knew he couldn't save her."

Ezekiel shook his head, wishing he could explain. "Men like Joe don't give up. Not ever. Regardless of how he felt about her, he would want to save her and he'd keep trying. He hesitated that little bit too long, and she was able to carve him up. Now he feels he failed everyone, you especially."

"Me?" Bellisia made an attempt to sit up, but when she winced, he put his hand on her belly, fingers splayed, stopping her.

"We're not talking about this if you're going to get agitated. You gave everyone a scare, baby. Especially me."

Her lashes fluttered and then she shook her head. "I'm used to running a mission by myself. I was fine. A little banged up, but I've been that way before and will be again."

Ezekiel didn't like that at all. "You're not alone anymore, Bellisia. You have people who worry about you. We work as a team, and when one member goes missing, none of us rest until we get him or her back."

"I'm sorry, Ezekiel. I know that sounded a little thoughtless. It wasn't that I didn't have someone looking out for me, I did, I just got beaten up now and then and took care of it myself. I counted on you coming. I don't know if I would have made it without you. It was pure luxury to have you come find me and bring me back to Nonny's home."

"*Our* home. This is our home until we get our house built. Just so you know, I brought in a local crew last week to work on the house. They'll do everything with the exception of building our safe rooms, hidden exits and entrances or the places on the roof to hide a sniper. We'll have an armory and explosives room. That's already been done by us."

Bellisia shook her head. "I'm fairly certain most couples don't have to have these extra features in their homes."

"Most couples aren't GhostWalkers. Our squadron bought up all the land around here from the Fontenot home to Trap's monstrosity, with the exception of one piece of property right in the middle between the two compounds. We can't find the owner. That's never a good thing. Whitney owned quite a bit of land here. Where Trap's home is, he owned a mental hospital with one patient, Dahlia. She's now married to a Ghost-Walker on another team, Nicolas Trevane."

Bellisia looked up at him from under her long lashes. He'd always noticed her eyelashes, but they seemed longer than ever. Taking one small hand in his, he brushed at her fingertips, feeling how soft they were, how unusual. His. He brought her fingertips to his mouth and bit down gently. Her eyes heated, went dark, moved over his face slowly, a little possessively. He liked that look.

"You need to tell me you're with me on this, sweetheart. You're going to make a life with me." Because he hadn't been able to breathe with her lying so still and small in the bed. He'd actually read up on the blue-ringed octopus. They were small and as a rule docile, but defended themselves aggressively. If she had any of that in her, she wasn't show-ing her docile side to him.

She took a deep breath, and his heart sank. When a

woman was all about talking and not just giving a man everything he asked for, everything could go to shit fast.

"You get that I'm not someone who needs protection."

"Of course you do, we all do. I expect you to stand with me every single time. Have my back when I need it, and you should expect the same from me."

"You're like Joe in some ways, Ezekiel. I've seen you. I spent a few weeks studying you, that's how I fell so hard for you. You're all about protection whether you realize it or not. I love that trait in you, and I'd love it for me, but I just want you to realize that being small doesn't mean I'm not lethal."

"I've seen the evidence of how lethal you really are, baby, I'm well aware." He tucked the pale hair behind her ear with gentle fingers. "You were happy to see me."

"*More* than happy to see you. I knew you'd come for me. I wasn't afraid because I knew I just had to hold out until you came. I would have died without you. I know that. It's just I don't want you to think I'm a girlie girl. I'm not like Pepper." Her gaze slid away from his face.

He caught her chin and turned her head toward him, forcing her eyes to meet his. "You're like Nonny. You'll stand with your man. Pepper will too, but in a completely different way. She's right for Wyatt, but not for me. *You're* right for me."

"Pepper's . . . sexy."

He studied her face for a long time. "Sweetheart, Pepper can't help the way she is. Whitney did that. There's a chemical in her body that builds up and it's hell for her, especially when Wyatt's gone, but she's his. We care for her and look out for her, but none of us covet her. She's more like a sister we all protect. As far as sexy, if you're comparing, for me, she has nothing on you. Just looking at you gets me hard."

She blinked at his crude admission and then her smile came, that slow, sexy one that she gave him sometimes. The one that stole his breath. "So tell me where you are on this thing between us."

"I thought I did."

"Not in so many words."

She smiled again and rubbed her forehead along his ribs. "You like words."

"I do. Are you going to fall asleep on me again?"

"Mmhmm. But I'll say the words first so you don't worry so much. Yes, we're on the same page, as long as you know I'm going to drive you crazy when I want to do things like waitress and you think it's too risky."

"It would only be risky to the triplets and Pepper because I'd put half the team on you and the other half would have to remain here. I have no objections to that." Like hell she was going to waitress and dangle herself out there as bait for Whitney.

Bellisia smiled again. He realized that smile he loved so much was going to get him in trouble. "I think we'll talk about that when I'm not so sleepy. But, Ezekiel, I really want to get back to why Joe would ever think he failed me. I know you distracted me on purpose, but he has nothing at all to do with me."

He stroked soothing caresses in her hair because he could tell she was agitated all over again thinking she might be the cause of Joe's worrying. He'd braided her hair in the morning, so it was out of her face. He didn't want her to have any excuses to cut it. He liked her hair. *A lot.* He liked how it felt on his skin and bunched in his fingers. He especially liked how it sometimes was spread out on the pillow around her face in his bed.

"Of course he does. He's the leader of our squadron, and he takes that very seriously. You're one of us and you've elected to stay here. That means you belong to all of us. In Joe's mind, he put you in a position of having to kill Violet, because he waited too long. Everything that happened to you after that was on his shoulders."

"That's ridiculous."

"That's how he thinks."

"I made the choice to go after Violet. I didn't have to; I wanted to. She was just as bad as Whitney, or worse, in my mind. She betrayed every single woman she grew up with. And she betrayed the rest of us, including those little girls in there. Her absolute worst mistake was when she tried to get my man killed."

He laughed softly. "Who knew you were a little hellion?"

Her lashes drifted again, two little bluish blond fans against her pale skin. "I'm perfectly within my rights to do that horrible woman in. She isn't one of us. She tried to have us killed, and she would have allowed Cheng to torture and experiment on you and then kill you. So it was my choice to go after her, for you, the children and most of all for all the women she abandoned to a terrible fate."

If he hadn't been halfway in love with her before, right then, in that moment, he knew he fell hard. Bellisia was a woman who would stand with him. She looked feminine and she acted it, but when push came to shove, she was a warrior through and through. He'd wanted a Nonny and he believed he had one.

He ran his hand possessively along her side, from her shoulder to her rib cage, rib cage to her waist and then hip. She might be small, but to him, she was gorgeous. She was going to lead him in such a dance, but that was part of the fun.

"Sing to me, Ezekiel," she murmured, already drifting. "I love when you sing."

He glanced toward the door. The house was quiet. Outside, it had begun to rain. The windows were open to keep the paint smell from being overpowering and the sound of the rain was like music. He could work with that. He stretched out beside her, wrapping her in his arms and dragging her close, right into his body. She never protested when he did that, she just snuggled into him. He wasn't certain if it was because she was so tired and couldn't be bothered to protest, or if she liked being that close to him. He meant for her to feel safe. He'd noticed she liked to curl into small places.

He sang softly, matching his melody to the rhythm of the rain falling, pouring his feelings into words he gave her. He made up the lyrics, giving her the song of his heart, the one she'd given to him when he first heard her in Jackson Square.

Feeling warm and safe, Bellisia's lashes drifted down as she inhaled Ezekiel's scent and drew him deep into her lungs. When he sang to her, she always felt as if she was in the middle of a dream—and maybe she was. After following him in the swamp, once back on the island she had spent an obscene amount of time daydreaming and fantasizing over Ezekiel. She sat on the porch of Donny's old camp cabin staring up at the stars, wishing on them that Ezekiel belonged to her. It was almost too much to believe he did, especially when he was singing to her.

She opened her eyes to look up at his face. He was beautiful. All man. His eyelashes were long, his jaw strong. His nose had been broken more than once and his mouth could have a distinctly cruel edge. He could look as cold as ice or as hot as hell. His voice was the voice of an angel, if one believed in such things. She believed in him.

"What is it, sweetheart? You're not sleeping."

"I love your voice, Ezekiel. I really do." She didn't want to complain. He'd waited on her hand and foot and all she'd done was sleep. She still needed to sleep, but truthfully, she kept asking for the water because she couldn't breathe in the house.

"Tell me."

She moistened her dry lips. "It's silly."

"Another bath? I don't mind." He pushed strands of hair from her face and bent to brush a kiss on her forehead. "I get to have you naked in my lap."

"I love the bathtub, especially when you're in it with me," she hedged.

"So not the bath." He cocked his head to one side. "I'm telepathic, in that I can push thoughts at you, but I can't read your mind, baby, so just tell me."

She sighed and rubbed at his forearm with her fingertips. She loved touching him, especially since she'd gotten to know him. "You've done so much for me already, but sometimes, if I'm cooped up for too long, I can't breathe. We had a dorm and it was fairly large, but we were locked in. I hated it, especially at night when it rained. I needed to be outside. I couldn't get to the rain."

"Of course you would want the rain. I should have thought of that. Give me a few minutes and I'll take you outside." Ezekiel pressed another kiss to her forehead and slipped off the bed.

She loved watching him move. He was like her beloved water, fluid, every muscle rippling as he donned clothes. She could watch him walk around naked all day and all night if needed. No problem. If he sang her a little song while doing it, so much the better.

Smiling because she couldn't help it, happy just to be with him, Bellisia forced herself to sit up. The pain she'd had when moving was mostly gone. The wound just below her heart pulled a little, reminding her she'd been too slow. She was going to have to improve her skills on land. She always considered that her actual missions were in water, but the lesson learned from this incident was she had to train harder on land.

Standing wasn't as difficult as she'd first anticipated. The pain was there, but it didn't streak through her body like white lightning, robbing her of breath and making her nauseated. She started over to the closet with the intention of pulling on her clothes, but out of the corner of her eye she caught a flash of color. Various shades of green, from vibrant to cool.

Bellisia made her way slowly to the wall with the light switch. She'd always had good vision through the water and in the dark, but she wanted to see what Ezekiel was up to. She'd woken often during the night and he had always been there in the room with her, but he was at the wall. She'd smelled the odor of fresh paint, and she knew he was painting, but she'd been too tired to pay attention before. Now she wanted to see, because, clearly, he wasn't putting a fresh coat of paint over what was already there.

She flipped on the light switch and gasped, her gaze sweeping around three of the four walls. Her man had created a masterpiece in the bedroom, surrounding her with an underwater sea. Her heart clenched and then began to pound. The walls were telling her a story. A love story. Ezekiel had turned her room into an under-the-sea wonder, but more importantly, she read love in every stroke of the brush.

The mural was actually painted onto something attached to the wall, not the wall itself, and she was grateful, because she wanted to spend her life surrounded by the painting. It was very detailed, with kelp forests and reefs, sea urchins and various fish. She found the tiny blue-ringed octopus curled up along a conch shell. Tears burned behind her eyes. No one had ever done such a thing for her. It was the most beautiful gift she could possibly conceive.

She stood staring at it, her heart so full and her eyes brimming with tears. She could barely catch her breath. Ezekiel Fortunes really loved her. More, he *got* her. How, in such a short time, she had no idea. She'd had weeks to fall in love with him, to see the man inside where no one else did, but how could he know her so well? The wall was their love story. Ezekiel and Bellisia.

"Sweetheart?" Ezekiel's voice came from behind her. His arm curled around her waist and pulled her back against his solid body. "You're crying. You're not supposed to cry, baby. You're supposed to feel comforted."

"And loved," she murmured, turning her head to look at him over her shoulder. Her vision was a little watery, but he was there, real and solid.

"That too."

"I don't have anything to give you, Ezekiel."

He turned her around and cupped her chin, bringing her face up as he bent down. He took her mouth gently, his tongue teasing at the seam of her lips until she opened for him. Then his kiss wasn't so gentle. She tasted possession. She tasted beauty and perfection. Fire. Most of all she tasted love. She knew what it looked like. She knew what it felt like because his arms were around her. She knew what love tasted like because it was all Ezekiel.

She kissed him back, her arms creeping up around his neck. The moment she lifted her arms high, she felt the protest in her body and winced before she could stop herself. Instantly Ezekiel lifted his head, his eyes searching hers. "Something hurt."

"Don't go all doctor on me. It was a twinge. Let's go back to doing what we were doing."

He laughed softly, kissed her nose and picked her up. He was dressed in a light shirt and his blue jeans. She was naked, her skin rubbing over the soft material, sending a little shiver of awareness through her body. She hadn't felt sexual desire the entire time she'd lain in bed, curled so tightly into him. Now, it was there, humming through her body, heat rushing through her veins.

"Ezekiel. I like kissing you."

"Good, because you're going to be doing a lot of that. Just not until you're feeling a little better."

"I *knew* it was a bad idea getting involved with a bossy doctor. Mordichai sort of warned me."

Ezekiel pulled a light sheet over her. She caught the thin material and dragged it around her as best she could as he strode down the hall.

"I'm *naked*," she whispered into his ear, afraid, even though it was night, one of the GhostWalkers with their acute hearing would be able to discern what she said.

"I'm well aware of your lack of clothing," Ezekiel said. "I wasn't stabbed. My body is in full working order. In case you didn't know what that translates to, I'll be more than happy to show you in another minute."

She buried her face against his shoulder. He wasn't in the least bit modest, but he was fully clothed and she wasn't.

"What exactly did Mordichai have to say?"

"It wasn't just Mordichai. Pepper and Cayenne warned me about your bossy ways." Purposely she made her tone snippy. "Mordichai just happened to come in and confirm it."

"He did, did he?"

He bent his head and nipped at her neck. The sensation of his teeth scraping over her sensitive pulse, his tongue easing the sting and his lips following with a kiss, sent more heat rushing through her veins. She squirmed a little, her body becoming *much* more aware of him.

"I really will have to beat the crap out of him."

She pulled back as far as her arms would let her, with her fingers linked together at the back of his neck. "Have you always had violent tendencies?"

"Yes." He was unapologetic. "Here we go, baby. Into the rain."

He walked right out the front door to the porch, using his long strides. The night was perfect. The rain came down in soft sheets of silver, falling into the trees where the drops hit the leaves and played a soft melody. The rain hit the surface of the river, creating pictures and adding to the rhythm of the song. More drops hit the pier, house and other structures, providing a drum for an accompanying beat.

Everything in her reached for the natural water. Rain. He carried her right off the porch into the middle of the yard. She turned up her face, held up her arms. The deluge saturated both of them. He didn't seem to mind in the least. He watched her face as she offered her skin to the downpour. She felt the impact of his gaze and looked down at him, drops on her lashes.

"Isn't it wonderful? So perfect? Thank you, Ezekiel, thank you a million times." The sheet was becoming transparent, but she didn't mind. The wet material clung to her skin, giving her body the chance to absorb the water so that she felt wholly alive and completely hydrated.

Ezekiel didn't answer, but she loved the look on his face. He didn't think she was a freak, or crazy. He had an expression of such beauty she wanted to cry just looking at him. He looked at her with love. She'd never seen that before, but it didn't matter, because she recognized the emotion. It was that clear.

He spun her around in a circle and then took her toward the river. Now that she was paying attention, she saw the large sun umbrella he used as a shelter. On the planks of wood was a blanket laid out with a small fire pit already lit. He carried her to the blanket and sat her down just beneath the umbrella so she could stick her legs out into the rain or be sheltered. He sat down beside her.

"You did this for me?"

"You wanted to be outside and I wanted you comfortable, so this is our compromise."

Bellisia's gaze jumped to his face. He sounded a little gruff. Her man didn't know how to take compliments, that much was easy to see. She leaned into him, and brushed kisses over his lips. "I like the way you compromise."

"I like the way you look in a sheet."

He took control of her mouth, a raw, possessive kiss that told her his body was on fire for her. He kissed his way down her throat to her breasts and latched on, his mouth a cauldron of fire over the cool sheet that clung to her. She cradled his head to her and let desire take her. The dark heat swept through her like a tidal wave, every nerve ending alive and hungry for her man.

He lifted his head, slowly, reluctantly. "I made both of us hot chocolate with whipped cream." He reached around her and pulled a thermos into view.

A whimper escaped before she could stop it.

He touched her lips. "You're pouting. Seriously, baby, what am I supposed to do with that?" He leaned down and caught her lower lip between his teeth, biting down gently and then tugging.

The sensation was electric and went straight to her clit. Her channel spasmed, and wept for him. He released her, and she reached for one of the mugs sitting in the middle of the blanket. "You are a tease, Ezekiel," she accused, pouting even more.

"You scared the hell out of me, Bellisia," he returned. "Your doctor hasn't given us the go-ahead, so you'll just have to suck it up."

That gave her ideas and her gaze dropped to his lap. Oh, yeah. Hard as a rock. She could work with that.

"No." He pushed the mug into her hands and then spooned the homemade whipped cream onto the surface of the chocolate. "Behave yourself."

"You're making me crazy."

He ignored the major pouting in her voice and poured himself chocolate, although he placed the mug on the wooden planks. "I have something for you. I'm going to warn you, it isn't expensive or particularly beautiful as you deserve, but it's important to me."

Bellisia studied his face. He looked as if he had been made of stone. His tone was mild, but that nonexpression on his face told her whatever he was going to give or show to her, was *extremely* important to him. She drew back and took a sip of the chocolate, keeping her eyes on his. The chocolate was delicious, not packaged for certain. She loved that he had made it for her. The first real meal he'd given her had been that very afternoon and it was shrimp gumbo, one he'd made with Nonny just for her.

She couldn't believe he had made it himself. For her. She had no idea if all men were that thoughtful with their partners, but she was eternally grateful that Ezekiel was that way with her. She'd really wanted to taste the gumbo Nonny had taught her to make. She loved seafood, and Nonny was such a good cook. She gave lessons twice a week to Pepper and Cayenne. The triplets always helped and were never treated as if they were in the way. Bellisia felt as if she'd learned so much from Nonny about life, not just cooking, in such a short period of time. The gumbo had been on the stove when Violet had come. Ezekiel had made certain she got to try it and it was delicious.

He pulled a small bracelet from his pocket. His fingers found the first stone. "When I was a kid and my brothers were born, I was so happy. I found this small rock on the ground right outside when my mother brought Malichai, my youngest brother, home. Later I found out the stone was something called black jasper. The rock was divided into threes by small red lines running through it. I thought it was fate. You know, a sign that the three of us belonged together against the world. I polished it every day and kept it in my pocket. This is it right here." He lifted the small stone and showed it to her.

Bellisia could see the rock was so polished it gleamed. It was very small, and oblong-shaped. The stone appeared to be black with faint red lines running through it, but it was clearly divided into threes just like he'd said. She thought it was beautiful.

Ezekiel touched the second stone. "I overheard my mother negotiating to sell my brothers to men so she could buy her drugs. Mordichai was five and Malichai was four. I took them out of there. When I found us an abandoned warehouse to live in, I found this small rock. It's hematite. It's actually the main source of iron."

She thought the stone was more than beautiful and she could see why it would have caught a young boy's eye. The stone had a rust red streak running through it that resembled a lightning bolt. This had to be professionally polished as well. It was thicker than the other stone. She wanted to cry, thinking of that boy taking his younger brothers out of harm's way.

"This one is for the first fight I lost. It reminded me that

I had to do better, to let loose that dark need for blood in order to feed my brothers. It's a red sunstone. I was beaten all the hell up and covered in blood and bruises. You can see I polished this so much I wore it down a bit on one side from my thumb moving back and forth on it. I kept it on me all the time as a reminder that I had to be okay with letting a demon loose in order to protect and feed my brothers."

She felt the burn of tears behind her eyelids. He was *such* an amazing man. The idea of him using his fists and feet for him and his younger brothers to survive made her feel as if her life had been easy. So what if she'd been experimented on? She had a bed and three meals. She'd been taught how to defend herself, and she ran missions that helped her country. She was falling harder for him every minute.

"This one represents the first time I won a fight. We needed food. *Really* needed it. I had to get medicine for Mordichai. He was sick, and there was no money. I knew if I didn't win, I'd be taking him to the authorities, he'd go into foster care and I'd never see him again." His fingers slid over the beautiful stone, a highly polished, gleaming black. "I lucked out. This is a black garnet. I was bloody and hurt like hell, but I had the cash in my hand. I looked down in that exact moment of awareness that I'd done it, gotten the money to save my brothers. I looked down at the blood dripping onto the ground, and there it was."

She couldn't help it. Tears slipped from lashes to her cheeks. She tried to dash them away before he saw them, but Ezekiel saw everything. He leaned in and kissed her eyes and then her cheeks, sipping at her tears.

"I won, baby. Don't cry. It was a good thing. It made me even stronger."

She nodded, trying not to think about that little boy clutching the money he needed for his brothers in his torn hands. "I know, honey, it's beautiful."

"This one is when a couple of rough boys from the Appalachian Mountains showed up. They needed help and reminded me of Mordichai and Malichai. Ready to fight at the drop of a hat, but good inside. Really good, baby. I had to help them survive, and in the end, they helped us, so it was good all around. This one is polished quartz and represents the family we formed together."

Ezekiel touched the next one. "This one is really rare. Trap gave it to me when I joined the service. Mordichai and Malichai followed me and then Diego and Rubin. It's called benitoite." The stone had several colors in it, including red, white and blue. She could see why it would represent his service to his country.

The next stone was gorgeous. Really, really beautiful, almost translucent. She loved the deep green of it. Ezekiel rubbed his fingers over it, clearly something he had done often. "This is green jadeite. My brothers got it for me when I became a surgeon. It means a great deal to me for that alone."

His fingers moved to the next one, an almost raspberry-colored gemstone. "This is from Afghanistan. It's a red pez-zottaites, a beryl actually, but has lithium in it, changing it slightly. Every mission I've gone on, I've collected a stone or acquired one that was native to that area. I've run missions all over the world and intend to make you a necklace from them when you have our first child."

The breath rushed out of Bellisia's lungs. A child? She didn't know the first thing about children. She wanted them, but the thought of having one was terrifying.

"This one is from a mission that went sideways. It was a hot zone, and there were Marines down. I ran two of them out of there on my back under heavy fire. I ended up wounded. I have medals, Bellisia, but for me, these stones mean milestones in my life. Things I conquered or overcame or achieved. I saved men's lives that day. Good men. And we got out alive."

She liked what his stones represented to him, and wanted to touch the beautiful red stone in the hopes that it would give her the same courage. She wanted children with him,

and looking at the bracelet with the rain falling down around
them and her man wet from both the rain and her soaked
body, she knew Ezekiel was the right one for her.

"This one is easy. I met Nonny. She's important, because
the only female influence I had up to that point was my
mother, and believe me, baby, she wasn't something I ever
wanted around the boys or me. This is a cabochon-cut oyster
shell. I found a red spiny one, shaped like a fan. She's a
firecracker if she needs to be and I just saw her like this.

"This one is a teal magenta Tahitian pearl. It represents
when I found you. You're cool like the ocean but have fire
in you. You're my most precious find, Bellisia, and I'll always treasure you." He opened the clasp of the bracelet and
held it out.

She knew he was handing her his life. She extended her
wrist, her hand trembling. To her, this was momentous. Ezekiel was giving himself to her completely.

"I had all the stones professionally polished and then I
had Mordichai take them to a very talented local jeweler,"
he explained as he closed the clasp.

She felt the weight of the bracelet on her wrist. She put
her other palm over it, holding Ezekiel to her. She never
wanted to take it off. Not *ever*.

"Stop crying, baby," he said softly and lifted her onto
his lap.

"I didn't know I was." But she did. How could she help
it? "You're the most beautiful, unexpected man. I'm so crazy
about you."

He nuzzled her neck. "That's a good thing. Drink your
chocolate. We can't stay out here too long."

"You're too good to me."

"Nothing is too good for you, Bellisia."

Ezekiel sounded like he meant it.

18

The house was going to be very, very large. Bellisia wandered around looking at it from the outside, while Ezekiel pored over blueprints with Mordichai and Gino inside. The house was completely framed in. Like most of the houses near the river, it was up high to give plenty of room for flooding. She liked the view. The house towered above the river, almost as if Ezekiel had known, when he bought the property and designed the house, that she would be his chosen partner.

It was perfect for her. The river was right there. The dock was already built, a long expanse of wood where Ezekiel's boat was tied up. The launch ramp was in as well. She walked a few more steps, shading her eyes, looking the house over.

"Babe, wait for me," Ezekiel called.

She glanced at him over her shoulder. She was healing fast and felt nearly 100 percent. She still got fatigued if she did too much, not that she would know because Ezekiel made certain she didn't do too much. He did it in a nice way, always sweet with her, like coming up behind her, spanning her waist with his hands and lifting her to the countertop when she was helping Nonny cook. He took over whatever she was doing smoothly, leaning in for a kiss and engaging with Nonny so that Bellisia didn't have a chance to protest.

"Catch up with me," she called back and rubbed at the stones on her bracelet. She *loved* her bracelet, although she did worry that if she had to dive into the river and disappear, something might happen to it.

"Wait for me, I'll just be another second," he repeated, and turned back to direct the men gathered around him.

She was tempted to keep walking, but what was the point? She liked being with him so he could point out every little detail of his plans. She might even give input, although she had no idea what she was doing. She didn't know what it took to build a house.

She wandered back to him, going inside the open, cavernous building. She could see they were framing the walls inside now, and the ring of hammers was loud. As she walked up to him, he held out his arm without even looking back at her, as if he knew exactly where she was every second, and he probably did. Ezekiel was not only observant, he had a highly developed sense of smell, and he'd told her everyone had a distinct scent.

She stepped close, slipping her arm around his waist. He instantly locked her to him, her front to his side, right under the protection of his shoulder. There was something wonderful and safe about the way he always held her to him. Her gaze slid around the room, taking in the various workmen forming up walls several feet away.

She stiffened, just for a second, an increment of time, but Ezekiel noticed. He always noticed. At once she had his full attention. "What is it, baby?" he asked softly, his eyes on her face.

Oh, God. She couldn't lie to him. She wouldn't do that, and she'd never get away with it anyway. She shook her head and attempted a small smile. Her face felt stiff. She curled her fingers in his shirt. Ezekiel's gaze drifted over her face, and then he lifted his head and studied the workers framing up the wall.

"They're here, aren't they? On the crew." He spoke softly. "We hired locally, a crew Wyatt and Trap used. I didn't think to check out each worker all over again, but I should have."

It was insane the way he was tuned to her. How would he know that? How could he possibly get that just because she hadn't controlled her involuntary reflex when she'd first spotted them? Gerald and Adam. Adam had been watching her, waiting for her to notice them. Just the fact that she hadn't right away told her she wasn't 100 percent—or that she was getting complacent. Adam had slowly shaken his head, warning her not to say a word.

She wanted to have the opportunity to talk to them before she condemned them to whatever fate the GhostWalkers would determine for them, but now it was too late.

"Bellisia." There was a hard note in his voice. "Take me over and introduce us."

She felt the darkness swirling in him, the powerful energy that rose when he expected a fight. It was that dark power that kept him alive, the power of sheer will and the need for violence—the acceptance of it. Her grip tightened on his shirt. "Ezekiel, maybe I should talk to them first."

"Take me over to them now."

She nodded and stepped away from him. He caught her hand as she started toward the wall.

Mordichai, Gino, with me. Spread out a little. Draden, get in behind them. Be careful no one is caught in a cross-fire, but first get the other workers out of here.

These the douchebags looking for our Bella? Draden asked as he beckoned to the three other men to follow him. He gave them orders outside, away from the building, before hurrying back.

The ones claiming to be her husband? Gino chimed in.

The ones about to get their asses kicked? Mordichai added.

"What are you doing?" Bellisia hissed, glaring at him. She felt the sudden rise in energy around them. It wasn't just the dark energy clinging to Ezekiel; she was certain he was talking telepathically to the others.

"Baby, whether you like it or not, you have our protection. These men were sent by Whitney to bring you back. That isn't going to happen, and we're going to make that very, very clear to them so they will make it very, very clear to Whitney."

She couldn't argue with that reasoning. She was never going back to Whitney. Her life was here, right beside Ezekiel. She wanted to save Adam and Gerald. They were good men. They'd gotten into a bad situation for all the right reasons, and had no way out, any more than she did. For all she knew, Whitney planted viruses in his soldiers the way he did the women who ran missions for him, but the bottom line was, she was Ezekiel's woman. She would fight by his side. She'd protect the people he loved as fiercely as he did.

She led him straight to the two men. Gerald slowly straightened, turning fully to face them. Adam didn't take his eyes from her face.

"I thought you both might want to meet Ezekiel. Ezekiel, this is Gerald and Adam." She lifted her chin. "I heard you were looking for me."

Before either could respond, Ezekiel did. "Some crap about Bellisia being your wife?"

The two men didn't so much as flinch. It was Adam who spoke. "You knew he would send someone after you, Bella."

"Of course, but I had hoped it wouldn't be the two of you."

"Better us than any of the other idiots he employs. We didn't want you hurt," Gerald said.

"He thought I'd come for you, didn't he?" she said.

"Why would he think that?" Ezekiel asked, his voice very low. Soft. Deadly.

Bellisia shivered. At once Ezekiel reached for her, pulling

her back into him, running his hands up and down her arms to warm her.

The moment she shivered, both of Whitney's soldiers took a step toward her as if they would take care of her. It was a telling step and one that would condemn them in Ezekiel's eyes.

"He paired us with Bella," Adam said starkly, uncaring that he might be inviting a death sentence. "At least he tried to."

"He did or he didn't," Ezekiel snapped.

Adam regarded him with a steady stare. "Bellisia is more a sister than anything else to us. Whitney can't possibly understand that. He doesn't get emotion. Sex, yes. That drive. He never did get that she was important to us in a lot of ways. We were already invested in a different way with her by the time he decided he would pair us."

Ezekiel frowned. "Are you trying to make me believe you don't feel physical attraction for her? Or she for you?"

Bellisia opened her mouth to protest, but his arm tightened around her in warning. She stayed silent, even though she was certain he would want to hear what she had to say.

"Bellisia was never paired with us, just us with her," Adam said. "She has never acted in any way as if she felt anything for us other than perhaps affection as a sister might feel. By the time Whitney decided to do his pairing, Gerald and I already were aware that the things he was doing with those women were wrong. Most of his soldiers were men with no morals and less scruples. We didn't want any part of his experiments."

"Yet you still carried out his orders."

"Better us than leave them to some of the other men," Gerald said. "It's easy enough to resist when you know what his motives are. Neither of us have any physical reaction at all anymore. At first we felt it mildly, but just barely, and then not at all."

"Whitney knows you killed Violet, Bella," Adam said softly, his gaze not on Bellisia, but on Ezekiel.

"He said to tell you if you don't come home, he'll turn you in. It won't be that difficult to prove that it was you who killed the senator," Gerald added. "We tried to talk sense into him, Bellisia, but he's pissed you escaped. You were always important to him."

"Not important enough that he didn't infect her with a virus deadly to her," Ezekiel pointed out. "Whitney can go to hell for all we care. Bellisia isn't going back. He can accuse her all he wants, but there's going to be a squadron of men willing to give her an alibi that will be unbeatable."

"Ezekiel," Bellisia cautioned, a hand to his arm. "We have to think about this. If Whitney does that, it could endanger the girls."

"Bella," Adam said softly. "It's an empty threat. You always think with your heart. Whitney won't go to the authorities, anonymously or otherwise. The last thing he can afford to do is draw attention to his experiments. He created you. You were a *child*. All those women were when he conducted his experiments. The moment you say that, he's as condemned as you are."

"Still, you came after her." Ezekiel sounded mild. Casual. Bellisia knew better.

"Like we said, better us than someone else. Once we traced her here, we didn't know you. For all we knew you could be every bit as bad as the motley crew he surrounds himself with," Gerald said. "We weren't going to have her go from the frying pan into the fire."

"That explains why you're here working on the house." Ezekiel made it a statement. "Now you can go back to him and deliver the bad news."

The two men looked at each other and then shook their heads. "No, we're not going back. Whitney will have to do without us."

"Ezekiel"—Bellisia put a hand on his arm—"maybe we can get the other girls out."

Adam shook his head. "He's already moved them. The

entire compound is deserted. I have no idea where he took them."

She felt bile rising and had to double over to keep from vomiting. Of course Whitney would move the other women; he probably had a plan every time one of them went out on a mission, just in case they didn't come back. She'd always had a vague idea that she'd find a way to free the others, but Whitney was always one step ahead.

"How were you going to contact him if you reacquired Bellisia?" Ezekiel asked.

"We had a number to call. He would give us instructions, and we'd bring her in. We're already past the time he allotted us," Adam answered.

Ezekiel's expression didn't change, but she felt that surge of power in him. Dark. Dangerous. The need to explode into violence.

"What exactly are your plans?"

"We thought we'd do a little fishing while we had the chance," Adam said with a shrug. "Find peace while we can."

Alarm bells went off in Bellisia's head. She started to take a step toward them, but Ezekiel's arm locked her to him. For the first time, she was really irritated with his proprietary ways. She glared up at him and was even more annoyed when he didn't seem to notice.

"What does that mean, Adam?" she demanded. "While you had the chance? Find peace while you can? That son-of-a-bitch infected you both with something deadly, didn't he?"

Neither answered.

"Didn't he?" she all but shouted at them.

"Baby," Ezekiel cautioned. "Easy."

"Don't 'easy' me. Answer me, Adam. He infected you, didn't he? You came here knowing if you didn't bring me back, you were going to die."

"We gave you as much time as possible to establish yourself, Bella," Adam said. "We wanted to know you were happy, so we just hung back and kept an eye out. The Fontenots are well thought of, and that was our first clue that you were in a good place. Donny, on that island, he lied for you, and he's got the reputation of not liking many people. You were already fitting in. We talked it over and knew this was going to be it for us, so our last gift to you was to help build your house."

For a moment she could barely breathe. Her lungs burned for air and her throat felt raw. "You're just going to die? You're going to let him kill you?" She wanted it to come out strong, but she sounded more like she was going to cry. Or maybe she was crying. "These men are doctors. It isn't too late."

"It was too late a few days ago. The capsules broke open. Your man is a surgeon. He isn't going to be able to figure out what Whitney concocted, certainly not in time before the virus takes hold," Gerald said gently.

"This was our choice, Bella," Adam added. "We're soldiers. We fight for our country. What Whitney had us doing isn't that. There was never anything left for us."

"Bullshit," Ezekiel said. "He made you into Ghost-Walkers. There's always a way to serve your country."

"We're a little flawed," Gerald said with a short laugh. "We didn't make the program."

"I read your jacket. You didn't flunk the psych eval. He enhanced you both." Ezekiel studied them. "Most Ghost-Walkers recognize one another. Not all. I couldn't recognize Bellisia. You really want out so bad you're willing to die to get out?"

"We tried numerous ways to stop Whitney. Nothing worked. Sooner or later he was going to have to kill us anyway, and I think he knows that it was only a matter of time," Adam said. "Those women need to be pulled out of there before it's too late for some of them."

"There has to be a way to find an antidote for the virus," Bellisia said.

Adam shook his head gently. "It's too late."

"It can't be. There are doctors, brilliant minds, here. If they aren't here, they know people. Right, Ezekiel?" She turned her face up to his, hopeful. Counting on him. Believing in him.

"Babe, you always look at me as if I can move mountains. In this case, I just might be able to, *if* I believe them."

"You can hear lies. Of course you believe them. They're telling you the truth," she insisted staunchly. No way was Adam or Gerald lying. She knew Whitney well enough to know he would rather kill the two men than lose them. All along they'd advocated for the women. More than once they'd beaten one of the supersoldiers Whitney had created for the things the man had done to one of the women. She *knew*, beyond a shadow of a doubt, that the two men were telling the truth.

Suddenly there was a terrible urgency about helping them. How much time had passed since the capsules had opened?

Ezekiel sighed. His woman looked at him with wide, trusting eyes, and he'd do just about anything for her, including taking on two more men. He caught Mordichai's knowing grin. His brother mouthed a single word, but sent it telepathically to all of them.

Whipped.

Ezekiel rudely flipped him off. "Let's go," he said abruptly.

Adam and Gerald exchanged a long look. Gerald shrugged. "There's nothing to be done, so if it's all the same to you, we'll just keep to our plan of fishing."

"Don't be an ass. Look at my woman's face. Do you think I'm going to leave you to die when she's looking like the world's coming to an end? Get in the car with Mordichai. He's nowhere near as nice as I am. He likes to shoot people just for the hell of it." He turned, taking Bellisia with him. "Come on, baby, let's get home. I've got to talk to Rubin."

Adam and Gerald could take his invitation or leave it. He'd extended a way out to them, but he wasn't going to talk them into it. They either wanted to live or they were talking bullshit. He almost wished it was the latter, but he had to admire them. Surrounded, they were cool under fire. They were fucking good soldiers, men you wanted at your back in combat. If they had hung back, waiting to see if Bellisia made a life for herself before making the decision to get away from Whitney, even though it would cost them their lives, he had to give that to them as well. They were brave, if a little foolish.

Bellisia went with him, looking back over her shoulder at the other two men, which pissed him off just a little. They could say all they wanted that the pairing didn't work, but she obviously cared for the two men, as they did for her.

"You're walking too fast," she protested, her voice low. "It's no different than the way you feel about Pepper and Cayenne, Ezekiel. You have affection for them, and that's all right. That's the way it should be. You all have created a family here."

He yanked open the door to the four-wheel-drive SUV, caught her around the waist and lifted her, all but tossing her onto the seat. He indicated the seat belt and shut the door with a controlled fury. Two more reasons why Whitney was going to continue to scrutinize the Louisiana swamp.

Bellisia didn't say a word as he drove back to the Fontenot compound. He drove a little faster than he normally would have with her in the vehicle, but what the hell did she mean by *that*? *You all have created a family here.* She was his family. She was part of what they were creating.

He caught glimpses of the second SUV, Draden driving, behind him. He parked, and Bellisia was already out of the vehicle by the time he'd turned off the keys. She rounded the hood of the car and as he closed his door, she leapt into his arms. He had no choice but to catch her. Her arms circled his neck, her legs wrapped around his waist. She pressed her body tight against his.

"Ezekiel." Her lips moved against his throat. "Kiss me. I need you to kiss me."

He knew what she was doing. She took the aggression from him with her kisses. She was afraid he was going to explode into violence. He'd been so close, *wanting* to annihilate everything and everyone around him. Damn Whitney to hell for wreaking havoc on so many lives. Bellisia would spend the rest of her life worrying about the other women she'd grown up with, partially blaming herself because she managed to escape and they hadn't.

He wrapped his arms around her, afraid of breaking her in half, trying to be as gentle as a man like him could be. He'd been totally unprepared for such overwhelming emotion for her, but it flooded him every bit as strong as that deep need for violence. He brought his mouth down on hers, lips teasing at hers until she opened for him and then he stormed inside.

Her mouth was hot and moist and perfect. He lost himself there, the need for her suddenly urgent and unchecked. It rushed through him like a firestorm out of control when just seconds earlier he'd had complete control. He didn't know if it was the mixture of sex and violence swirling in him, twining together until he wasn't certain he could control the need for her, but the fire burned hotter than it ever had.

Her mouth was a scalding paradise. He kissed her over and over, possession and love warring with each other. He felt primal, savage, a wild animal claiming a mate, and yet at the same time, his love for her was so damn deep he could barely breathe with it. She gave him everything in return, her body soft and pliant, molding to his, accepting his primitive claiming, doing a little claiming of her own, returning kiss for kiss.

When he lifted his head, the sound of snickering cleared his mind. The other vehicle had parked and the men were out, watching them, shaking their heads.

She blushed furiously and hid her head against his shirt. "Mordichai will never let me live this down, will he?"

"Never going to happen, little sister," Mordichai answered, proving his hearing was nearly as acute as his brother's.

"Take the two of them to the room in the laboratory," Ezekiel ordered, uncaring that the others saw him staking his claim on his woman. He rather liked it. Let them all know she was off-limits, particularly Gerald and Adam.

"You're growling," Bellisia whispered, her lips moving against his shirt. He felt the warmth of her breath through the thin material. There was a surprising intimacy about the movement, one that sent heat spiraling through his body.

"I don't like the idea of you close to those two men."

"I'm close to you right now, not them," she reminded, an invitation in her voice.

It had been a long couple of weeks, going on three now, and he'd woken up every morning wrapped around her naked body. He had more pent-up sexual aggression and need than he knew what to do with. Her voice made him hard, let alone any invitation given to him.

"Behave yourself."

She sent him a quick, mischievous grin, one that said she might not listen to him. He hoped she did, because he'd had enough of sainthood. Ezekiel took her hand and led her toward the garage that had been made into a laboratory and surgery. Rubin waited just outside for them.

"What can Rubin do that you can't do, Ezekiel?" she asked, plainly worried.

Ezekiel loved that she thought he could move mountains, and right now she was counting on him to save Gerald and Adam. She couldn't see that Rubin might have a different skill or gift than he did. In her eyes, no one could save them if he couldn't.

"There's a psychic gift that is extremely rare. Some of us can see into the body straight to the problem, but we have to use instruments and drugs to heal. There's only three men that I have heard of who can heal psychically."

"You're not talking about healing a psychic talent, but really healing the human body using psychic means."

He nodded. "Yes. It's a rare and extremely valuable talent. It doesn't always work, but when it does, it's a fucking miracle."

"Who can do this?"

"There's a young man on Team Three, our Marine Recon Team, who is particularly talented. We lucked out on having two on this team. Joe is a psychic healer and can do a very good job most of the time, but Rubin and the man on Team Three both are psychic surgeons. Rubin is extremely powerful. No one talks about it, Bellisia, and we can't. No one ever discusses it, especially not in front of the children. We don't ask Rubin or even Joe to use their gift that often because there's a cost to the healer. It would be a disaster if Whitney ever got wind of it."

"And no one on any of the other teams can do it?"

"Not that we know of. Because it can be done, I'm certain eventually someone else will show they have the talent. Maybe one of the women."

"Not me," she declared solemnly. "Rubin can really save them?"

"Trust me, Bellisia, Rubin can do it if it's at all possible to stop the virus." He pulled open the door and let her in.

She hesitated before she stepped through the doorway. He glanced down at the top of her head, feeling anger wash through him all over again. He hadn't been there to protect her. He knew Joe had been doing his job. Hell, he would have done the same thing, but that didn't stop him from wanting to beat the crap out of every one of them.

Her hand slipped into his. "I'm all right. It was necessary and you know it, Ezekiel. I'm sorry I made you think I was upset about it."

"You should be upset about it. It's a crappy way to have to be introduced to the men I call brothers."

Adam and Gerald sat in the small examining room, Mordichai draped against the back wall, looking casual, and Gino lounging by the door, looking anything but casual.

Rubin nodded to Bellisia as they entered. "You certain about this, Zeke? You certain Whitney didn't send them here to spy on us?"

"I cleared them," Ezekiel assured. "Mordichai was with me. Even if I missed something, he wouldn't have."

Rubin nodded slowly. "All right, one of you stretch out on the table for me."

Gerald and Adam exchanged a long look. "What exactly are we doing here?" Adam asked. "It isn't as if anyone told us anything."

"Just lie down and let me take a look at you," Rubin repeated. "I might be able to figure out what's wrong and fix it."

Adam stood up slowly, his gaze on Ezekiel, even though he was addressing Rubin. "What's wrong is Whitney shot a little capsule into us just before we left and told us we had fourteen days to bring Bellisia back to him. We knew we weren't bringing her back. The capsule broke open some time ago. Both of us have symptoms already. Nose bleeds mostly, cramps, that sort of thing." A faint grin stole over his face. "We figured he'd make it as painful as possible in retaliation for not doing what he wanted. He's like that."

"So let me take a look," Rubin said, indicating the table.

Adam sauntered over to the table and stretched out. Bellisia started to move as if she might go to him. Ezekiel locked his arm around her chest and pulled her to him, her back to his front. What the hell was she thinking? Was she going to hold Adam's hand?

Her heel landed against his shin. "You're growling again. You need to stop before I have to tell Mordichai to put you in that cage over there, and you know he'll be happy to oblige," she hissed, glaring at him over her shoulder.

Mordichai made a little sound of pure derision. Even Gino turned his face away to hide the ghost of a smile.

Instantly, Bellisia subsided against him, clearly unused to the teasing the men did with one another.

Rubin walked around the table, removing thin gloves he wore, his eyes on Adam's body. Ezekiel had only seen Rubin working a few times and he was always astounded at the sheer focus in the man, the complete concentration. No one else was in the room, just Adam and Rubin. How he blocked everyone out to that extent, Ezekiel would never know.

Rubin closed his eyes and put his hands just inches above Adam and began running his palms along his chest, over his heart and down the rest of his body. He frowned and then shook his head. The hands moved toward the head, and then over the entire brain. Without opening his eyes, he spoke softly.

"Bellisia, I need your confirmation that these men are worth saving. It won't be easy, and there's a risk involved."

She bit down on her lip before blurting out confirmation. "Risk?"

"I need your confirmation. You've been around them the longest. I know they're good soldiers, but are they good men?"

"Yes." There was no hesitation. "They tried to shield us from the others."

"I can't do both at once, Ezekiel. I'll need a few hours' rest in between. A few days would be better, but they don't have that kind of time before it would be too late for me to work on them."

Adam started to sit up, but Rubin's hand on his chest prevented him. "If you can only do one of us now, and you really think it's going to work, save Gerald."

"No." Gerald leapt up out of his seat. "That's not happening."

"I'm going to save you both," Rubin said. "So don't be an ass. Just sit down and don't bother me." Already his hands were moving in patterns, as if he couldn't stop the compulsion.

He gave the order distractedly, his focus on the body lying beneath his hands.

"Talk to me, Rubin," Ezekiel said.

"Inside the body I see and feel patterns. It's all about those patterns to me. I practically see in patterns even when I'm not being a medic. Something can invade and disturb those configurations in a person's body. Psychic energy can do that. Like you, Zeke, you have that dark energy that's strong and eclipses just about all the patterns in your body when it swallows you whole. Bellisia has light patterns, a rhythm that ebbs and flows in her body. Everyone with psychic energy has very distinct threads or spools."

"Is Adam's psychic ability strong enough to read his patterns? He tested very low," Ezekiel said. "That was the only reason why he wasn't brought into the program. Everything else was there."

"Whitney said he tested low? That's bullshit. He's got talent and it's strong. Each pattern I see is unique to the individual and their particular set of gifts. Most people with psychic talent have more than one, some much stronger than others. Pepper has a lighter weave in her brain, so when energy created from violence swarms toward her, she's unprotected and absorbs far more. The violent energy actually punches holes through her patterns, giving her brain bleeds. She could die if she was surrounded by violence for too long. Her brain would just bleed out. Your weave, Ezekiel, is much more dense. Adam's patterns are very dense as well."

All the while Rubin explained, he kept moving his hands over Adam's body, weaving his own patterns, as if he was conducting a symphony. His eyes remained closed and sweat beaded on his forehead. His voice was even and low.

"If this is a virus, what does it matter if my patterns are dense?" Adam demanded. "It's a virus, like the flu, right?"

"Whitney would never give you anything that mundane. This particular virus attacks your brain and the psychic threads you have. We're all using parts of the brain never used before. Whitney activated neuropathways that aren't static, they grow and branch out. He didn't believe Adam had psychic ability, or rather, thought that it was very small, so he really revved up the enhancement to the brain. I'm certain his thinking was that Adam would have a mediocre talent, but instead, he has an extremely strong one. That's why this virus he injected into you hasn't killed you already."

"How bad is it, Rubin?" Ezekiel asked.

"The forms in Adam's body are broken and shredded in places, eaten away by tiny little holes all through the patterns, but the worst damage started in his brain."

"Can you repair him?" Gerald asked.

"I am repairing him. It takes time to gather those threads back together. I use a healing energy for that, but when I attack the virus, I have to use a different kind." He frowned again, and moved closer to Adam's head. "You must have a whale of a headache. How did you manage to work on Ezekiel's house? I can't imagine the pain you were in."

"Our last gift to Bella," Gerald explained. "We thought it would make her happy when she found out we'd helped build her home."

"The brain looks as if it took a terrible beating, the holes in the patterns much worse. I have to use a magnetic type of energy to gather the virus and then destroy it with a laser energy. I can't talk while I do that, and would appreciate everyone else staying quiet."

Sweat poured off of him. Gino wiped his face with a towel and stepped away. The temperature in the room had gone up several degrees, and the heat source was clearly Rubin. His skin nearly glowed, definitely giving off a copperish cast. Ezekiel swung Bellisia around so she faced the wall, shielding her with his body as the heat became a furnace blast.

Rubin worked for a good hour, his body beginning to tremble, his hands never stopping as he fought to burn out the virus. His patient appeared to lose consciousness and lay very still. When Rubin did eventually step back, he staggered and would have gone down had Gino not caught him.

"I need to lie down." Both hands went to his head, pressing as if in terrible pain. His face had deep lines cut into it. "Somewhere dark. Give me a couple of hours, and then I'll start on Gerald."

Ezekiel didn't see how Rubin could do that, not when he was in such bad shape, but he wasn't going to argue. He nodded to Gino. Holding Rubin upright between Mordichai and him, Gino took the psychic surgeon out.

19

Ezekiel woke with his body on fire. Sensations like molten lava ran from his toes to his groin. Fingers of desire played on his thighs. He opened his eyes to the dark of the room. Bellisia's hair swept over his thighs, soft silk brushing his skin like the tips of her fingers. She lay with her head in his lap, her hands moving over his body, those microfibers stroking his sac into twin cauldrons of boiling hot seed.

Her mouth slid up and down his shaft. Tight. Hot. Wet. Her tongue danced. Caressed. Stroked. Blood thundered in his ears. Her mouth was so wet and soft, slipping up his shaft and back down until he thought he might lose his mind. Her tongue was a miracle, finding the underside of his crown, teasing at it and then licking along the thick vein.

Her mouth closed over him again, wet and tight, the suction beyond his ability to imagine. He looked down, his fingers finding her hair, bunching it into his fist and lifting it away from her face so he could watch her. His woman. Perfection. He loved that moment in time with her mouth and lips around him, her eyes on his face, love there. Lust there. Pleasure. She loved what she was doing, waking him up, giving him that look she had on her face. Adoring. She might never give him the words, but right then, he knew she didn't have to, because she felt it. She was everything he could ever want.

He indulged himself for a long while, getting off on the incredible sensations, finding even more pleasure in the slow deliberate thrust of his hips while he held her head still just to see the trust in her eyes. He was getting close, too close. He didn't want to lose control and let go in her mouth, although he could tell she wouldn't pull away if he did. The temptation was strong, but he wanted more for her.

"Come here, sweetheart," he urged, transferring his hold from her hair to beneath her shoulders. "I don't want this over yet and it will be if you keep it up." He could barely get the words out, his breath already rushing out of his lungs. His belly was on fire right along with his balls. Somehow he found the strength to pull her up over his body. "Kneel up on the bed for me. On your hands and knees."

She did so immediately, looking back at him over her shoulder. She looked sexy as hell, her eyes slumberous, her mouth swollen from sucking his cock. He knelt behind her, stroking his hands over her body, feeling the silk of her, the softness, all the while breathing deep to get himself back under control.

One hand circled his inflamed cock, fisting it hard, using a slow slide while he cupped her mound to make certain she was as wet as he needed her to be. The evidence that she enjoyed her mouth around him nearly as much as he liked it was thankfully right there, between her legs. He hadn't been certain he could hold back long enough to get her ready. She was small and tight and he was large for her.

He pressed the crown of his cock into her burning entrance, his breath hissing out of his throat. It felt so good, the way her muscles clamped down on him, strangling him.

There was always resistance with her body, no matter how ready she was. She made a little sound, a moan of need he felt vibrating all the way up his shaft. He caught her hips in his hands and drove home, pulling her body into his as he powered through her tight muscles.

Scorching heat surrounded him. So tight. Wet silk gripping like a fist. He lost himself in her, driving deep over and over until he thought he might go insane with pleasure. He never wanted it to end. Twice her body rippled strongly around his, adding to the friction, but he didn't stop, didn't let her come down. He drove her up over and over until her cries were frantic, a musical melody that added to his lust.

He liked that she was small and that he was a big man. He liked that his hands could almost span her waist. He liked the feeling of power he got when he was towering over her, or, like right now, into her. He loved it when her lips were wrapped around his cock and she was looking up at him.

He held her pinned right where he wanted her as his body surged in and out of hers, locking them together. He took one hand and pressed it on her back right between her shoulder blades, forcing her head down, until she dropped the way he wanted her, ass in the air for him, her breasts on the sheets. Hopefully her nipples rubbed along the sheets, adding to her pleasure.

He especially liked driving her out of her mind. He loved when she was dazed and hungry for him. The moans she made. The little cries. The way his name came out in pleading gasps. Her voice, so desperate for him to give her release.

The fire was close to consuming him. So close. He wanted her with him. "Again, baby, give it up for me again."

"It's too much."

"It's never too much," he declared ruthlessly.

Ezekiel reached down and found her clit. She exploded, her body clamping down, milking, wringing every scalding drop out of him. There was a kind of ecstasy in having her body draw his seed out, so that jet after jet splashed her sensitive walls and she spasmed more, again and again, drawing out the tidal wave consuming her.

He collapsed over her, his lungs burning with the need for air, his mind soaring somewhere and he couldn't quite rein it in. He could feel the beauty of those flames rolling over and into his skin, burning through his belly and down his thighs, centering in his groin, until all there was for him was this woman and her body. She did that to him. She wiped out every ugly thing in his life and gave him paradise.

When he could breathe again, when he could force his body to move, he inched back, enabling him to press kisses down the length of her spine. "You're so beautiful to me, Bellisia." The words were muffled against the cheek of her butt. He loved the way she was so silky soft, but firm. "I've somehow gotten to a place where I don't just want you, I absolutely need you in my life. You make everything so much better."

She made a muffled sound, and turned her head so she could look at him, her face partially buried in her sheets.

He bit her cheek and then laved the sting with his tongue. "You make me feel alive and . . ." He trailed off, feeling raw and broken open. "All those long years, baby, you're worth every single minute of those long years."

She smiled and brought one hand toward her face. He saw she wore his bracelet and she brushed a kiss over the stones. His heart stuttered. She was killing him. *Killing* him. That adoration he didn't deserve and never would was there in her eyes. He vowed to himself it would always stay there. He was never going to let her down. He didn't say it out loud to her, because there was only so much idiotic poetic truth a man could spew to his woman without looking like a complete and utter wuss. She had him wrapped around her little finger, but he wasn't about to tell her so.

"You're growling," she murmured sleepily, her smile widening.

"I feel like growling." He hadn't pulled out of her. He couldn't. He felt cocooned, wrapped in her love, surrounded by her wet, tight, scorching-hot body. He glided. Slowly. Easy. Still semihard. Still stretching her.

"I need to lie down, honey," she said.

He wrapped his arms around her and took her to the bed, so that she was on her belly, and only he supported her hips. "Go back to sleep."

He heard her muffled laughter. "Like this?"

"Fine. You're such a high-maintenance woman." He poured pretend concern into his voice.

He loved when she laughed. Not just because of the sound, which was beautiful, but because when he was connected like this, the vibrations played along his shaft like fingers. Her fingers. He pulled out, rolled so he was on his back and draped her over top of him, his cock once more sliding deep. She sprawled across him, legs spread wide to accommodate his hips, her head pillowed on his chest, her fingertips lazily tracing the muscles in his arms.

"I'm in love with you, Bellisia." It was the absolute stark truth. "Absolutely in love with you."

She lifted her head, chin to his chest, looking at him with her bright, sea blue eyes. "That's a good thing, Ezekiel, because I didn't even know there was such a thing as love until you. You taught me what it is. I don't want to ever do without you either."

"So you'll stay here and make your home with me."

"I said I would."

"I want to marry you, Bellisia. Have children. Plural."

She was silent for so long he was afraid he'd pushed her too hard, but she didn't look away from him. Eventually she sighed. "You sort of intimated the children thing before, Ezekiel, and I've thought a lot about it. I have DNA that is messed up. I don't have any idea what I'd pass on to our children."

"You aren't the only one he genetically enhanced, baby," he reminded her softly.

She turned her head and lay back on him. Her fingertips drew lazy circles over his chest muscles. He felt the warmth of her breath over his skin. "I accepted your bracelet, honey. They'll have to take it off my cold dead body. So if we figure out the children, that we're not going to screw them up, then yes to them. I already said yes to you. I'm tired again. I think I'll sleep for a while. Wake me up when it's time to eat."

He woke her up long before it was time to eat. Not once, but twice.

~

Breakfast was a feast. Cayenne had helped Nonny prepare it, and they'd made enough for an army. Gerald and Adam were sitting at the table for the first time. Ezekiel could see they were a little uncomfortable, but he remembered he'd been that way the first time he ever sat at Nonny's table. He'd never felt more awkward in his life. It wasn't as if his brothers and he had sat at very many tables with an older woman before, one they admired. They didn't exactly have the best of manners either. He also knew Nonny would put the two newcomers to ease fast.

"Where's Pepper?" he asked. She was absent, but all three of her girls were there. She rarely left their care to the others. She always had help, but she was adamant about doing it herself. He'd never even known her to sleep in when Wyatt was there—and he knew Wyatt wore her out.

"Mommy's puking again," Ginger announced. "She doesn't want breakfast."

Ezekiel frowned. "How often has she been sick? Why wasn't I told? She can get very ill when she's been around violence, and she shouldn't let that go." He looked at his brother. *It can be life-threatening. I can't imagine having to tell Wyatt we lost his wife because we weren't paying attention.* He didn't want to lose Pepper. She was a gentle soul, sweet and kind to everyone. She was a force to be reckoned with if anyone threatened her children, but it wasn't in her nature to be a fierce warrior.

Nonny cleared her throat. "I don't believe it has anything to do with the fight, Ezekiel."

"Still, I'd better take a look at her."

"I think she'll be perfectly fine in a few months," Nonny insisted, her tone telling him to leave it alone.

A few months? He sat back in his chair. Pepper was pregnant with Wyatt's baby. "I'll take a look at her a little later, just to make certain everything is all right and she has the necessary vitamins."

"Ezekiel, I would never let her go without," Nonny said quietly.

The two looked at each other. He was a doctor, and he needed to make certain Pepper and the growing child had the best start possible. He knew Grace Fontenot was a *trait-eur* and men and women around the swamps and bayous sought her out for health care. This was Wyatt's wife. A GhostWalker. Part of his family. He wouldn't back down.

Nonny sighed softly and inclined her head, the queen giving her permission.

"I would want Wyatt to look after Bellisia for me if it was the other way around," he said, by way of apology.

Without thinking, he laid his hand over Bellisia's stomach. What would it be like to know his child was growing inside of her? He hadn't used protection, and he knew she wasn't on anything. The thought of feeling his baby kicking inside of her brought a warmth to him he hadn't ever experienced.

"Don't," she said softly.

"Don't what?" He raised an eyebrow, trying to look innocent.

"You know what."

Warmth blossomed in him. He never thought he'd have this. Not once in all those years when he couldn't sleep did he think he would have a woman, let alone one who made him so happy just by frowning and playfully censuring him.

"Come here, woman," he ordered, his arm along the back of her chair. He needed to kiss her, needed to feel her mouth under his.

Bellisia leaned toward him, never thinking to deny him, not even there in front of all his men. She'd catch hell for it too, they'd never let her hear the end of it, but she still leaned close and lifted her face toward his. The window over the sink shattered and behind her, something hit the wall hard. The reverberation of a gunshot ravaged the peace of the morning, the bullet passing where her head had been only a half second earlier.

Ezekiel all but slammed Bellisia under him, rolled and came up on the other side, near the door. Gino took Ginger and Thym to the floor. Mordichai swept Nonny down and was over her in a heartbeat. Draden had Cannelle protected. Rubin and Diego hit the floor along with Gerald and Adam.

Ezekiel ran his hands over Bellisia, intellectually knowing she wasn't hit, but his heart and body couldn't stop the reflexive action. His heart was in his throat. He'd come that close to losing her that fast. Wyatt was getting bulletproof windows installed just as Trap had in his house. Ezekiel would damn well get them as well.

Stay with the children, Nonny and Pepper, Diego. Draden, you're on Joe and Bellisia. I'm going hunting. Gino?

With you.

Mordichai and Rubin, get to the roof. Rubin, take the back of the house in case we've got company sneaking up on us while these fuckers are holding our attention.

He gave his next order aloud, putting every bit of command he had into his voice, the years with his brothers, the years of taking charge of other men in combat situations. "You stay put, Bellisia. I fucking mean it. You protect the others if you have to. Joe's still out of commission and you back up Rubin and Diego. Under no circumstances can you go outside where I'm hunting." Even as he gave the commands, he was already out the back door and running along a covered path. One of the first security measures Wyatt had ever put in his home was the cover around every doorway.

He made it to the yard and waited. The sniper was patient, not giving away his position, not firing again without a target. Ezekiel crawled through the brush until he was into the trees, Gino right behind him. Once in the cover of the bushes and trees, they circled around to allow the wind to carry information to them. The wind blew in off the river, blustery, a whip that stirred up leaves and a larger puff that sent them dancing in whirlwinds in the air.

Both hunters raised their heads to scent the air. Gino pointed to his left and held up two fingers. Ezekiel nodded. He'd caught the faint odor of sweat and skin. He went right, the two splitting up, Ezekiel going straight at them while Gino circled around to get behind them. By now, Mordichai would be moving into position on the roof. Draden and Diego would stay close to the women and children. Rubin would guard their back, but his Bellisia was a wild card. He hoped she'd listen to him.

Mordichai would know that he only had to worry about two friendlys in the forest—Gino and Ezekiel. Anyone else would be treated as an enemy and get shot. When Mordichai fired, he didn't miss.

The dark, deadly rage inside him began a slow rise. Someone had tried to kill his woman and he wanted to know just who had been that idiotic. Whitney knew him. Knew what was inside of him. Nothing would stop him hunting the man until he was dead if he came after one of his brothers or someone he loved.

Peter Whitney was a monster, but he was one with certain characteristics holding true. The man was a die-hard patriot. He would test his GhostWalkers, but he wouldn't kill one of them for no reason, not even if they'd pissed him off. The women weren't subject to the same rules—he despised women and thought it was perfectly fine to experiment on them. Whitney had his own code, as skewed as it was. He just couldn't see Whitney sending an assassin for spite.

Ezekiel dropped to his belly and moved into a small, almost nonexistent trail made by a swamp rabbit. He used elbows and toes to propel himself forward. He took his time, careful not to give his position away by moving bush limbs or leaves even gently. An experienced sniper would spot that. Whoever this was had to have patience.

Gino and Ezekiel had both scouted through the swamp numerous times and never picked up a trail. Both had been edgy, but there was never anything concrete to tell them that anyone was stalking their family. Still, they'd stepped up security and patrols. Days had passed, and turned into almost three weeks since the last attack on them.

The shooter was a distance away and most likely had a spotter with him. They would be up high. Ezekiel was a sniper, a good one, and he knew every tree in the swamp surrounding the Fontenot compound. The kitchen faced away from the river, so the shooter wasn't across from them. He was somewhere in the dense grove of trees, the taller, stronger ones in the middle. The shooter had made a good choice.

That particular grove was an area he would have chosen to set up for a shot because it had several locations that would give him access to the kitchen. He'd mentioned it to the others many times, but Wyatt and his brothers had made the decision not to use bulletproof glass in Nonny's home. Ezekiel and his brothers had argued, but in the end . . . Aside from the money, and that wasn't an issue, he couldn't figure out why they wouldn't take that extra precaution to protect Wyatt's family and Nonny.

He understood Nonny had lived there most of her life and the house was already changed so much. They wanted normal for her, but GhostWalkers weren't the same as everyone else. Pepper and the girls weren't the same. They had to be protected at all times. Nonny would understand that, if someone explained it to her. The Fontenot boys had over-ruled him in favor of giving Nonny her last years in her home as peaceful as possible. What the hell difference did it make if the glass was bulletproof?

Bellisia had nearly died because no one wanted Nonny to know exactly how much danger they were all in. Maybe it was that they didn't want to think they could be picked off, one at a time. As a unit, it would be tough to kill them all, but pick away at them one at a time, and someone could annihilate them.

Every few feet he stopped and listened to the drone of insects. To the birds in the trees. He lifted his head just enough to scent the air. Yeah, the stench of sweat was getting stronger. It was still drifting through the trees and brush, letting him know he was on the right track. He paid attention to the wildlife in the area. Two raccoons off to his right ambling their way back from the river. Squirrels running along a branch, another clinging to the trunk of a tree. Lizards making stops and starts up a tree trunk.

He started forward again. He could remain still for hours, so still squirrels ran over his back and a couple of times up his leg. He wasn't alone in that ability, which meant wildlife could have settled and they were close, but he didn't think so. The smell was still too faint.

The trick was to keep getting closer to them without giving himself away by accidentally moving a leaf or snap-ping a twig. It was slow, inch-by-inch work, but he was born to be a hunter and his training had honed his skills until he was elite. He covered the next few hundred feet without a problem, staying under cover of heavy brush, but suddenly the bushes gave way to a wide swath of bare ground. He knew immediately he was close to the shooter. Not only were the trees tall enough and sturdy enough to set up a blind, but anyone coming at them would be spotted the mo-ment they emerged from the brush.

In position.

Give me another five, Gino said.

Gino was nearly as strong a telepath as Ezekiel was. The two of them could easily hold a bridge for the others when needed and often did in combat situations when it was necessary for complete silence and yet they needed to communicate. Gino was making his way around behind the suspected grove of trees. It would take longer but be easier to travel because he could use the outer edges of the swamp to move in.

Ezekiel lay relaxed, waiting for the moment he was anticipating. He breathed in and out, contemplating the fact that he felt alive for the first time in his life for the right reasons. Really alive. Before he'd felt that way when he fought with his fists, a raw insanity that he doubted was too healthy. He lived to protect his family, but he hadn't given much thought to a wife and children. That was for other people—specifically his brothers and Rubin and Diego. He planned to keep them alive until they could find happiness.

Nonny had gotten him thinking. There was something very special about the woman and the way she shared her life with all of them. She referred to them as her boys. He knew she had a special place in her heart for each of them. She took in Pepper and Cayenne as if they were her daughters. She did the same with Bellisia. The woman was generous and open, yet fierce and protective of her family.

She'd given him something he couldn't quite put a name to, but he knew it was real and it was extremely important. The traits he'd grown to love in Grace Fontenot were the ones he looked for in women. He realized Pepper and Cayenne had them, just in different ways. Bellisia had them in very similar ways.

Ezekiel allowed his gaze to move through the trees, up in the heavier branches where the trunk met the limbs, providing a thick cradle. Someone up there had tried to take his woman from him. He could have killed the triplets or

Nonny—or his brothers, and that included every member of his squadron, who had chosen to be GhostWalkers. They had chosen to serve their country. They knew and accepted the risks, but they did it expecting that their families would be safe.

In position. Do you have them in your sight?

Ezekiel's eyes moved up the long, thick tree trunk. The bark was disturbed in three places that he could see. His gaze continued up to the cradle and yeah—he saw them. They'd built a makeshift blind that wasn't good enough to fool a goose, let alone an eagle—something he was often called when his brothers were teasing him.

I have them.

How much time do you need? Gino asked.

Give me sixty seconds and I'll take them. I'll kill the spotter and question the shooter.

I'm on your six.

Gino didn't have to reassure him. Of course his brother would watch his back. That was a given. That was something else he'd been lucky enough to have. He'd given up his childhood, but he'd gained a lifetime of absolute loyalty from his brothers.

Two minutes later all hell broke loose behind the shooters. Gunfire, explosions, the sounds were horrendous, disrupting the early morning silence. Birds rose in a heavy migration, filling the air with startled, flapping wings as they exited the swamp and flew toward the open river.

Both men spun toward the danger and Ezekiel was up and running, breaking cover, sprinting across the open area to leap onto the side of the tree trunk. He went up it fast, using his strength to climb. He moved like a lizard, going up the trunk with blurring speed, uncaring about stealth. The men above him were moving, trying to get into position to see what was happening behind them, so they didn't notice the slight shaking of the tree, or if they did, they'd put it down to their own actions.

Ezekiel came up and over the limb serving as their platform, kicking the rifle over the edge and simultaneously sinking his knife into the spotter's left kidney. He withdrew it and stabbed a second time, this time slicing through the back of the neck. He used his boot on the man's back to send him tumbling out of the tree, already dead before he hit the ground.

The sniper came at him, seeing death, knowing he was next. He'd made the mistake of leaving his rifle set up, the Fontenot kitchen in his sights, so he had to scramble to pull a weapon. He was late, far too late. Ezekiel was still in motion, driving forward the moment the spotter's body fell. They came together, Ezekiel's knife sinking deep.

The sniper screamed and went to his knees, nearly toppling from the tree. Ezekiel held him there, settled him almost gently in the cradle, his hands moving over the body and flinging weapons away.

"Who are you?" Because the man was no soldier. Ex-soldier, probably, but he wasn't in the service. A mercenary then. Since when did Whitney employ mercenaries? Whitney made his own supersoldiers. Granted, they didn't last long, but while they were alive, they were a force to be reckoned with. This wasn't one of his creations.

"Stan. Stanley Jordon."

That didn't tell him a thing, and Ezekiel knew just about every sniper out there—at least the ones with the good reputations.

"You're not in the service." He made it a statement.

Stanley Jordon pressed both hands to the wound in his gut. He bled profusely through his fingers. His breath came in ragged pants. Still, he managed a sneer. "Losers. Any man stupid enough to take the crap pay to risk their life deserves to die."

"So a killer for hire."

Jordon nodded again, trying to look superior and tough—a little hard to do with a knife wound bleeding all over the place.

"You were hired to kill Bellisia?" Ezekiel kept his tone mild.

"Any of the women. *All* of them, including those little brats."

That dark swirling rage, always inside Ezekiel, pushed close to the surface. He took a breath and resisted the urge to kick the bastard out of the tree.

"Senator Smythe hired you."

A crafty look crept into Jordon's eyes. "Get me out of here and get me medical help and I'll tell you everything you want to know."

Ezekiel was fast, and he used blurring speed, slamming his knife right through Jordon's left thigh. He wasn't in the least gentle about it. Or careful. Jordon screamed and tried to throw himself to the side, away from Ezekiel, but Zeke just caught his shirt, settled him back against the trunk and casually wiped the blood from his blade on the sniper's other pant leg.

"That's not very respectful, calling the girls brats. I wouldn't want you thinking I'm not being upfront with you. I'm just fine cutting holes in you all day. I know a thousand ways to keep you alive. I'm a doctor. Did Violet mention that? A surgeon. Bellisia is my woman, and you royally pissed me off. So if you want to get along with me, I suggest you answer the questions."

"You're a doctor?" Now the breathing was more than ragged. Jordon was hyperventilating. "You can't do this. You took an oath. Doesn't that mean you have to fix me up?"

Ezekiel deliberately looked around him. "No one's here but the two of us, Stanley. I guess that oath doesn't count much unless I want it to." He tapped Jordon's right thigh with the point of his knife so that little dots of blood welled up, and the man's leg jumped with every prick. "I think it best if you talk to me about Senator Smythe."

"You're psycho." The accusation came out somewhere between a scream and a sob.

"Possibly. But no one's going to save you. You've got to talk, Stanley, or it's only going to get worse."

"Smythe is a cold bitch. She sleeps with anyone to get her way."

"She sleep with you?"

"Yeah. She did. At first she was a little whore, eager to do anything I wanted her to do, but then I was doing things for her I didn't even remember agreeing to." He shook his head. "I swear it was like I was hypnotized or something. I did a couple of jobs for her, and all the time we'd be together she'd talk about these disgusting experiments Whitney was doing with some women. Using insect DNA or something to mutate them." A shiver of revulsion went through him.

Clearly Violet had done her job, using her twisted talent of influencing people with her voice to turn a number of supporters against the women Whitney had experimented on. Ezekiel had seen the same hatred and loathing stamped on the faces of the mercenary soldiers Violet had in her employ.

"Keep talking."

"She kept saying we had to wipe them out, that she was planning to do it herself, to save America. That if we didn't get it done, the world would eventually be overrun—that they were like cockroaches, multiplying."

"I thought you only worked for money."

Jordon's body shuddered with the effort to keep going. He shook his head several times to clear it, to try to focus. He shivered continually, but didn't seem to notice. The sniper frowned in an effort to remember.

"She paid me part. When I get the job done, she'll pay me the rest. The bounty was high too, one of the best contracts I've ever taken. A mil each for the little bra . . . the kids," he hastily corrected. "A million apiece for the women. I didn't get a thing for killing any of you so I didn't bother, although I had you in my sights a couple of times. That should buy me something."

"Did she hire anyone else for the same job?"

He coughed. Spat blood. "No, it was all supposed to happen when she initiated the attack. She was the Trojan horse, coming to make peace talks with Spagnola. Said we weren't to touch him. She wanted to do him herself. That would be the signal to start the war. Everyone else was to kill all of you, and we were supposed to do the women and kids. She'd hired three other mercs to help with the job besides her own private little army."

"But you didn't have a shot."

He sighed. Coughed. Spat more blood. "No, so we waited. Watched them all get massacred. Of course the bitch got away. I knew she would. Decided it would be better to let things settle down. Almost took those kids when they were let out to play the other day, but too dangerous, too many guards on them."

His entire body shuddered. "I'm cold."

Ezckiel ignored that. "As far as you know, no one else was hired to kill the women and children?"

Jordon shook his head. "You got to do something. There's blood everywhere."

There was. It ran in long trails down the man's body and onto the branch to leak down the trunk of the tree.

"What else did Smythe say?"

Jordon closed his eyes and leaned his head back, as if unable to maintain the weight of it. "She's going to be president. She's made an alliance with Cheng. Big badass in China. The government there protects him, but he makes deals all over the world. He's loaded, and he's backing her to be president."

"She's dead." Ezekiel leaned toward the man and raised his chin with the blade of his knife. "She didn't get away. Bellisia killed her. Even if you did the job, you wouldn't have gotten paid." Jordon resisted raising his head, but Ezekiel held the blade of the knife steady. "Look at me."

The head shook. "No. No. Why are you doing this? They're

insects. *Insects.* Like cockroaches. Snakes. They spit venom. Don't you understand? The nest has to be wiped out."

"You don't do causes. You don't save America. You hold all soldiers in contempt. Why would you want to deviate, risk your life for a cause?" Ezekiel kept his voice very quiet. Nonthreatening.

Jordon frowned. Blood leaked from his mouth. He shook his head, his eyelids flickering continually. "I don't . . ." He trailed off. "The meeting. Three senators there. A roomful of us. Her voice. The way she talked. There was a general too. A bigwig."

"How many people?"

Jordon didn't respond. He closed his eyes and shook his head.

"You don't want me to hurt you again," Ezekiel said softly. "Just answer. Soon this will be over and you can sleep."

"About sixty of us, mostly her army and the mercs. No women."

"The senators. I need names."

"Crane from Mississippi. Delgato from Florida. Jenson from California . . ." The voice trailed off.

"The general?"

"General Ivan Newman."

Ezekiel's heart jumped. The man had the ear of the president. He was the Air Force's military service chief, and outside of his duties for the Joint Chiefs of Staff, he worked directly for the secretary of the Air Force. It was no wonder that their squadron found themselves deployed in several places, leaving them without guards for the women. Violet had prepared carefully and gotten people in key positions to aid her. Had she been able to have a little more time, she most likely would have eventually succeeded in wiping the women out.

Jordon drew in another deep, shuddering breath. Blood bubbled and foamed around his lips. More did the same around his hands. His fingers were coated. He didn't seem to notice. His throat rattled. There was silence. A moment went by. Another. Again there was a deep, shuddering breath, and then his body began to slowly topple over.

Ezekiel stood up, pushed him with his boot so that the man fell from the tree, landing practically at Gino's feet.

Gino looked up at him. "Take care of that weapon. He made a great shot with it."

"Too late. I kicked the damn thing out of the tree already."

"Do you always have to be such a badass?" Gino demanded, hands on his hips.

Ezekiel smiled at him, crouched low and then jumped down. "Yeah. Otherwise Mordichai and Malichai wouldn't recognize me." That much was true. He wasn't going to admit he was never a badass around Bellisia, he just tried to be.

20

Grace Fontenot sat in the rocking chair her husband had built so many years earlier. Pipe in hand, she looked out over the river. Her three great-granddaughters played in the little play yard only a few hundred feet from her. She could see them as easily as she could her beloved river. The sound of their laughter drifted to her on the slight breeze coming in from the water. She remembered her grandsons playing and laughing. The sound was better than any symphony she'd ever heard.

Cayenne, Pepper and Bellisia emerged from the house, smelling of spices from the kitchen. She'd given them another cooking lesson. They didn't know it, but she enjoyed those lessons a lot more than they did—and she could tell it was one of their favorite things. She'd never had a daughter, and having the opportunity to spend time with her grandson's wife, Pepper, and Trap's wife, Cayenne, and Ezekiel's woman, Bellisia, filled her days with laughter and joy.

"I love the way pork roast smells," Cayenne informed

Nonny, as she leaned down to brush a kiss on the paper-thin skin of her cheek. "Especially when it's in the slow cooker and takes all day. The house smells like home."

Cayenne, Nonny speculated, had come a long way in a very short time, from that girl who had been raised in a small cell with no family and no knowledge of what a family was. Nonny was proud of her. Showing affection for anyone other than Trap had been difficult for her, but now, she was good with the three little girls, Pepper and Nonny. She definitely was going out of her way to help Bellisia find her way with the others.

"Me too," Pepper said. "When I'm not throwing up. When Wyatt comes home, I might have to kick him very hard, Nonny."

Grace couldn't help laughing. "At least you're not having to hide in the bedroom because you've turned into a little sexpot, Pepper."

Pepper burst out laughing. That was another good thing. Pepper could laugh at the effects of the chemical that built in her body forcing her to need sex. She was able to joke with the women about it, where before she could barely open her mouth because she was so ashamed and guilty.

"That's true enough. Wyatt thought if I got pregnant I wouldn't produce that chemical, and he was right. He'll crow about being right."

There was so much love and pride in her voice, Nonny had to close her eyes, remembering the way she felt about her husband for all the years of their marriage. For a moment her eyes burned. Her man. So beautiful. He was a man's man, much like her grandsons and their friends. She was so blessed to have them surrounding her, making their homes with her or close by.

She'd had a few lonely years when she thought she could join her husband, but now, she had her boys to look after again. She wanted them all to be happy like her Ezekiel.

They needed to find good women, and she planned to help each of them do that very thing.

She worried the most about Joe. Joe was quiet and calm, a steady leader commanding respect from men who commanded respect. That said a lot about him. Now, recovering from his wounds, he rarely spoke and he never smiled, not even when he looked at the triplets. Grace thought they could make anyone smile, heal any wound, but maybe not. Maybe the scars Violet had put on Joe went much further than on his skin or bone. These went to his very heart and soul. She would have her work cut out for her making him whole again.

She couldn't help smiling when she finally opened her eyes and looked at Bellisia. Little Bellisia. She was a strong woman. Fit to walk beside her Ezekiel. She would walk through fire for her man. She had done as he asked and stayed in the house while he had gone hunting the men shooting at her. Grace had seen how difficult that was for her.

"How are you coming with your wedding plans, Bella?" she asked.

Cayenne and Pepper coughed behind their hands. "Yeah, Bella," Cayenne said, nudging her. "What about those wedding plans?"

Bellisia blushed. "Well . . . Um . . ." she hedged.

Grace sat up straighter. "That isn't an answer. Ezekiel has hired more workmen. They're nearly finished with that house of yours. He's got special walls so you can see the river and bulletproof glass everywhere. The moment he's finished, he'll expect you to move in. I told that man I'd be getting out my shotgun if he doesn't do right by you."

"It's just that . . ." Bellisia trailed off again, turning tomato red.

Pepper laughed. "They start talking wedding plans and Ezekiel gets all hot and bothered, and the next thing you know, he's worn her out and she's asleep dreaming about her man and what he can do, not the wedding part."

Grace had practiced her stern look from the moment she'd had sons and then grandsons living in her home. She had needed that look in her arsenal many, many times. She was very grateful she had it, because it allowed her to keep from laughing as she turned that particular expression on her latest "daughter." "Is this true, Bella?"

Bellisia nodded. "In my defense, Nonny, the man can kiss. Like truly kiss. You have no idea. He starts kissing me and every sane thought goes right out the window."

That was the trouble—she did have an idea. Grace Fontenot knew all about a man's kisses and what they could do to a woman.

"Did you get the license taken care of?" She knew very well they had. Ezekiel had done the paperwork first thing. He was a man who knew the importance of paperwork. They had faked Bellisia's birth certificate, and the license had been issued over seventy-two hours prior. More, now.

"Yes, nearly a week ago."

Grace pulled out her cell phone. She loved the little phone Raoul's wife, Flame, had given her. Flame kept her supplied with the latest gadgets and always took the time to teach her how to use them. She could text with one thumb, a useful tool in situations like now, when she didn't want to spook the bride. First she texted Ezekiel, then his brothers and finally Papite Vallier, an old family friend.

"That's good, *chère*. At least you managed to get that done." Nonny studied her. Bellisia was a beautiful woman with her pale hair, a thick pelt that looked sleek like that of an otter in the water—and she spent a great deal of time in the water. "Do you really want to marry Ezekiel? He's your choice for certain?"

"Absolutely," Bellisia stated. "Not a shadow of a doubt. Well, sometimes I worry about our children and what my DNA could do to them, but he says his DNA is every bit as enhanced as mine. Still, that in a way makes me worry more."

"I worry about that as well," Pepper said, one hand sliding

over her stomach. There was the slightest pouch there, barely showing, so that if one didn't know, there would be no guessing. "We consulted Lily Whitney before we decided to try. The girls were in vitro, and Whitney added his enhancements, so we have no idea what will happen with this baby, but Lily says the baby will be just fine and will be born with skills and talents like the other babies born to GhostWalkers."

Grace's cell phone made a little noise and she glanced down at the text from Papite. Anything for you. On my way.

"That's what Violet used to turn her army against us," Cayenne said. "The children. She wouldn't have stopped with just our children and the three of us, she would have gone after the others as well."

Grace believed that to be true. Violet Smythe had been a troubled woman. A true sociopath, caring nothing for others. If they got in her way, she removed them. She wanted power, and she wanted to be the only female GhostWalker. There had been no hope for her, although her white knight Joe had tried to save her.

Grace's cell pinged, and she glanced down at the text from Ezekiel. Want to marry her ASAP. If you've got the preacher, I'm on my way back with my brothers.

Sometimes you just had to take matters into your own hands. There was plenty of food. She always made enough to feed a small army. Usually she had that around her dinner table. Tonight there would be a celebration. Music. Dancing. She texted her friend Bernard to come with his band and then Donny. He would want to come to the celebration.

"You need to see to Bellisia's hair and makeup, girls. Find her a pretty dress. I'll be working in the kitchen to make certain we have enough food for tonight."

Bellisia turned slowly from where she was leaning against the railing, looking out over the river, just as Grace liked to do. Both were drawn to that body of water. Grace liked to think that Bellisia would be living just down the road, looking at the same river in the morning over her coffee.

"My hair and makeup?" she echoed.

"That's right, girl, unless you want to be married just as you are. Ezekiel won't mind, but I suspect you'll want to look your Sunday best."

"Married?"

Cayenne and Pepper caught her arms. "Come with us."

"Now?" Bellisia said.

"Your man is on his way, and so is the preacher. We don' mess around here in the bayous, not when it comes to our women marryin'." Nonny pointed to her shotgun. "I wouldn't want to have to hold that on you durin' the entire ceremony, but I will if I have no choice."

Bellisia burst out laughing, when just a moment earlier she'd looked faint. "I'm really getting married? Today? Right now?"

"That's right. Preacher's comin'. Band's comin'. Groom and his brothers on the way. You're holdin' things up."

"I'm being railroaded."

"Never heard of a woman puttin' off her weddin' just to get kissed, even if the man is as hot as Ezekiel. You're the one draggin' your feet, not him. And you're probably in the family way, the way you two have been carryin' on. So you're gettin' married, Bella."

Bellisia laughed as the SUV swept into the yard, doors popped open and her man and half the team leapt out. Ezekiel started toward her, a grin on his face. Nonny shook her head, stopping Ezekiel in his tracks. She pointed to the house, and Pepper and Cayenne grabbed Bellisia and rushed inside.

The wedding took place two scant hours later. Bellisia was decked out in one of Pepper's dresses. It was far too sexy for her to feel comfortable in front of the others, but Ezekiel's face lit up when he saw her and she decided she might like it after all. It wasn't that she was all that modest, but she still wasn't used to so many people surrounding her with love, warmth and camaraderie.

"I love you, Bellisia," Ezekiel whispered as he took her hand and drew her beneath the protection of his shoulder. He turned her to face the preacher.

"I love you too, Ezekiel," she whispered, putting her hand on his chest and fitting her front to his side. '

Both turned their heads toward Grace Fontenot, who was beaming. The preacher cleared his throat, and they turned back to take their vows.

AUTHOR'S NOTE

I grew up with a deep respect for the military. My grand-father, my father, all three of my brothers, one sister, my sons-in-law and my nieces and nephews were all or are now in the military. I spent a good deal of time listening to stories and sending care packages, so once I became published I knew I wanted to extend my feelings of admiration and respect in a meaningful way.

I was determined to show appreciation for our soldiers and have been work' s with Support Our Soldiers to send books to soldi; who were deployed overseas. Prior to working wi. -oki, in 2004 I began to send care packages and, a year later, books to soldiers. I found Kelley Granzow, who worked with SOS in Columbus, and in 2006 I began sending books through her. I have no idea how many books I have sent over the years, but for every new book release I sent thirty to fifty books along with the money for postage. (I have a lot of new book releases per year and Kelley sends hundreds of packages.) It had been my intention to send gifts to our soldiers, but in reality, I was the one to receive gifts as emails and letters came in from those soldiers sharing their thanks and stories of how my books had, in some small way, helped them. Whether through offering escapism or offering hope, the soldiers shared how the books affected them.

It was always important to me that there be realism in my books, especially with my GhostWalker series, which features military men and women from a special program I created in which the soldiers were enhanced psychically. Knowing that this science fiction–thriller aspect would need to be offset by as much real-life military information as I could include, I set out to find experts in different fields of the military to ensure the fictional missions were accurately portrayed, the weapons were correctly used and the other aspects of military life were familiar to those serving or those who had served.

I have had a tremendous amount of help from generous soldiers both currently serving and retired. I was fortunate enough to have soldiers from every branch of the service help me. In the Marine Corps I have two Master Gunneries, one retired, one not, who help me. I also have two Navy SEALs, one retired, one not, and a retired Naval doctor who assist. In the Army, I have a retired Ranger and a retired explosives and weapons expert who help, and I have help from the members of the Air Force as well. I'm always looking for good contacts willing to help me, especially to plan out missions. I still make mistakes. I'm rather inept with guns, but those mistakes are mine and not those of the wonderful men and women willing to help me.

As a civilian with a strong respect for the military, I hope my books always portray my admiration through my hours of research and attention to detail, through my focus on military personnel as heroes and heroines, and through my own support by sending my books and care packages to those who have paved the way for me to realize my own dreams because of the freedoms I enjoy.

KEEP READING FOR AN EXCERPT FROM THE NEXT

SHADOW RIDERS NOVEL BY CHRISTINE FEEHAN

SHADOW REAPER

NOW AVAILABLE FROM BERKLEY

Ricco Ferraro wanted to punch something. Hard. No, he *needed* to punch something, or someone—preferably his brother. It would be satisfying to feel the crunch of his knuckles splitting open flesh. Cracking bone. Yeah. He could get behind that if his brother didn't shut the hell up. They were in a hospital with doctors and nurses all around. If he really went to town and made it real, Stefano wouldn't suffer for too long. Of course, it might not be such a good idea when he could barely stand . . .

"Ricco," Stefano hissed again, using his low, annoying, big-brother tone that made Ricco feel crazier than he already was feeling. "Are you even listening to me? This has got to stop. The next time you might not make it. You were in surgery for hours. *Hours.*"

Stefano had been lecturing him for the last ten minutes; Ricco figured no one could listen that long, let alone him. He didn't have the patience. He knew damn well how close he'd come. They'd replaced every drop of blood he had in his body not once, but twice on the operating table. He'd hit the wall at over two hundred miles an hour, but he knew he hadn't driven into it. Something broke and the suspension went, driving pieces of metal through his body like shrapnel. He'd lived it. He still felt it. Every muscle and bone in his body hurt like hell.

"I'll listen when you make sense, Stefano," Ricco snapped and finished buttoning up his shirt. It wasn't easy. The pain was excruciating when he made the slightest movement, but he was getting out whether the doctor signed the release papers or not. Six, almost seven weeks in the hospital was enough for him. All he could stand. Even though he'd spent three of those weeks in a coma and wasn't aware, it still counted. He'd had enough of all of them—doctors, nurses, surgeons, the neuro doc, but especially his older brother.

He turned to face them, his four brothers and one sister, with their faces looking concerned. Grim. But there was Francesca, Stefano's wife. He focused on her and the compassion in her eyes. She had nudged Stefano several times to get him to stop. It had worked both times, but only for a moment or two.

"I'm going to say this one more time and then never again. You don't have to believe me." He spoke to Francesca because, surprisingly, it was Francesca who believed him. They all should have—they could hear lies. That gave him pause. *He* could hear lies. If no one believed him, it was because he had to be lying to them—and to himself.

He turned his back on them. Just that little motion hurt. His body protested the slightest thing he did. "At least wait until you get the report on the car before you jump to conclusions. I didn't have control. The car's system just shut down." That much he was certain of. He drove at speeds of over two hundred miles per hour and had no trouble; his hand-eye coordination and his reflexes never failed him. The car had failed. He knew that with absolute certainty, so why couldn't he convince his brothers and sister that he hadn't tried to end his life? Why couldn't he convince himself?

It took everything he had to stand there, trying not to sway when his body broke out in a sweat and he could count his heartbeats through the pain swamping his muscles. What had he done to try to save himself? Nothing. He'd done nothing. He'd let fate decide, closing his eyes and giving himself up to the judgment of the universe. He'd woken up in the hospital with needles in his arm and pain in every single muscle and organ in his body in spite of the painkillers.

His room was filled with flowers. There were boxes of cards, all from people in Ferraro territory, the blocks considered off-limits to any criminal. Their people, all good and decent. He hadn't looked at the cards, but he wanted to keep them. He didn't deserve those cards any more than he deserved the concern on his brothers' and sister's faces, or the compassion Francesca showed. Still, he was alive and he had to continue.

"Something went wrong with the car, Stefano," he repeated, turning back to look his brother in the eye.

"We're checking the car," Vittorio assured. He was always the peacemaker in the family and Ricco appreciated him. "We immediately towed it to our personal garage and it's been under guard. Only our trusted people are working on it."

Ricco flicked his brother a quick glance that was meant to serve as a thank-you. He didn't say it aloud, not with Stefano breathing down his neck.

"You almost died," Stefano said, and this time the anger was gone from his voice and there was strain. Apprehension. Caring.

That was Ricco's undoing. It was impossible to see or hear the stoic Stefano torn up. He was the acknowledged head of the family for a reason. Ricco didn't deserve for them all to care so much. There were too many secrets, too many omissions. He'd put them all in jeopardy and they had no idea. Worse, he couldn't tell them. He just had to watch over them night and day, a duty he took very seriously.

He shook his head, sighing. "I know, Stefano. I'm sorry. I lost control of the car." That was true. He had. He remembered very little of the aftermath, but in that moment when he realized the car wasn't an extension of him anymore, that it was a beast roaring for supremacy, separate from him, he had felt relief that it was over. If he had died, it all would have been over and the danger to his family gone.

"Are you convincing me? Or yourself?" Stefano asked quietly. "We're taking you out of here, but you have to pull yourself together. Enough with the craziness, Ricco, or I'll have no choice but to pull you off rotation even after you're physically cleared for work—which, by the way, won't be for some time."

Gasps went up from his brothers and Emmanuelle, his sister. Francesca uttered a soft "no" and shook her head. Ricco's heart nearly seized. He was a rider. A shadow rider. It was who he was. What he was. A rider had no choice but to do what he'd been trained for from the age of two—even before that. It was in his bones, in his blood; he couldn't live without it.

Stefano stepped directly in front of him, close, so they were eye to eye. "Understand me, Ricco. I won't lose another brother. I'll do *anything* to save you. Anything. Give anything, including my life. I'll use every weapon in my arsenal to protect you from yourself and any enemy that comes your way. You do something about this, whatever it takes, and that includes counseling. But there aren't going to be any more accidents. You get me, brother? There will be no more accidents."

Ricco nodded his head. What else could he do? When Stefano laid down the law he meant every word he said. It wasn't often that Stefano spoke like this to them, but no one would ever defy him, including Ricco. He loved his brother. His family. He'd sacrificed most of his life for them gladly, but Stefano was more than a brother. He was Mom, Dad, big brother, protector, all rolled into one.

It was Stefano who had always been there for him. His own mother hadn't even come to the hospital to visit him after the accident, but Stefano had barely left even to eat. He looked haggard and worn. Every time the pain had awakened Ricco from his semiconscious state, Stefano and his brothers and Emmanuelle had been right there with him. They'd stuck by him throughout those long six weeks. That solidarity only reinforced his decision to keep them safe. They were everything to him.

"I get you," he assured softly.

"It's done, then. You don't train any more than the regular training hours, and that's after you've done your physical therapy and the doctors okay you for training again. You sleep even if you have to take something to get you to sleep. You stop drinking so fucking much and you talk to me if you are having trouble doing those things."

His heart was pounding overtime now. He couldn't promise Stefano that he would stop with his extra training hours once he was cleared. He had to make certain he was in top form. That he didn't—couldn't—ever make a mistake again. That was part of him as well. But how did he explain that to his brother when he couldn't explain why? He just nodded, remaining silent so no one could hear his lie.

He drank sometimes to put himself to sleep; he could stop drinking with no problem, he just wouldn't be able to sleep. He wasn't about to say anything more to Stefano. It was impossible to lie to him and he didn't want his brother to worry any more than he already did.

Staring into the mirror as he finished buttoning his dove gray shirt, he looked at the vicious bruises and the swelling, at the side of his head that felt as if it had nearly been caved in, causing the severe concussion. Beneath the shirt his muscles rippled with every movement, a testimony to his strength—and he was unbelievably strong. According to the surgeon, a miracle and his superb physical condition had saved him from certain death. His frame was deceptive in that his roped muscles weren't so obvious the way his cousins' were, but they were there beneath the skin of his wide shoulders and powerful arms.

He reached for his suit jacket. The Ferraro family of riders always wore pin-striped suits. Always. It was their signature. Even Emmanuelle wore the suit, fitted and making her look like a million bucks, but then she could wear anything and look beautiful. He sent his sister a reassuring smile because she looked as if she might cry. He knew he looked rough. He felt worse than rough, but his sister didn't have to know that.

"I'm fine, Emme," he reassured softly. He wasn't, but then, he hadn't been for a long, long time.

"Of course you are," she said briskly, but she looked strained. "Walking away from a crash like that is easy for a Ferraro."

He hadn't exactly walked away from it, but he was standing now, and that was what counted. He forced himself not to wince as he donned his jacket. Once the material settled over his arms and shoulders, he looked the way his brothers looked—a fit male, intimidating, imposing even. No one could see the bruises and internal injuries, or inside his head where someone was taking a jackhammer to it.

There was a rustle at the door. His brothers Giovanni and Taviano moved aside to allow the doctor and nurse to enter. The doctor glared at all of them. The nurse kept her eyes on the floor. He noted her hands were shaking. She didn't want to confront the Ferraros, but had no choice when the surgeon insisted on saying his piece.

"You shouldn't be up, Mr. Ferraro," Dr. Townsend said. "You were in a coma for three weeks and your operation took hours to repair all the damage to your organs. You need rest and extensive physical therapy."

"I've done nothing but rest for the past six weeks."

"You're going to have headaches, blurred vision, dizziness on and off for a while. You need care."

"I'm fine," Ricco assured. "And very grateful to you." That had to be said whether or not it was a lie. And it was a complete lie. He had the headache from hell, was dizzy and his vision was blurred, but he was leaving.

"I refuse to release you. You could have blood clots, an aneurysm, any number of complications," the doctor continued.

"I won't," Ricco said, giving them the look every Ferraro had perfected before their tenth birthday. His eyes were cold and flat and hard. Both the doctor and nurse immediately moved back. That, at least, was satisfying. He took another step toward them and they parted to allow him through. He might look like hell, and feel worse, but he was still formidable.

"I want the boxes of cards, but you can distribute the flowers to other hospital patients," Ricco continued, ignoring Stefano's frown. He knew what that meant. Stefano would want to talk to his doctor. A shadow rider could hear lies and compel truth—even from someone in the medical field. He kept walking, knowing his brother would never let him walk out to face the reporters alone.

"You're leaving against medical advice," the doctor reiterated.

Ricco didn't slow down. Immediately, his brothers and Emmanuelle fell into step around him. Surrounding him. Shoulder to shoulder. Solidarity. The moment he was one step outside his hospital room, his cousins Emilio and Enzo Gallo moved in front of them. Tomas and Cosimo Abatangelo, also first cousins, dropped in behind. The cousins always acted as bodyguards for the Ferraros, and Ricco knew he needed them. He might say he was ready to leave the hospital, but he wasn't. His body needed rest desperately, as well as time to heal. He just couldn't do it there.

The press had been all over the accident, trying to sneak into the hospital and get photographs of him covered in bandages. One nurse had been suspended while they investigated the allegation that she'd taken numerous pictures of

Ricco unconscious and sold them to the tabloids. There had been several other attempts by orderlies and a janitor. Anyone getting a picture of playboy billionaire Ricco Ferraro after he crashed his race car in a fiery display stood to make hundreds of thousands of dollars.

"Did Eloisa come to visit you?" Stefano asked, walking in perfect step with him.

Ricco glanced at him, one eyebrow raised. "I crashed, Stefano. Not perfect. Why would you think our mother would ever come to visit me when I showed the world I was less than perfect?" Stefano had raised them, not Eloisa.

Stefano glanced at Francesca. "I thought she was attempting to turn over a new leaf. Guess I was wrong."

Ricco didn't answer. He knew Francesca had been trying to make peace with Eloisa, but his mother didn't seem to have one maternal instinct in her body. He couldn't care less. They'd had Stefano while growing up and he'd watched out for them—just as he was doing now. His eldest brother might be annoying, but he loved his siblings. A. Lot. And he looked after them. It was something they all counted on.

Ricco hated that he'd caused his brothers and sister so much concern. He knew he had to change his life around. It was time. He just didn't know how.

"Ready?" Stefano asked as they approached the double doors leading to the parking lot. No one broke stride, all moving with the same confident step. The town car had already been brought to the entrance. It was only a few feet, but the paparazzi, several rows deep, already had flashes going off.

"Yeah," Ricco said. He wasn't. He could barely walk upright. Every single step jarred his body and reminded him he was human.

The doctors had told him that if he hadn't been in such good shape physically, he wouldn't have survived. That was both a blessing and a curse. He knew more sweat dotted his forehead even before he could reach the privacy of the car, but he kept walking. He had to get out of the hospital before he lost his mind. He'd had his own private wing paid for by the Ferraros, complete with bodyguards, but that hadn't stopped the madness of the press and his fear that they'd catch him at his most vulnerable.

Stefano and the rest of his siblings had stayed the three weeks he was kept unconscious; at least that was what Francesca had whispered to him. They only left if a job was imperative. Once he was awake, it was mainly Stefano with him while the others took care of work. He felt their love, and in that moment, facing the paparazzi with his siblings surrounding him, he knew it had all been worth every sacrifice he'd made to protect them. He'd do it all over again in a heartbeat.

Ricco kept his head up as they moved as a single unit to the town car with its tinted windows. Emilio and Enzo cleared a path through the reporters. None of the Ferraros even looked at them. Ordinarily they were friendly with the paparazzi. They needed the reporters and photographers to provide alibis for them. Today, the family just wanted to get Ricco home.

To his dismay, Stefano slid into the car with him. Ricco sighed and shook his head as Tomas shut the door on the frantic cameras and shouted questions. Enzo slipped behind the wheel.

"Stefano." God, he was tired. He lifted a hand to wipe at the beads of sweat dotting his forehead. "You don't have to escort me home."

"I wanted a private word with you."

Evidently the fact that Enzo was driving the vehicle and Emilio was in the front seat with him didn't matter.

Ricco laid his head against the cool leather. "I'm listening."

"I've been patient since you returned from Japan. More than patient. You've not been the same since Japan and I've waited for you to tell me what the hell happened to change you, but you pretend it's all good. It isn't, Ricco."

Ricco stiffened in spite of all of his training. It was the last thing he expected Stefano to bring up. He was barely fourteen when he'd been sent to Japan and had just had his sixteenth birthday when he returned. It seemed a lifetime ago. He'd tried to bury those memories, but nightmares refused to go away. They haunted him no matter how much liquor he consumed.

"You have to talk to someone about what went on there. It's colored your life. You're the best rider we have, Ricco, but you're too reckless. You don't care about your own life, and that's something I won't allow you to risk. You've gotten worse, not better."

He couldn't deny that. "I've never once failed a mission. Not one single time, Stefano." Ricco could barely breathe when he told that truth that wasn't the entire truth. The thought of having his legacy—what he'd been born to do—taken from him was enough to kill him. He wouldn't survive. Doing his job kept him alive. His brother couldn't possibly be saying what Ricco thought he was.

"No, but you don't give a damn about whether you live or die."

It was the fucking truth, and if he opened his mouth, Stefano would hear it. He forced air through his lungs and stared out the window at the buildings as they drove through the streets of Chicago. Outwardly, he looked calm. Confident. There was one truth he could give his brother. He turned back to face him. "There is no surviving without being a shadow rider. You take that away from me and I've got nothing to hang on to."

Swift anger crossed Stefano's face. "That's fucking bullshit, Ricco. You have us. Your family. How do you think I will do without you? Or Emme? The rest of them? You're important to us. Do you even give a damn about us?"

He loved his brothers and sister fiercely. Protectively. He'd alienated himself from them—for them. Fury burst through him, that rage that sometimes threatened to consume him.

"What does that mean? You think I would do this if I had a choice . . . ?" He broke off. That was a mistake, and shadow riders didn't make mistakes. He couldn't afford to have Stefano launch an investigation. It was the painkillers, loosening his tongue when he knew better.

Stefano fell silent. That was a really bad sign. He was highly intelligent and little got by him. Ricco tried desperately to think of something that might distract his brother, but nothing came to mind. He hurt too much. Every muscle. Every bone.

Most people didn't realize how physically demanding it was to race a car for as long as a race took, let alone wrecking at such a high speed. Even with all the safety measures built into the car, the jolting and spinning on one's body was incredible. Add an actual crash into a wall of thick concrete and metal, and his body felt as if it had been beaten by an assembly line of strong men with baseball bats—or run over by several very large trucks.

"I get what you're saying to me, Stefano, and I'll do something about it. I have to be a rider. You won't have to replace me in the rotation. As soon as I'm healed, I'll be back to work." He poured truth into his voice, knowing his brother could hear him.

That wasn't going to be enough and he knew it. He made a show of sighing, so it would be more believable when he caved. "I need to change my life." There was nothing truer than that. "I can't wait for a woman to walk down our streets throwing shadows out like Francesca did. I have to find someone now. I've been giving it some thought, but I had decided it wouldn't be fair to find someone, allow them to fall in love with me, and then have to give them up to marry a rider so I can produce children."

All riders were expected to marry another capable of producing riders, even if that meant an arranged marriage. Emme had it the worst because she was a woman, and if she didn't find her man by the time she was thirty, her marriage would be arranged. The men had a few more years before they were forced into an arranged marriage, but there was no falling in love and getting married to just anyone.

Stefano's dark gaze never left his, and Ricco forced himself to continue. "I've thought a lot about this. I'm an artist. I know I need physical therapy before I'm ready for work again, so I think now would be a good time to work on my art. I've continued studying Shibari, and I love the artistic elements, but the only place to actually display or practice my art is in one of the clubs."

Stefano blinked, his only reaction.

Ricco nodded. "I know what I do can't be protected in the kinds of clubs I'd have to frequent. Sooner or later the paparazzi would find out and it would be in every magazine from here to hell and back. But if I find a good rope model, one I can work with in the privacy of my home, I can photograph my art. I've always wanted to do that. I have my own darkroom and can develop the photographs myself. Eventually I can put them on canvas or in book form. I just have to find the right model. I'm hoping if I do, I'll feel a strong connection with her."

Stefano rubbed the bridge of his nose as the car slowed and then turned through the heavy throng of paparazzi standing on the sidewalk and nearly blocking the drive up to Ricco's home. Both men ignored them as Enzo inched the car through the crowd to the high iron gates. "It's a risk, Ricco. Not the art. The woman."

Ricco nodded. "I'm aware of that. I want to find someone I can connect with on a more intimate level. Someone who could love me and maybe understand if I have to be with another woman."

"That's highly unlikely."

"I know. I know that. I just can't live like this anymore." Staying up all night, drinking himself into a stupor or partying with multiple women at the same time until the sun came up. Never feeling anything. He watched as the gates swung open to allow them inside. He didn't realize he was holding his breath until they closed behind the car, locking out the paparazzi.

"Someone threatened us, didn't they?"

Stefano asked it quietly—so quietly Ricco almost missed it and almost asked what he meant. Stefano said it like he already knew, that he was just confirming. Of course he would figure it out. He'd been the head of the family for years, since he was a teenager. He'd taken care of them all when he was even younger than that. He would know. He'd probably considered that possibility all along.

"I can't talk about it." That was confirmation and it wasn't.

Stefano swore, a long tirade of Italian. He kept his voice low, vicious, and Ricco heard the promise of retaliation there.

He shook his head. "Just let it go."

"Let it go?" Stefano looked at him as if he had grown two heads. "They threaten my brother, a fellow rider, and you want me to let it go? We have an international council— "

"Don't. I mean it, Stefano. Let it go. There are reasons."

"There are never reasons for one family of riders to threaten another family."

"It was a long time ago. I'm asking you to let it go." He didn't allow desperation to show on his face, no matter that he was feeling it. Stefano would go to war in a heartbeat over him, but there was no way to know how many families in Japan would unite against them. Ricco wasn't willing to risk his brothers, sister or cousins.

He'd remained silent for years. They'd been long, hard years of always looking over his shoulder and training harder than ever. Often, when he couldn't sleep, he'd go to one of his family's homes and watch over them, paranoid that something might happen to them. After several years had gone by, he was certain they were safe, and he didn't want his brother to stir up trouble, but he still checked on them throughout the night.

"I think finding a partner for your art is a positive move, Ricco. Looking for a woman to be your partner when you know you'll have to walk away later is something else altogether."

Ricco already knew that, but he was losing too much of himself. Going too wild in a desperate attempt to feel something. Anything. He was already too far gone and didn't know if there was anyone who could bring him back. He'd deliberately separated himself from his family, spending less time in public with them and more time racing or partying in the hopes that others would think he didn't care about them. He must have done a good job for Stefano to ask him if he cared.

Ricco dropped his hand to the door, needing to escape. Stefano shifted in his seat as if he might follow him. "I need to lie down," he said, knowing his brother would hear the ring of truth. He did need a bed, and fast, or he was going to topple right over.

Stefano backed down. "Angelina Laconi is going to come check on you, and don't give me any trouble over it. She's a nurse."

"She makes eyes at me." Now she'd have excuses to touch him. Life sucked. He wasn't going to get out of having a nurse drop by; he could tell by Stefano's expression.

"Live with it. Emmanuelle made certain your fridge is stocked and Francesca made several meals for you. They're in the freezer. One's in the fridge."

"Please thank them for me." Ricco shoved open the door and forced his legs to work. It wasn't easy, but he had discipline in abundance, a trait every rider needed. He was very, very aware of Stefano's eyes on him as he made his way up to the door.

❦

"Francesca." Ricco bent his head to brush a kiss along his sister-in-law's cheek. The weeks of healing had helped. Pain didn't crash through him every time he took a step, and he'd begun training again, although Stefano watched him closely. His older brother was still unaware of the training hall Ricco had installed in his home a few years earlier. Most gatherings were in Stefano's penthouse in the Ferraro Hotel.

"Ricco." She flashed her amused smile, the one that mocked him a little for his greeting.

He rarely said hello or good-bye. He said her name and she responded by saying his. He loved that about her. He loved everything about her, mainly that she loved his brother more than anything or anyone.

He'd never really learned the art of relaxing. He could play his part out in public, but at home, with his brothers and sister, he had always been the one to pace around; to help Taviano, his youngest brother, in the kitchen; or to find his way to the training room and work out while the others conversed. Since the accident, he'd made attempts at being better.

"Smells good."

"I hope it tastes good. I've been working with a few new recipes for the artichoke sauce you said you liked and I think I've got it for you now. I'm serving homemade pasta with artichoke sauce, zucchini flan, guinea fowl and fried stuffed flowers. Oh, and for dessert, tiramisu."

"Nice. I've never had anything you've ever cooked that I didn't like." It was the truth. He wasn't into flattery, but Francesca was truly the nicest woman he'd ever met and she cooked like a dream. She loved and accepted all of them right along with her demanding husband. "Where's the boss?"

She laughed. "He only *thinks* he's the boss. I still have my job at the deli, don't I? You know how much he hates me working."

"Here's a little newsflash for you, honey," Ricco said. "We all hate you working. We've got enemies."

"I don't."

They'd taken care of her enemy. Permanently. "They can get to us through you," he pointed out. It was an old argument, and one he was certain Stefano had tried many times. Francesca might be the sweetest woman he knew, but she was no pushover.

The fact that Francesca still had her job surprised him. He couldn't imagine his oldest brother allowing his woman to put herself in danger, and Stefano had no trouble bossing all of his siblings around.

Ricco shrugged out of his jacket and let her take it to hang up along with his tie. "Just us tonight?" He was already unbuttoning the top three buttons of his shirt.

"Yes." She made a face at him. "Family business."

He found himself relaxing. He was good at family business. Francesca would have told him if Eloisa was present. As a rule, his mother didn't show up for family events at Stefano's—which meant she was almost never present.

Taviano had come to him three weeks earlier with his findings. A casing had cracked on the shock absorber. The family had put out the word to other teams to stay away from that particular company for their casings. Stefano had yet to talk to him about it, so he was fairly certain that was what this night was all about. He didn't really care what it was that brought the family together, only that they were together.

"Stefano told me you're advertising for a rope model again," Francesca continued. "How's that coming?"

"There's a lot of fucked-up women in the world," he said.

She laughed. "You're just finding that out?"

"Since meeting you, I had high hopes." That was partly true, but mostly he was teasing her. Something new for him with an outsider, although he'd never considered her that. Francesca fit right in with his brothers and Emmanuelle. She was family, and every one of them would lay down their lives for her.

She gave him another smile. She really was a beautiful woman. Stefano was lucky to find her. Not only was she sweet, intelligent and beautiful, but she also could have been a rider had she been found and trained from the time she was a child. She was rare. Very rare. She had accepted their way of life, shrouded in secrecy and living outside the accepted laws of the land.

Ricco sighed. He'd secretly hoped that by advertising for a rope model, the woman of his dreams would appear. She would be tall, with red hair, because he liked that look, slim like a model, and very willing to accept him as the focus of her life. More, she would be an untrained rider, one who could give him children so his family would be happy. So far he'd gotten every body type, every hair color and a variety of curves, a lot of women willing to do kink and more who wanted money. A lot of money. He hadn't connected with any of them, not even physically—and that was a first for him.

He hadn't conducted the interviews, but he'd been there, in the shadows, watching where they couldn't see him. Trying to find one woman that aroused him at least emotionally, if not physically. But nothing happened. It was depressing.

He'd always liked women, especially when he came out of the tunnels after a job, but really all the time. He never connected with them on any level but physical. He never wanted to spend any time with them outside of having sex. He was adventurous sexually and surrounded himself with women who were the same way, but he played and he left. He always made that clear. He wasn't a man who stayed. Lately, even that was fading. He played with the Lacey twins occasionally, but he wasn't into it any longer, and hadn't been for some time.

He envied Stefano his ability to have a relationship. He wasn't certain he could do it. Now that he'd been in on the interviews with the various women applying to be a rope model, he was fairly positive he would never be that man. He wanted it, but he just felt indifference or annoyance. None of the women knew who the rope master was, but they'd tried to find out, and several suspected it was a Ferraro—specifically Ricco, as more than once in magazines his love of rope art had been written up. He'd been careful to have Emilio conduct the interviews in a neutral location—the conference room of the Ferraro Hotel, where many interviews for various businesses took place.

"It's going to happen for you, Ricco," Francesca said, walking with him through the enormous open room toward the kitchen where the family usually gathered. "I know you don't think it will, but I feel it. She's close."

He glanced at her sharply. Francesca wasn't given to fantasy. He shook his head in denial. He'd given up that dream a long time ago. "Done too many things in my life to ever have a decent woman throw in with me."

"I'm a decent woman and I love you," Francesca said.

"Yeah, but you're my sister."

"I love you, too." Emmanuelle joined them, slipping her arm around his waist as well. "But then, I'm your sister too, and it's well known by the lot of you that I have no sense."

Ricco couldn't help but laugh. Emmanuelle could always make him smile, no matter how bad his nights had been. She was a ray of sunshine to all of them.

She turned her face up to his, her eyes moving over his features, seeing things he didn't want her to see. At once the smile disappeared. "You aren't sleeping."

He shrugged, trying to look casual. "Never been good at sleeping, honey. Tell me what's happening in our neighborhood. I've been out of the loop for a while." Isolating himself as much as Stefano would allow it. He wanted to be with his family but had always considered that it could be dangerous for them.

"Francesca knows far more than any of us. Working at Masci's, she hears everything, don't you?"

Francesca went to the stove where Taviano was turning the guinea fowl in the frying pan. Using olive oil, he'd sautéed garlic and scallions and then placed the fowl skin-side down before adding sage. He glanced up and winked at Ricco. "She was just going to let this burn."

"She never burns anything," Giovanni objected. He mixed the homemade pasta noodles with the artichoke sauce. "Stefano scored big-time with this one. He just needs a few bambinos running around, with her pregnant and barefoot, and the man will be happy."

"He's already happy," Francesca said smugly.

"Well, I'd be happy," Giovanni clarified.

Francesca blew him a kiss and sat up on the bar stool

between her brothers-in-law. "Lucia and Amos are having the time of their lives with their new daughter, Nicoletta. Extremely happy." Lucia and Amos Fausti owned Lucia's Treasures, a small boutique that Francesca and Emmanuelle often frequented.

"Is Nicoletta going to a regular school yet?" Stefano asked, coming up behind his wife and circling her around the waist with his arms.

Ricco had noticed Stefano couldn't get near Francesca without touching her. He envied his brother that and wanted it for himself. He just wanted to feel for someone. Connect with someone.

"She's smart," Vittorio said. He stabbed his fork into the pasta and took a bite, then held up his thumb, indicating it was good. "But she doesn't want to go to a regular school. Amos asked me to talk to her. I did, but I don't think she was impressed. She didn't say much, just looked at me. I don't envy them. The girl is gorgeous. Every young man from here to hell and back is going to be knocking at their door."

"Why do you all want her in a regular school?" Taviano asked. "More trouble, if you ask me. All those horny bastards leering at her. Do we really want that kind of problem? One of us would have to go scare the crap out of them, and then she'd be embarrassed or pissed and we'd get the blame. Keep her home. Locked up. It's for her own good."

"It's her last year of high school," Francesca said. "She deserves to have fun."

Ricco wasn't positive Francesca was right about sending the girl to the local high school. Nicoletta had come from New York from a terrible situation. She'd been brutally abused—physically, sexually and emotionally—by her three uncles, men belonging to the notorious Demons, one of New York's bloodiest gangs. Stefano and Taviano had rescued her, but the damage had been done and it had been severe. Ricco knew the girl, like him, didn't sleep. He knew because he often pulled guard duty.

Nicoletta was one of the rare potential riders, her shadow throwing out feeler tubes to connect with the other shadows around her. The riders all took turns watching over her. He took the night shift because it suited him, and she went out her bedroom window and sat on the rooftop listening to music. He kept watch, but he didn't interfere. She looked so young and alone, and he knew he'd just scare her if he suddenly appeared beside her.

"She likes being with Lucia and Amos," Stefano said. "I've talked to her often and she wants to stay with them."

"Who wouldn't want to be with them?" Taviano asked. "They'll spoil her rotten. She's good for them as well."

"It was a cracked casing, Ricco," Stefano said abruptly. "On the shock absorber. Not you, a cracked casing. The wrong metal alloy was used and passed off to us as the real deal. I've already informed the other racing teams and they are boycotting the company."

Ricco didn't look at his brother. That was the most Stefano was going to give him, when both knew that everything else that had been said between them still stood. He just nodded and sank down into the chair at the table beside Emmanuelle. It wasn't exactly news anyway. Taviano had come to him immediately a good three weeks earlier and told him. Taviano preferred to race Indy cars, and he was the one, along with Vittorio and Emmanuelle, who designed their engines. Stefano had been pulling extra jobs, taking Ricco's place in the rotation, and the family had been very, very busy.

"How are you coming along on your hunt for a partner?" Vittorio asked, sliding into a chair at the long table.

Ricco shrugged. "I guess I've got to choose someone soon. I'm doing one more round of interviews and then I'll have to pick someone."

"Or not," Francesca said. "Seriously, hon, don't hook up with just anyone. It won't work."

He knew that, but he was determined to try. He had to if he was going to survive.